D1561405

Ancient Illumination

by

Rod Van Blake

Copyright © 2015 by Rod Van Blake

All rights reserved.

This book or any portion thereof may not be reproduced or used in any manner

whatsoever without the express written permission of the publisher except for the use

of brief quotations in a book review.

Printed in the United States of America

First Printing, 2015

ISBN: 978-1-62217-541-3

Contents

Chapter One

JARED OMEGA, AN IMPOSING FIGURE of granite, enters the secret meeting place on Jupiter IV. The king of the Kison Tontu surveys the rest of the chamber with his intelligent, dark eyes. The other leaders rise to show proper respect, and Omega greets each one as they approach, mentally taking roll. Omega is nearly two and a half meters tall with smooth, ash gray skin, and gold titanium cuffs glistening beneath his flowing cape.

"Where is he?" Omega whispers. Jared Omega rarely, if ever, has to raise his voice.

"He's just arrived, as you have, great king," Athena replies. Athena is the blindingly beautiful queen of the Limbia Johari. The crystalline tresses and diminutive stature help conceal her lethality.

Hironike, the emerald-skinned leader of the Jade Assassins, inquires, "Why should we listen to the mystic's babbling?"

"Have some patience, Hironike. The galaxy respects his wisdom for a reason, and he may know how to put an end to this bloodshed," Omega cautions.

All eyes go to the entrance as the doors slide open to admit a cloaked figure. He strides confidently to the center of the chamber. The voluminous folds hide a slim, athletic build, despite his considerable age. Babylon pulls back his hood to reveal long white hair and a deep turquoise visage with glowing amber eyes. Omega signals for the others to take their seats. As everyone takes their places, the ruler of the Kison Tontu addresses the new arrival. "Babylon the Wise, I thank you for coming, and welcome you on behalf of all those we represent."

A look of surprise passes over Babylon's wizened yet somehow youthful features. "Wise am I now. Welcome, too? I can see in de eyes of some who stare pon me that all don't tink me wise. Crazy and old yes, but not wise," Babylon rasps.

Out the corner of his eye, Omega sees a man-shaped blur on the wall, ten meters to his left. The image is inching its way toward him. Perplexed by the king's suspicious expression, Babylon watches the stone warrior pull out a small video screen surrounded by keys with glyphs on them. Athena shoots a questioning glance at Hironike, who merely shrugs but is also aware that something may be wrong now. Omega taps a couple keys, and a floating sphere with a cone-shaped diamond attached to it enters the chamber. The diamond blossoms, revealing a glowing lens that scans the room, halting on the area the blur occupies.

The king nods at the screen, as if confirming whatever he suspected, and puts the device away. Hironike is about to speak but stops when the leader of the Kison Tontu rises. Then with incredible speed and grace that should be impossible for a being his size, Omega sprints toward the phantom. The ghost attempts to flee, but the distance is closed too quickly. The stone warrior king's hand shoots to where the neck should be and finds his quarry. Invisible hands reach up at Omega's wrist, struggling to escape the vice-like grip. Smiling cruelly, Omega turns to the others, saying, "Let's see what gift the general has sent me now."

They all watch as the king seems to take the head off of the wraith. With the helmet removed, the struggling figure appears. Comprehension dawns on all of them as they stare at a man clad in strange battle armor. A man with close cropped blonde hair and ice blue eyes glares at Omega with a mixed look of fear and hatred. Omega inspects the helmet, noticing the numbers etched on the back, 1086 followed by three chevrons and cross rifles.

"Who sent you?" Omega quietly demands.

"J. Anderson, Sergeant, 123-55-0069," the Marine replies.

Hironike and Omega recognize the response. Marines are trained to give name, rank, and service number when captured. Even if beaten or tortured, that is the only information the sergeant will divulge.

Knowing it will be futile to ask again, the king signals everyone to one side of the chamber. The head of the Jade Assassins moves to approach but stops short at the look and negative shake of Omega's head. Sensing the others' intentions, Hironike backs up, as if shielding the rest of the gathering. Anderson, who expects to be tortured, is thrown against the wall. He lands hard on the floor five meters away. Dazed, he rises. He is confused by the temporary freedom. Knowing he won't have much time to contemplate the situation, Anderson reaches for his holstered dual-barreled sidearm, draws it with blinding speed, and squeezes the trigger twice.

Moving with amazing agility, Omega dodges the projectiles as they narrowly miss him; instead one of his personal guards at the entrance is hit. Omega rushes Anderson, punching him in the midsection. Ribs crack audibly despite the body armor as blood sprays from the Marine's mouth. The pain forces Anderson to drop his weapon as he flies, once again, into the wall. Landing on his feet this time, Anderson kneels, hugging his fractured ribs. Hand-to-hand combat with an unbound stone warrior is suicide without weapons more potent than what Anderson has at his disposal. The blade of his special issue Ka-Bar can cut some metals, but for some reason, most rockheads skin has proven nearly impervious to this weapon. Besides, even if the blatanium blade could breach the skin, most men aren't quick or strong enough to push deep enough to hit anything vital. Considering his options, and realizing there are none, Anderson decides to try anyway. Athena, Hironike, Babylon, and the others watch the trapped soldier reach down to unsheathe a gleaming black blade. Some stifle laughter as they realize what's about to be attempted. Babylon is more wary in light of the fact that the Marine is wearing a wraith suit, and armed with weapons they have not seen before. It's doubtful, but the blade may prove to be another deadly surprise.

Anderson hates the arrogant look on the rockhead's face, but knows the stone warrior king's confidence is justified. He raises the ka-bar in a reverse grip, gathers himself, and then charges. Admiring the foolish bravery, Omega meets the attack, grabbing the knife-hand. Swinging up and across with his other arm, Omega forces Anderson's elbow to bend in the wrong direction. Screaming in agony the sergeant lets go of the ka-bar. The stone warrior backhands him, keeping hold to the mangled limb to ensure Anderson stays on his feet. When Omega sees solidarity return to Anderson's shaky legs, he releases the injured arm, saying, "Now, Askari, I will show you my new toy."

Once again, the floating sphere hovers into view. The cone on the orb begins to spin like a diamond-tipped drill. Omega reproduces the video screen and taps a key. In response, the sphere streaks into Anderson hitting him in the chest, exiting out his back, and leaving a fist-sized hole in his torso. His body falls over, pooling blood on the floor.

The mess is cleaned up as Omega checks on his injured guard. Kamal is the guard's name and new to the detail, if the king remembers correctly. When he is sure the guard will live, Omega goes back to the business at hand. Conventional ballistic rounds do not have much effect when used on the Kison Tontu, unless vulnerable spots are hit, and to do that, you either have to be an incredible marksman or at close range. As mentioned before, being in close proximity without proper control measures is not advantageous, but the corp is full of great marksmen. Although the shot only resulted in a glancing blow, they are all disturbed to discover it did have some effect. Had the attempt actually been meant for Kamal and aimed at a vital area, the results would have been fatal. The Galactic Marine Corp (GMC) depends on constant technological advancement to keep control of its subjugated people.

The Kison Tontu, used as slave labor for mining, are controlled by manacles on their wrists and ankles. If a revolt takes place, large, powerful magnets are activated throughout the facility. The slaves are forced to the walls and floor by the magnetic system. If any escape the facility, the GMC is called to corral them or eliminate them, if necessary. The Stone People are working on eluding these measures and are having some success. They are also developing some technological weapons of their own from the mining equipment given to them. The latest development seems to be another step toward freedom. It is not yet the time to fully press the issue, but it will be soon.

Omega uses the new invention to scan the entire area for more would-be assassins before reconvening the meeting. Once everyone is back in place, Babylon, once again, begins to address the leaders. "You must unite the people ... and I mean, all people. Even de ones who sent a Marine to come dead you. Hard to believe, I know, but dem your brodas."

Hironike throws skeptical glances at Athena and Omega, stopping only to finally gaze back at Babylon.

The ancient Atlantean continues, "Let me tell you from de beginning. When you hear how it all start, den you know I say true. If not, you do what you wish anyway, right?"

Omega, Athena, and a less enthusiastic Hironike reassure Babylon that they will listen to his historic tale.

"Good dat you listen. Better you do what needs to be done when you know what it means," Babylon warns.

Closing his amber eyes, Babylon mentally gathers himself to speak to the respective leaders of the Umano, the slave races. "Hear me now, so I only have to tell you once. I know you can't tell, but Babylon be getting old. Might be giving up m'last breath if I have to tell ye twice." They all laugh at the jest as Babylon continues, "Eons ago, around de time when man was what dey call Cro-Magnon, people from de other side come to observe, ya know? Dey watch and tink we inferior to dem and others dey know. After centuries of watchin', we make some progress, but not fast enough for dem, I guess. So dey decide to do us a favor and help mankind along, you know. At first it was hard for dem to communicate with man 'cause we were too scared to listen to dem. Dese people like nuttin' man had ever seen before! It would hurt your eyes to look pon dem 'cause deir bodies made of pure light! When dey come down to teach looking like a bunch of little suns, boy, everyone run as fast as legs make dem go! So in order for dem to help enlighten man dem take on human-like form, ya know, but dey still have a glow. Some people take dem for gods when dey start to teach rudimentary knowledge of mathematics, astronomy, and other sciences. I call dem de Ancients. For de most part, dey were good beings who could control deir bodies on a molecular level, and dey come to help us. Dere was one a dem dat tink man too backward and stupid to learn what dey tryin' to teach. Ya follow me? Soon he become frustrated wit de slow progress, so him start killin' and doin' other cruel acts for pleasure. When de Council of Twelve for de Ancients found out, dey were outraged! Violence is supposed to be a last resort when threatened. Since man was no threat to de Ancients, dey decide to punish de renegade. As punishment dey banish him from returning home. He had to live in exile on Earth, and guess what else?"

Unable to resist the rhetorical question, Hironike answers, "What? No meal before bed?"

Babylon shoots him an annoyed glare before going on. "No, smart ass! Somehow dey take away his ability to change back to his original form, and de only way for him to leave is to enlighten man himself. When man gets close to de Ancients' level of knowledge de banishment will be lifted. Although he could not go back to his pure light form, de renegade Ancient could still change form and had vast powers compared to man. Angered at being humbled and given a seemingly impossible mission, de renegade goes to work. He goes on to influence man to advance, and left many amazing scientific and architectural monuments in his wake. Stonehenge, I believe, is one of his earliest. Even now we don't know exactly what it is. Ever wonder how dey had star charts thousands of years ago, listing planets and star systems we supposedly only just discovered fairly recently?"

Sensing another sarcastic remark, Athena gently elbows the Jade Assassin leader in the ribs while trying to keep from smiling herself. Unaware of the silent exchange, Babylon continues his tale. "De renegade continues to travel all over de Earth, teaching some, while manipulating others dat came to see him as a god. Because he can take on many forms, he is de cause of many different religions dat sprang up around de world. Dat's also why a lot of religions are similar. He also used a lot of different names throughout time. I believe he was known as Neptune when he was with my people, but de name he used most recently was Pharaoh."

Finally, unable to contain himself, Hironike interrupts, "Are you trying to tell us YOU knew this Pharaoh?!"

Shrugging off his audience's incredulity, Babylon continues, "Listen to me now! After years of work, he became bored and decided to take the elite of his students to create a kingdom. Dis is when he used de name Neptune. De society he started was located in a mountainous region between Cuba and the northwestern tip of South America. Dis was de most advanced society at dat time called Atlantis. Dese were my people. When I was young, Neptune decided he want to rule all lands on either sides of the Mediterranean, so he took an army of 750,000 and easily conquered all of what would become Southern Europe, along with most of what would become Northern Africa. What would become Greece and Egypt had no intention of being ruled and somehow freed the conquered lands when Neptune went back for reinforcements. Dey followed de returning army of Atlantis to deir home, dey want to make sure Atlantis keep to demselves. Just as both armies reach Atlantis, a huge bloodclot earthquake hit, killin' both armies and destroyin' everyting built dere! A few family members of mine take me, and we barely escape wit' our lives. I'll tell you my story some other time. Later, Neptune set himself up as a god-king in Egypt. Dis is when he use de name Pharaoh. Dis is why dey tink of deir rulers as god-kings. Pharaoh used his powers as he ruled Egypt. Pharaoh suspected Atlantis was destroyed on purpose by de Ancients for trying to set up a kingdom of his own. Soon after erecting de pyramids and giving dem doctrine to follow, Pharaoh left, but de name stayed behind. It was a title given to each successive ruler of Egypt."

After waiting to allow the group to digest the first part of the story, Babylon continues his tale. "Now after him leave Egypt, Pharaoh goes on to raise many civilizations, only to see dem eventually fall to natural catastrophes, cycles of war, slavery, disease, and famine. He found dat, on a small scale, he could manipulate some of dese conditions, and get entertaining results. It was chaos, and Pharaoh loved it. With his ability to change form, Pharaoh found it easy to play many gods to many different peoples around de world. The oppressed and enslaved races asked for empowerment over deir conditions. De prayers to deir respective 'gods' were answered and dey mutated in order to survive in dangerous environments. The most robust of dese mutants were sent to work in conditions nobody else could survive. Before dey were mutated, dese conditions where dey were sent to mine was killin' dem by de thousands! Dat's why dey asked to be changed to de now proud Stone People. Soon deir newfound strength allowed dem to revolt. Frustrated in deir efforts to control de subjugated mutant races, man asks for technological advancement. Wit'out dat, dey know dere's no way to control people who are tremendously stronger dan dey are, and are slowly becoming nearly adamantine when confronted with conventional weapons. Deir wishes were granted. De wars resultin' from dis were spectacular and escalated to new levels wit' each advancement or genetic mutation. Pharaoh, pleased by dis chain of events, promotes division and conflict among all races for his entertainment. So listen to me now, one of you must unite de races and stop de real instigator of all dis bloodshed."

After a short meal, the enigmatic Babylon says his farewells and hops into a very alien-looking personal transport. Most interplanetary transportation is limited to bulky rectangular ore haulers that have been converted to accommodate passengers. Personal ships are almost unheard of, unless you're very wealthy or high up in the military or government. The technology is very new; plus the resources and costs are too high for everyone to have access to. This is a situation Omega plans to change. He has dreams of secretly forming a fleet for his people, and from the envious stares aimed at Babylon's vessel, it is obvious everyone is curious as to its origins. The hull is triangular with stingray-like wings with multi-directional attitude thrusters on the tips. The ship is very sleek. It is metallic blue with two small protrusions on the nose, and main thrusters aft of the spacecraft. When the engines roar to life, the ship begins to float, and retracts its landing gear, giving the illusion of an organic life form before racing for the stars.

When everyone returns from the landing bay, Omega turns to the others and asks, "So what do you think?"

Unsurprisingly Hironike is the first to respond. "As usual, the old man gave us background history and supposed facts that we cannot refute or substantiate. How can we know what's true and what's mere legend?" the Jade Assassin wonders aloud.

By the conclusion of the discussion, they all know what is to be done. In order to confirm Babylon's tale, Pharaoh has to be found. If the story is true, he's confined to Earth. Theoretically if they trace the path that leads to the common roots of the religions, they'll find him.

Chapter Two

SITTING AT THE TOP OF Margherita Peak, in what was once called Uganda, is a lone, benighted figure. This obscure human-shaped being is none other than Malice, the infamous assassin, and number one henchman of Pharaoh. Like its master, Malice has had many names and legends associated with it. The descriptions of Malice are always vague and vary because no one has been up close and lived to tell the tale. Height, weight, and gender have never been accurately discerned for the same reasons. Plus, it seems to have the ability to change some of these characteristics at will. All agree that Malice is a tall being with glowing crimson eyes. These bright malevolent orbs gaze down from within a black hood. From a distance, the eyes seem to float on their own, and as Malice gets closer its phantom-like body takes on a shape that is almost certainly human. By the time its prey realizes the floating form is tangible, it's too late.

If one could clearly see the countenance of Malice, frustration would be etched on it. For tonight is not the time to hunt, but to observe. To the southwest is a large gathering of Kison Tontu in what was once called Zaire. The bloodthirsty Malice focuses its evil gaze in their direction, so a report can be made later. These are mine workers gathered from the diamond mines in Namibia and South Africa, as well as the mine workers from the copper mines in Zambia and Zaire. What Malice does not know is that similar meetings are happening simultaneously around the globe. For years, the Stone People have been searching for a way to escape their yoke of forced labor. Finally a discovery has been made on Jupiter that could be the key to their freedom. During a mining expedition, an alloy was found that is almost identical to what their shackles are made of. The only differences are that the new alloy has a slight gold tint to it, but more importantly, it is not attracted when the powerful electro-magnets are turned on.

In a clearing amid a thick jungle, Simeon waits for the rest of the mine workers to file into the meeting area. Simeon is not tall by the standards of the Kison Tontu, but neither is he short, and he's very powerfully built. He is the head foreman from the biggest diamond mine in South Africa. His voice and charisma more than make up for his stature. As the stragglers make their way into the gathering, Simeon announces, "Today is the proudest day of our lives! For today we initiate the breaking of the chains of bondage for our people!"

This ceremony was planned after the discovery of the new alloy, and so the other foremen took their places. They gather in a formation shaped like a giant wheel. The spokes of the wheel are lines of Kison Tontu, and at the head of each line are two foremen with tribal hammers to break the shackles after they are heated. Before the ceremony commences, the towering form of Jared Omega steps to the center of the formation to address his people. "No longer shall we be Umanu, slaves to man! No longer shall we be merely Kison Tontu, but now we shall be Kison Askari! My foremen are now all generals, and we will train to be warriors in the great kwa that will bring us our freedom!"

Thunderous cheers rise from the Stone People as Omega continues his speech. "Generals, let God know we appreciate His blessings!"

The deep sonorous voices of the foremen rise in song, and hundreds of voices join as hammers clang against shackles. Both are heard for miles around.

> "Our God is an awesome God,
>
> He reigns from Heaven above,
>
> With wisdom, power, and love,
>
> Our God is an awesome God!"

Hans isn't the smartest man in the world, but he knows when something is not quite right. As the lead overseer at one of the largest diamond mines in South Africa, it is his job to keep an eye on the disposition of the laborers. Ever since the mass ritual the Stone People had in the jungle, he can tell their attitudes are slightly different, but the administration of the mining company says they don't care, as long as the ore and diamonds are still coming in normal quantities. Money is the bottom line. As long as a profit is still being made, the Stone People can have all the primitive rituals they want. "Besides we still have the means to subdue them if they try anything," the administration officials say.

Looking around, Hans sees a confidence in the Stone People that was absent before. They don't seem as subdued as usual. Simeon, his head foreman, is a touch less respectful than is normal for him. Production has slowed enough to arouse suspicion, so Hans sends James to the line to admonish the foreman. The hairs on the back of his neck stand up as soon as he realizes he hasn't seen James since the errand had been given to him. Fear and anger blossom in Hans as he pulls on his boots and grabs a sonic rifle before going to investigate. The rifle will do little more than knock a few Stone People down, but that should make them see reason if they become unruly. If the barbarians persisted, he could always lock them down electromagnetically.

On his way to the observation station, he notices a lot of peculiar things. First, he senses it is much too quiet for there to be diamonds being mined. This is easily explained because no one is working. Furthermore, he sees no other humans throughout the facility. Not only is James missing, but nobody, except Stone People, are in evidence.

Upon arriving at the observation station, Hans sees a group of Stone People gathered in front of the entrance to the control center. Immediately he notices a shattered porthole with a body-sized hole in it. There is also what curiously looks like blood around the edges of the hole, as well as some spattering of the same along the walls and floor.

"What's the meaning of this?!" Hans demands.

The group turns to look at him, but make no reply. Slowly, with trembling hands, Hans removes the sonic rifle from its sling and aims it in the general direction of the Stone People.

"Come see for yourself, slaver!" the smallest of them finally answers.

It is then that Hans recognized the speaker as Simeon. Hans feels his heart leap into his throat, and it takes all of his self-control not to hastily pull the trigger. He does, however, reach down and pull out his personal remote that will activate the magnetic system throughout the facility.

As Hans approaches the shattered window, a horrible scene materializes before his eyes. At least, four figures lay prone, in malposition, in a bloody heap on the other side of the window. Not one of them is recognizable. Unconsciously Hans has been repeatedly hitting the activation button on his remote. When he realizes the Stone People are not held to the walls or floor by their shackles, a look of confusion flashes across his face. He looks up to see an evil smile on Simeon's hardened visage. The expression is mirrored by his companions as they surround Hans. The man notices the shackles have a golden hue to them he hasn't seen before. Finally free from his paralysis of fear, Hans attempts to bring his weapon to bear. Before he can complete the move, as well as determine the significance of all that has happened, his head suddenly leaves his shoulders. After beheading the overseer with the ceremonial hammer that was strapped to his back, Simeon and the others watch the head, along with most of the spinal column, thud against the wall and clatter to the floor.

Simeon turns to gaze at his fellow warriors, because that's what they were now. No longer are they slaves to men. They will live or die as free beings from now on.

"Come. Let us properly arm ourselves. Those remotes, when used, send out automatic distress signals. When no communication comes back, others will come to see what happened. Those who are sent to investigate will be military in nature, if not by name. We must be prepared," he proudly tells his brothers. Simultaneously, similar incidents take place at mines all over the world. It has begun, the revolution has erupted.

* * *

For Lance Corporal (LCpl) Aragon, time is both passing too quickly and not quickly enough. The young Marine has black hair with dark brown eyes, and he is the machine gunner for his fire team. Time is going slow because Aragon is anxious to use the training he's received, along with the rest of platoon 3035 Lima Company 3rd recon Battalion. At the same time, he knows that training might not be enough to keep everyone alive. There are going to be casualties, and Aragon is praying that he won't be listed among them as the verdant jungle of Central Africa races beneath him. Distress signals have gone out almost simultaneously from nearly all mining facilities in the region. The Marines dispatch as soon as possible when no return communication is received from the miners. Riots are not uncommon, but are usually short-lived, and the miners have always been good about letting the authorities know when they had things under control.

Three Night Eagle troop transports land in a triangle formation in a clearing near a copper mine. The heavily armed and armored transports carry one platoon each. They are slightly slower than fighter aircraft, but have the ability to take off and land vertically, as a result of being fitted with antigrav engines. Before the landing struts actually touch down, the rear hatches swing open, and Marines boil out of the transports to secure the area.

Nothing can prepare Aragon for the gruesome carnage that greets him. It is deathly quiet, and bodies are everywhere. Lifeless eyes stare accusingly as open mouths hang silently screaming for help that has come too late. The horror of it threatens to freeze his blood until Corporal (Cpl) Garrison calls out, breaking the trance, "Hey! Snap out of it, Marine! The major wants us to take two squads to check out the facility. Make sure you're all locked and loaded."

Aragon follows his squad leader's orders and makes sure his rail rifle is loaded properly. Everyone also has their issue of frag grenades, which might help.

Two squads of Marines head into the mining facility. Inside, there are more corpses in random locations. Due to the heat, the bodies have started to decompose, despite being dead for only a short amount of time. The smell of death and desperation invades the Marines' nostrils, and Aragon needs a moment to compose himself. Cpl Garrison waits until he's sure none of his squad members are going to be sick before moving on. The two squads split up with Aragon's group going to the main observation center and the other to the employee quarters. The search goes on without incident, in dead silence. Not one living being is found. The squads re-group near the entrance, and it is then they hear what vaguely sounds like weapons going off. They scramble outside to find all hell breaking loose.

The jungle thrashes and writhes as various ballistic and energy pro-jectiles plow through it in all directions. Marines on patrol outside the mining facility disappear as the lush foliage seems to come to life, snatch-ing or engulfing unsuspecting sentries.

In preparation, the Kison Tontu have covered themselves with moss to blend in with the jungle. The camouflage proves effective as they are able to get within arms' reach of the Marines, often killing or neutralizing them before they can get a shot off. Terror begins to gnaw at the Marines' sanity until they begin to fire at enemies, real and imagined.

When enemy casualties start to appear, some of the 3rd Battalion's confidence returns. When the Marines finally see the enemies are, in fact, Stone People and not the jungle itself, their training takes over, orders are shouted, and what started out as chaos becomes an organized counter-at-tack.

As Aragon rushes to return to the platoon, two of his squad mates are eliminated. To his right, one of the Marines' chest explodes. The young man falls to the earth with his face frozen in horror, a silent scream on his lips because he lacks the lungs to give voice to it. Aragon glances to his left in time to see Cpl Garrison's leg fly from his body, leaving a ragged stump. Immediately Aragon hits the deck as he realizes that they're taking fire from their own weapons. He looks over at Cpl Garrison pointing to a copse of trees fifty meters ahead of them. When he sees movement amid those trees, anger wells in Aragon. Taking a railgun from one of his fallen squad mates, he sets both to fully automatic and begins to charge the area his squad leader has pointed out.

Opening fire as he approaches, Aragon mows a swath of trees down to reveal a group of green-hued Stone People with commandeered military weapons. Two of their number fall back taking sustained bursts to the head and torso. Screaming in a rage, Aragon watches the tough, natural armor of his targets, slowly but surely, chip away until vital organs are reached. When the weapon in his left hand clicks empty, Aragon tosses it aside and pulls a grenade from his LBV. Tossing the grenade, he dives to avoid return fire, as well as to seek cover from the blast. The explosion is deafening, and when the dust settles, Aragon raises his head cautiously.

Surprisingly there are two more bodies among the first two. Slowly Aragon rises to get a closer look at his handiwork. Upon reaching the first two bodies, Aragon senses motion to his left. He whirls to finish the job when the head of the fallen warrior suddenly evaporates into a purple mist before he can bring his weapon to bear. Confused, he looks back to find Cpl Garrison in the prone firing position and waving weakly before collapsing. Aragon rushes back to his squad leader's side. After digging out his med-pack, Aragon pulls away the shredded pant leg to apply a tourniquet. Satisfied that the bleeding is staunched, he injects Garrison with a painkiller and sedative combination.

In reaction to the prick, Garrison's eyes flutter open. Grabbing Aragon's arm, he croaks, "You did good, devildog, but I don't think I'm going to make it."

"I'm not leaving you," Aragon says, and before the corporal can reply, he's hoisted up in a firemen's carry.

Heading back to the transports, the two squad mates meet with no further resistance, and that makes Aragon suspicious. Upon seeing the Night Eagles, they notice that two of them are grounded; the third is still hovering a meter off the deck. There are corpses strewn everywhere, and other Marines are struggling with similar burdens, hastily making their way toward the functioning troop transport. A captain looking more dead than alive catches sight of the two Marines coming back from the mining facility and says, "Put a fire under it, men! We've been granted a reprieve. Let's move before they change their minds."

A corpsman comes to relieve Aragon of the duty of carrying his squad leader. They are ushered into the transport, and it starts to ascend. Nearly two-thirds of the company have been annihilated. Apparently the hostilities have gradually lessened, and the Marines are allowed to regroup and retreat. A message is being sent. At the realization of how close to death he has come, Aragon begins to tremble. Fury stabilizes him as he silently vows to answer their message with one of his own.

Chapter Three

THE SEARCH FOR PHARAOH HAS begun in earnest. The small task force given this mission has representatives of all the oppressed peoples. The Kison Tontu, Limbia Johari, and the Jade Assassins are all in on this. They have, also, hired guides who are native to the areas being searched. Some wonder where servants can get money to pay guides, but greed overrides curiosity most of the time. The main task force includes Takimura and Megumi of the Jade Assassins, Angelo and Julius of the Limbia Johari, and finally Kamal and Nefer of the Stone Warriors.

The quest leads them all over Earth, as well as to other planets, where upstart religions are spreading. The newer religions are more than likely dead ends since they have no direct link to the older religions being derived from phenomena on the other planets. It seems fruitless until, gradually, clues begin to pop up. Most of the evidence found points to Egypt. The Stone Warriors have to wear cloaks to disguise their identities. Reports over the Sat-Net describe the galaxy-wide uprising. To avoid unwanted attention and hostility, they cover up as best as they can. The cloaks do well to hide their species, but not their stature. Kison Tontu are bigger than most normal humans, and in some places in Egypt, the cloaks draw attention because of the climate.

The small group is led by the heavily muscled form of Takimura. The broad-shouldered Jade Assassin is dressed in a tan linen suit beneath a light trench coat to conceal twin diamond bladed kitanas sheathed at his sides. His diminutive but dangerous counterpart, Megumi, is dressed much the same way. The two assassins are opposite in size but similar in their efficiency at their jobs. The Limbia Johari or walking jewels are likewise dressed in linen suits, but theirs are fitted with hoods to make them more discreet. They are also armed with an assortment of blatanium and diamond-edged blades. It is decided that only melée weapons are to be carried. Ballistic and energy weapons tend to be loud and will leave evidence behind if used. The two Stone Warriors carry no arms. They don't need to; they are living vessels of death and destruction. Since this is considered an information gathering mission, no one expects to meet with violent resistance and, therefore, sees no reason to be heavily armed. The Jade Assassins and the Kison Askari are both skilled fighters, and the Limbia Johari are espionage masters. All their skills are going to be needed to make it back with the information they find.

Angelo has set up a meeting with a contact in Cairo who is to lead them to the Valley of Kings, and to various pyramids to see if they could find evidence of the elusive Pharaoh. Professor Charles Jones-Bey is the contact. The tall, brown-skinned scholar can read Sumerian text, hieroglyphics, and cuneiform. The professor is also working on a biological study in genetics. He believes all species of man are genetically linked. He is pleased to discover that the group he is charged with guiding has two representatives of each race. Now all he has to do is get DNA samples from each of them.

* * *

Corporal Garrison's eyes flutter open. He blinks a couple times to clear his vision because, for some reason, he can't shake his head. When his vision is no longer blurry, he sees harsh lights above and apple green curtains drawn in his peripheral vision. The air has a very pungent antiseptic smell to it. Garrison tries to recall where it would be necessary to have such a sterile environment. Hospital, he thinks. The thought only inspires more questions.

"Why would I be in a hospital?" he asks no one in particular. The memories all come flooding back into his mind, like a tidal wave, threatening to mentally capsize him.

Rod Van Blake

In an instant, he is back in the jungle with his heart thundering in his ears as he runs through plush foliage. The smell of sulfur, burning flesh, and ozone fills the air. There's a cacophony of gunfire and agonizing screams as he and his squad try to make it back to the platoon. Time turns sluggish as fire erupts around them and railgun rounds begin to chew up soil and bodies. Garrison sees Private First Class (PFC) Carter; at least, he thinks that is his name.

Carter's heart and lungs are jettisoned from his body in a shower of blood. Nothing you can do. He's gone, Garrison thinks as rounds come at him from different directions. Adrenaline slows the realization that he's been hit, and hit hard. Strangely, the bottom of his right foot strikes him in the small of his back before pinwheeling a few meters away. Time returns to normal speed as Garrison falls face-first to the ground. Lying on the jungle floor, he thinks, Did I just kick myself in the ass?! Is that even possible?

Pain robs him of all thought, and he reaches for the injured area to see that it's ... gone. Or, at least, it's not wholly there. Resigned to his fate Cpl Garrison releases his bloody stump so that he can point out to Aragon, the only survivor of his squad, where the fire's coming from. That accomplished, he watches Aragon pick up a rifle from their fallen brother, and run off, guns blazing, in the direction indicated. Well, if I can't go out in a blaze of glory, the least I can do is take some of them with me, the corporal thinks to himself.

Closing his eyes to shut out the pain and hell around him, Garrison pulls his weapon into his desperate grasp. He assumes the prone position since it's the only one he can manage at present and searches for targets. Screaming like a banshee, Aragon flushes seven rockheads from their cover. Garrison focuses on three running away from Aragon, starting with the furthest one. As he aims at the first target, the mantras from marksmanship training run through his head. Sight alignment, sight picture, control your breathing, exhale, and squeeze the trigger. Off in the distance, a face is obliterated. Garrison repeats the process twice, having to lead his final target because it is faster than the first two. Satisfied that his job is done, he considers dying when there's a grenade detonation from Aragon's direction. He watches as Aragon approaches a group of fallen bodies and realizes too late that one is still alive. Without thinking, Garrison sights in once more. This time, his front sight tip settles on a Stone Warrior's mouth. "That's right, you bastard. Open wide." With that happy thought, Garrison sends the warrior to oblivion...then darkness takes him.

Corporal Garrison opens his eyes and finds himself back in the present, in the impersonal hospital room. He still cannot move his head, so he strains to look at his damaged leg. To his surprise, it looks as if the sheets are covering two feet. Silently, he questions himself, "I lost one leg, didn't I?"

His arms are restrained at his sides, so he painstakingly pulls the sheets back with his fingers to reveal two metallic boots.

"Magnificent, aren't they?" the speaker, a gaunt-faced man in a lab coat, says.

"Who are you?" Garrison asks.

"I'm Lieutenant Commander Jameson. I'm the surgeon who fitted you with your new cybernetic legs. I apologize for the restraints, but not all of the neuro-processors have been installed. We have one last procedure to do so that you can fully control the legs."

Tears well up in the Marine's eyes as he responds, "But I only lost one leg, and now I can't feel either."

"Yes, but we couldn't simply give you just one cybernetic leg. It would have thrown your equilibrium off. Your new legs are vastly more powerful than your old ones," Lt. Commander Jameson replies.

After digesting all this, Garrison looks up and asks, "What now, sir?"

The Lt. Commander clasps his hands behind his back and answers, "Well, you are to be promoted to sergeant, and given the Medal of Honor for actions above and beyond the call of duty. After we get these neuro-processors installed, you'll be sent to Saturn for rehabilitation and to get used to the legs. Upon completion of that, you'll be sent home for leave and then back to Saturn for some type of training, but I'm not cleared to know what type. Your orders come from Headquarters Marine Corp signed by General Krulak himself. You'll receive a copy before you ship out after this final procedure. I suggest you get as much sleep as you can. We don't know if the neuro-processors will adversely affect your sleep cycle. Oh, and congratulations, Sergeant."

"Thank you, sir," Sgt. Garrison replies and closes his eyes, hoping he'll wake up in a different reality, where he'll feel more thankful.

* * *

Deep below the surface of the Valley of Kings, Malice waits on bended knee in one of the many chambers in a huge obpyramidal structure. He knows that to move before acknowledgement can bring tremendous pain or death. Malice has no fear of pain, but if death comes to him now, he'll be deprived of the privilege of being the deliverer of those things. Being the giver of pain and death, instead of the recipient, is the whole of Malice's existence.

A tall, imposing man with light bronze skin, deep brown eyes, and long ebony hair bound in a long braid sits upon a golden throne dressed as a pharaoh of old. Even though he can take on many forms, the original god-king feels most comfortable with this one.

Pharaoh looks on as Malice obediently waits to be called upon, despite being the only one present. "Rise, my servant." Pharaoh rumbles.

Only then does the intense gaze shift from the floor to focus on his master. Malice stands to his full height before speaking. "We have visitors, master."

"Who, and what do they want?" Pharaoh asks.

"It's a mixed group, master, and I believe they are searching for you," Malice replies.

Pharaoh ponders the implications of that before responding. "Follow them and curb their enthusiasm. Hurt them, if necessary. I don't like being disturbed."

Bowing as he replies, Malice smiles inwardly at the prospect of inflicting pain. "As you command."

* * *

As the small band makes their way through the dusty corridors of the underground labyrinth, they can't shake the feeling that they are being watched. The feeling is mutually shared by all, and to hide his nervousness, Professor Jones-Bey tries to distract everyone by translating the ancient hieroglyphics that decorated the walls. Angelo and Julius are the most appreciative of the academic aspect of the tour, while the others are more interested in the results. Jones-Bey leads the expedition, with the Limbia Johari close behind, followed by the Jade Assassins, and then the Stone Warriors. Two of Jones-Bey's assistants and fellow scholars bring up the rear.

Mysteriously when the halls became too dark, the floor and ceiling begin to glow of their own accord. The light is not bright, but it is good enough to help them find their way. Malice enjoys stalking his prey. Silently he follows their progress, occasionally making noise to startle them. The Umano become more alert but don't scare easily. The two humans at the back of the group are visibly terrified. Malice thrives on their fear. It is delicious to him, but it is time to reveal himself.

One of Jones-Bey's assistants begins to whimper. It has been going on with every scratch and skitter of rodent or insect that spooks the taller of the two novice scholars. Takimura has grown tired of his whining and is about to demand that the professor shut the student up; since they have not been introduced by name, the Jade Assassin cannot do it himself, at least, not verbally, but Takimura has more direct methods at his disposal. Luckily for the scholar, they are not needed. Everyone stands stock still as a fog, ankle-high sweeps through the large hall they've just entered. All eyes follow the approaching fog in search of its source when they notice a figure at the end of the hall shrouded in darkness. Glowing ruby red eyes glare balefully from beneath a hooded cloak. Malice's deep grating voice seems to come from the very walls. "Leave or die. You are not welcome, and my master does not wish to be disturbed."

"Charming," Angelo observes and then asks. "Who is your master, and how may we gain audience with him?"

Silence follows. There are mutterings from the teary eyed students about leaving not being a bad idea. Unable to control himself, the taller of the two students sprints toward a door in the middle of the passageway. Malice knows they can't be allowed any closer to the master's sacred chambers and bolts into action.

The dark phantom seems to glide atop the fog as it blurs past the group. Upon passing the student, there's a brief flash of metal with no immediate results. The group stares at the spectacle, confused, until the student's limbs and head drop from the body. Malice wheels on the rest of them. The Stone Warriors move to protect the professor as the Limbia Johari and Jade Assassins unsheathe their weapons simultaneously. Malice speeds toward them. Blades ring off one another, and there are accompanying grunts as Malice moves liquidly through the small gauntlet. Finally his blades send sparks flying when deflected by the arms of the Stone Warriors as he passes them. Dive rolling, Professor Jones-Bey draws a handheld laser cannon and fires at the retreating apparition. Unscathed, Malice runs his hands over some glyphs on the wall before disappearing. His task completed, he relishes the idea of future battles with these foes who may prove to be worthy opponents.

"What the hell was that?!" Megumi demands of the professor.

Before he can respond, the whole structure begins to slowly shift. Seeing the danger of being trapped, the group forestalls the discussion until after they are safely back on the surface. Before leaving the chamber, the professor takes some samples from the ground. As the rumbling grows louder, Kamal forcibly lifts Jones-Bey, and they proceed through a deadly shifting obstacle course, narrowly escaping to the surface. Frozen in horror, the other student is left behind with his dead comrade.

When the warriors and the professor are outside, they stop, under the cool desert night, to catch their breaths. Nefer glides seductively over to Professor Jones-Bey, grabs him harshly by the arm, and asks, "Who or what was that?! And why would a scholar have such weapons as you do?"

Angrily, the professor replies, "I have no idea what that was, but it may be what you're looking for. As for the weapons, we live in dangerous times. I'm travelling with a group of beings that I can't protect myself against. Yes, I deal in knowledge, but I doubt that thing wanted to have an intellectual conversation. It could have killed me, just as easily as it did my student!"

The Kison Askari eye him suspiciously. Professor Jones-Bey's bald head is sweating profusely as he bellows, "Don't look at me like that! It's true! Have you seen the Sat-Net news reports on yourselves, my fine stone-faced friends? The revolts south of here, all over the globe, and throughout the galaxy are being called bloody massacres! As for you two emerald-skinned beings, wherever you are, death is soon to follow, and your bejeweled companions know about it before anyone else. I don't necessarily distrust you all, but you can't blame me for being cautious."

Nefer releases his arm, still eyeing him warily. "If you thought we would endanger you, why would you agree to guide us?"

Professor Jones-Bey tiredly wipes his brow and answers, "Research takes funding, and you had it. Plus, the direction of your inquiries piqued my curiosity. It's rare to see three different peoples together on one agenda. I have a theory that we are all closer than we think. I'll let you know if I'm right."

The professor takes them to a secret spaceport before heading to his lab at the University of Cairo. Once off planet, the others split and seek passage to their respective leaders to report on the mission.

* * *

The rehabilitation sessions are excruciating for Sgt. Garrison on Saturn. With time, the pain goes away as his body heals. The heavier gravity proves to be another problem. The neuro-processors are implanted without difficulty, and though his cybernetic legs are powerful enough to handle the gravity, the rest of him cannot. The simplest tasks are a torturous workout. Garrison's torso feels as if it has been dipped in liquid alloy and then dried so that he is constantly weighed down. For weeks, he can't even walk upright. Gradually his body becomes acclimated to the gravity, and with the aid of a special steroid, he becomes strong enough to train. His upper body strength will never match his lower body, but at least, he can move like a normal human being now.

Sgt. Garrison receives his orders, stating that he's being transferred to a new unit based there on Saturn. Most of the men have been raised there, so he knows they'll be immensely stronger than the men on Earth. His old battalion has been nearly crushed. Maybe this new First Battalion unit has a fighting chance. He hopes so. Garrison thinks to himself, Platoon 1086, here I come! It's payback time!

Chapter Four

AT HIS PRIVATE LABORATORY, WHICH is also his home away from campus in Cairo, Professor Jones-Bey is analyzing the "samples" he collected. Among the dirt, he has flakes that have been chipped off of the Stone People during the attack in the underground labyrinth. Whatever type of blade that thing uses has to be very sharp. The Stone People are not harmed, but it is still remarkable that there are any results at all. Most blades are ineffective against these people, but he counted himself lucky that they are in this case. Professor Jones-Bey has what he needs to test his theory, a sample of Kison Tontu DNA.

Further examination and comparison of the DNA samples prove his theory to be correct. The DNA of the Kison Tontu and that of normal humans are almost identical. There is a mutated gene that's not found in normal humans. Once the professor isolates this gene, he is able to discern what trait is connected to it. It is tedious work, but once completed, the professor is amazed that he has not guessed what is different.

The only difference between the Stone People and the others is their skin. The mutated gene gives them a calcium buildup that grows on their epidermis and acts like an exoskeleton. They breathe oxygen like everyone else, and the same food sustains them. The new gene must have come about as some type of evolutionary survival measure. Professor Jones-Bey's excitement grows. There are only two problems — who to tell, and what to do with this information. The so-called Stone People are our brothers!

* * *

Jared Omega sits on his throne, brooding. He has just received Kamal and Nefer's report on the search results. Omega holds a vid-conference to seek the opinions of the other leaders who have received similar reports from their subordinates. At first the others think that, perhaps, they'd found the being they are looking for, but Omega is quick to point out that the red-eyed phantom referred to a "master." It attacks to cover his master's escape. The king of the Kison Tontu figures the "master" is more than likely the ancient being they seek. After considering this, the others agree. The thing found at the Valley of Kings is another mystery. The leaders all want to seek Babylon's counsel to see what he knows of the creature, but no one knows where he can be found to ask. Babylon has eyes and ears everywhere; he will show himself when he wants to be involved further.

Meanwhile Omega mobilizes thousands of warriors and, with the help of the Atlanteans, is building a strong space navy. The Kison Askari have acquired an abundant amount of ore and other resources during the initial revolt. These resources are combined with technology from the Atlanteans to give them the ability to fight space battles, as well as transport laborers and materials. Once the technological advantage the humans have is nullified, the war should end quickly.

Many of the Stone People spend a lot of time away from Earth because of mining expeditions. Most mining facilities on other planets soon turn into flourishing colonies. These colonies are either beneath the surface or domed cities. Both are equipped with atmosphere controls and gravity compensators. Domed cities are more convenient because they can be made bigger, but the underground cities are easier to defend. Neither of the growing space navies are battle tested. Up to this point, there have been no interstellar conflicts, but all know, sooner or later, planetary bombardment will be a key offensive tactic. Most assume the underground developments will be protected by the surface. In a lot of cases, this would be true, but not all. Omega sets up base camp for his family and himself on Jupiter. There are military training facilities on its various moons. Humans have, also, colonized some of the other planets, but it is much harder on their bodies, and the fatality rate is very high. The harsh conditions mean that, away from Earth, the Kison Tontu have a lot more freedom, but that will not last long. The most recent revolt has been a devastating blow to the economy, as well as to the pride of the GMC.

* * *

After various skirmishes throughout the galaxy, the GMC has taken significant losses. Uranus and Mars have ended in bloody standoffs. General Krulak, commandant of the GMC, needs an outright victory to boost morale. He also needs an opportunity to use the new navy to press the attack. The career military man has closely cropped, brown hair that is turning silver, tanned skin, and intelligent brown eyes. Krulak is of average height and well-muscled, as a result of constant training. He has been taught that officers lead from the front. How can you do that if you can't keep up? To keep from having to answer that question, he drills himself murderously. The entire Marine Corp knows this, and all respect and admire him for it. Most officers try their best to follow his example.

The general, along with his most trusted military advisors, including Lt. General Jones and newly frocked Vice Admiral Featherson, come up with a possible target. All they need now is a way to implement the attack. There are various aerospace shipyards in and around some of Saturn's moons. Each is working feverishly to crank out space-worthy attack craft for this initial assault. Luckily, the Galactic military possesses enough ore and has enough material stockpiled to last fifty years or so. During the revolt, the Stone People have managed to steal untold amounts of ore and resources for themselves and their allies. Krulak knows they are up to something. He only hopes that his people would win this arms' race in time to land the first blow. That blow will hit a small colony on Pluto. The humans have been hurt during the uprising. It is time to return the favor.

* * *

Meanwhile the workers in the newly constructed shipyards around Jupiter are no less busy building war craft for the Kison Askari, and thousands of warriors train in underground complexes deep beneath the surface of the largest planet in the Milky Way. There the Stone Warriors rigorously train in hand-to hand-combat, as well as weapons training, using shoulder fired laser cannons made specifically for them to wield. They already have a vast physical advantage in size, speed, and strength. Proper knowledge of what to do with it will only widen the gap. The commandeered weapons they have are of good quality, but they have limited ammunition for them. The custom-made laser cannons are more comfortable to fire and handle; thus accuracy is much higher. They are determined that the next ground battle will be won decisively without the need for surprise or subterfuge.

Not to be outdone by their counterparts, the Marines are on Saturn arduously sharpening their deadly skills. The recruit depots on Earth and other planets continue to train Marines, but the ones on Saturn are the elite. The conditions there make the days strenuous. Heavier gravity, a shorter day cycle, and an atmosphere they can't breathe in makes things tough. Not all of them survive. The average surface temperature is negative 218 degrees Fahrenheit. All P.T. runs are done in full vac-suits. These are highly uncomfortable, but they are better than freezing to death while their lungs burn for oxygen. Soon after Sgt. Garrison makes a full recovery, he begins training in earnest. When he can move his body in concert with his legs, he is made one of the first drill instructors on Saturn. Thus, drill instructor Sgt. Garrison leads many such P.T. runs on Saturn's uninhabitable surface. Strangely enough, he enjoys the challenging runs through the barren alien terrain. The sun beats down on them, offering no heat through a weird purple haze. Garrison revels in the strong voices echoing through the comm units built into their helmets.

"Left, left, left, right, layo!"

"Left, left, left, right, layo!"

"Lo, right, layo!"

"Lo, right, layo!"

"Left, right, layo!"

"Left, right, layo!"

"Lo, right, layo!"

"Lo, right, layo!"

"Love to double time"

"Love to double time!"

"We do it all the time!"

"We do it all the time!"

"Up in the morning with the Saturn sun!"

"Up in the morning with the Saturn sun!"

"Gonna run all day til the runnins done!"

"Gonna run all day til the runnins done!"

"Night Eagle floatin' down the strip!"

"Night Eagle floatin' down the strip!"

"Me and eighty-six gonna take a little trip!"

"Me and eighty-six gonna take a little trip!"

"Get down, buckle up, shuffle through the door!"

"Get down, buckle up, shuffle through the door!"

"Jump right out and shout Marine Corp!"

"Jump right out and shout Marine Corp!"

This is his platoon. These are his brothers. In society, he is now an outcast, but here, among his brothers in arms, he belongs. Sgt. Garrison has a new purpose in life, and that purpose is to inflict as much pain as possible on those that harm him or his brothers.

* * *

Ms. Levine waits in her private chamber prior to an important press conference. She's dressed in long gray senatorial robes. The left breast pocket is embroidered with the new executive insignia. It's a silver eagle surrounded by nine stars. The insignia is new, as is the bill she's about to announce tonight. The senator's short blonde hair, clear blue eyes, and cherubic face masks the hatred in her heart. The outward appearance makes one think of fairness and goodwill, but it hides spitefulness and cunning. How dare these savages turn against us! The senator thinks to herself.

Angered by the recent revolt and the constant questioning of her sexual orientation, the senator sulks. She had been having a good political run until rumors about her and her security chief, Officer Thomas, having an affair began to spread. The senator feels it is irrelevant that she has no use for men in a physical sense. She has to put all these thoughts aside to concentrate on the task at hand. In moments, the senator will be addressing the galaxy to propose a bill that will restore order.

If made into law, not only will the Stone People be rounded up, but so will sympathizers to their cause. They'll all be deemed enemies of the government. A woman with sandy blonde hair, brown eyes, and dressed in a black security uniform enters the senator's private chamber.

"Are you ready, baby?" CSO Thomas asks, watching the sole object of her loyalty and affection.

The senator gives her a disapproving glance and replies, "Yes, I am quite ready, and you know better than to address me so casually here. You never know who could be listening."

Thomas rolls her eyes, then sarcastically said, "Very well, Senator. I'll be expecting some sort of corporal punishment later."

Before the senator can respond, the door slides open and four orbs, known as hovercams, float into the chamber, trailed by three top media executives. All of the executives nod politely as the senator composed herself at her desk. Thomas takes her place out of camera shot, a meter behind and to the left of the senator. When the senator looked up to make eye contact with the hovercams, the light on each one goes from amber to red. All four hovercams hang stationary in midair as the senator addresses the galaxy.

SAT-NET programs throughout the galaxy are interrupted simultaneously. Perplexed viewers watch in confusion as the screens in their homes or work places go blank. When the screens come back on, they are looking into the cool blue eyes of Senator Levine.

"Greetings, my fellow citizens of the Milky Way. I apologize for disturbing you, but what I have to say is of great importance due to recent events. For those of you that don't know me, I am Senator Michelle Levine. As I'm sure most of you know, by now, there's been an uprising by miners resulting in many innocent deaths. The miners have now begun to mobilize hostile forces on Pluto and Neptune. Such acts of violence cannot be tolerated or condoned by our government. We need your help to neutralize this situation in a lawful manner."

* * *

Disgusted, Jared Omega watches Senator Levine propose the new "Loyalist Act," which, if made into law, will allow her and the government to set up control camps. These camps will be used to isolate wayward "miners" and anyone sympathetic to their cause. Omega sneers every time the senator refers to his people as "miners," acting as if this is just some labor dispute and not a fight for freedom. His anger rises as he listens to this politician twist the truth, making it seem as if she has everyone's well-being in mind. Omega sees the Loyalist Act for what it is — a tool by which the government can put the Kison Tontu back in shackles and silence all criticism of this with the control camps. Under the umbrella of the law, they will be able to round up anyone they deem as enemies of the government or a threat to the status quo. The only surprise is the mention of Pluto and Neptune. They are not strategic locations, and the only significant installations there are mining outposts. Colonization is there, but it is minimal due to the location and atmosphere of those planets.

The senator closes the speech by urging the citizens to vote for the Loyalist Act to ensure a return to normalcy and to help suppress the insurgents. The monitors throughout the galaxy go blank, once again, and then return to normal programming. Some are caught off guard by the announcement, but happy to hear the government is willing to deal with troublemakers. Others, however, are not fooled by the charade, no matter how sincere the senator seemed.

In Senator Levine's private chamber, the hovercams shut down and float out of the room. The three anonymous media execs mumble their thanks and follow the hovercams out.

"How was it?" Levine asks when she is sure they are alone.

"Inspirational as usual, Senator. I'm sure the citizens will see reason and approve it," Chief Thomas replies stiffly.

The Senator stifles a chuckle at the obvious sarcasm while preparing to go home. Thomas and the other two members of the security team escort the senator to the balcony to await their transport. Moments later, a long, sleek car with anti-grav engines pulls up to the balcony. After visually clearing the vehicle, she watches the senator climb in and then follows. The other two security officers board up front. When they are underway to the senator's palatial home, a mischievous glint comes to Levine's eyes as she says, "I believe we can contemplate your punishment now, Chief."

Chapter Five

LT. GENERAL JONES SITS ON the observation deck in the immense space station surrounding one of Saturn's moons. The space station is built around the furthest moon from the ring of Saturn, giving the illusion of a small replica of the planet. In between the station and the planet floats the newly constructed shipyard. General Jones watches the galaxy's first hyperspace capable fleet performing combat maneuvers. There is a look of pride in the general's stern brown eyes. Hyperspace technology has been around for a while, but this fleet is being manufactured with linkable navigation computers. Now military units in their entirety will be able to make hyperspace jumps simultaneously. This capability was not needed before. Most of the hostilities, up to this point, have taken place on Earth. This, however, will begin a new era in warfare. The hatch hisses open, and General Jones turns to see Rear Admiral Halsey enter.

The admiral snaps to attention and smartly salutes the general. "Good evening, sir!" the admiral barks,

"Good evening, Admiral," General Jones replies.

The two officers turn to face the main porthole through which a colossal Centurion class space carrier and a third of its normal contingency of ships can be seen awaiting orders for their maiden simultaneous jump. The ships without hyperspace capability are swarming into the docking bays on the underside of the hyoid-shaped floating city. The Centurion class space carrier looks like a gargantuan gunmetal gray horseshoe bristling with weaponry. The sub-light engines are located aft of the ship, the two tips of the "horseshoe" leading the way are the bow. The command decks are located in the interior of the U-shaped vessel seemingly shielded by the rest of the ship. The sub-light engines glow softly waiting for the other ships to dock before the jump.

The general and admiral could pass for brothers. Both men have silver, close-cropped hair, brown eyes, and a rigid military posture. Though still muscular, the admiral's build is slightly thinner. Both officers swell with pride as they gaze out the viewport at the precision formation flying of the newly minted battle group. Four smaller but still huge Man of War class space frigates flank the Centurion. The sub-light engines flare, and the hulking Centurion slowly lumbers forward. When the last of the small fighters finish docking in the bays of the carrier, the huge craft stops its forward progress. Gigantic attitude thrusters ignite, orientating the ship for the jump.

The two officers stand, transfixed by the size and military majesty of the Centurion carrier. Lt. General Jones is the first to break out of the trance. "Ops deck to the bridge of the *Peacemaker*." There is a small chirp, and then the screen comes to life showing a man with a shaved pate and cool gray eyes.

On the bridge of the *Peacemaker* stands Captain King; he waits at modified parade rest with his hands clasped behind his back, staring out at the void they are about to travel. The short, prematurely bald naval officer is in his dress white uniform with golden eagles gleaming on his collar. All that he has endured now seems worth it. The captain thinks to himself, All those who laughed at me will now shiver in fear at the power I have at my disposal. The thought brings a smile to his lips. There is a chirp, and the comm officer, a redheaded lieutenant, tells him there is an incoming transmission from the observation deck of the lunar space station. The captain checks himself over and goes to stand before the monitor.

"Put it through," he orders.

When the blank monitor is activated, the captain finds himself looking at the two (nearly identical) officers.

Seeing that stars adorn both of their uniforms, the captain salutes crisply and greets them, "Good evening, gentlemen."

"Good evening, Captain," they chorus.

The admiral steps closer to the monitor to addresses the captain. "At ease, George. I trust all is ready to get underway."

"Yes, sir. She's ready, and the men are ready to take care of business," replies Captain King.

The admiral glances at the three-star general, and the general nods before addressing King. "Very well, Captain. Proceed to the target and turn it into a parking lot. I want those rockheads to get the message."

The captain snaps to attention and salutes. "Aye, aye, general!"

Both monitors wink out.

"Think our boy will make it?" the admiral asks Jones.

"I hope so. Those ships are state of the art ... and expensive, to boot. He's got a good astronavigation crew, so as long as they get there, the soldiers and fighter jocks should take care of the rest."

Neither of them look very confident, because, even though Captain King is highly motivated, he sometimes takes unnecessary risks.

It turns out they are not far off in their assessment. As soon as Captain King is given the order to proceed, he turns to the helmsman and asks, "Ensign Sims, did you get the new plot coordinates I sent to your console?"

Incredulously, the brown-skinned, heavily muscled young officer with wavy black hair replies, "Yes, sir, but —"

Before he can finish, the captain overrides him. "Set a course for the route I calculated. It's faster and safe. I want to get to Pluto, excise our society of the cancer there, and be back in a reasonable time."

A few of the crewmembers exchange nervous glances, but they can tell, by the look on the captain's face, that he will brook no argument.

What the Captain doesn't realize, since his rank and station are due mainly to family connections and money, is that plotting a course through space is a very complex endeavor. There are many black holes, celestial bodies, and many other anomalies that have to be taken into account. It's not a simple matter of plotting from point A to point B. Most of the crew doubts the captain has considered beyond routine obstacles during his calculations. After looking longingly at the captain for some sign of common sense or intelligence and not seeing it, Ensign Sims reluctantly does as he was ordered. He turns to his console while muttering, "Aye-Aye, sir," under his breath and pulls up the route calculated by Captain King. The young ensign then punches in the coordinates and prays silently before engaging the hyperdrive systems. The whole ship begins to roar as the crew feels invisible hands pushing them into their seats. Outside the main viewport, the stars turns into bright streaks, and the ship quiets to a low hum. The inertial compensators in the hulking ship return everything to normal, and it is announced that the crew is free to move about the ship.

Two days later, when Ensign Sims is on his way to the galley, the great vessel begins to shudder. Sims stops the lift with the press of a button on a small console beside the hatch. A female voice comes from the intercom requesting, "Destination?"

"Bridge," the ensign replies.

The lift, then, reverses its direction, heading back up to the bridge. After two days of uneventful flight, the suspicions about the captain's calculated route have died down some. The entire ship shuddering, however, brings Simms's fears back to the forefront of his mind. Upon reaching the bridge level, the hatch hisses open, and Sims springs out racing down the gleaming white corridors to reach the command deck of the bridge. Sims enters the bridge to see his fears confirmed by the horror-stricken looks on the faces of the crew, including Captain King's. Something is definitely wrong, but no one seems to have the heart to voice what it was.

Sims throws a questioning glance at the red-headed lieutenant. Anger blossoms in her eyes, and she breaks the silence. "It seems our esteemed captain has led us into a singularity!"

The captain, fuming, roars, "I will not tolerate belligerence and insubordination on my bridge! I could charge you with treason!" he adds lamely. The captain closed his gray eyes, taking a moment to control his rage before continuing, "To redeem yourselves, put your effort into finding a way to avoid this obstacle. These things are known to move. How could I, or anyone, have predicted this?"

'These things' that the captain refers to are singularities or black holes, and, to the best of everyone's knowledge, are stationary phenomena. No one, however, is eager to argue this fact. The crew works diligently, but nothing stops the *Peacemaker* from being pulled toward the black hole. The ship shudders again, and then it is terribly hot. The crew sweats profusely, and this shouldn't have been the case. The sudden heat increase is inexplicable because the hull of the ship is comprised of highly endothermic alloys. The black hole is the ultimate void. Slowly the outer hull begins to break up, setting off a chain reaction of explosions until, finally, the entire ship is ablaze, floating lazily into the maw of the insatiable black hole. The frigates, slaved to the carrier, are pulled to the same horrible demise.

* * *

Back on Earth, Athena, queen of the Limbia Johari, is fulfilling her role as spy and knowledge broker for the oppressed peoples. The Limbia Johari, or walking jewels, are commonly used as servants in affluent homes and businesses. As a result, they usually have access to top secret information before it is disseminated. It is only natural that espionage would be the contribution her people would make to the cause. Moments like these almost make up for the humiliation the Limbia Johari have suffered at the hands of the so-called elite. Through diligent work, they are able to intercept an encrypted message from the senate to the military. The beauteous lavender eyes of Athena are furiously scanning the decrypted missive. The contents of the message appall and enrage her. The Loyalist Act has not officially been passed, yet here are instructions for the military to begin detaining, not only Stone People, but all abnormal humans deemed threats to the establishment. "Abnormal," meaning all mutated races. This means her people are in danger of being detained if they are caught siphoning information, or even if they weren't. Even normal humans, who show any inclination to sympathize with the oppressed mutants, are to be taken immediately. A possible early strike on Pluto is also mentioned. It seems as if the senate is taking the initiative as the foremost instigator, and has signed off on all of this.

Athena quickly compiles a list of the senators who have authorized jumping the gun, and sends the list, along with the message, to Jared Omega. Once he gets this information, Athena knows Hironike would be notified. When that happens, the Jade Assassins will be called into action. Athena does not agree with some of their methods, but the senate is playing dirty. Sometimes things have to get worse before they can get better.

* * *

To most of society, the Jade Assassins are no more than a vague myth. The name is used to scare wayward children. For the most part, the reality of the organization's deadly activities are kept secret. Hironike and his people work hard to keep it that way. They are, by no means, anonymous, though. The Jade Assassins are known, far and wide, by another name. Their alter ego, as you might call it, is Ongakujin, the world-renowned group skilled in all manner of music, theater, and dance.

Ongakujin is sought after by the highest echelon of society. Their myriad talents give them not only relatively easy access to their targets, but also an abundance of venues in which to ply their lethal trade. Heads of state and military leaders have always been targets of assassination attempts, especially at public gatherings. This is a widely known fact, and the high and mighty will have their entertainment, regardless of the risks. The beauty of the operation is that the Jade Assassins don't always strike. Their musical, dance, and theatrical performances are well-deserving of the acclaim and praise they receive. The performances lull their targets into a false sense of security. Targets are often unaware that their assassins are right in front of them. Ironically some of the Jade Assassins/Ongakujins' targets have been some of their most avid fans. More often than not, the police and security teams look everywhere but the stage after someone is killed. Even if Ongakujin is questioned, the effort is only a formality. After all, they are revered and nearly above suspicion. All this caters to Hironike and his people. He's just received a list of potential targets from Jared Omega and Athena. The Jade Assassins were born of necessity, and Hironike and his emerald-skinned warriors know it would be "show time" again soon.

In Kyoto, Hironike sits in his private garden, meditating among bonsai trees and cherry blossoms. Upon receiving the message from Omega, the head Jade Assassin calls the others. Takimura and Megumi will arrive soon. Toshi, the brains behind a lot of their instruments/weapons, is on Jupiter collaborating with the Kison Askari on a fighter ship design. Hironike will have to call Toshi in before any attempts can be made. The planning will be meticulous, but, at least, he can bounce some ideas off Taki and Megumi before anything can be finalized.

As the leader of the Jade Assassins sits in the lotus position, meditating and enjoying the tranquility of his garden, there is an almost inaudible sound similar to a light breeze. Hironike knows he is no longer alone. Without moving or even opening his eyes, he greets his two stealthy companions, "Konbonwa watashi no tomodachi."

The two smaragdine-skinned assassins (one tall and broad shouldered; the other female, petite and lithe) stop at a respectable distance and bow simultaneously to their leader. Takimura replied, "Good evening, Sensei. We came as soon as we could."

Megumi searches the garden with her almond eyes before asking, "Toshi wa, doko des ka?"

Hironike answers, "Toshi's on Jupiter working with Omega and Babylon's aeronautical engineers. He's working on the designs for the Kitana and Shibokaze class star fighters. They should be just about finished. Meanwhile we should check the guest list from our performance against the list of government and military conspirators. Once we see how many matches we have, we can figure out who and how many we want to take out at a time. Toshi should be back soon, and he'll probably have some new toys for us. Are there any questions?"

They all wait, gathering their thoughts, until Takimura breaks the silence. "Are we going to target the heads of administration first to slow down their decision making?"

Hironike mulls this over before responding. "No, actually we're going to start a little lower to send a message to the big wigs. We're also going to wait until they strike first. Sort of let them tighten the noose on their own necks. I know this will be costly, especially in terms of lives, but no one will blame us for retaliating. This will soon be an all-out war, but for now, we have to use guerilla tactics. Our forces are mobilizing now, but the fleet is not big or strong enough to be a challenge to the GMC. The Kison Askari have openly confronted them, and soon, we all will. We're not used to war on a large scale, and they are, so we're a little behind the curve. Toshi says we're catching up fast, so let's be ready for him when he arrives. Get the list compiled for me."

"Hai!" they both respond and leave to complete the task.

* * *

It didn't take long for word to travel back to the lunar space station at Saturn about the failed mission to Pluto. In a rage, General Krulak gives Lieutenant General Jones all power and authority to rectify the situation. With orders from the commandant in hand, no doors are closed to Lieutenant General Jones; all assets are immediately available to him. Painfully aware of how detrimentally expensive the loss of the Centurion space carrier and the ships that went with it are, Jones is determined not to make the same mistake. For the second attempt on the same mission, a much smaller battle group is chosen. Jones is leaving nothing to chance. He will lead the mission himself from the bridge of a Praetorian class cruiser, the smallest of the capitol ships. The Praetorian is designed to protect the flanks of the cumbersome Centurion carriers with speed and formidable firepower.

The Praetorian looks like a big metallic bird of prey with wings fully extended. The wingtips house laser cannons, while launch tubes are on the underside of the wings. It will be crewed by a mix of approximately thirty Marine and navy personnel. That is all that's needed, and that's all that Jones is taking on the cruiser, but they are to be accompanied by a squadron of prototype Thor class bombers. Air-to-air, or rather space-to-space, resistance is not expected, but just in case, the bombers are to be escorted by a flight of space harriers. Both the bombers and space harriers are to be flown by Marine pilots. The lieutenant general handpicks the crew for his cruiser and chooses Lieutenant Krulak, son of the commandant, as the squadron leader for the Pluto offensive. The younger Krulak is a capable pilot with plenty of ambition. The name doesn't hurt either, and for these reasons, Lt. General Jones leaves it up to the discretion of the junior Krulak, who the other pilots will be. After this is accomplished, the smaller battle group gathers in formation outside of Saturn's lunar space station and prepares to jump to Pluto. On the bridge of the Praetorian cruiser, the *Dante,* Lt. General Jones is seated in the command chair. "Open a line to the squadron leader," he commands.

"Aye-aye, sir!" the communications officer replies, and immediately a monitor slides up from the deck in front of the general, showing the obscured face of the younger Krulak in full flight gear.

"Lieutenant, have the squadron link their nav-computers to the *Dante's.* The route we're taking is the most recommended, if you actually want to make it there. I don't want to lose anyone to any 'special routes,' and remember this actually is rocket science, so no heroics from you or the other fighter jocks. Is that understood?"

"Yes, General!" Lt. Krulak replies.

"Good. Now once we come out of the jump, you are authorized to go weapons free and complete the mission. We'll be there to supervise. When the squadron's linked, give us a double click, and we'll initiate the jump. Godspeed. General Jones out."

The general turns to the communications officer and the helmsman and says, "When you receive confirmation of the link from the squadron leader, commence the jump."

"Aye-aye, General!" they both reply.

A minute later, the confirmation is received, and after a nod from the communications officer, the helmsman initiates the jump. The stars turn into streaks of light, and the engines roar into a steady hum as the battle group hurtles toward Pluto.

Chapter Six

A FEW HUNDRED MILES OUTSIDE of Pluto's atmosphere, the *Dante* and its retinue come out of hyperspace. The stars that are streaks of light reverted to pinpricks of light. As soon as he realizes that they are back in real space, First Lieutenant Krulak opens up a secure com-link frequency to the bomber squadron.

"OK, leathernecks! You heard the man. Before the jump, we are weapons free and cleared to designated targets. There's not much here, only a few settlements easily seen because of the scarcity of any other signs of civilization. There should be holographic mapping images on your H.U.Ds, I've assigned a target for each flight. This is pretty simple stuff, gentlemen. Let's make this place uninhabitable again. I don't expect any trouble, but you flyboys in the Harriers are to watch our backs in and out. Let's do this!"

In reply, he receives double clicks from his squadron.

Thrusters flare as all three flights and their SpaceHarrier escorts push their throttles forward to speed over the designated targets. The Thor class bombers are shaped like double-bladed battle-axes, with the rounded handles leading the way. The launch bays for ordinance are located beneath the curved wings or "blades" of the huge battle-axe. The cockpits, mysteriously enough, are also located beneath the craft at the end of the "handle." They are bubble cockpits that can move like an eye in its socket with small laser cannons to either side of the pilot. The SpaceHarriers look like bigger versions of their archaic predecessors. The main differences are that SpaceHarriers are space-worthy, as well as atmosphere capable, and the armaments were laser- and proton-based. By contrast, the Thor is only viable in space, equipped with laser cannons, and its sole purpose is to drop ordinance on planetary targets. Each flight of Thor's are led by a Harrier, the squadron leader's flight has an additional one covering their aft en route to the designated target area. When they are just outside the gaseous envelope of Pluto's atmosphere, the bomb bay doors beneath the axe-like wings open to reveal racks of hammer-shaped shells. These are called mjollnir shells; each carries a quarter ton of thermal explosive inside the "head" of the hammer. The "handles" of these hammers are fitted with mini-thrusters, which are sufficient enough to push the shells through the atmosphere. For this operation, it should be relatively easy because Pluto's atmosphere is so thin. Once the mjollnirs are released, however, something happens that is not predicted, but should have been.

As the mjollnirs approach the atmosphere, there is a blinding reaction when the mini-thrusters break the plane. Not only is Pluto's atmosphere thin, it, also, contains a high amount of methane. The heat from the mini-thrusters ignites the methane, temporarily transforming the dwarf star into an incandescent sun. The squadron barely escapes being engulfed in blue-white flames as they head back toward the *Dante*.

* * *

In the domed city on Pluto's surface, Ngoni begins to worry. A lot of the facility life support systems are on the decline. Now it seems as if he is going to have to add the temperature gauges to the list of things to work on because it is extremely hot. This was strange because the average surface temperature outside the dome was -369 degrees Fahrenheit. The Kison Tontu are not known to sweat, except in the most extreme of hot climates. Pluto is the opposite, and yet the old but large slate-skinned warrior tasked with system maintenance is sweating profusely. He goes to the viewport to look outside, and his worry turns to perplexity as he sees it is bright and getting brighter. His bewilderment turns to anger as he realizes the temperature is still inexplicably rising. Others are just as confused as they flood the maintenance quarters to see what has gone wrong. They are all blinded as the heat becomes unimaginable. Screams are silenced before they can fully form as hardened skin melts away, and the flesh beneath sizzles to nothing in a hellish inferno. It took nearly a full day, but it seemed instantaneous as the fuel for the flames eventually burned out. What was left behind was a planet-sized smoldering gray rock cooled by the vacuum.

Most of the crew aboard the *Dante* is amazed at the speed and ferocity of Pluto's decimation. A significant amount of lives have just been extinguished without a hint or chance of resistance. This does not sit well with many of the men and women in uniform, but orders are orders. As dishonorable as the mission feels after its completion, Lt. General Jones knows that, sometimes, such actions are necessary. This is war after all. The battle group resumes their previous formation, link navigation computers, and jump back to Saturn to await further orders.

* * *

Back in Egypt, Professor Charles Jones-Bey has just returned from a seminar in Paris. Ever since his discovery on man's genetic link to the Kison Tontu, the brown-skinned clean-shaven scholar has been diligently searching for more knowledge, and he has found it. He has discovered that man is also related to the Limbia Johari as strange as that seems. He has known this in his heart, that this is the case before the research is complete. It is just a matter of proving the theory is correct. Jones-Bey is still trying to isolate the mutated genes, which, for some odd reason, is proving to be far more difficult than it should be.

The professor believes that knowledge is power, and upon acquiring proof of his theories, he quickly spreads the information. The way he sees it, the galaxy is on the brink of an all out civil war. With this newfound knowledge, he hopes to promote brotherhood and end the hostilities. Unfortunately, the government doesn't see it that way. Although they cannot refute Jones-Bey's findings, they publicly deny them. The recent seminar and pamphlets produced and distributed by Jones-Bey spark much protest about what the government is doing. The Loyalist Act passes easily behind a veil of deceit, and now the general public's eyes are being opened to reality. The professor will have to be dealt with soon.

Outside of Professor Jones-Bey's apartment, the motion sensors detect activity in the entryway. This automatically activates the vid-cams in the area. The professor is surprised because he is not expecting visitors, but he is not worried because the threat alarm hasn't gone off. He is more confused by the fact that he does not recognize the late-night intruders. What is immediately familiar to the professor are the uniforms they wear.

Four men stand at the ready with military grade personal laser cannons. They are clad in black body armor, with blue metallic shields on their left breast plates, and on the front of their black helmets are visors. There is a fifth man dressed similarly, who brings up the rear. The only thing that distinguishes him from the others are the silver bars on his shoulder plates.

The professor approaches the door to ask the reason for this unlikely visit when it explodes inward, knocking him off of his feet. Door fragments fly everywhere as the men in the security forces uniforms enter the apartment.

* * *

When the professor comes to, he finds himself staring at the ceiling. He shakes his head to clear it when the security forces leader speaks, "Professor Charles Jones-Bey?"

"Yes, what the hell is the meaning of this?" Jones-Bey says.

"You're under arrest," the leader replies.

"For what?" the professor growls.

The leader pulls out a small data pad, looks down, and begins to read aloud, "For conspiring against the government, inciting riots, mayhem ... uh ... need I say more?"

Before Jones-Bey can respond, the leader commands, "Take him!"

Two of the security force officers pull out stun rods, and for the Professor Jones-Bey, all goes black.

* * *

Pharaoh sits in the uppermost chamber of the pyramid in Guatemala, meditating. He sits in the form that has become most comfortable for him. He has golden brown skin, long jet black hair, and brown eyes. The light being is truly savoring the enjoyment of manipulating Earth and the rest of the galaxy for the sheer entertainment of it. Instead of making things simple, man always has to further life's complications. This is one of the only things Pharaoh admires about man. It keeps things interesting. Fear and greed, also, help Pharaoh, and these are abundant. Man constantly seeks technological advancement for the wrong reasons, and Pharaoh is always there to provide or push in the right direction. After all, he is only doing what the elders demand of him. Pharaoh's eyes burn with hatred as he remembers the exile imposed on him millennia ago.

Sometime long ago, when prehistoric man was roaming the Earth hunting and gathering, the Radiant Ones came among them to bring the gift of knowledge. Pharaoh (then called by his unknown original name) had been working with these dull, shortsighted beings for centuries now and was highly frustrated by their lack of progress. The others of his kind didn't seem to mind being in the presence of these vermin and this further disgusted Pharaoh. The first sign that these fools were undeserving of respect was when Pharaoh showed himself in his true form and the humans fled in fear. Later they would worship him, and he would take advantage of that. The Radiant Ones would have to assume a form similar to man's own in order to interact with them at all. This took some experimentation, but soon was an easy task. Pharaoh found this tedious and demeaning. Soon Pharaoh started taking his frustration out on the slowest of his pupils by putting them through hideous and painful mutations. Pharaoh had finally found something he liked here. The anguish of man was utterly delicious and hilarious. He figured the others were enjoying themselves in a similar fashion. To his surprise, they were not. In fact, some had become aware of Pharaoh's actions and were appalled. They did the unthinkable and reported him to the elders.

Pharaoh opens his eyes, coming back to the present, leaving the past image of twelve living beacons handing down a sentence to one of their own. The betrayal he felt was staggering. Enlighten man? Impossible! They had also ordered him not to harm these backward beings. This Pharaoh gets around easily. Man shows an affinity for all things violent, and nothing is said about man hurting himself. Pharaoh merely provides a means and nudges them along the way. Honest attempts have been made to enlighten these people, but boredom leads to further experimentation, and then other tools are discovered that help violence flourish. The most prevalent tool is diversity. For some reason, man fears anything different from himself. To promote this, Pharaoh genetically pushes groups of men in different directions. When they overcome certain prejudices, Pharaoh creates reasons for new ones. This has become a seemingly endless cycle. Now someone is trying to stop the cycle. This, Pharaoh cannot allow.

The exiled Radiant One mentally calls out to his most trusted minion. The hooded ghostly figure of Malice glides into the chamber. The glowing crimson eyes burn a hole into Pharaoh as he asks, "Yes, Master?"

Both pleased and slightly angered by the lack of fear in his servant, Pharaoh answers, "The scholar who found us in Egypt should be eliminated. The knowledge he is spreading could bring man together."

Malice silently broods and then says, "Master, no man has ever been able to unite more than an insignificant group together. This scholar shall be no different." Sensing his master's anger, Malice quickly adds, "I don't question you. Of course, it will be done."

"Good. Be sure that it is," Pharaoh replies. It doesn't seem possible, but Professor Jones-Bey's troubles have just gotten worse.

* * *

Deep in the petrous caverns beneath Jupiter's surface, Jared Omega sits pondering the progress of the war. As the king of the Kison Tontu worries about the senator's announcement and the intercepted message, his anxiety only increases when no communication from Pluto has come back to him. The Stone Warriors have sent scouts to check on their brethren there in prototypes their aerospace engineers and Toshi have put together. The navigation systems are top notch, but the weapons packages have some bugs to be worked out. It is not certain if they will encounter hostile forces or not. Omega prefers not to battle test the new star fighter until they are sure of the weapons.

Tunisia, an ebon-skinned Kison Askari and the wife of Jared Omega, walks up behind the king to put a strong but slender hand on his broad shoulder. The coal black eyes and dark gray visage of Omega's turn to concentrate on the liquid brown, almond-shaped eyes of his queen. One look at the breathtakingly beautiful look of serenity on her face drains the anxiety from him. They embrace, and Omega is grateful for her presence and the calming effect she has on him. "Still the worrier, I see," she tells him.

"It is my responsibility to be concerned," Omega answers.

"No, your responsibility is to lead your people in the right direction. This you have done. We knew there'd be risks before we began. Share the burden of concern with others. You are our king, our strongest link. Too much strain, and it might break when we need it most," Tunisia chides.

Omega considers this and says, "I have you to worry about, also. Are you still not feeling well?"

"I am, and I am not," she replies.

Confused, the king asks, "How is that?"

"Calm down, beloved. I am feeling better because nothing is actually wrong with me. The reason for my sudden ailment is because I carry another life within me." Omega's eyes go wide in surprise. "Yes, I'm afraid you have, at least, one more thing to be concerned about, but I hope you're happy as well," she adds.

Taken aback, Omega finally blurts, "Of course, I'm happy, but we must get you to safety. A son would make me most proud."

Annoyed, Tunisia retorts, "What if it's a daughter?"

Chagrined, the king replies, "Then I'll be equally proud. I must fight all the harder to make the galaxy a better place for him or her to live in."

"I'll take that, Omega," she replies not entirely convinced and then goes on, "How can I leave with all that's going on?"

Omega quickly answers, "We'll smuggle you back to Earth somehow on the next transport going there. Too many things are happening here. It could be catastrophic if the baby is born here."

What the king of the Stone Warriors says is true. The gravity there is slightly higher than Saturn's. A newborn's skin will not be tough enough yet to protect its internal organs and skeletal system. This strain can stunt its growth or cause deformation. They definitely need to get Tunisia to a safe haven, if not Earth, so the baby can be born in relative peace, but that might prove difficult.

* * *

On a planet at the edge of the galaxy, there's a clandestine meeting being held by six living beacons. This planet is always mistaken for a star because of its inhabitants. It could be the most wonderful place in the entire universe, even the vegetation shimmers. Most of the dwellings are transparent, and the occupants glow for all to see. The brilliance of millions is so bright that it is visible from light-years away.

However, the living beacons of this meeting are not on the surface, and no one knows they are in the thalamic place that hid them. Satori, Ra, Heru, Amsu, Avsar, and Nubia, all ancient beings of light, sat in a circle in their purest form, like a gathering of small suns. Satori the most constant of them, is leading a discussion, if you can call it that about what they are witnessing in the Milky Way. It can't quite be called a conversation because they are communicating the way they are most comfortable — telepathically. It is more akin to brain synapses firing off at each other, rather than a conversation, and it is hard to keep track of which thought belongs to whom. It is almost as if all their identities become jumbled together during the spirited debate.

"This is madness. All of man seems bent on destroying each other/I know and I'm ashamed that one of our own is responsible. We should advise the Council of Elders/They already know; besides, intervention was denied as an option. They say Pharaoh is actually teaching them./Yes! In only martial matters for his own frivolities./Oh, come on now. They have made some progress. They travel the galaxy after all./The fact that they still need vehicles to travel shows how small that progress is./What can be done? Has all been decided?/We can ignore the Council and intervene!/ Then we'll be no better than the exiled./Not so, we do what we do of our own accord, not because we are forced to, and we do not act solely for our own personal gain./The question still remains, what can be done?/If we go to Earth, surely we'll be noticed./True, but we can travel to other planets without raising any suspicion./I doubt that will put us in any position to confront Pharaoh; he's confined to Earth./Will they exile us for interfering?/ We already interfered in the development of these beings. Hopefully we can right the wrong done to them, and I have found a way so that you won't be exiled./How?/I will exile myself to personally confront Pharaoh./No, Satori!" They all yell mentally. "I am decided," Satori replies.

* * *

Anyone on the surface of the planets furthest from the sun might have caught a glimpse of Satori's transplendent form streaking toward Jupiter from beyond the realm of the Milky Way. Satori has a mission to complete. He has to find a way to Earth to confront Pharaoh. The direction the exiled Light Being is leading the galaxy in can only result in its destruction. The Living Beacons have no need for vehicles or vessels to travel, unless they carry possessions. "Things" are mundane and can be lost when they most needed them. Satori has no need of things, but he does need to go undetected by those of his kind who might be watching. Therefore he needs a vessel, and there is only one vessel he can use for his purposes, the body of a being from Earth. Satori will have to unite with one on Jupiter, and then go to Earth. This will be a precarious predicament because Satori will lose most, if not all, of his consciousness, not to mention the potential risk that might be done to the host. It is a risk that has to be taken.

Satori floats down to the surface of Jupiter and continues on throughout the caverns the Kison Askari dug below in search of a fitting symbiant. The Light Being dims himself to a soft glow as he floats through the caverns, finding none that were suitable. Satori touches the minds of those he passes just enough to erase their memories of him. He feels as if one being in particular is drawing him to it. Satori follows his instinct into a private chamber where a beautiful onyx-skinned Kison Tontu female lay sleeping. Confused Satori looks deeper into this female only to realize it is not her that lured him, but the life growing inside her.

This may solve, at least, one of the difficulties. Since the mind is not fully developed there is a smaller chance of driving the being mad. The drawback is that two would become one entity, and Satori would grow up as a member of this little being's race. Curiosity about such an experience takes over. Satori condenses himself, dives into the womb, and joins with the unborn child.

Chapter Seven

SEVEN SLEEK BOOMERANG SHAPED STAR-SHIPS burst out of hyperspace near what used to be Pluto. Toshi is in the lead; the Shibokaze Star-Fighter checks his instruments to be sure they have jumped to the right place. The instruments further confuse him by confirming that they are indeed in the right spot. Further investigation reveals no signs of life, no evidence of the domed structures known to exist here, and more alarming is the uncharacteristically high heat signature coming from what used to be the planet's surface. Upon receiving confirmation from the others in his flight, Toshi decides to go back and tell Omega the grim news. Pluto has been ruthlessly decimated. As one, all seven star-fighters turn and streak into hyperspace. Seconds later, there is a sonic boom.

* * *

Back on Earth, the recently promoted Corporal Aragon attempts to relax while on leave. After being nearly wiped out, all survivors of the initial revolt in Africa are immediately transferred to the First Recon Battalion based on Saturn. The next six months are nothing short of pure hell for Aragon and his fellow survivors. At first, it is nearly impossible to function on a basic level until the new supplements kick in. After dealing with that environment, Aragon figures they are the hardest physical specimens in the galaxy, aside from the Stone People. He feels they might have a fighting chance if everyone in the armed forces are similarly augmented and trained. As far as he knows, that is not to be, platoon 1086 is an elite group. Aragon has even been surprised by being reunited with his old squad leader. Somehow Garrison has been raised from the dead and put back together with cybernetic implants. Cpl. Aragon is now a squad leader in his own right, and Garrison is now his platoon sergeant. When their eyes meet for the first time, a chill runs through Aragon's spine as he realizes a part of his old friend has, in fact, died and been replaced by an indescribable bitterness. As frightening as that is Aragon does not shy away from his fellow Marine because, on some level, the same transformation has taken place within him. Recognizing their kinship of tortured souls, Sgt. Garrison soon takes a special interest in Aragon, pushing him. Not wanting to disappoint the man who saved him during his first combat action, Aragon does not crumble in the crucible but stands firm.

The platoon commanders have briefed the newly hardened warriors that, upon their return to Earth, their newfound speed and strength will appear superhuman. They are advised to appear as normal as possible. This frustrates Aragon mightily as he has to make a conscious effort to move with the speed perceived to be normal by his family and friends. Numerous times, he shatters glasses while trying to drink, earning strange looks from his mother. Aragon puts in some calls to some of his fellow service members and discovers they are having similar problems. There are also rumors of a preemptive strike on non-combatants on Pluto. As angry as he is, the rumor still bothers him. Since enjoying a drink has become difficult, Aragon decides to try something new.

Time and technology constantly move forward, making some things obsolete. One thing that remains constant throughout time is the need for chemical recreation. Alcoholic beverages are still around, but the Marines and sailors trained on Saturn are having difficulty enjoying them without attracting attention or without the aid of reinforced drinking vessels. To remedy this Aragon and a few of his friends decide to try the latest phenomena called *nitroclubs*. He catches a transport to the nearest one and is met outside by Corporals Simms and Jordan. They are also squad leaders but from different platoons in the company.

"About time, Aragon!" Simms says.

Aragon exits the transport. "Well, I assume you boys reconned the establishment. What's it like in there?" Aragon replies.

With mock formality, Simms brings his muscular form to attention, intense brown eyes staring at nothing, and states, "It's like no E-club I've ever been to, Corporal. Strange is the first thing that comes to mind. We didn't do more than look."

Jordan just shakes his head and motions for them to get on with it.

Before entering the building, all three Marines check each other's civilian attire. The clothing is appropriate, but at first glance, there is no denying they are military personnel. They are of different ethnicities — Jordan, a blond-haired, brown-eyed Caucasian; Aragon, dark- haired and Hispanic. Simms is of African descent and lacks the high and tight haircuts his companions are sporting, but his bearing and build match theirs perfectly. They are all having problems controlling the speed of their movements. To civilians, they look like slightly epileptic gym freaks. Because of their imposing size, nobody mentions this.

They file into a metallic and highly reflective building that seems to hum. Once inside, they are met with an eerie silence. What makes the quiet so strange is that they are standing at the beginning of a corridor with rooms running along the sides, and large windows allow them to look into various chambers where, for the most part, patrons are dancing. Some of the partiers are moving in unison while others are obviously either out of sync or are dancing to a different tune. Yet Aragon, Simms, and Jordan hear nothing.

Before their apprehension can get the best of them, a receptionist appears out of nowhere. The Marines are surprised but hide it well.

"Welcome to Cloud Nitro! How may I help you, boys?" she intones cheerfully. Her nameplate over her left breast states that her name is Mariko. She has large, dark, almond-shaped eyes, and long shiny black hair. She is dressed in a high-collared red dress that shows off her slim but curvaceous body. Seeing their indecision, she smiles and says, "First timers?"

They nod dumbly, steadily scrutinizing her. Ignoring their intense attention, Mariko steps back, and some kind of mini-bar pops up from the floor between them. A wide cabinet pops up behind her and slats slide to the side to reveal shelves with various canisters with glowing labels on them. Aragon squints at the labels lingering on two of them. The first says "Mirth," and "Ambrosia" is on the second.

"Well, since it's your first time, let me tell you how this works," Mariko begins. "It's ten G-bucks to get in the public chambers, with an additional five every three hours to keep the nitro flowing. Those are the basics, and if you like, you can always come back and try the VIP package."

Jordan and Aragon reach into their wallets to pull out the global currency when Simms stops them to ask, "What's the VIP package, and how much is it?"

Mariko smiles and replies, "Unlimited access to all the public chambers and most of the private ones. We'll take an image of you for our computers to analyze for musical purposes, or you could tell us what type of music you prefer. Most people like to see what the system will come up with before telling us. That's four hundred G-bucks for a two-month period."

Perplexed, Jordan asks, "What does our image have to do with music?"

Mariko rolls her eyes playfully as if it is obvious and says, "The computers will analyze your features to determine your racial makeup and tailor the music accordingly, along with the preferences you mention. If you're by yourself, you get your own personal theme music. As more VIPs enter, more elements are added to the mix, unless they're closely related to one of the other VIPs. It sounds complicated, but it actually keeps the music similar and fresh at the same time. The only way you'll hear the same music is to go to the same chamber by yourself or with the same friends."

Simms stifles a laugh and says, "Damn! Racist music? I like it!"

Slightly perturbed, Mariko retorts, "No, no! It's not racist. The image analysts are not a hundred percent accurate, but they're close. We haven't had any complaints. Plus, that's the reason you have the option to tell us your preferences. I personally think it promotes diversity, since a lot of people will ask others from different ethnic backgrounds to accompany them just to get a different mix. Now what will it be?"

Simms looks at his partners before taking out his military debit chip and handing it to Mariko. "We'll take three VIP passes. I've got to see this."

Aragon shrugs; Jordan looks like he's about to object, but Simms waves him off. "Don't trip. I've got this. Besides, with all the hazard pay I've got saved up, this is nothing, and it looks like we'll be getting plenty more. Might as well take advantage of what liberty and leave we have."

Mariko scans the debit chip and starts typing information on a console on top of the bar. Floating cams come out and begin recording images of the three Marines from different angles. When they're finished, the cams float back down the corridor. Mariko looks up from the console. "OK, gentlemen, what's your poison?"

Simms looks to Aragon, who nods toward the canister labeled "Ambrosia."

"Ambrosia, it is," she replies.

Jordan speaks up, "Can we try a private chamber first?"

Simms nods. "Yeah, I agree. Civilians should be taken in small doses."

The bar and cabinet retract into the floor. Mariko proceeds with three large ambrosia canisters in her arms. She turns down the corridor and orders, "Follow me."

Watching her retreating backside, all three respond, "Yes, ma'am!" and follow.

* * *

In the lobby of the Ryoko-gekijo, Athena, queen of the Limbia Johari, stands surveying the incoming patrons in search of the Jade Assassins' first government target. Dressed in a shimmering, formfitting silk gown that perfectly matches the amethyst color of her eyes and crystalline hair, she scans the crowd, looking for a match to the image displayed on a small

PalmPilot in her hands. The Ryoko-gekijo is a mobile theater that floats on huge anti-gravity engines. The theater usually stays in coastal areas over the water, but on rare occasions, it can hover high over an inland city for special events. From the outside, the floating playhouse looks like a shining castle suspended over the ocean. Inside, its luxury and opulence are without equal.

Tonight, the venue is near the Hawaiian islands in the Pacific Ocean. The swarm of hovering transports dropping off and picking up patrons and staff members is reminiscent of a gigantic beehive.

When a tall, brown-skinned man with waves meticulously brushed into his hair, wearing tacky gold-rimmed glasses, walked in, Athena holds up her PalmPilot to compare the images. There is a nearly inaudible tone as the device confirms that the new arrival is indeed the target. Anyone observing Athena's actions would assume she is checking herself in a compact mirror of some sort. Athena, then, saunters over to an information terminal near a refreshment bar and casually sets the small device on the interface plate. With the name and image already displayed on the device, it automatically pulls up the seat reservation information for the target. After another inconspicuous tone, the data is transmitted to an identical device in Hironike's possession. Before the elimination can be completed, the target's identity must be confirmed and reconfirmed by various ushers, surveillance devices, and other seemingly random passersby throughout the theater.

The subject of all this maleficent attention is Senator Beasley, a government yes-man extraordinaire known for his inability to form his own ideas or views. Ironically, this is what got him as high up in the government as he is. Other politicians saw a future, easily-influenced colleague in the former correctional officer and coaxed him into running for various seats and offices. Now that he is a senator, those politicians are not disappointed. The investment of time and backing have paid off in big dividends for them. Unfortunately for Beasley, taking the seemingly sound advice of his political benefactors and signing off on the Loyalist Act, and also helping to approve the pre-emptive strikes on Pluto will be his undoing.

Unaware that his time is about to be cut short, Senator Beasley is a happy man. Attending tonight's performance is one of the perks of being among the elite. This is a small self-reward for having the courage to stand up and do what's right in the face of adversity. Michelle Levine, his fellow senator and friend, is right, the Stone People should have taken their labor grievances up the proper chains; they should not have revolted. It is still a mystery how they defied the electromagnetic infrastructure throughout the mines, but they will be dealt with harshly. The loss of lives and other difficulties will be painful but necessary to restore order. All of these thoughts are pushed from Beasley's mind as he follows other finely dressed patrons to the elevators that will take them to their various seating levels. Once he arrives at his designated balcony, the ushers are very obsequious and helpful, as they should be. The senator is a very important man, after all. As he requested, Beasley's seat is not too close and not too far from the stage and orchestra pit. Ongakujin is performing tonight; they are the best! This place is supposedly designed so that the quality of sound is the same no matter where you sit. Beasley knows better because his friends have told him there are sweet spots where the sound will be best. Senator Beasley is also not a snob who needs to be right up front to show how important he is. In fact, he is happy to be here at all. This performance will be the experience of a lifetime. Besides, he can tell the staff knows how important he is. He can tell by the deference they show him, and more than once, they have referred to him by name and title. Dignitaries are to be well-respected.

Senator Beasley relaxes and lets the seat conform to his body as the lights begin to dim. Tonight's performance will feature music, interpretive dance, and a holographic light show. Ongakujin is a fusion of performing arts, old and new.

In the semi-darkness, Hironike assembles his special flute. Sweat makes the tuxedo cling to his green skin as he concentrates on the task at hand. In the orchestra pit, the other musicians are putting together their instruments, but only Hironike's flute has dual purposes. Of course, it plays beautifully and is masterfully crafted. The head Jade Assassin's flute has an extra piece that will collect moisture throughout the performance. He will freeze it to create a cryo-needle. Once the cryo-needle is formed, the device will slide back toward the assassin, who then sights in on the intended victim, aiming for the neck or head. Once expelled, the sharp frozen projectile can kill easily if used properly. The senator is seated well within range of the weapon. Moments before the lights begin to dim, Hironike has sighted the balcony where Beasley is seated. Now the Jade Assassin tunes the flute, so he can play his part during the performance. Once he's finished with that task, he waits with his fellow orchestra members for their cue.

For a long moment, darkness and silence reign in the theater. They are both soon shattered by an azure spotlight and the high, mournful tones of wind instruments followed by subtle violins. The focus of the spotlight is on the petite form of Megumi, laying center stage with her long black hair spread out in a huge fan above her head and shoulders. The audience involuntarily gasps as she slowly raises her head to glance at them, gracefully rising in accordance with the music, as if she is pulled by invisible strings. Gradually Megumi begins to sway; the flowing gown she wears glows softly, giving her a ghostly quality as she moves. The dance routine goes through stages, starting hesitantly, growing in fluidity and confidence to outright boisterousness. The accompanying music follows suit, going from sad to playful to triumphant, and back again. Holographic projectors make it seem as if she's dancing among the stars.

The audience is spellbound as three more figures join the dance and the music turns ominous. Broad-shouldered Takimura strides center stage like tightly coiled violence waiting to be unleashed. He's flanked by two less prominent players. They are all dressed in dark gray body suits with their shaven emerald heads, gleaming in the night. The story behind this piece is about a glowing flower-like entity that lives deep in space. The beauty and brilliance of this entity attracts a throng of space explorers who come to admire it. One of the explorers, played by Takimura, decides he wants the entity all to himself and wards off the other admirers. Once they are out of the way, the zealous explorer attempts to totally possess the flower-entity, destroying it in the process. Despite there being no words, the audience follows the action and high drama, as lasers and holographic images flash. The music varies in tempo, and cymbals crash to accentuate the ballet. The audience is astounded, baffled, and inspired by the dancers. Some of them think to themselves while others whisper aloud, "Surely they must be using some type of zero-g technology on stage! Nobody's that fast and agile. How else could anyone keep their positions moving that slowly without simply falling?"

The performance is nearing its climax as Takimura acrobatically chases Megumi around stage through a myriad of holo-images. The music and dances are perfectly matched, frolicking at first, to frenetic and finally terrifying as Takimura catches up to Megumi. In obvious anger, Takimura grabs Megumi in a crushing embrace punctuated by a high shrill note from a flute. There is a collective horrified gasp as Megumi's gown and body cease to glow as her body goes limp. The spotlights blackout and pop back on to show Takimura alone on his knees, with his head bowed, seeming to float freely among the stars. There is a sorrowful final piece being played as he lifts his tearful face to the audience in anguish over what he has done.

* * *

During the scene where Takimura finally catches up to his quarry, Hironike has spotted the target on a balcony, not forty meters above him. There is a sharp whisper covered by a high flute note as the head Jade Assassin presses the nodule, ejecting the cryo-needle at high velocity. The needle punches through Senator Beasley's throat. After lodging itself near his medulla oblongata, it instantly begins to melt. The senator is utterly confused by the chain of events leading to his death. One moment he's riveted to his seat by the artistic spectacle he's witnessing, the next he's inexplicably slugged in the throat by some invisible force. Fighting for breath and tasting blood, he looks around for help, and finds none. Everyone is still caught up in the performance. The sound of the impact is hidden by the entire theater's sudden noises of surprise at the vicious treatment of the precious flower. Many people in the audience weep when the flower's light is extinguished. The strange gurgling noises coming from the senator are probably interpreted as an audience member who has fallen deeper into the emotional turmoil of the performance. The senator's final kneeling posture is mirrored by many people throughout the theater. In the dark, it is hard to tell anything is amiss. The lights are brightened after a long standing ovation. Some patrons in the lower balconies glance up to find that the dark liquid dripping from above is not tears. Screams erupt from the terrified patrons and pandemonium breaks loose.

Chapter Eight

Back at Cloud Nitro, Corporals Aragon, Simms, and Jordan follow Mariko to a small VIP chamber with a lone occupant. The door hisses open in recognition of Mariko and the three new VIP members. Mariko bends to screw the canisters into the sockets to the right of the door and waves the Marines inside. Trance music is blaring inside the chamber; the solo occupant, who is bobbing his brown-haired head, opens his eyes when he realizes he's no longer alone. African drums with undertones of twentieth century hip-hop blend into the music as Simms steps across the threshold. Spanish guitars and bagpipes are insinuated to complete the mix as Aragon and Jordan enter. The door slides closed behind them, leaving them to try and figure out who's responsible for each musical element.

"I'll assume, from the haircuts you're sporting, that you're Marines," the stranger says by way of introduction. He is above average in height by several inches, closely cropped brown hair, brown eyes, and is in reasonable shape.

Clearly offended, Aragon answers, "What's wrong with our haircuts? It's not all that different from yours."

"You got something against Marines?" Jordan adds.

In order to calm things down, the stranger quickly replies, "Take it easy, jarheads. It's only obvious. Our haircuts may be similar, but yours are a bit more ... aggressive. I'm Petty Officer Second Class House, and I have nothing against Marines. In fact, I help put them back together."

"You're a corpsman?" Simms asks.

House nods in confirmation. Simms smiles.

"Squid are ok with us," Aragon quips.

Introductions are formally made. The vents in the chamber release the contents of one of the canisters, and seconds later, they are all extremely happy.

In a collective state of euphoria, House is the first to recover. "You gotta love that," he states.

Simms nods his head in agreement.

"It's different," Aragon hazily adds.

"Yeah" is all Jordan can manage.

Twenty minutes later, they all go through a fit of laughter, but no one seems to know what's so funny. When the sensations of elation and supreme well-being come back around, House reinitiates conversation. "The mirth always confuses things somewhat. So where are you guys stationed?"

Aragon answers for them all, still feeling a bit giddy. "First Recon Battalion. We're on leave. The rest of our outfit is training on Saturn. What about you?"

Stifling giggles of his own, House answers, "Actually, I'm on administrative leave, and in between commands. My old unit was pretty much destroyed during the uprising. On top of that, I had a difference of opinion with the company's first sergeant. A friend of mine, who works in admin, thinks I'll be heading to Saturn, but everyone's being hush-hush about it."

The Marines exchange knowing looks as all of their previous units were nearly wiped out, forcing a vast personnel shift.

"What was your disagreement with the first sergeant about?" Simms asks.

"Apparently he thought I should be skilled enough to reattach a severed head. Can you believe that?" the corpsman answers.

They are all taken by another fit of laughter, but at least this time, it seems appropriate. This time, though, Simms is the first to recover and resumes the conversation. "I've got a cousin that's a spaceswabbie like you. He was all excited because he's assigned to one of those new carriers. I'm waiting to hear from him. He still talks to me, even though I'm enlisted and a jarhead."

A strange look comes over Petty Officer House's face. Noting the look, Aragon asks, "What is it?"

"Probably nothing, but do you know the name of the carrier?" House asks in return.

Before Simms can answer that he doesn't know, the military men are all overcome by a dreamy, hypnotic state. Their bodies take on an almost weightless quality as the music seems to permeate their very beings. The door hisses open, and East Indian horns are infused into the music as a dark-skinned man in a Marine's dress blue delta uniform with golden oak leaves on the collars steps into the chamber. The four of them attempt to shake off the trance-like effects to look at the newcomer.

"Who are you?" they say dumbly in unison.

In a thick Hindi accent, the man replies. "I am Major Vashti! I'm sorry to tell you that all leave and liberty has been cancelled. The threatcon level has been raised as a result of an assassination, and something is happening at one of the new detention centers as we speak. All active duty members are to report to their local unit liason."

There's a soft hiss within the chamber, and shortly after that, they are all seized by fits of laughter. Teary eyed from cracking up, Jordan and Aragon manage to blurt simultaneously, "Are you serious? You mean now!"

Stifling giggles of his own, Major Vashti replies, "I'm afraid so."

* * *

In a dark cell in the newly constructed detention center in the Arctic, Professor Jones-Bey sits, trying to hold on to his sanity. For weeks he's been subjected to pointless interrogations. The absurdity of it all baffles him mightily. The truth shall set you free, he thinks. Unfortunately for the professor, it has done the opposite. Now he is stuck in the middle of nowhere with no way of escape. Even if he manages to get out, there is no place to go; he'll freeze to death before he gets anywhere. All the captives are constantly reminded of their chances of survival in subzero temperatures without proper supplies and clothing. A tropical person by nature, Jones-Bey does not do well in such environments. However, this is not the source of his near mental breakdown.

The reason for the added anxiety results from the cell's other occupant, who for some reason, copes with the situation that he and Professor Jones-Bey find themselves in by talking perpetually. The professor's cell mate is a short, stocky, dark-skinned man with dark brown eyes, a prominent nose, and a gravelly voice that grates on the nerves. He is sure the man has given his name, but for some reason, Jones-Bey cannot think of it. The man is constantly asking pointless questions and making mundane statements. The drab slate-gray walls seem to close in on the professor. When Jones-Bey thinks the blessing of silence has been granted, the man starts up again. "Say, man, what you in fo'? Heh heh! I always wanted to say that. Man, these fools trippin'! What you think they goin' to do with us?"

Jones-Bey rolls his eyes and interjects, "At this point, a swift death would be merciful."

"They can't do that, man!" the man replies.

Rolling his eyes again as he puts his bald head in his hands, the professor says, "We can hope, can't we?"

Somewhere outside, there's a muted boom, and Jones-Bey wonders if he only imagined it, or if that was his head beginning to pound.

The detention center is a huge cube-shaped building with its bottom half embedded in the ice layers. The top half houses all the administrative and security forces personnel, while the half below the surface houses all the inmates or malcontents in two-man cells. There are four main entrances, one at each wall of the building. Ten meters in front of each entrance are small guard shacks equipped with heaters and computers connected to cameras atop the building behind them. From within the shacks, three armed guards can view their posts and a great distance out in front of their designated areas. The building and the shacks are eggshell white, slightly duller than the surrounding area but still able to blend in well. At a distance, it would be hard to see a break in the flat landscape. The views on the monitors from each guard shack are nearly identical. A sea of undisturbed white as far as the eye can see.

The guards are all well-trained and armed with old rail guns. They aren't expecting to face any opposition out in the middle of nowhere in a facility that has no name, and was conveniently left off most maps of the area. The lack of action and monotony of sitting there day after day chips away at the once razor-sharp edge of their training. The elements help to further their lack of motivation. Despite the heaters and their parkas with matching snowsuits, it is still unbelievably cold here. The guards are supposed to tour their areas occasionally, but the lack of activity combined with the cold has led to log entries stating the areas have been patrolled when they have not. The prisoners don't seem to be dangerous at all; they just have views or opinions that could be potentially dangerous to the government. In other words, there is no sense of urgency in anything they do. For the most part, they stay huddled in the shacks near the heaters, randomly glancing at the monitors.

A few hundred meters away from the perimeter outside the detention center, Simeon, one of Omega's generals stands with the task force given the job of rescuing Professor Jones-Bey. All of the Kison Askari there are short of stature, just as the general is, and they are all dressed in white body suits with hoods to help them blend in. Stone People's bodies are better insulated than normal human bodies, so the cold doesn't bother them. They also don't have much of a heat signature, so they are probably safe from infrared scans. Once again, valuable information has been supplied by the Limbia Johari spy network that includes schematics of the detention center, as well as the prisoner roster for it. The plan is to break in and free Jones-Bey, along with the other political prisoners, and get away as soon as possible in one of the stolen Night Eagle troop transports. Once that is accomplished, they'll get to the nearest underground hiding place and figure out a way off planet.

This group of warriors has been picked for this mission because of their size and because most of them have spent a lot of their mining time on heavy grav worlds. As a result, on Earth, they are faster and somewhat stronger than anyone who's been earthbound most of their lives. Silently they begin to low crawl toward the detention center. The facility has the capacity to house two hundred prisoners; fortunately only forty are present, according to their information. As they get closer, their speed increases, causing the snow drifts to kick up like a white sand storm, masking their approach further. They carry no weapons, but a few of them have explosives strapped to their backs in white canvas bags. Awakened by the feeling that something is amiss, one of the guards in the shack in front of the west entrance glances at his monitor. At first glimpse, he thinks it's a storm of some sort blowing toward them, but something still doesn't seem right. The guard turns around to kick one of his slumbering co-workers and says, "Hey! Check this out." All three guards are bundled up in their parkas and snow suits with the hoods pulled over their heads, drawstrings tight. The newly disturbed guard sits up and pulls the drawstrings to loosen his hood, freeing an unruly mass of brown hair. He wipes the sleep from his brown eyes before looking at the monitor. Stifling a yawn, the second guard mutters, "Yeah, a storm, so what?"

The comment makes something click in the first guard's mind as to what's not quite right about this. It suddenly dawns on him that what the monitor shows looks more like an avalanche, except that can't be right either because they're on flat land. By now, the third guard is up and wondering what all the fuss is about. Switching the sensors in the cameras to infrared and seeing no heat signatures, the first guard decides to step outside to eyeball this mystery personally. Once outside, the guard's ears are assaulted by a deep hissing sound as the avalanche-like phenomena rushes closer and closer, getting larger by the second. Frozen with shock, rail gun in hand, his trance is finally broken as a part of the "storm" co-alesces into a small humanoid form.

"What the —"

Before the guard can finish the exclamation, he is hit in the midsection with incredible force. His ribs crack as the rifle flies from his hands. The Stone Warrior forces the guard to the ground quickly, and as the squat Kison Askari straddles his chest, he simultaneously punches the man in the face. Brain matter, blood, and skull fragments spray the once pristine white snow and ice outside the shack. When the other two guards come out to investigate, they are savagely eliminated as well. There are no war cries to accompany the killing, just silent but deadly efficiency. With the guards on this side taken care of, hopefully without an alarm being raised, the Stone Warriors begin placing explosives in strategic places along the west wall. After setting the charges, the Kison Askari goes a safe distance away before blowing them.

* * *

Inside the professor's cell, the explosion is deafening.

"Hey, man! What was that?" his cell mate exclaims.

* * *

On the inside of the west wall, two guards making their rounds are thrown against a rail on the tier. They try to shake off the disorientation as their ears bleed, and their heads ring. The biting cold rushes into the gaping holes in the wall, followed by a swarm of dwarfish figures in white body suits. The cold helps to unscramble the guards' dizzy brains, and both now have the presence of mind to bring their weapons to bear, squeezing the triggers.

There are loud cracks as rounds from the railguns smack into the chests of some of the small warriors, sending them back out of the breached wall they entered. The eyes of the guards widen when most of those that are hit reemerge, seemingly unscathed and undeterred. The guards try to regain their feet to take better aim, but never make it. One of the warriors they'd missed is already upon them with a strange hammer-like object. There is a sickly wet thud as Simeon swings his ceremonial hammer through one guard's chest, sending the heart and a lung flying down the tier. A reverse swing sends the head of the other guard flying from his shoulders.

Simeon glances at his schematic and sends five of his task force to what is labeled "central" to unlock the cells. Four remain at the makeshift exit, and the rest are to round up the prisoners and lead them out. Seeing the results of their co-workers combat training, the administrators try to run or hide. The Stone Warriors let them. Annihilation is not their mission.

* * *

Professor Jones-Bey and his cell mate listen to the mayhem going on throughout the facility, wondering at its source. "Aw, man! You was right. They gonna kill us all!" the man yells.

The professor replies, "I'm not so sure. Calm down."

The noise continues for a few minutes more until the cell door slides open. A small figure in white confidently strides in and inquires, "Professor Charles Jones-Bey?"

Before the professor can respond, his cell mate goes into a frenzy screaming, "You can't just take him! You gotta take bofus! I'm serious, man. If bofus don't go, nobody goin'!"

The short Kison Askari raises his hands in a gesture to calm the man. "Be at ease, brother. We've come for everyone."

Not entirely convinced, the man inhales preparatory to going on another tirade, but the professor cuts him off. "Shut up already! *Bofus* is going. Now let's move!"

With a nod, the Stone Warrior exits, and they follow. On their way through the corridors and up the levels of the detention center, the two prisoners are nearly paralyzed by the gore they pass.

Outside, the task force of Kison Askari are trying to hold the armed guards at bay now that the alarm has been sounded. The scholar and his former cell mate are the last to reach the west wall. Both notice the other prisoners running through a virtual war zone in the freezing cold.

"We ain't got nowhere to go, man. I don't want to freeze to death!"

Finally frustrated with the man's outbursts, the Stone Warrior points skyward. "Shut up, Bofus! Transport is on the way."

All heads turn toward the sound of antigrav engines. In the distance, riding the night horizon came a GMC Night Eagle troop transport. A ragged cheer goes up from the armed guards, thinking the cavalry has arrived. The Stone Warriors know better, but let the guards celebrate and think what they will. The truth of the situation will be a rude awakening.

The transport hovers a meter off the ground as the hatch at the back swings down to the snow-covered ice. Confusion and horror crosses the faces of the guards as it is not Marines that have come bustling down the ramp, but huge Stone Warriors wearing strange shoulder harnesses. There are thick rifle-like appendages attached to the harnesses behind the warriors in what would be considered sling arms.

The warriors fan out as the prisoners run to board the transport. When one of the guards fire at the line of escaping prisoners, the appendages move in unison and seemingly, of their own accord, in front of each warrior into a firing position. There is strangely no noise to accompany the multiple flashes of light. Cries ring out in the chill night air as flesh sizzles, and heads explode. The guards quickly scatter, seeking cover that is nearly nonexistent. Meanwhile the Night Eagle takes off with its cargo.

* * *

Speeding over the vast arctic tundra in a hoversled is Malice, coming toward the detention center. The red, glowing eyes have seen the smoke from afar and know something is not as it should be. Cautiously Malice halts the vehicle a good distance away. Soundlessly Malice stalks toward the shattered wall, watching humans scurry to and fro, carrying their dead or tending to the wounded. One of the medical techs from the facility, in a black and orange snow suit, is walking around aimlessly when she catches sight of Malice. She stands stock still in terror, staring at the nightmare before her.

Malice mentally reaches out to touch the woman. She falls to her knees in agonizing pain as he telepathically whispers, "The prisoners, where are they?"

Her brain feels as if it is on fire as she screams her reply, "Gone! All gone! They escaped!"

Malice's eyes turn into glowing slits as he glares at the cratered west wall of the detention center. Feeling the truth in the med-tech's words, frustration and anger break the heavy chains holding them back. Malice surrenders to the anger and stealthily glides past the med-tech as she continues to writhe in the snow.

There's a soft hiss as the blades of an unknown metal are unsheathed. Blades are a passion of Malice's. Technological toys are good, but blades are personal. To Malice, a blade says, "I want to look you in your eyes and drink your fear before you die." Malice will drink well this night. At the unfamiliar sound, heads turn. Malice zigzags, dodging railgun rounds as he wades into the crestfallen guards, med-techs, and administrators. Seeking only to maim, disarm, or otherwise incapacitate on the first pass, Malice revels in the carnage as hands and limbs fly, further staining the snow with splashes of blood. Turning to sweep through the people with blades flashing, the killer puts them out of their misery, leaving only the med-tech he mentally contacted alive.

Done with the momentary respite for entertainment, the frustration comes back full force. The professor, being out of the government's hands, will make Malice's task more difficult. Pharaoh has spies among the oppressed peoples, but they are not as far reaching as the ones in the government. Plus, gaining access to them would alert his master to this failure. Malice decides it would be better to find the trail on his own and report back only when the task is complete. Delays can be overlooked if they aren't too long. Failure is not an alternative.

Chapter Nine

NERVOUSLY WAITING ABOARD A "DERELICT" automated ore hauler is Tunisia, dressed in the wraith suit taken from the failed assassination of Jared Omega. The huge, boxy freighter is en route from Jupiter to Earth, and filled with ore. Most of the automated haulers have been deactivated now that the revolt is in full swing, but Omega needs a way to get his queen to Earth, where she can have his child in relative safety. War is about to erupt on a greater scale, spreading out to the other planets. Omega has no doubt that the GMC will strike out at what is deemed the heart of the revolution, Jupiter. This is taken into consideration, along with the environmental dangers to a newborn on a high grav planet.

The plan is to have the GMC detect the ore hauler exiting hyperspace, followed by Shibokaze Star-Fighters attacking it. They will suspect a trick, but hopefully greed will override any suspicions. As soon as anyone comes to intercept, the star-fighters will break off the attack, and retreat to hyperspace before the enemy can engage. When the GMC boards the hauler, the wraith suit should conceal Tunisia's presence, allowing her to find a way to the surface and rendezvous with Simeon.

There's a thunderous boom followed by several smaller ones as the enormous ore hauler comes out of hyperspace near Earth. The smaller booms announce the arrival of seven Shibokaze Star-Fighters in pursuit. The sleek boomerang-shaped fighters begin peppering the hauler with laser fire. Inside the ore hauler, Tunisia winces with each impact on the ships' hull, knowing this is all according to plan, but wary nonetheless. The unscheduled entry of vessels into Earth's star system is detected, prompting two flights of Space Harriers to lift off from the lunar space station to challenge the intruders.

* * *

In the cockpit of the lead Space Harrier, Major Vashti suspects a trap of some kind, but he can't put his finger on it. Satellite sensors have reported the entry of an automated ore hauler with no life signs aboard it, chased by seven unknown star-fighters. The Space Harrier's scanners concur with that analysis as the two flights draw closer. It is assumed that the unidentified space craft are fighters since they are obviously armed, but they are either underpowered or playing possum. The scene before them makes sense to the fighter pilots, and this is why Major Vashti doesn't trust it. It makes sense that, if an automated hauler full of precious ore gets away, the Stone People will try to keep it from falling into GMC hands.

Ore haulers aren't known for their maneuverability, and the fighters should be able to destroy it, at least, unless they didn't truly intend to stop it. When the space station is notified of the situation, Vashti mentions his thoughts to his superiors. The warning goes unheeded. Greed and arrogance cloud better judgment. Greed because they simply covet the ore, and arrogance because they figure the Kison Askari's first attempt at making space-worthy fighting vessels will fall technologically short of the GMC's initial efforts. The scene being displayed does nothing to change their assumptions. The major smells deception but will not get a chance to gauge the enemy.

As the Space Harrier pilots all throttle forward to just within maximum weapons range, the unknown craft stops firing, turns in unison, and simultaneously jumps into hyperspace. Now unhindered, the hauler heads for the ore depot on the other side of the moon. Disappointed the major opens up the communications frequency to his squadron mates and speaks in his heavy Hindi accent, "No action today, gentlemen. Escort the hauler to the depot. If it breaks for Earth, take out the engines. Destroy it only if we can't stop it from reaching the planet. Vashti out."

In response, there are three double clicks.

Aboard the hauler, Tunisia hears a monstrous thunk as huge magnetic grapnels latch onto the vessel. Donning the helmet to complete the wraith suit, she quickly makes her way to where the molten ore is contained in heated bins. The suit should keep her concealed from visual scrutiny for as long as she can keep still. The chamber should mask her heat signature from any infrared scanners. Once the boarding party is sure there are no life forms or weaponry on the vessel, she will have to sneak off when they leave.

Several hatches hiss open simultaneously by remote from the ore depot. Marines, dressed in vacuum suits to guard against nerve gas or any other nasty surprises, storm into the hauler. The black vac-suits the Marines wear are somber compared to the suits of bright yellow worn by the hazmat crew that follows them. Loud exclamations of "Clear!" are heard repeatedly over the encrypted frequency the Marines and hazmat crew are using as they search the vessel, chamber by chamber. The last place to be checked is the ore storage bins.

Standing next to an ore bin, Tunisia's heart thuds loudly in her ears as she hears heavy boots announce a search party's arrival. The hatch hisses open and in stomps two figures in oversized yellow vac-suits. After, they wave handheld scanners in a multitude of directions, passing over Tunisia several times. With military precision, four Marines sweep into the chamber in black vac-suits brandishing large laser cannons followed by a fifth with a new ominous looking dual-intensity high powered rifle. Satisfied that the chamber is clear, nobody knows that their group has gained an unseen member as they go to report in.

*　*　*

After reviewing the footage of the ore haulers emergence near Earth and the flight of unfamiliar spacecraft, Major Vashti's suspicion only grows. The major isn't comfortable not knowing the enemy's strength and capabilities. He's voiced these concerns to his superiors. The top brass are reluctant, but can't ignore the value of good intel. They will not authorize sending a large force to Jupiter where the Stone Warriors are headquartered, even though that is probably where the strange fighters have jumped to. The risk is too great, sending a large force where the enemy was strongest. However, there are alternatives that may give the GMC an opportunity to assess enemy star-fighters while minimizing the risk.

Neither star-fighting corp of the GMC or the Kison Askari are seasoned, and it is time to start testing the waters. Rumor has it that the Stone Warriors are practicing maneuvers near Mars in unknown craft. Major Vashti will soon be heading an expedition with a Praetorian class cruiser, and a squadron of Space Harriers at his disposal. If the Stone Warriors are going to make a push toward Earth, Mars is the most logical staging area. The GMC does not want to go into the lion's den just yet, but if any stray cubs can be found they'll eliminate them before they mature.

Lt. General Jones temporarily gives Major Vashti the *Dante* for the mission. The *Dante* and its crew are the only members of the new space fleet with a successful mission under their belt that is more than a live fire exercise. That is if you count the Pluto bombardment. Most of the crew would call that action, while others in that same group are sickened by the thought of what they witnessed. The navigation computers of the *Dante* and the squadron of Space Harriers have been synchronized. Major Vashti, who nervously paces the length of the bridge in his white dress uniform, finally sits in the command chair. Swallowing his sudden apprehension, he orders everyone to battle stations and nods to the helmsman.

To the left and behind the cruiser hang six Space Harriers, an identical formation waited on the starboard side. In the cockpit of the first star-fighter on the port side sat First Lieutenant Krulak. As they waited for the jump to hyperspace, he pulled on his gloves, closed his eyes, and meditated. It would be a fatal mishap if his hands were to slip off the stick or throttle at a crucial moment during combat. That is exactly what will be when all thirteen vessels emerge from hyperspace combat, not the bombing of an unarmed stationary target. The thought hardens his resolve and scares him at the same time. The lieutenant opens his eyes to see the stars elongate into bright streaks.

Circling one of Mars's few satellites is one of the Kison Askari's WarDragons. The WarDragon is an interceptor designed by Toshi with the help of some Atlantean engineers. It is twice the size of an average star-fighter, and shaped like its name sake with wide, flaring wings. Mounted on the wingtips are heavy laser cannons, and the fuselage tapers into a long neck ending in a cockpit where the dragon's "head" would be. On either side of the cockpit, two small laser turrets are mounted. The cockpit can swivel up or down, in addition to nearly 180 degrees from side to side. The pilot and gunner sit up front in the cockpit, while a third crew member sits in a bubble-like compartment in between the wings near the base of the fuselage topside. There are rear laser cannons on each side of the main thruster, and a launch chute on the belly of the interceptor. The forward laser cannons and turrets can be used in tandem or independently. These are controlled by the gunner seated forward and slightly below the pilot, but the pilot can use them also, especially when there are multiple targets. For the most part, though, the pilot flies and the gunner shoots. The third crew member controls the rear laser cannons, sensor array, main nav-computer, and the launch chute which could release astral depth charges.

After the short lived search for Pharaoh, Kamal, and Nefer return to Omega's side. Upon learning about the development of the WarDragon, Kamal asks to be trained to fly it. Predictably Nefer does the same. Kamal proves to be an adept pilot, but Nefer is far more accurate as a gunner. Thus, this is how they ended up patrolling Mars space, joined by Muturi, another Kison Askari, and the third member of their crew. Muturi is a dark brown-skinned Stone Warrior with a short, compact muscular body as a result of mining on heavy-grav planets. Therefore, he doesn't mind the smaller rear compartment. The only gripe he has during training is that he doesn't get to use his laser cannons or depth charges as much as he liked, unless they are far outnumbered. As a former foreman, Muturi refuses generalship in the infantry for the opportunity to fight among the stars.

The peaceful tranquility and silence is shattered by multiple booms as several ships burst from hyperspace in close proximity to the WarDragon. Kamal becomes evasive immediately while Nefer begins counting and assessing targets. Muturi begins scanning and recording the vessel's images, simultaneously alerting the base on Mars's suface. Help will be there shortly, they just have to survive long enough for it to arrive.

As they emerge from hyperspace, Major Vashti nearly jumps out of his command chair at the sight of the strange spacecraft in the viewport hastily speeding away. The major mumbles, "What the hell is dat?!"

Being close enough to hear, a young officer at the sensor console replies, "Unknown, sir. It's a little bigger than a regular fighter, and it looks nasty!"

The major frowns at the man and says, "Rhetorical question, Ensign. Of course, we don't know what they've got. That's why we're here. Comm, open up a line to the squadron."

"Aye, sir!" the comm officer replies. There is a quiet chirp, signaling the frequency's readiness.

Major Vashti speaks, "Lieutenant Krulak, deploy one flight to engage that...thing. Be cautious, I want to see what she's got."

Through clenched teeth, Krulak responds, "Aye aye, Major."

Frustrated at being left out of the action, the lieutenant opens the squadron's frequency and orders the first flight to split into pairs and engage the enemy. He receives four double clicks in return and watches the corresponding Harriers speed off toward the target. Clamping down on his anger, Krulak realizes that Major Vashti is handling the battle this way for political reasons. It would not look good to lose the commandant's only son during the first engagement. Despite this reasonable train of thought, he still yearns for battle. He will not have to wait long.

Meanwhile the first flight has split into wing pairs with one trying to speed ahead of the larger craft, and the second pair in hot pursuit behind. The idea is to catch the enemy in the crossfire. The idea might have worked had not the WarDragon been constructed with that exact tactic in mind. Playing possum, the WarDragon allows the Harriers to surround it. Suddenly dark space is made brilliant by the exchange of superheated light energy. Almost as soon as the Harriers open fire, the WarDragon's laser cannons, both forward and aft, answer simultaneously. There is a glancing blow to the strange craft, not doing any real damage to the fuselage. The Harriers forward of the WarDragon break off their attack to dodge the return fire. The two to the rear try to do the same thing but one is not so lucky. Tendrils of laser fire lance into the Harriers starboard engine, causing a short explosion which is quickly quelled by the vacuum. In the process, the engine bursts into flames, melts into slag, and quickly cools into a misshapen metallic lump beneath the wing steadily smoking. The Harrier begins to list toward its starboard side. With speed that belies its size, the WarDragon turns about. The flames of the WarDragons rear thrusters go from orange to blue as it races to finish off the kill. The forward laser cannons and turrets work in unison, spitting bright yellow laser light into the Harrier's other engine, cockpit, and fuselage. This time, the explosion is still short but much bigger, sending mangled debris everywhere.

Stifling a scream of anguish, Lt. Krulak's left hand pushes the throttle forward as his right grabs the stick, guiding him in the direction of the melée. Noticing their squadron leader's departure, the rest of the squadron rockets off after him to lend support and hopefully avenge their fallen comrade. There is soon another explosion heralding the destruction of an additional flight one Harrier. On the bridge of the *Dante*, Major Vashti stares in horror and amazement at the efficiency with which the monstrosity repels the Harrier's attack, and counter strikes. The Major is snatched out of his trance by the officer at the sensor console exclaiming, "Sir! We have bogeys streaking in from the other side of the planet!"

Regaining his composure, the major sits in the command chair manipulating the remote embedded in the left armrest. Before him, a holographic image of the red planet materializes, showing yellow blips coming from the night side of the planet. As they get closer to the engagement area, the nondescript blips take shape into the now familiar form of the boomerang-like fighters from the ore hauler incident. There seems to be about fourteen of them. Belatedly realizing that Lt. Krulak and the rest of the squadron have taken off unbidden, the major opens a comm frequency to them himself from the command chair so as not to waste the time it would take to order it done.

"As you were, Lieutenant Krulak! Reverse your course. We have hostile vessels en route from the night side attempting to flank us. We estimate a squadron-sized group. Take second and third flight to engage them. We'll do our best to scatter them for you."

Battling the urge to disobey the orders the, lieutenant replies, "Acknowledged *Dante*," and pulls back on the stick until he's headed in the opposite direction. The rest of the squadron follows in his wake, imitating his maneuver when he rolls to re-orientate his fighter topside up. The two Harriers left from first flight stay behind, continuing their deadly cat and mouse game, trying to flank the WarDragon with little success because of its turrets mobility.

The *Dante* presents its left flank to the incoming Shibokaze Star-Fighters. As soon as they are within range, the star-fighters open fire with laser cannons mounted on the nose and wingtips of their craft. In response, the major orders his crew to fire at will. The launch tubes on the port side open all at once, and proton torpedoes erupted from them en masse. Four of the torps find targets, making temporary fireworks of them. The rest of the Shibokaze scatter, easily dodging the remaining torps. By then the Harriers have split into wing pairs and have begun to dogfight it out.

Taking advantage of the enemy's disorientation, Lt. Krulak and his wingman slip behind one. Hearing the tone that signals torpedo lock, the lieutenant flinches in excitement, but he's still able to instinctively pull the trigger in time, to be rewarded with his first kill. The torpedo goes straight into the boomerang-shaped fighter's main rear thruster. The resultant explosion splits the craft into two nearly perfect halves. Unfortunately for his wingman, Krulak's flinch makes him veer to keep the lieutenant out of his firing lane. The movement brings his Harrier into the sights of a Shibokaze that is tailing them from above. Laser-fire punches straight through the cockpit, killing the pilot instantly while leaving the star-fighter mostly intact, floating dead in space.

The elation of Lt. Krulak's first kill vanishes when an alarm signals that someone has a target locked on him. Heart thudding in his chest, Krulak goes into a series of jukes and jinks to break the target lock. The alarm eventually subsides, but his pursuer is good because he cannot get him off his tail. Through his anxiety Krulak notices he is flying solo, but he doesn't recall hearing or seeing his wingman getting blazed.

Seeing that the WarDragon has destroyed the remnants of first flight and is quickly coming his way, Major Vashti orders the starboard launch tubes to be fired. By individually targeting the torpedoes with the forward laser cannons and laser turrets together, the pilot and gunner make short work of them before they get close. Not liking the results of that attempt, Major Vashti decides they have enough data and issues the retreat order. The signal goes out to all seven remaining Harriers that they're about to attempt another synchronized jump. They immediately break off their engagements, fighting to get into alignment with the *Dante* while avoiding being shot down in the process. Still being chased doggedly, Lt. Krulak is, for once, happy to comply with the major's order, and is relieved when the stars outside his canopy turn into bright lines. Sweating profusely in his flight suit, he collapses in the cockpit, savoring his survival during the jump home.

* * *

The shuttle to Earth is cramped. The most difficult thing for Tunisia is remaining undetected, despite being in such close proximity to the other passengers. Bumping into an invisible but solid object will alert them that something is wrong. As far as the GMC knows, everything the ore hauler is carrying is still being scrutinized at the lunar ore depot. Once the shuttle lands, it is relatively easy for Tunisia to slip away unnoticed. When she feels she is a safe distance away, Tunisia takes out a small transponder, activates it, and waits for Simeon to pick her up.

Chapter Ten

SIMEON WAITS WITH HIS TROOPS and a select group of evacuees in caverns deep beneath the Earth's surface. The underground complexes are constructed in preparation for the revolt that will inevitably happen. The Kison Askari is proud of the foresight and hard work it takes to construct the place in addition to the oppression his people endured. Only Stone People would be comfortable in a place like this, but the men and women rescued from the detention center don't complain, having no alternative place of sanctuary.

Professor Charles Jones-Bey stands in one of the smaller underground caves, encircled by fellow refugees, explaining the theory of a genetic link binding all races that got him in trouble. The scholar is grateful for his freedom, but wishes that some of his fellow outcast humans would enjoy their freedom elsewhere. In particular, Jones-Bey wants to banish Bofus forever from his presence. The professor has to endure the dark-skinned, gravel voiced man's ravings for their months' long incarceration at the detention center in the Arctic. Bofus isn't even the man's name, but that's what everyone calls him as a result of him crazily shouting the nonexistent word in protest of possibly being left behind prior to the extraction. Eventually his further protest (that his name is not Bofus) has stopped. Now he answers to nothing else.

The man's voice grates on Jones-Bey's nerves because he always has an annoying comment or never ending stream of pointless questions. Worse is the fact that, most of the time, Bofus won't wait for an answer before spouting off more queries and comments. The professor is further dismayed that no one else seems to be frustrated by the intellectual impediment the often one-sided exchanges result in. In fact, the scholar sometimes feels that those who witness the interaction between Bofus and himself are amused by his discomfort with Bofus's antics. Jones-Bey is just coming to the conclusion of his impromptu lecture when Bofus can hold his peace no more. "Come on, man! How could we all be related? How come they changed and we didn't, huh?"

The professor rubs his brown bald head, ignoring barely concealed giggles behind him so as to regain the composure to speak. "I've already explained repeatedly to you that I don't know the exact catalyst that triggered the mutations, only that study of our DNA points to a common origin."

He is saved from listening to one of Bofus's tangents by the appearance of Simeon. All eyes go to the small but sturdy Stone Warrior as he speaks, "We've just received the signal we've been waiting for. I'm taking a small force to make another pick up. Professor, come with us." As an afterthought, the general added, "Bofus, you come, too."

Simeon turns quickly to hide his grin as he leaves to prepare for their departure. The professor, indignant but resigned to his fate, rolls his eyes and follows, with Bofus jovially trailing.

* * *

Fearing retaliation for encroaching on the Stone People's territory, once again, the GMC calls in a huge U-shaped Centurion class space carrier from the shipyard at Saturn to orbit Earth.

They hope the show of force will prevent or, at least, delay any reprisals. In the wardroom, Major Vashti is narrating as a holographic reenactment of the skirmish at Mars plays out. Some of the top brass are listening intently while survivors of the battle, such as Lt. Krulak, are trying to hide their nervousness. The presence of his father, General Krulak, and other officers with multiple stars on their shoulder boards only make things more intense.

As the scene plays repeatedly for the officers' analysis, it is obvious that the pilots on both sides are inexperienced. The younger Krulak shows some promise, as well as some others that remain. One of the pilots in the strange boomerang-shaped ships displayed more skill than his companions, but most disturbing was the accuracy, speed, and agility shown by the dragon-like ship. The authoritative voice of the commandant addresses the wardroom. "I don't like that thing one bit. It's been slow going, building our fleet, and I don't think anyone predicted the rockheads coming up with such formidable weapons in so short a time. Gentlemen, I want the answer to that thing, and I want it yesterday! Give me something that will knock it from existence. It took out a flight of Harriers by itself, and held its own with a Praetorian cruiser. Unacceptable odds, if you ask me. General Jones, Admiral Halsey, be sure R and D gets on this. We don't even know the full capability of these things. Major, good job. Dismissed!"

The lights come on as the general turns to leave.

"Dismissed!"

"Aye, sir!" all the officers chorus.

Major Vashti feels vindicated and confident now that his superiors see the enemy fleet as a threat. Lieutenant Krulak is sulking, feeling snubbed by his father's swift departure, even though he understands why he can't be paid too much attention in front of the others. The major catches the dejected look on the young officer's face and approaches to give some encouragement. "You did well to survive, even though you jumped the gun, Lieutenant. I advise you to heed my orders, and put in some serious simulation time, if you wish to fulfill the high aspirations we all know you have."

Lieutenant Krulak stiffens at the rebuke and stands to leave, muttering, "Yes, sir," as he does so.

* * *

On Jupiter, a similar conference is being held by Jared Omega. The head Kison Askari is discussing tactics and the performance of their new star-fighters with Toshi, the Jade Assassin who had flown in the lead Shibokaze. The crew of the lone WarDragon is also present, along with the remaining pilots from the Mars engagement. Toshi, with the help of some Atlantean engineers, developed both of the craft used in the brief fight. Most are pleased with the speed and agility of the boomerang-shaped Shibokaze (death wind), but want heavier fire power to go with it. The hull of the Space Harrier is thick, meaning it takes concentrated fire from the weaponry carried by the Shibokaze, while often glancing blows in return could take them out. All are pleased, thus far, with the performance and possibilities for the WarDragon.

Toshi goes to work immediately with some of the other engineers on plans for

designing heavier fighters that can afford to sacrifice some of the speed the Shibokaze has in exchange for the ability to give and take more punishment. Jared Omega decides one good turn deserves another. They will, indeed, strike back, just not where the GMC expects it.

* * *

In the main mess hall at the training facility on Saturn, Corporals Aragon, Simms, and Jordan sullenly eat their meals. Their gloomy attitudes are a result of being pulled from leave early. There was a breakout at a supposedly secret detention center. Plus, there have been multiple assassinations of government officials, which has put the military on high alert. Things are heating up in the galaxy. The newfound amusement in pranking the newest member of their group is wearing off. Petty Officer House is a Navy corpsman they met at a nitro club. Upon having his leave revoked, he immediately received orders to report to the facility on Saturn and support the First Recon Battalion that Aragon, Simms, and Jordan are already attached to. It takes time to get acclimated to the shorter day cycle and heavier gravity. Special supplements and steroids are taken to help speed the process, in addition to help from soldiers who've already gone through it.

The three Marines decide it might be fun to "help" the naval cousin they met at the nitro club while on leave. For the latest attempt at helping, they figure the corpsman might get cold despite the environmental controls throughout the facility. So they sneak into House's barracks room while he is sleeping to replace the blankets with heavier ones lined with lead. Then they use a small device to play the reveille signal and watch Petty Officer House through old night vision goggles as he struggles to rise from bed. He has to admit it was pretty funny, after the fact, but House vows he will have the last laugh, especially after the previous instances where the three squad leaders decide to reverse the gravity's polarity in House's barracks room. Petty Officer House returns to his room to find the furniture on the ceiling, and upon entering finds himself floating in that direction. At first, it seems like an amusing trick, but unfortunately it is temporary, and House is given no warning when the default settings kick back in. Luckily for the corpsman, the supplements have taken effect now, strengthening his bone structure, so nothing is broken when it all comes crashing down. House takes it all in stride, and the three Marines are surprised, even disappointed that he has made no attempt to retaliate. What they fail to realize is that he already had, but his efforts are more subtle. When they all first met, House had mentioned he had friends in administration.

A bulletin catches House's attention, it is asking for volunteers for a flash training experiment. He puts in a call to one of his friends in admin and tells him three of his friends in the Marines wish to volunteer but didn't know how to go about it. After he's gives the names and ranks of his three Marine buddies, House is asked what program they wish to try.

The corpsman smiles and says, "Piloting." It has all been arranged without them knowing. House will, also, be surprised because the program will be implemented sooner than expected, and not just as an experiment.

* * *

Heading to a conference in what used to be Eastern Bloc Europe, Senator Levine rides in an armored limousine propelled by powerful anti-grav engines. Anxiety is etched on her face as her blue eyes dart this way and that, looking for would-be assassins. The last few months have been terrifying for the senator, as a lot of her governmental confederates have been systematically knocked off, some of them brutally so. In the most recent incident, a legislator named Cyndi Nguyen was beheaded at a public restaurant. The crazy thing is that no one noticed anything was wrong at first, and nobody saw the attacker.

Whoever did it was phenomenally swift and precise. For long moments, she looked as if she was simply sitting there. The illusion was shattered when Nguyen's clothes were soaked inexplicably by copious amounts of blood. People stared in shock as they noticed something was definitely amiss. Screams rang out when the head finally toppled to the floor. At first, Senator Levine dismissed these events as random acts of violence, but then a secretary found a correlation between the victims in these incidents and those who supported the Loyalist Act. Even more telling is another discovery made by the senator's Chief Security Officer Thomas. Not all who support the Loyalist Act are being killed, but everyone who both supports the Loyalist Act and approves of the Pluto offensive are. All the victims of assassination and suspicious accidents have this in common.

Sitting across from the senator in the limo is CSO Thomas. She is worried for and about her charge. Being lovers complicates things further. After discovering the pattern, security has been beefed up tenfold. In some cases, hovercams are used, and the security detail has to check and recheck to make sure areas are clear. It makes movement tedious. The paranoia is necessary though because someone out there is chiseling away at the foundation of the senator's power base and working their way up. The really disturbing thing for CSO Thomas is that whoever is doing this is privy to personal information on their targets, such as schedules, indulgences, and secret vices. This could be an inside job, and the senator could become the target eventually. Thomas's job is to stop these people before it gets that far.

* * *

Out of everyone in the group that went to retrieve Tunisia, only Simeon is not caught unawares as she seemingly appears in their midst out of thin air. Bofus nearly jumps out of his skin, drawing an infrequent smile from Professor Jones-Bey. However, Jones-Bey's amusement is short lived when they board a subterranean railcar that takes the group to another underground haven. The professor is nauseated and disorientated throughout the fast, twisting ride through the Earth's bowels. The heavy protective suits he and Bofus have to wear, because some points in their route take them dangerously close to the core, aren't helping. Meanwhile Bofus is thoroughly enjoying himself like a youth at some amusement park, hooting and hollering nearly all the way. This further agitates the professor but lifts the others spirits. Simeon is just relieved the trip has gone so smoothly, and without a confrontation.

* * *

Tunisia, after getting down to the surface, had kept herself hidden in a secluded area, miles away from a military installation in Colorado. Simeon knows the reason Omega has had her smuggled back to Earth, and this only heightens the tension that comes with the responsibility now placed on his shoulders. The queen is pregnant with Omega's heir; their safety is paramount. After the baby's born, it's to be raised in the cavernous network of safe havens throughout Earth's underworld that the Kison Tontu have so arduously constructed. Simeon is to train the child in combat and mining techniques. Professor Jones-Bey will handle the formal education. When the child is developed enough to live on planets where the gravity is heavier, they will seek a way to safely unite the child with its father. The initial separation will be painful and hard to explain, but necessary. Omega knows that Tunisia understands the precautions they are taking, and can only hope that, later, the child will also.

* * *

Eight months later, Darius Omega is born. The king of the Kison Askari witnessed the birth of his son via an encrypted sat-net video link.

He thought there had been a malfunction with one of the hovercams because the little brown baby seemed to literally glow. When Tunisia expressed a similar observation, he figured it was simply the shared pride in their child.

* * *

General Krulak sits in a meditation chamber several decks below the bridge, aboard the newly minted *Peacemaker II*, the replacement Centurion carrier for Captain King's fatal and costly error. The carrier is orbiting Earth as the commandant meditates, stripped to the waist, brown eyes shut tight in concentration. He is trying to influence some type of technological breakthrough. It's not praying exactly, but close to it. The people in research and development believe only in their scientific knowledge, but there are others in the military and society in general who have faith in a higher power of some sort. In the military, these people are labeled as "superstitious." Religion is still around but has become subdued throughout the years.

The general is not a particularly religious or superstitious man, and the fact that he is trying this tactic shows how worried he is. If he can get a spiritual nudge in the right direction, he'll take it. Krulak has heard there are documented cases of it happening before. The small engagement at Mars has slightly unnerved him. Nobody expected the Stone People to advance so quickly. They must be getting help. The GMC will have to find out from whom, but more importantly will have to get back the technological advantage they usually enjoyed. There are several things in development that would keep things even, but that isn't good enough. The Stone People always have the physical advantage, while man has the upper hand technologically. If the Stone People are to leap far enough ahead of man technologically, the balance could be tipped so far as to reverse their roles in society. For man to be enslaved by the very beings they used to oppress is General Krulak's worst fear.

* * *

In the upper most chamber of the pyramid at Giza, Pharaoh hears the half-hearted petition of man's military champion but ignores it. The light being is angered by the prolonged absence of his servant, Malice. Besides man already has the materials and tools to match what the Kison Askari have done. Pharaoh refuses to hold either side's hand throughout the conflicts. That's what made this galaxy so interesting, seeing what direction they would go after pulling back the outside influence. Things look to be heading toward a deliciously destructive climax. The beings in this galaxy have supposedly learned their lesson during the nuclear fallout era, but Pharaoh can hope for a relapse. That timeframe is highly entertaining. After all, history often repeats itself.

* * *

Jared Omega sits in an empty meeting chamber, contemplating the next move for his people. Things have become really complicated in a relatively short time. The war is escalating and may soon spiral out of control. The king's life has become more strained with the added worry for his wife and child. To Omega, the additional stress is well worth it. Recalling the images of his newborn son, the ruler of the Stone People is further determined to make the galaxy a better, safer place to live. If things continue in the direction they're headed, children will inherit nothing but barren wastelands. This cannot be allowed.

Omega's thoughts are interrupted by approaching footsteps. Looking toward the sound the Kison Askari immediately recognizes the cloaked figure of Babylon. The old Atlantean pulls back his hood to shake out white dreads, and turns an intense amber stare upon Omega. Blue lips part in a bright smile as he says, "Greetings, King Omega. Did I tell you true?"

The big Stone Warrior stands and goes to clasp hands with his friend. "Our investigation ran into a dead end, but not before getting, at least, a partial confirmation of Pharaoh's existence. Things are heating up, but we'll pick up the trail once they cool down some. I never doubted you. I am surprised to see you, though," the King answered.

A grim look passes over Babylon's turquoise features as he replies, "Me knew you'd believe me, dread, but not yer little green friend and the pretty crystal woman. Dem needed convincing. Me knew dat all along, but I'm not here to talk 'bout dat. I have sometin' for you." Babylon reaches into his cloak and pulls out a small disk. The disk seems even smaller once placed in the huge ash gray hands of Omega. The Kison Askari sits down in a throne-like chair and nods for Babylon to do the same in a smaller but similarly stone crafted chair.

"Fetch a hovercam," Babylon whispers as he settles into his seat. Omega pulls out a data screen with glowing glyphs on it and presses one of the command buttons. The door to the chamber silently opens to let in a floating conical orb that the Atlantean recognizes as the modified mining tool/weapon that Omega had used before. The device comes to a stop and hovers in front of the king. A small slit opens in the rear of the globe-like portion, and he deposits the disk into the opening.

The cone-shaped part of the device opens, giving it the appearance of a floating stem-less flower. The lights in the chamber dim as a three dimensional image of Pluto is projected from the mining device. Part of the image blurs as seventeen ships jumped in system. There is one larger vessel that Omega recalls from recordings of the small battle at Mars, and sixteen smaller ships. The king also recognizes four of the smaller ships as the type of fighters that had initially attacked the lone War Dragon patrolling Mars's space. One fighter escorts each flight of four of the other unknown craft with the exception of the lead flight. The lead flight has two fighters to escort it as they split up. The purpose of the unknown battleaxe-shaped ships becomes apparent when they begin dropping hammer-like objects into Pluto's atmosphere, forcing the bombers and to flee in order to escape being destroyed themselves. There's a blinding flash throughout the entire image, as the flames surrounding the dwarf star intensifies. When the light dies down only a smoldering rock remains, and the ships jump out.

Omega has already seen the aftermath of the attack on Pluto from images his scouts brought back, but seeing the bombing firsthand makes the cruelty of the act more obvious. The Warrior-King stifles the anger that has welled up at the tragedy of so many lives snuffed out to prove a point. The image disappears, and the lights in the chamber brighten to their normal luminosity. Omega asks, "Where did you get this?"

Babylon replies, "Some of me people went to investigate after we heard de news. Dey found de remains of a fried and mangled satellite. De log disks were de only tings salvageable. Dere were more but dis only one significant. I know you plan to strike back. After seein' what dey did, me come to tell you dat I'll help you make a comparable bomber using our technology if you promise to choose military targets only."

Omega nods his assent and says, "I'd have done that anyway, and your people are already helping us build our fleet."

A strange gleam comes to Babylon's eyes. "We've been guiding you dread, and only in the basics. Now we gon put our hands into de construction instead of just guiding yours. When you get a glimpse of what's possible it gon blow your mind!"

Chapter Eleven

VICE ADMIRAL FEATHERSON HAS BEEN given the task of researching the most strategic targets for the GMC to hit that would weaken the new fleet the Stone People are building with stolen material. Routine sensor scans are out of the question since the rockheads have become considerably smart enough to begin destroying satellites near installations they controlled. For once technology cannot be depended upon for intel. Recon is being done but that is putting new technological, as well as personnel assets, at risk. The theft of weapons and material had hurt economically, as well as forced the GMC to be cautious in how existing assets would be deployed. Never in his wildest dreams did the Admiral think there would ever truly be a threat to their way of life in this galaxy, which is why General Krulak has conveyed the importance of regaining control as quickly as possible.

Up until now there has been no threat whatsoever here, and despite the theories and storylines from science fiction, there have been none that have shown themselves able to topple the hierarchy in the galaxy. It is known that there likely had to be life elsewhere, but they had always come to observe and do nothing more. How ironic that the threat to mankind comes from directly beneath their boot soles.

The admiral sits at his desk reading reports at a secret interrogation facility. Since technology cannot be relied upon, more arcane methods are being used to gather information. Lt. Commander Jameson, the talented neurosurgeon, is borrowed on temporary orders to help the admiral speed the process along.

Ordinarily tasked with rehabilitating and augmenting fallen or injured Marines, the doctor is now using his expertise to extract information, by any means necessary, from a handful of POWs captured after conflicts at Mars, Neptune, and Uranus.

On the subject of human anatomy, Lt. Commander Jameson is an expert with no known peer, which is why he was able to join cybernetics and flesh together almost seamlessly to the point that his work could be mistaken for a natural occurrence. During his research on the Stone People, their neural network looked eerily similar, yet the doctor could not swallow the theory that these savages were in any way closely related to humankind. That is the propaganda being spread by some crazed scholar. Despite the scientific soundness of the theory given the similarities, Jameson ignores that and focuses on the task at hand. That task is to torture these people until they give up the information the admiral wants.

The difficulty is that these are hard people both literally and figuratively. The tools needed have to be precise enough to break through their adamantean skin in order to tap into the neural network to inflict pain without killing them or leaving them useless. This is proving to be a challenge. Experimenting with the size and intensity of various laser scalpels is getting some progress but not the results the top brass want in the time they need it. Something has to give and Lt. Commander Jameson is determined they will give in before he does.

* * *

Corporals Aragon, Simms and Jordan sit nervously in a large class room at Camp Puller on Saturn. There are thirty other service members with them, all are wearing the same strange helmets. On the outside, they look like pilot's helmets, except they are not connected to any hub systems that they can see. There are retractable cables coming from the back of each helmet, and they would be remarkably heavy had not this collection of Marines and other service members been through the training/supplement regimen here. Aragon looks to Simms and Jordan. "There has to be a way to get House back for this!" he exclaims.

"Damn right!" they reply.

Jurassic thuds are heard heralding the arrival of Sergeant Garrison. All conversation stops. Garrison has the ability to walk quietly, but he has since embraced this new part of him. He likes to make an entrance; plus, fear helps him train Marines. His slim yet heavy gleaming metallic legs come to a halt in front of the class with an audible clunk and hiss.

"Good morning, Marines!" he bellows.

"Good morning, sergeant!" the class responds. He further addresses them, "You all know who I am. Today we will begin flash training to immediately replenish the ranks of fallen fighter pilots should the need arise! Now those of you who know me firsthand know that I am a grunt to the core, yet I am here because I am commanded to be a part of this. I like to do my killin' on the ground where I can look into the enemies' eyes. Hoorah!"

"Hoorah!" they chorus. "Now there's more than one way to fry a fish," the sergeant continues. "So as long as I get to kill, dead is dead in my book from air, land, sea or space! They took my legs, and Uncle Sam gave me better ones. I am also equipped with a neural interface that allows me to tap into the flash system like a computer. I don't quite know how that works, but the CO says I don't have to. Now apparently I have already had the training uploaded to my brain during surgery. You all should have noticed by now the cables hanging from the back of your helmets. When I tell you to, take that cable and insert it into the corresponding jack on the front left of your desk. I will then choose the flash training for pilots. Your face shields will become opaque, and when I jack in, you will see what I see. Is that understood?!"

"Yes, Sergeant!" they cried. "Good. JACK IN!"

Everyone did as commanded and at first nothing happened. They all jacked in, and the face shields went black, and they could see nothing. Just as they were getting restless, a blinding light flashed before their eyes and a multitude of images streamed by at an incomprehensible speed. Information was coming in, and it felt painful at first as their minds were trying to register everything all at once and could not. Once their minds seemed to get into a sort of rhythm they became numb as their brains adjusted.

* * *

Deep in the catacombs beneath the Earth's crust Simeon watches in amazement as young Darius crawls with the speed and dexterity that takes most babies a lot longer to exhibit. Tunisia is relieved to have her baby in a safe environment. Jupiter or, more accurately, most of the known galaxy is going to be a huge war zone soon. This hidden underground network is the safest place to be at the moment. More and more camps are being constructed and filled on the surface. The way things are escalating, civil war where every people will be involved one way or the other seems inevitable. Down here, Darius will be given the chance to be a child for as long as it is possible.

Bofus has taken a liking to the child, and it seemed the feeling is mutual. The small dark-skinned man plays and wrestles with the baby as if he were being thrown around until the child giggles for hours on end. Professor Jones-Bey will often suggest the display of the baby's strength advantage over Bofus is reality, not just a joke. Everyone watches the child in wonder. He has a glow in his eyes and not just the glimmer of new life or enjoyment. There, of course, is the literal glow that most simply ignored and never speak about, but there is also a look as if he fully understands what is being said and done at all times. Professor Jones-Bey finds that knowing look to be frightening because that should have been an impossible state of being for one so new to the world.

* * *

Toshi is summoned back to Jupiter IV by Jared Omega, and Hironike allows him to go, keeping in mind what happened to the mining colony on Pluto, as well as the announcements made by government officials recently. The leader of the Jade Assassins prefers to handle business in the shadows, rather than out in the open, yet he knew it was only a matter of time before his people would be targeted and put away. They were different and, therefore, would be deemed a threat. It is rumored that Babylon is heading a project to build a weapon to strike back with, and Toshi wants to be a part of it. Despite Takimura and Megumi's report lending some credence to the old man's story, Hironike feels more comfortable with Toshi keeping an eye on what is being planned.

With half the fleet of commandeered, ore haulers that have been modified, so they could be linked, the Kison Askari create a mobile ship yard of sorts, which could be disassembled to relocate at a moment's notice. This is a smart move, considering the game of strike and counterstrike is about to begin in earnest. This way the GMC will have a hard time figuring where the most beneficial target will be. The initial revolt is the first haymaker, the second is the attack on Pluto, and now there have been a few jabs between the two sides. Both sides are now trying to get a measure of the other's strength. Hard to do when this scale of warfare has not occurred before. This is an arm's race where both sides are testing new technology that will be put to use before it can be perfected. A dangerous prospect for all involved.

On the observation deck of one of the transformed ore haulers, Toshi, Babylon and Jared Omega view schematics for a prototype bomber. This ship is of a similar shape to Babylon's personal ship, but it is three times as large with more weapons' placements and huge bay doors at the bottom of its manta-shaped hull. There are laser cannon emplacements fore and aft of the ship. The front cannons are fixed while the rear cannon can rotate beneath the tail, giving this bomber the ability to cover its six. There is also another nasty surprise Toshi had worked into the design — depth charger chutes under the wings with EMP ordinance as the final touch.

The Space Harriers are maneuverable, not as fast as the Shibokaze, yet a sight faster than these new bombers. What the Morningstar gave up in speed would be made up with firepower and other capabilities. "Toshi, dis ting be wicked, mon! Omega, be sure to use technology and force only when absolutely necessary. Try not to become too much like de oppressors you fight against," Babylon rasps.

"Don't worry, wise one, if there were any other way I would not use force at all, but violence seems to be the only language the GMC understands. My people will no longer be cowed by their weapons. We did not start this, but it is time for us to end it. If we cannot find this Pharaoh, bring him to light so that all can see the true schemer behind our strife and differences, then sadly enough beating the GMC at its own game may be the only way to have peace," Omega responds.

Toshi could care less about who had the moral high ground, the reason behind things, or the methods. He is more concerned about what simply is. Reality is what it is. The oppressed people are in the position they are in because others put them there, and in the end, it has been allowed. The only way out is with a violent reaction, so these people will be taken seriously. Babylon can posture about using too much force all he wants. The truth is that, throughout all time, force is the one thing everyone understood regardless of whom they were or what language they spoke. From sticks, rocks, arrows, and ballistic projectile weapons to energy and anti-matter technology, whoever was on the wrong side of the people holding the weapons got the message pretty quickly. The Morning Star might be a step closer to making this government get a clue.

"Let's get some test pilots up here," Toshi says.

Omega and Babylon nod their heads in agreement.

* * *

Lt. Commander Jameson walks into a room at the interrogation facility. Shackled to a medical magnetic table is an unconscious Stone Person. Trailing the silver-haired neurosurgeon is a hover table laden with various laser scalpels. Roughly kicking the table, Jameson glares at the unfortunate Kison Tontu and says, "Waky waky, my stone-faced friend."

The prisoner's eyes flutter open, and when his eyes get used to the lighting and sterile hospital-like environment, they focus intently on the intense green eyes and gaunt, pale face of his captor. By the looks of the tools on the table floating nearby, this is not going to be good, and this is definitely not a friend.

Seventeen hours later, the Kison Tontu is barely breathing, life is seeping out of him as the maniacal Lt. Commander Jameson stands over him, satisfied yet strangely disappointed at the same time. Confirmation of where they already knew the stone people had to be based is a good thing. That is a positive in that the top brass will have a direction to go in with their plans of attack. Jameson is also hoping to extract something more, something secretive, and this captured pilot should be able to provide that. This being has proven to be a hard nut to crack. Jupiter is not only far, but there were many moons near, which any one of them could be a shipyard or staging area. A report will be sent immediately to Marine Corp headquarters.

* * *

Aragon's eyes open to see a blank screen too close to his face. Moments later, the screen clears to show a face shield attached to the ungainly helmet he and the others in the training room are wearing. Throughout the training many of the service members lose consciousness, as if the speed of the flash training is too much for their brains. Corporals Simms and Jordan take off their helmets and approach Aragon.

"You guys feel any different?" Aragon asks them.

They both shake their heads. There is a strange whirring noise, and everyone turns in the direction of the sound to see the gears spinning on Sgt. Garrison's cybernetic legs. The slumped torso of the sergeant rises as he disengages from the monitor and computer system that link them all during the training.

"All right, ladies. Time to see what we learned. All of you head to the flight deck. Space Harrier live. Air time in twenty mikes!" he bellows.

"What?" many inquire incredulously.

"Shouldn't we try some simulation time first, Sergeant?" Corporal Jordan asks.

"No sim time, boys. Your fist run will be with the real deal. Now act like you got a pair and let's fly!" With that, Sgt. Garrison marched out the room and everyone filed out after him.

They boarded shuttles to one of the GMC's flagships, which was a monstrous Centurion class battleship assigned to Saturn's sector of the galaxy. All were apprehensive as they have had no practical application of what they were "supposed" to know. This is insanity! Marines are trained well and hard. This goes against all previous experience. Things are simple; you are issued a weapon, and then you go to the range to get qualified. This flash training in theory should have given them the proper knowledge to fly and fight, yet no one feels like they know anymore after the training. Some remember images but nothing more than that. This is going to be one hell of a ride. Aragon, Simms, and Jordan just hope it won't be a short one.

* * *

Deep beneath a pyramid in southern Mexico, Pharaoh sits in his meditation chamber, pondering the whereabouts of his minion. It's been months since Malice disappeared. He does not want to have to destroy one of his first creations. Malice is a work of destructive art, and a lot of Pharaoh's power went into mutating it into what it is. Eventually the plan is to somehow regain his original form and have the strength to leave this forsaken place. Earth has become quite entertaining. Despite all the expansion and developments, Pharaoh has no plans to stay.

Malice is an important tool. He serves as external eyes and ears while also serving as hands to do whatever needs to be done in the name of keeping things going according to plan. Pharaoh feels his powers are not enough to overcome the hold the elders have on him, but he is getting stronger. Creating another minion like Malice might set him back, but there is also some value to creating one that is not quite as powerful, in case his servant does not return. The question now is which organism to use for this new minion. Man is excellent material. With the right amount of intellectual nudging, they can be useful as trackers, hunters, or agents of destruction.

There are plenty of life forms here that are physically more impressive yet lacking in sophistication which quickly lose any amusement value with Pharaoh. Lying down in the meditation chamber, Pharaoh empties his mind, letting his consciousness leave his corporeal body to search for a satisfactory subject. Maybe sophistication will not be needed for this minion. Pure brute force might be just the thing to reign Malice in, and then what a tandem they might be once he is back in the fold!

* * *

Malice rides the tracks throughout the underground rail system sans vehicle or suit. He simply puts his appendages on the tracks and begins to propel himself under his own power taking on speeds that would rival some of the railcars this system is made for. Malice senses he is close to his quarry. This Professor Jones-Bey has proven to be a nuisance. Should have been easy to catch him at the prison camp, yet the Stone People have interfered by breaking all of the prisoners out, but soon the trail was picked up in Colorado, leading to an entrance to this supposedly abandoned subterranean rail station.

This wild goose chase has taken months but will soon be over. Malice has let his frustration and anger build. It will fuel his speed until he catches up with Jones-Bey, and he will use his frustration and anger to annihilate him, as well as everyone unfortunate enough to be in his company. Malice will revel in their screams and misery. He will take his time and see if sound can travel all the way to the surface. He will not let them escape this time.

Chapter Twelve

ARAGON, SIMMS, JORDAN, AND A host of other service members double-time to the shuttles behind Sgt. Garrison. They stop in front of a space worthy NightEagle modified to work as short distance troop transports strictly at military installations like the one on Saturn. Saturn is for the elite to be based at, whereas regular troops are trained on Earth. The conditions make men into more robust fighting machines. Now it will be a source of pilots as well. More installations are to be made in the future, if these operations are a success. They all file into the shuttle, and wait for the short ride to the Centurion class ship that orbits the planet.

As the shuttle rose through the heavy gravity, Simms can feel himself being pressed into to his seat, as if an elephant is sitting on top of him. He can tell the others are feeling the same until someone piloting the bucket they are in gets smart and turns on the inertial dampeners, thus taking the pressure off the passengers. All of their hearts, however, still weigh heavy in their chests. Apprehension about the first time in the cockpit of an aeronautical fighter after experimental training with no hands on experience is how most sane people would feel. These are, for the most part, battle-hardened Marines and soldiers, yet they could not escape fear of some things.

As they approach the nearly city-sized Centurion class battleship the activity around it is akin to looking at a bee hive with a frenzy of activity surrounding it. Ships in formations fly in, out, and around it. They cruise, until at one hundred meters distance, a magnetic guidance system takes over, guiding the shuttle into a landing bay. They settle in with an audible clunk. Sgt. Garrison is the first to unstrap and stand before yelling, "Flight Deck 145 men, on the double! There will be some fly boys to help you suit up, and direct you to your new rides!"

* * *

Babylon sits at the controls in the pilot's seat of a new Morningstar bomber as Omega and Toshi sit behind him at the weapons and navigation consoles.

"Head to the sixteenth moon, we will do a test run there," Omega booms.

Babylon eases the stick forward, and smoothly the ship's engines roar to life, surging ahead. Toshi calibrates the weapons system in preparation for dropping its payload. Toshi has devised and armed the Morningstar with anti-matter ordinance. The stuff is highly volatile in that there is no telling how much destruction it will do. For that reason, Babylon makes everyone involved promise it will only be used on military targets. They all know that, in the wrong hands, this kind of weapon can prove disastrous.

After orbiting the massive planetary body that is Jupiter, they cruise around the various moons until approaching the sixteenth. Unnecessarily, Omega announces that they are at range. Toshi begins a series of dial and button manipulations at the weapons console, and when he finishes, the bay doors slide open at the underside of the ship, letting drop in an inanimate shell. Seconds later, small wings sprout near the tip of the rocket-like ordinance and a single thruster comes to life, and as the experimental weapon begins to hurtle toward the surface of the targeted moon.

"Bombs away!" Toshi declares.

* * *

Malice jumps off the rail deep within the Earth as he senses his prey. Professor Jones-Bey is near, but there are also a large number of presences with him. If the company the professor was keeping the last time they had met is here as well, that might make things difficult. It is no matter. There will be no acceptable excuse his master will allow for failure. The minion approaches an entrance to a labyrinth of underground corridors and caves. Bending down to touch the floor of the entrance Malice extends its senses throughout the structure to gauge the number of beings occupying the nearest cave.

Two hundred meters within the cave, Simeon, Tunisia, Professor Jones-Bey, Bofus, young Darius, and a large group of Kison Askari are all getting ready to lie down for the night. Bofus, as usual, is harassing the professor to the amusement of most everyone there. Sentries head to the entrances to begin the night's watch. Two of them go toward the entrance closest to the rail system. One of them thinks he sees a strange red glow up ahead, but ignores it. Determining whether or not he has been noticed, Malice decides to crawl on the ceiling of the cave to stealthily get by the guards. Completing his mission holds more importance than feeding his blood lust. Once the professor has been eliminated a different game can begin.

Tunisia is resting with her sleeping baby in her arms, stroking his smooth head. His skin is beginning to become rough but has not hardened yet. The boy is breathing deeply, and she wonders how long this type of peace will be enjoyed by her son. She will not have to contemplate long on the subject. Seemingly, for no reason, the baby becomes restless and begins crying. The queen tries to console the child, to no avail. Simeon and some of his men rush in to see what is wrong. Suddenly he stops crying and opens his eyes. To everyone's astonishment, they are glowing pure white. Darius is glaring up at the ceiling, his cold stare is met by an eerily similar pair of eyes, except they are an angry crimson.

Everyone turns to look up to see what the child is staring at. Whatever it is, it looks menacing, a cloaked figure with glowing red eyes clinging to the ceiling. Simeon is the first to react. The cannon on his harness is raised to the shoulder and fired instantly. The semi-dark cavern is lit up as five other Askari join in. Tunisia grabs her baby, scrambling back away from the firing, fearing that the ceiling may cave in. Dodging the fire, Malice skitters across the ceiling to the floor with unbelievable speed. Blades appear in his hands as he scans the group for his target. The professor is at the rear of the cave, huddled with another human. The issue is running the gauntlet of warriors fanned out before him.

Grasping tightly to the professor's arm, Bofus exclaims, "Hey, man! What the hell is that thing?"

Seeing the crimson glare from a distance, the professor immediately recognizes that very same being as the one he saw in Egypt months before. "We've met, and I can't say it was a pleasure," he replies.

The Askari are trying to get a read on the creature, but it will not stand still long enough for them to get a clear shot, so they try to fire, so that when it dodges, it will run into the crossfire from another cannon. So far, the tactic has not been successful. In a blur, Malice weaves through the crowd, clashing blades with the hardened skin and weaponry of the Kison Askari in an effort to get to the professor.

It seems the two sides are at a stalemate. Malice is too quick to get a good shot at, yet the Kison Askari have hide that nullifies his blades. In addition, they have formed a barrier of bodies and weapons that, along with their shooting, effectively keep Malice too far to get a shot at the professor. For the professor, Bofus, Tunisia, and young Darius, it is nothing short of chaos-filled with cannon fire, ringing blades, and grunts accompanied by shards of rock flying everywhere. Baby Darius begins to wail again, and all the action stops as everyone takes notice. He stands up and walks out of his mother's arms.

Turning his intensely bright, shining eyes to Malice, a deep, unearthly, resonant voice comes out of his mouth as he addresses Malice. "Be gone! I will not tolerate your ilk in my presence!"

Malice's eyes narrow; then seemingly of their own accord, his limbs move as he sheathes his weapons, leaving swiftly without knowing why exactly. After the minion leaves, Darius collapses, and everyone surrounds him worried and mystified, and some were a bit frightened.

* * *

Nervously Aragon steps out of the Night Eagle, onto the deck of a huge docking bay within the Centurion class capitol ship they learned had been dubbed "The Ex-Wife." Most agree it has to be a nickname, but none have noticed anything emblazoned on the huge ship. Even if it has been there, they are all too distracted by the sheer size of it to notice. Sgt. Garrison seems to be the only one not awed by the ship's dwarfing of nearly everything in the vicinity, except the planet itself. Stepping out onto the deck, Garrison's mechanical feet clang loudly against the metal flooring, causing some to cringe at the noise. Wordlessly he marches to the lifts to the flight decks for fighter craft, and the others follow him to a hatch labeled 145.

Once they are all in the large lift, the hatch shuts abruptly, and they are swiftly whisked a long ways up at an incredible velocity. Most are nearly dizzy as they step out into a cacophony of noise and commotion. Fighters are being worked on, and the air is abuzz with flying sparks as mechanics use tools to refit engine housings or trim rudders, and computers beep while calibrating weapons systems. A Marine in coveralls with red hair and bright green eyes comes over to greet them. "I am First Lieutenant Maplethorpe, your instructor. I will be grading your flight time in the Space Harrier class fighter. You are all supposed to have a working knowledge on how to fly these beasts, as well as other craft. Either that is true and you will make fine fighting pilots, or it is not and some of you will end up as debris floating in space. Muster in locker room echo to collect your gear and meet me back out here in ten mikes!"

"Aye, aye, sir!" they all chorus and race toward the locker room.

Garrison stays behind and approached the young officer. Crisply saluting, he bellows "Good evening, sir!"

Returning the salute, Maplethorpe replies, "At ease, Sergeant. You think the flash training worked?"

"Not sure, sir. We shall soon find out. It worked with me, but that's not really a good barometer. The training came along with the programming for my legs, so at least, part of me is somewhat computerized. These men are all flesh and blood. Sounds like trying to electronically hypnotize people into knowing what they had previously not known."

"Think high speed, low drag, Marine. It's a little deeper than that from what they tell me. Depending on the results, these docs will either seem like geniuses or frauds. All of this was done in an effort to mitigate predicted losses of pilots in battles we all know are coming," the officer states.

In the locker room, pilots stationed on the *Ex-Wife* help the trainees into formfitting jump suits which are surprisingly heavy. The suits are made of a combination of Teflon, Kevlar, and a molded acrylic-like substance with small strips of metal throughout the suit.

Standing in front of a mirror, Cpl Aragon examines himself. "I feel like I am in a big black condom."

Corporals Simms and Jordan come to join their friend. "That's ironically appropriate and inappropriate on multiple levels," Simms jokes.

Jordan laughs and adds, "Hey, I've read up on these suits. They're supposed to be pretty badass in a cockpit. I wouldn't want them in a firefight, though. Temp controls, wirelessly connected to a miniature computer in the helmet, as well as the flight and weapons systems of whatever you are piloting."

The weight of the suit is designed to help pilots deal with the amount of G-force applied to their bodies during certain maneuvers or at certain speeds during a dog fight. To the Marines, the suits seem heavier than usual for clothing, and the pilots aboard the *Ex Wife* have been given supplements similar to their ground force counterparts to help the process. Normal human beings would not be able to move in these suits.

Each of the Marines is paired with a pilot. Aragon nervously makes his way up the boarding ladder of a Space Harrier followed closely by his new instructor, Lieutenant Maplethorpe. This particular set has been modified so that two can fit into the cockpit. Weapons systems can be controlled by the officer seated in the rear, while the pilot up front will primarily fly. Aragon is ordered up front after a questioning glance at the lieutenant. After helping the corporal strap in, Lt. Maplethorpe straps himself in and begins talking the nervous Marine through the checklist routine.

"Ok, Marine. Here we go. Directly in front of you is the dashboard. On the center of the console, there should a button slightly above and to the right of your left knee. When you are sure that your helmet is properly sealed, which it should be because real pilots helped you put it on, press that button."

So far nothing seems familiar, and there is an empty feeling in the pit of Aragon's stomach that is beginning to spread throughout his being. Hesitantly, he pushes the button. There is a flicker from inside the helmet as the HUD system came online as the gauges that are lit on the dashboard go dark and miniature gauges appear in his field of vision. Without his view of anything else, he might need to pay more attention to being hindered.

Slowly Aragon begins to relax as the lieutenant keeps speaking. "With your left hand, ease the throttle forward slowly while adjusting your direction with the pedals. The pedals control the rear attitude thrusters. They are automatically dialed down while inside a docking bay. Once we are in vacuum, they will be at full power so that you can quickly adjust the orientation at will."

The fighter eases forward, and without really thinking about it, Aragon uses the thrusters to navigate through the bay, as if he has been doing so for years. Looking out, Aragon notices that there is a line forming, four columns to be exact. Sirens blare as red lights come on inside the bay, alerting all personnel that the airlock is about to open. All the ground crew scrambles to batten down any loose equipment, and secure tools in their proper places before making a mad dash to the hatches. Just as the last man's foot clears the entrance to one of the locker rooms, hatches quickly slam shut as the huge bay doors begin to slide open vertically. Everyone gapes at the starry abyss they are about to enter. Without being told, they all form small four-fighter diamond formations and take off in groups.

"Well, I'll be damned!" Lt. Maplethorpe exclaims.

"What's wrong, sir?" Aragon asks.

"In case you hadn't noticed, Corporal, we or should I say, you are flying in formation with twenty-eight other pilots, all of whom have never sat in a cockpit until right now, and I barely even got to tell you anything. I'm guessing the other instructors are having similar experiences. What was it like?"

Perplexed by the question, Aragon answers, "Not sure, sir. There was a glitch or something in the helmet after the cockpit readouts went dark, and then I just...knew."

"Well, the big wigs at HQ will be happy, as this will likely cut down on training time. Open up a line to all flights. This is Lt. Maplethorpe. You boys seem to know parade formations already. Let's see what combat maneuvers you learned," the lieutenant ordered.

* * *

Although there is no sound to accompany the detonation of the bomb hitting the surface of the targeted moon, the results are immediately evident.

"Lord, 'ave mercy!" Babylon exclaims.

"Indeed," the king responds.

Toshi sits in silence, staring at the wreckage. It looks as if some giant has taken the moon and decided to take a huge bite out of it as if it were an apple. The core is not visible, but multiple layers of the ravaged moon's crust can be seen. The small moon has not stopped spinning, but the momentum has slowed as it seems off balance now that it is proportioned differently. Now it kind of wobbles as it has no true axis on which to center like other planetary bodies. After all the pertinent data is gathered by Toshi, the Morningstar turns around, heading back to the mobile shipyard.

* * *

With the creature gone, Simeon is the first to regain his composure from its sudden appearance, and short skirmish.

"My lady, we must move to put some distance between us and that thing...whatever it was."

Most agreed with Simeon's assessment, but the professor is not so sure. "I agree we should get everyone to the rail cars and leave, but I am not confident we will be able to outdistance that thing."

Finally the queen speaks up. "Simeon is right! We must load up the cars and keep moving. Sitting will only make us an easy target."

Nobody speaks about what is really on their minds — the child and the voice that came from him. Some are far more worried about that than the creature that just appeared in their midst. Bofus is huddled in the back of the cave, watching the sleeping child warily, but does not have the heart to distance himself as some have silently vowed to do. "Possessed," "cursed" are some of the things people are thinking. The queen herself is worried but holds fast to the belief that her baby is just special in ways most cannot comprehend, and that he is destined for greatness in these troubled times. All will see that soon. A shame they cannot see it now after all the creature left at her son's command.

* * *

Speeding through tunnels as fast as his empowered limbs can carry him, Malice bounds through various caves before forcibly stopping himself. There is something strangely familiar about the child among his prey. This does not line up with what he saw, yet there is more to this being than that. Something evoked fear in Malice that usually only has one source... his master. This fear will have to be conquered in order to complete his mission. Professor Jones-Bey has to be eliminated, but the warriors he is traveling with will be a deterrent, and more will have to be learned about this child. Perhaps Pharaoh will take a warning of this new player, temporarily diffusing the anger over his failure to assassinate the one being that is seemingly trying to unravel the discord among the people of this galaxy.

Meanwhile Pharaoh senses the fear emanating from his minion even at a great distance. This is highly disturbing to the exile since there has been nothing to evoke such a strong emotional response in his servant. This development will need to be researched, and Malice needs to be brought back into the fold. Whatever the reason for his absence, it will be excused for now. Pharaoh attempts to communicate that sentiment through the vague link he and his minion seem to share at the moment, but he's not sure if the message goes through.

In the meantime, he will continue his search for another candidate to empower. Things are escalating, and he does not like the direction things are going. More hands may be needed soon.

Since the exiled light being is outside of his body scanning for suitable minion material, distance is not a factor in the search. While travelling once, he came upon a group of silverback gorillas. Pharaoh decides to approach the alpha male, slightly nudging his consciousness to see what the reaction will be. Confused the beast looks around in search of the disturbance. Not as much intelligence as a man, but it is not so far behind that he will not be useful. It will take some effort, but with some mutation, this animal can attain some level of understanding and boost its capacity to rationalize or reason. The simplicity of the mind the beast has may be of more value. With pain to aid in the initial instruction, perhaps this minion will not disobey or go astray as Malice has. A little competition may also help keep Malice in line. The threat of possibly being replaced should work wonders to adjust his attitude.

Chapter Thirteen

AFTER VIEWING FOOTAGE OF THE damage, the new ordinance has on the targeted moon, Omega, Babylon, Toshi, and some of the prominent Kison Askari are planning their first offensive strike. It is agreed that strictly military assets will be the focal point when the weapon is used. The avoidance of collateral damage is a high priority. A message will be sent, but they don't want to be seen as new oppressors, taking the place of the old ones. The scale is beginning to tip in favor of the oppressed, and balance for all will need to be restored or else they might as well leave things as they are.

Base camp on Jupiter IV is full of activity as the Kison Askari stock three flights of Kitana to be accompanied by a WarDragon for each group. All will be escorting the new Morningstar on its maiden live-action bombing run. The plan is to jump in, deliver the payload, and jump back out. Their numbers aren't strong enough to fight an all-out battle, and the assets being taken for this mission are too valuable to lose. There is plenty of materiel for building, but Omega sees no need to waste what they have assembled so soon in the game. Babylon and his generals agree.

In the hangar bay, Muturi is aboard a WarDragon, calibrating the rear depth charger deployment system and laser cannons while Kamal straps in to start the flight check process. Finally, Nefer climbs into the gunner's seat slightly above and aft of the pilot's seat in the cockpit.

"You boys ready for this?" she asks.

Kamal replies, "Of course. It's about time we started throwing our weight around, give them something to fear. These people have been comfortable with doing whatever they want for too long."

When their eyes meet, Muturi simply nods to confirm his readiness. Once they receive the launch order, Kamal eases the throttle forward to taxi out of the hangar bay. In truth, they are all nervous. Battle is to be expected, but pulling escort duty for a new bomber class ship piloted by the leader of their people, the leader of another group, as well as an important member of another group, adds pressure to an already high-profile situation. Many think the Kison Askari should begin with disruption of supply routes to put the squeeze on the GMC. Others feel that retaliation for what took place on Pluto is exactly the right move. Omega feels this move would achieve both. By hitting Saturn, they will hinder ship production by destroying some of the ore and other material being mined there while simultaneously striking at the heart of the military. After all, Saturn is supposed to be where their very best train.

Once all vessels communicate their readiness, the order is given to jump. All pilots and navigators watch simultaneously as stars blur into streaks of light, engines roar prior to forcefully making the transition into hyperspace. Some find this mode of travel nauseating, but most think it necessary. Toshi is secretly cringing inside. Sitting aboard the Morningstar with Babylon, Omega and some other infamous figures make it all the more difficult to hide his anxiety. The problem is not the experience of hyperspace travel, but it is the full understanding of what a mistake can do to those taking this wild ride and those who may be caught in their path.

It is rumored that one of the GMC's officers made one such mistake and has paid a hefty price for it. The pressure of knowing that even the most miniscule miscalculation could have disastrous effects makes Toshi's stomach broil and his skin a paler green than usual. Babylon approaches the young Jade Assassin to see why he looks so sickly right before battle. After all, he should be accustomed to bloodshed, and this will be from a distance, at least.

"What's wrong, boy? You look sick as a dog! Don tell me you nervous bout dis little rump we goin' to. Should be short, ya know," the old Atlantean rasps.

Toshi can't help but smile when looking at the old man with his long dreadlocks, the mischievous glint in those amber eyes, and the creases in his cerulean skin. This being has lived a very long time, seen an untold number of events, both mundane and monumental, yet here he is unfazed.

Much to his relief, the jump goes smoothly. No casualties, no random anomalies to complicate things, and the group stays together for the entire trip. The jump is clean, one would say almost perfect. There is, however, an element to spice things up. They jump into a large group of GMC craft and fly in military formations as if they are supposed to be there. Both sides are equally surprised. The Askari prove to be the better prepared to recover as they are carrying live ammunition, but the GMC pilots in training ...are not.

* * *

Speeding his way through various maneuvers as if he has been doing it for years, Aragon is exhilarated. The rush of combat when all is going as planned or the adrenaline rush of having made it through a tough spot is the only things that tops what he and his brothers-in-arms are experiencing right now as they slice through the stars at speeds they have not dreamed possible. The close precision with which they fly adds to the euphoria most are feeling. That all comes to a crashing halt as a flurry of ships seemingly magically appear in the midst of their previously organized formations. Chaos ensues.

Just outside of Aragon's cockpit a large bestial ship materializes, seemingly, out of thin air. As his heart leaps into his throat, Aragon yanks the stick hard to the right barely avoiding what would most likely have resulted in a fatal collision. Aragon pushes the throttle as far forward as it will go to put some distance between himself and these unwanted participants in their training exercise. Turning about, Aragon toggles the switch to go weapons free when Lt. Maplethorpe yells, "What are you doing, idiot?"

"In case you hadn't noticed, sir, we have unwanted guests!" Aragon responds.

"Yes, but in case YOU hadn't noticed, we are armed with TRAIN-ING rounds!" the officer bellows.

This is not good.

* * *

As soon as they come out of the jump, Kamal has to pull up hard in order to avoid pancaking three fighter ships. One of the star fighters breaks hard to the right, separating from its wingmen before turning about as if to attack. Before he can give the order to fire, Nefer already has the laser cannons primed and begins stitching bright purple lines in space, harassing the lone pilot, but it is proving to be a hard target.

Meanwhile Corporals Simms and Jordan are having troubles of their own trying to stay out of the crosshairs of some boomerang-shaped ships that came with the enemy.

Sgt. Garrison's voice blares over the comm system, "All units get your asses back to the *Ex-Wife* double time! We won't last long out here shooting spitballs at the enemy. Evade and get to base!"

General Krulak immediately orders the forward batteries to give their fighter pilots some cover fire. This is proving to be a difficult task as they attempt to cover the retreat without clipping their own people. Friendly fire will not be looked upon favorably. The fact that what they are being asked to do is like performing surgery with a broad sword, instead of a scalpel, will not make a difference to command.

So distracted by what is happening out beyond Saturn's atmosphere, the commandant notices the larger manta-shaped ship flying over their planet side headquarters when it is too late. The call is put into anti-air units on the ground to eliminate that ship. Krulak is furious. Whatever that ship is doing will not bode well if it is successful. Communications from the ground confirms that something is afoot. Reports of the strange ship dropping what is assumed to be some sort of ordinance is quickly disseminated.

Planet side, Lt. Commander Jameson looks skyward through the purple and lavender haze that is Saturn's atmosphere, to see a dark orb fast approaching the surface off in the distance. He waits in anticipation for the accompanying boom or explosion after the orb dips below the horizon, away from his sight. Eerily, there is no such sound or even an explosion. There is, however, a dark cloud fast approaching. Despite his macabre and growing curiosity, the doctor decides it will be best to watch the results from a distance or perhaps view a recording of it. Grabbing what research he can Lt. Commander Jameson quickly makes his way to the nearest shuttle that will take him off planet.

Aboard the Morningstar, Babylon, Toshi, and Jared Omega look on as they pull away after dropping their payload. Seeing the look of consternation on Toshi's face, Omega approaches to see what is troubling him.

"Did we hit the target?" the king asks.

The Jade Assassin looks up shamefully and replies, "Wasn't a direct hit, but we were close enough to do some damage. I was hoping to level the entire facility. We won't know what the extent is until the drones finish recording and come back."

"Dat is assuming da GMC won't shoot dem down before they gather any real data," Babylon retorted.

The king of the Kison Askari walks over to the display showing the deployment of ships as well as activity groundside. "They are in a mad scramble right now and may be more worried about licking their wounds at the moment. Toshi, tell everyone to jump home to regroup," the king orders.

* * *

Corporals Simms, Aragon, and Jordan sit in the ready room aboard the *Ex-Wife*. After Aragon landed in the docking bay, it took him a long time to realize his hands were shaking. Some of the others had similar experiences knowing how close they had come to death during what was supposed to be a training exercise. Here the three sit together, internally contemplating what it all means. Jordan is the first to speak, "Where did they get their tech? There's no way they should have anything close to what we have after being nothing but miners for who knows how long now."

"Someone is definitely helping them. Intel needs to find out who and quick. If we can cut them off, we can regain the advantage," Aragon replies. Silently Simms sits in agreement with his fellow Marines.

Lt. Commander Jameson and a research team go back to Saturn's surface in full environment suits to assess the damage, as well as to gather information on this new weapon the enemy has. The findings are not encouraging. Luckily it wasn't a direct hit, or there would be nothing of the facility to study. Whatever was dropped the stuff does not simply destroy everything it touches. It eradicates its very existence to the point where it is hard to prove the object existed at all. This proves to be a particularly bad attribute when dealing with the injured. There are around a thousand casualties and twice as many injured service men and women are soon to join them. Many Marines simply bleed out because lost limbs seem as if the part that was taken had never existed, the tissue left does not clot, scar, or more importantly, heal.

The medical staff has taken to using lasers to burn the existing tissue in order to cauterize and close the wounds. Painful yet effective, and Jameson has a theory of what this weapon is but needs more conclusive evidence. The young team of ensigns and lieutenants are baffled by what they are studying and have no answers. Organic or not, anything caught in the blast radius is utterly destroyed. The ground and foliage are a blank slate as if this part of the world is just a painting that is left unfinished. Some areas are smoothed over, as if thousands of years of water wear happened in an instant. With incendiary weapons matter is burned up but there are ashes and other remnants left behind. Anti-matter technology is a theory that has been discussed but nothing has been done to solidify anything useful. Lt. Commander Jameson has to get a handle on this and fast, or they might just be in serious trouble.

* * *

Back deep in the underground network beneath Earth's crust, Tunisia, Simeon, Bofus and Professor Jones-Bey and the rest of their retinue keep moving to stay away from whatever that creature is, and watching young Darius grow at an alarming rate. Tunisia is proud of her son. His skin tone is a marbled mix of hers and the king's. Ash grays and browns swirl throughout his body, and there is that strange glow that occasionally comes out. This happened mostly when the boy seems to be distressed. Among the group, the opinion of blessed or cursed is varied. Most tend to believe he is blessed since nothing bad has befallen them since they began their journey.

What they did not know is that the creature known as Malice is not far away, waiting to try again to eliminate the professor. Whatever hold the infant has on him will not last, and his mission will be completed no matter what obstacles get in the way. Nothing is worse than the master's ire. Failure is not accepted. Perhaps when they bed down for a night, when the sentries are the only beings alert, that will present a better opportunity. Full-frontal assault will not work. The Stone Warriors are tough and now are using technology that goes well beyond what Malice is used to seeing from them. Pharaoh thinks this makes things interesting, but his minion thinks it's annoying since it complicates things. Either way, the professor has to die.

A few caverns away, Malice listens intently to the activities of Professor Jones-Bey, young Darius and the rest of the group that have gone into hiding while the revolution rages on the surface and throughout the galaxy. With this hunt, Malice will have to be patient, waiting in the shadows and listening for the perfect time to strike. This method lengthens the timetable more than he likes but raises the probability of success.

Nearby Professor Jones-Bey sits with young Darius as he plays with toys of various shapes and size to teach spatial relationships. The toys are also of various colors.

Darius easily grasps the concepts of these toys and seems to need more advanced learning aids. This is remarkable to all who see him play, but lately the lesson has taken an even more astonishing turn, and the professor has no idea what this new discovery means. Hastily the professor rushes into the adjacent cavern to gather the others, so they may witness what he just saw.

"Your highness, Simeon sir, you must see what the boy can do! Hurry please!" he exclaims.

Bofus is the first to answer. "Man, what's yo problem, and why you all out of breath?"

Tunisia, Simeon, Bofus, and a few others hurry to see what the fuss is all about. Flustered and breathless, the professor rushes in to hand the child a few of the toys. Darius immediately begins to organize them by size, shape, and color. Upon completion of that task, the boy looks up at Professor Jones-Bey beaming.

"Um ... I've seen this show befo'," Bofus jovially says.

"No, no, there's more. I assure you. Go ahead, Darius. Show them!" the professor implores.

Darius grabs one of the smaller globes at his feet, walks up to Jones-Bey, and hands him the ball.

"All right. What happens now?" Simeon asks.

"I promise, a few moments ago, the boy showed extraordinary abilities! The only way I can describe it is to call it telekinesis," Jones-Bey replies.

"Teleki-what? Man, you lost yo mind! I'm out," Bofus exclaims and exits the chamber abruptly.

Puzzled, Simeon turns to the professor. "So he floated these toys with his mind, huh? I think you might have spent too much time below ground, my friend."

The professor is crestfallen, and with a few giggles, the group leaves Darius to finish his play/studies with him. After they are completely alone, Darius gathers several toys and drops them at his feet. Sitting in the middle of them, he closes his eyes and begins to glow slightly. The toys, singly at first and then simultaneously, begin to rise. They are lifted higher and higher until they are near the roof of the cavern. The toys start spinning and rotating as if caught in a hurricane, building speed until they are a blurred mass.

Amazed, the Professor watched until he realizes that the child had just played him. Jones-Bey screams in frustration and surprise as the swirling mass of toys unexpectedly launches themselves at him. The toys stop before impacting with the professor's cowering form and fall harmlessly to the floor. Darius giggles and then falls out laughing. Still angry, the professor cannot help but join in.

Tunisia comes back to see what the commotion is about. Seeing the look on her face, the professor reassures her. "It's all right. I was startled by something I thought I saw, but nothing but a figment of my imagination I'm afraid. Perhaps they were right about being here too long."

The queen walks over to pick Darius up and then leaves the professor to his thoughts. Cruel as the exhibition was, it justifies the Professors excitement. Who knows what other abilities the boy has, and research will need to be done to find out why none of the others showed the talents Darius had. That will need to be a careful line to walk. Professor Jones-Bey will have to find a discrete method of gathering information.

* * *

Aboard the *Ex Wife*, Lt. Commander Jameson walks with General Krulak to give his report in the aftermath of the attack. Standing in front of one of the large viewports, the general gazes down at the strange and misshapen crater on Saturn's surface, watching the ground crews attempting to clean up.

"Let's have it, Lt. Commander. What are we dealing with here?"

Jameson stands next to the general. "Sir, it's got to be some form of anti-matter or dark matter that we've only seen in theoretical terms. It's bad if they've found some way to harness it; I don't think we have any way to nullify its effects."

The general looks grim. This is not a good sign. They are baffled at how these people could have developed a weapon this potent before the GMC.

"Find me some answers, Lt. Commander, and find them quick! Can it be replicated?" General Krulak asks.

The lieutenant commander takes off his glasses and pinches the bridge of his nose while shaking his head negatively before answering. "No, sir, this stuff is volatile. We have no way of containing the substance. How they made ordinance out of it is a mystery. There's very little to study at ground zero. We may have to come up with something else, maybe something that can be just as devastating. I'll have a team go to work on it, sir. Meanwhile, we will piece together what we can in an effort to steal their tech. It would be a beast of a mission, sir."

General Krulak clasps Lt. Commander Jameson's shoulder. "I'll find some Marines crazy enough to attempt it. Don't know how many of those bombers they have, but we have to get that weapon out of their hands before this spins out of control more than it already has. You'll have whatever you need for your research. Dismissed."

The lieutenant commander smartly salutes, about-faces, and heads to the ship's lab.

* * *

As soon as the strike force jumps back into Jupiter's airspace just outside of the atmosphere, Omega gives the order to have the mobile shipyard prepare to relocate. Toshi looks a little perplexed but relays the order to the crews aboard the shipyard's ore haulers and assembly ships. Quickly the shipyard turns into a frenzy of commotion and movement as docking arms retract into the haulers, and various bots collapse into themselves and attach to the outer hulls of the larger ships. Soon the shipyard is a mini-fleet ready to move out.

"What now, great King?" Babylon asks.

Omega turns to the old Atlantean to reply. "They will regroup and seek to retaliate. We caught them with their pants down, so to speak. I'll not return the favor and let them do the same. I'll have the shipyards jump to Mars. We can use that as a staging area while they come here to strike."

Chapter Fourteen

DEEP IN A FOREST OF central Africa, a disorientated gorilla awakens with a splitting headache. Holding its head, he attempts to shake off the pain while trying to remember what the cause was from last night. The animal's jaw goes slack, and his eyes dilate as the strangest realization comes upon him. A new form of self-communication has suddenly developed. The gorilla thinks of himself as "I," and now looks at his surroundings subconsciously, designating descriptions to the land, plant life, and animals here in his "home." The pain now is either gone or forgotten. Distracted by the discovery that he has somehow learned to think using words, he begins to contemplate further. For he knew there was another use for these "words."

The gorilla has no idea how he has come to this epiphany or why it has come to him at this time. The beast gets up on all fours and manipulates his mouth to try and form his first verbal utterance when a voice suddenly thunders in his head. "Come to me!"

He knows the voice to be "master," and does not like the idea. He will go to master because master is responsible for his recent pain. Yes, he will go to seek "retribution" — a complicated yet fitting word he suddenly knows and likes. Then he thinks, "I am coming master."

The reply fills his mind again, "Good."

The beast then heads off toward the direction from where the voice is coming at an alarming speed. Words, complex thought, and intelligence are not the only things that have changed for this creature.

Pharaoh can feel the creature's aggression and anger. This comes with the partial enlightenment. It is no matter the beast is more powerful than it was before and immeasurably more intelligent, but it is still no match for a pure light being. It will be cowed and controlled as all of its pre-decessors have been. All previous minions were human to begin with, so this is technically new territory. Any amusement that can be drawn from this is tempered by the dire nature of the possibilities developing if this backward group of beings ever truly unites. There are disturbing whispers about an ancient Atlantean augmenting this movement to unite all beings on this miserable planet. When this Professor Jones-Bey is taken care of, this supposed ancient will be next in line for an untimely demise.

* * *

Back on Saturn, in part of the barracks where the base hadn't been destroyed by the strange ordinance, Corporals Simms, Aragon, and Jordan sit, playing cards.

"They are still trying to figure out what we were hit with," Simms states.

"Yup, and you know we're not going to take this lying down. Head-quarters is planning a counterstrike as we speak" Jordan adds.

"True, but we have to be careful. Don't want to run into the belly of the beast, if they've stored up a bunch of that ordinance or utilized it in other forms of weaponry we haven't thought about. They're a people with a grudge. Anger can breed a pretty inventive and sick imagination," Aragon replies.

Just then, the hatch swings open, and Petty Officer House strides in with something behind his back.

"I come bearing gifts of truce! The last prank could have got you boys killed. Please accept my apologies, Marines."

From behind he produces a small steel canister that looks oddly famil-iar. Instantly the guys perk up.

"Is that what I think it is?" Jordan asks.

"No way! There are no nitroclubs here, so how did you get that?" Aragon asks.

"I can't tell you my secrets. I have my ways, so just enjoy and stop with the questions. By the way, I don't know what blend it is, but it should be good. I think it's called 'surprise,'" House tells them before exiting.

Simms shouts, "Hey! Where are you off to so fast?"

"Fire watch!" House shouts from the hall.

The canister sits in the center of the room as the three Marines stare at it, distrustful of the gift despite the fact that House called it a "truce." This could be another elaborate prank. They are all wary of a trick yet need the temporary respite the gift might give them if it's genuine.

"What the hell!" Aragon says as he walks over to twist the top off the canister.

Jordan jumps and yells, "Secure the hatches and ports!"

Simms and Aragon do so, making sure that even the vents are closed, making the room airtight.

A loud hiss emits from the canister, and they all look at each other in anticipation. After a few moments, none of them are feeling any different. Corporal Jordan narrows his blue eyes. "Man, I think that just made me more serious than I was before. Do you guys feel anything?" he asks.

"Nope!" Simms and Aragon chorus.

"I think we've been had again, Marines. That's ok, though. We'll get the last laugh on that spaceswabbie yet," Aragon adds.

Simms and Jordan smile, thinking of their devious revenge. Simms finally says what he is thinking. "You know when you think of it, this prank was kind of a dud. The only 'surprise' was that nothing happened."

* * *

Heedless of the strange looks and screaming of beings he passes, the silverback makes his way through jungle, desert, and cityscape when he cannot avoid it. The impulse to come to the master is unbearable. Not only does the voice not leave his mind, but it is accompanied by pain now. If this master is the cause of the new pain in addition to the pain experienced earlier, retribution will need to be slow and as drawn out as possible. Giza is fast approaching, and the real mystery is how he knew where to go. The beast runs directly to a secret entrance at the base of the north wall of the pyramid.

Pharaoh can feel the beast as he approaches his stronghold. The anger emanating from it is palpable. In a mindless rage, the silverback navigates the serpentine labyrinth easily and quickly. Sitting in the bottom most chambers at the zenith of the ob-pyramidal structure with his eyes closed, he waits. A portal opens through which the beast comes roaring in, gaining entrance to where Pharaoh waits. Screaming, the silverback hurls itself at Pharaoh. At the last second, Pharaoh's eyes open blinding the beast with piercing light.

Skidding to a halt on the cold stone floor, the beast shakes its head to get stabilized before another attempt. Pharaoh stands to face the enraged animal. "Did you really think you could defeat a being as powerful as me? I made you! Well, not originally, but call it spontaneous evolution. A gift, if you will, is what this is, to use logic and reason, and this is how you repay me?"

The gorilla blinks, gathering his thoughts. "Master...hurt me. Pain is no good," the silverback mumbles.

"Ah, verbal speech! Another ability you were lacking before I enhanced you. Understand this. I am your master! I can crush you with a thought. Obey me and live. Defy me and know that your pain will only be magnified, and I will restore you to the state I found you in!" Pharaoh bellows.

Almost in a genuflecting pose, the silverback bows. "Master," he stammers.

"Good, you see your place in my presence. Be sure not to forget. Rise. I must give you a vast amount of experience and knowledge in a short period of time. This means more pain. It is the price you pay for greatness. I need you to know a great deal if you are to help and do my bidding. Now we need to call you something. What name would you take, beast?"

After a moment, the silverback still remained on the ground. Pharaoh commands, "Rise." The beast rises up on all fours. "No, no, that won't do," The light being says. Closing his eyes, Pharaoh begins concentrating. Immediately there is a tingling sensation in the gorilla's lower back and legs. Soon, it is standing upright without awkwardness. "Better, yes?" he asks.

Strangely it does feel better despite never having been in that posture for any extended period of time. The beast closes its eyes and said, "I shall be called ...Typhoon!"

Pharaoh chuckles deeply and replies, "As you wish. I like it! An irresistible force like a force of nature that is what you will be. Do my bidding, and you shall always be feared and respected. No one or anything shall stand in your path. Fail me, and you will be blown away like so much chaff."

Newly named Typhoon bows in obedience yet knows in his mind that he will indeed take the strength and power granted by this strange being. He knows he would much rather be respected than feared, and he also knows that one day he will use the powers granted to him in an attempt to strike down his new master. That knowledge, along with his newfound intelligence, strikes fear in his very core because he seriously doubts he will ever be successful. The expansion of his formerly primitive mind helps quell that fear. There is so much more to learn, and the furthering of his education will bring more possibilities.

* * *

A task force is sent to Jupiter to give answer for the attack at Saturn. Cpl. Aragon and Sgt. Garrison are ordered to fly point when they jump into Jupiter's star system. The others in their group are flying escort for two flights of heavy Thor class bombers. Only light activity is detected on the giant planet's surface, and for the most part, this installation looks abandoned. There is a lot of debris around a few of the moons. The rockheads must have packed up quick and got ghost. Aragon presses his chin to the mic in his helmet, opening a frequency to his wingman.

"What's the plan, Sergeant? This looks like a lot of dead space."

Before the sergeant can respond a voice with a thick Hindi accent fills their ears. "All bombers do a surface sweep and deploy your packages to areas with the strongest heat signatures, fighters watch their sixes. This could be a trick. Weapons free."

All pilots double click their mics to acknowledge that the order has been received and understood. The ships fan out to execute Major Vashti's orders. A few areas were lit up quickly as mjollnir cluster bombs are dropped, penetrating parts of the surface, shaking some of the underground network but doing little overall damage. The contingent that stayed behind are deep enough to be safe from the bombardment. They are ordered to stay in hiding until the strike is over. There will be a time when they will reassemble the mobile shipyard here.

The GMC does not fare well in ground engagements on Earth and will likely not do well in the conditions on Jupiter, so they know that boots hitting the ground are an unlikely tactic. Technological advantage has been the GMC's ace up their proverbial sleeves previously. This attack is pointless, but no action at all would have been worse, and it was an opportunity to do some recon on this part of the galaxy. Everything is being analyzed. Every bit of space is being scanned for a hint of jump scars. If the direction the shipyard has gone along with the other ships that had to be in tow can be sniffed out, then the GMC will give chase. Acts of war have to be met with equal violence, even if the effect will not be equal. General Krulak is not the type of man who will turn the other cheek after being punched in the face.

Major Vashti gives the order to withdraw, and the task force turns about to dock aboard the Man of War class frigate he was overseeing the operation from. Sgt. Garrison and Cpl. Aragon are two thousand meters away from the docking port when several vessels simultaneously jump in and begin firing off pot shots at the remaining ships. There is a brief but brilliant explosion as one of the rearmost bombers gets skewered with laser fire. Without discussing the maneuver, the Marines both pull up on the sticks to reverse course to intercept the new arrivals. Major Vashti calls to them over the comm, "Negative, Sgt. Garrison! Turn those fighters around, we were ordered to attack with minimal loss of assets!"

Sgt. Garrison clicks the chin mic and replies, "Sir, if we do not get them off our tails, they will be able to pick off most of the stragglers! Aragon and I will run some interference, so we can jump out of here."

"Roger that. Make it quick!" the major exclaims. Turning to the officer at the sensor scanner station, Major Vashti bellows more orders. "Record any possible jump scars and calibrate likely trajectories. Once we get that intel, we will return in force. I am sure by then HQ will have something in mind."

Without looking up from his station, the young ensign manning the sensors says, "Aye, aye, sir!" with fingers whirling in blurs over the control panel.

Meanwhile, Aragon and Garrison are giving chase to two boomerang shaped fighters as they jink and juke to evade laser fire. They head around one of the sixteen moons as Aragon clips the wings of the Kitana class star fighter that is in his sites only to end up staring into the laser turrets of a much larger WarDragon.

"Break hard to port!" Sgt. Garrison screams into his mic.

Silently complying, Aragon suddenly has to fight the urge to giggle. The move is executed just in time as the area their two Space Harriers had just vacated is now filled with hot streaks of light.

"Damn! That was close!" Aragon manages between bouts of gut-busting laughter.

Pulling hard on the stick to avoid follow-up fire after avoiding several volleys from the ambushing WarDragon, Garrison's eyes narrow as he screams at his wingman, "I'm not sure what you find so amusing about being fired upon, but you need to get your head in the game, Marine!"

Still trying to clamp down on his sudden uncontrollable laughter,

Aragon is experiencing the strangest mix of emotions he has ever known. At any moment, he could be blasted by laser fire that would open the hull of his ship and lance him through the chest and then instantly freeze him as vacuum joined him in the cockpit. This was hardly a hilarious predicament, yet he found it to be deathly terrifying and, simultaneously, very humorous.

Fighting through tears from intense laughter, Aragon manages to avoid certain death and even takes out another Kitana when he realizes what is wrong. "Surprise..." he murmurs.

Most of the task force has made it back to the frigate with the exception of a few bombers and Space Harriers too slow on the sticks. Aragon, along with his wingman Sgt. Garrison, who pealed back to give the group time to dock, is among this group.

Major Vashti's orders come blaring into their helmets. "We are clear! Get back so we can jump back to base. Repeat! Break off pursuit and disengage!"

"Surprise. I mean, yes, sir!" Aragon mumbles.

Sgt. Garrison doesn't know what is wrong with Aragon, but he was determined to get to the bottom of it if they survive this. The corporal is usually one of his most reliable men. This is the absolute wrong time to start acting like a goofball. Meanwhile Simms and Jordan are having similar experiences, except they are manning turrets on the Man of War frigate designated as the command ship for this task force. They are picking off fighters in pursuit of the friendlies trying to get back aboard for the jump to base, all the while, laughing loudly as they squeeze the double triggers. Finally the dock hatches were battened down as the last ship comes in and the order to jump is given. Sgt. Garrison and Cpl. Aragon had narrowly escaped a final barrage that skittered off the closing hatches.

* * *

Through the cams of the drones left around Jupiter, Toshi watches the entire engagement along with Jared Omega and Babylon.

"Impressive, yet surprising," Toshi comments.

"They knew we would leave no resources for them to take, and there was no strategic target for them to hit. This was more of a reconnaissance run than an attack. They likely scanned to see if they could figure out where we are now," Omega stated.

"Don get too cocky. The need for revenge will eventually override the commonsense of avoiding losing battles. Soon the devastation of Saturn will matter less to the GMC," Babylon warns.

Toshi turns to the group and says, "Then maybe we will have to periodically remind them."

This kind of situation is exactly what Omega wants to avoid. Things will only continue to escalate from here until they either destroy each other or the Kison Askari are forced to become oppressors in an attempt to maintain order.

Sole power for any one group would bring corruption eventually, no matter how good the initial intentions are. They all knew this, but it seems as if compromise is an intangible thing for this conflict. If the true culprit from which all the conflict began cannot be found then the alternatives will not be pleasant. As much as it disgusted him, a contingency plan has to be put together to take out the current leadership. Perhaps whoever took their place will have a change of heart and sue for peace, instead of keeping the conflict going. More than likely, the next generation of leaders will be even more pugnacious.

"Toshi, see if you can invent some kind of nonlethal weaponry. When it is an available alternative, I would like to begin neutralizing, instead of eliminating, perhaps something that will attack their weapons systems, so they will have no viable way of fighting back," Omega suggested.

"I'll see what I can do, but you know these people will throw dirt rocks at us if that's all they have at their disposal. Reason, sadly enough, is not one of their strong suits," Toshi replies.

"Try anyway. Someone among dem has to have some sense. It will be noticed by dem when they see we are not about wholesale slaughter," Babylon interjected.

With that, Toshi begins to work on nonlethal measures, while on the other side, Lt. Commander Jameson and his team are working on a weapon that will rival the anti-matter ordinance, if such a thing can be done. The balance of power is slowly shifting the question, determining if this is a good or a bad thing. Nobility of character, as well as corruption, is present in all groups of people. Despite many differences, there are also many similarities in all species. One miniscule variable can influence the realization of huge consequences. This circumstance is expressed repeatedly throughout the universe. If there is not a scientific law stating this, then there definitely should be.

Back on Earth, Athena and her network of spies have been keeping abreast of all the craziness that has taken over the galaxy in a relatively short amount of time. The Kison Tantu that initially went on the expedition with Taki and Megumi of the Jade assassins are busy fighting a war among the stars, but the search has to continue to find this mysterious Pharaoh. Hironike has released the two assassins to pursue the search again, along with Angelo from the Limbia Johari. It may be a long time before another show is scheduled, and if there is a show, it is not known who will show up. Dignitaries are scared to come out in public, and the military is on a witch hunt for anyone "deemed" an enemy of the current regime.

Chapter Fifteen

BACK AT GIZA, TYPHOON STANDS before Pharaoh upright in a flowing cloak, giving an illusion that he might be human. His movements are swift and more fluid now. Not quite as smooth or quick as Malice's, but he is more physically powerful than his predecessor. The beast has spent time practicing skulking and stalking to get accustomed to his new abilities. Pharaoh is pleased with his progress. He is amazed at what can be done with this species in so short a time, yet the human race seems to advance at a snail's pace, once they reach a certain level. Last week, this brute of a primate was content to sit in the forest foraging for prized foliage. With the help of slight mutation and some mental nudging, this primitive animal can actually hunt.

It has tasted flesh and reveled in it. Rudimentary tools are a thing of the past as Typhoon can now wield weapons and has actually gone beyond mere melée weapons or blades, as Malice preferred. This particular advantage may prove useful over Malice. Whether it will be enough to even things up, Pharaoh is not sure. It will make the conflict an interesting one, though. Malice must be brought back into the fold and quickly before things unravel. The fact that Typhoon recognizes his speed and flow disadvantage is a good sign, so he takes up ballistic weapons in case he has to strike from a distance. There are others who have tried the same tactic against Malice with less than desirable results. None who have tried before knew exactly what they were up against.

"Kneel," Pharaoh commands.

Typhoon obeys scraping the sand with a plethora of scabbards strapped to his hairy legs while closing his eyes. Tapping the gorilla on the forehead and then stepping back, Pharaoh commands him to rise. Upon rising Typhoon opens his eyes which have changed from a docile deep brown to a glowing bright cerulean blue. "Now you are recognizable as my servant. I command you to go and find my wayward servant and bring him back to me alive, if possible. Disobedient as he is, he is still valuable. Understand this, beast! He will be severely punished once the tasks I had bid him to complete are accomplished. Fail me, and you will join him in immeasurable agony," the light being states flatly.

Typhoon rises. "Yes, master" is all he says before gathering and propelling himself into motion, as if shot out of an unseen cannon. There are reports of a small sandstorm moving throughout the desert. Inexplicably, Typhoon can feel Malice and knows where to find him, similar to the way he knew where to find master. Unsure of what he will do once he is before the fellow servant, he is content to follow his instincts for now; strategy will come later.

* * *

Deep in the catacombs, Malice is still tailing the group as they travel great distances throughout the world in an intricate subterranean rail system he did not know existed. Suddenly he feels a presence that is vast a distance away but approaching at great speed. This presence is unfamiliar yet strangely known to him in some way. One thing is certain; he is now a target. It is imperative that he overcomes this inexplicable fear of the child. Malice has tried to wait until the boy is fast asleep, but whenever he gets near the group to strike at the professor, something in the boy awakens, and Malice feels it, feels its knowledge of his approach, and he retreats each time.

The youngster is not at his peak in power, which is something else that makes Malice wary. He isn't simply growing as all young do; it is apparent that he is also becoming more and more powerful. Malice has no idea what the source of the power is, but it is obvious that it outstrips the prowess he has obtained through Pharaoh's manipulation of his molecular structure. Something will have to be done; failure was not an option. The professor has to die, and if Malice has to die completing this mission, then so be it. Whoever or whatever is coming will be another confrontation that could be a distraction, so Malice will have to figure this out fast.

Unaware that they are still being stalked, Professor Jones-Bey and Bofus sit in a cave deep in one of the caves near one of the access points where the group has stopped to rest. The subterranean rail system is a huge advantage as they can travel over larger distances in a much smaller amount of time than conventional methods. The humans along for the ride have to wear protective gear similar to the G-suits pilots wore in the past to keep from passing out during flight. Bofus is watching the professor struggle mightily to take the heavy, cumbersome suit off. He is enjoying the squealing commotion.

"You look like you need help." Bofus chuckles.

Looking up in surprise that someone is witnessing this debacle, the professor angrily replies, "Glad my misery is a constant source of joy for you."

Bofus approaches the professor, grabs one sleeve, and begins to pull. Grunting with effort, as the suit proves to be quite stubborn, the professor then begins wheezing and whining throughout the struggle.

"Hey, man! Sit still! You must have glued this thing on or something," Bofus complained.

"No, I certainly did not! How on Earth did you get yours off?" Professor Jones-Bey demands.

Bofus looks at him and replies, "Mine had a button that deflates the inner sheath thingy. It's above the left shoulder blade."

"Get off me!" the professor yelps as he pushes Bofus away and proceeds to press the button. Instantly the pressure within the suit lessens until it is loose enough for him to easily slip out of it. The professor angrily stares at Bofus before speaking again. "That should have been the first thing you did when you came here to make fun of me."

With a bewildered look on his face, Bofus scratches his head and says, "Didn't come to make fun, just thought maybe yours was broke. That's all. How was I supposed to know you didn't know how to take it off? You are a doctor or something, right?"

Infuriated, the professor storms off.

After the professor leaves, Bofus stands there, thinking, Things have taken such crazy turns. He has gone from being a small-time hustler in Chicago to a supposed political prisoner on the run with professor and a group of mutants. The last was according to the professor's studies. The rest of the world believes them to be monsters with no relation to the rest of the human race. They are incredibly fast and strong, but in some of them, Bofus sees his own eyes when he looks into theirs, so to some extent, he believes Jones-Bey, despite not understanding the scientific jibber jabber the man has taken as a second language. Plus, they have saved him, along with the others, and that was the most important thing he needs to know about these people.

Suddenly his deep thoughts are disturbed by a strange scrabbling noise that seems to be heading in the same direction the professor has taken, yet Bofus has seen nothing to accompany the sound.

"Hello?" he offers the silence, a sickening feeling filling his stomach. There is no reply, and Bofus starts to walk, following the sound, knowing that he does not want to, but his feet seem to have a mind of their own, much to his dismay. The noise has quickly passed overhead, and he slowly follows it toward the exit, into the next cavern where the angry professor entered mere seconds ago.

Instinctively Bofus knows he should, at least, hide somewhere rather than follow that noise. Yet for some reason, he cannot refrain from doing so. He feels as if he is stuck looking through the eyes of a character in some strange horror film. The beast is just around the corner, and somewhere in his subconscious a loud movie patron is screaming, "Don't go over there!" As with every cinema experience the character never listens because, after all ... they cannot hear the patrons.

* * *

In the hangar bay aboard the Man of War frigate, Sgt. Garrison jumps out of the cockpit tossing his helmet in the process and sprints toward where Cpl. Aragon, who is doing the same a few Space Harriers down from where he docked. The loud clanking of the cybernetic legs make everyone turn to see what the commotion is. Garrison skids to a sparking halt in front of Aragon's Harrier, rushing up to him while grabbing the Marine to hold him up by the lapels of his jumpsuit.

"What was your malfunction out there?" he screams into Cpl. Aragon's face.

Aragon struggles to be released from the Sgt.'s iron grip while also trying not to laugh and further infuriate Sgt. Garrison.

"I don't know, Sergeant!" Aragon manages while swallowing giggles.

Five others rush in to break Sgt. Garrison's grip on their fellow Marine. Reluctantly he releases the still smirking Aragon and stalks off in a huff. Dragging his metal feet to scrape the deck, he forces all around to cover their ears at the hideous screeching sounds on his way out. Lt. Maplethorpe rushes to the now heaving Aragon.

"What's up with that, Marine?" he askes.

Cpl. Aragon stands in semi-control of his giggles. "Got a little loopy out there, sir. The sergeant didn't like it. Not feeling too well, sir," Aragon replies. "Report to sickbay, and when they clear you, stay in your quarters and get some rest," the officer orders.

Corporals Simms and Jordan come into the docking bay, looking inquiringly at Aragon, but he waves their unasked questions off before they can open their mouths. "I'll tell you later. We need to find sickbay and then get some shuteye," he tells them.

"Ok, good. We heard something about Sgt. Borg going crazy on you!" Simms states.

"Borg?" Aragon askes.

Cpl Jordan interjects, "Short for cyborg ... get it?"

All three burst out laughing and quickly stifle it at the steely glances they receive from the other pilots and deck hands.

* * *

Bofus rounds the corner into the next chamber only to see the professor in the grasp of a huge shadow come to life with gleaming crimson eyes, his feet dangling inches from the floor of the cave. Suddenly, the professor is thrown across the cave, into the wall. The thud of him hitting the ground wakes Bofus from his paralysis.

"Run!" he screams.

Turning, Malice streaks toward the source of the noise. Bofus yelps and turns to run when the apparition is intercepted by another hulking form. The new arrival looks like a gorilla with some strange outfit on similar to what the first monster is wearing. Gathering himself off the floor, the professor hurries over to Bofus.

"We must warn the others!" he whispers.

As the two powerful beings collide, there is a thunderous boom as they skid into the cave walls. They separate briefly. Malice shakes his head slightly to get his bearings. "What is the meaning of this? Are you some shameful imitation?" the crimson eyed minion rasps.

The silverback's glowing azure eyes narrow with disdain. "No, I am something else. The master requires your presence. You've been absent too long," the beast replies.

Suddenly Typhoon lunges toward Malice, but this time, he catches the snarling beast locking grips with it. Bofus and the professor desperately need to leave, and yet to their horror, cannot leave the incredible spectacle of these strange beings wrestling. One seems like a phantom that solidifies from time to time, and the other is an enormous cloud of rage chasing the former. The struggle is both beautiful and terrifying to behold.

The professor is the first to break out of the trance. Grabbing Bofus by the arm, he whispers, "Let us take our leave while these two ... beings are preoccupied!"

Mouth agape, Bofus gives no answer, but the two turn to bolt around the corner to the next cavern, only to run headlong into the approaching Simeon. The stout Kison Askari puts both arms forth catching them both, pressing his hands to silence the screams that seem about to erupt. Quickly he whispers to them, "What's all the ruckus in there? Sounds like someone is terraforming, or drilling!"

Bofus is the first to respond. "That ...thing that came and attacked earlier is back, but another one followed, and the new one has blue eyes! I thought the doctor was finished, and then the other one attacked the red-eyed monster, so we got out while we could!"

Simeon looked to the professor for confirmation and the academic simply replied, "What he said."

"Get everyone to the rail system and prepare to move!" Simeon bellows as he rushes off to see what they are blabbering about. Rounding the corner into the next cavern, he sees that the lanterns have been smashed, and it's almost pitch black now, where formerly it had been well lit. Whatever or whomever had been struggling in here had done so over every square inch of space, crashing into walls and the ceiling, and the lanterns had been destroyed in the process. Simeon squints, trying to discern the vague shapes snarling and scraping in the darkness. Slowly his eyes adjust, and he is able to see with some clarity the two forms locked in battle. There is a break in the action as the heads of the two combatants simultaneously turn to face Simeon.

Temporarily paralyzed as he is nailed into place by the glowing orbs staring holes into his chest, Simeon immediately raises his shoulder cannon and prepares to fire. Super heated plasma-like projectiles erupt from the barrel of Simeon's weapon, sending both minions sprawling to avoid being hit. Portions of the walls melt into slag when the rounds hit them. As the dust settles, Malice and Typhoon gather themselves to spring upon the new attacker. Not wanting to give them a chance to converge on him, Simeon continues firing, forcing them into evasive action in order to avoid being wounded. They are very powerful beings, yet superheated plasma rounds puncturing the body while simultaneously cauterizing the wounds will take its toll on most beings, robust or not.

Rounding the corner, out of breath, Bofus and the Professor can barely speak as they approach Tunisia and the rest of their group. The queen walks up to meet them and puts her hand on the professor's shoulder to straighten him.

"What is it?" she asks.

Before Professor Jones-Bey can respond, Bofus blurts out, "That thang is back! The one with the crazy glowing eyes, and it's not alone!"

Darius walks into the cavern, and everyone turns to see his eyes take on a ghostly white glow. Tunisia quickly scoops Darius up before he can do whatever it is he is about to attempt. All she knows is that danger must be fast approaching, and they need to get to the rail system as fast as possible.

After turning up the power on his plasma cannon, Simeon aims at the cavern walls, not the two things streaking toward him, and fires multiple rounds ahead of them, collapsing most of the cavern, blocking their advance. Turning to catch up with the queen and the rest of the group, the warrior sprints head long through various corridors, feeling his way through. He catches the group just as the last few are loading into the rear car. Tunisia hands Darius off to the professor and runs to Simeon, looking for news of their pursuers. Out of breath, Simeon answers her unasked questions. "There are two of them now. They look like the thing we saw a few weeks ago during one of our first stops. I've buried them in rubble, but I don't know how long that will hold them!"

No sooner do the words leave his mouth when there is a huge explosion sending rocks and debris through the caves and corridors Simeon had just vacated, pushing dust toward the railcar everyone has piled into. Shining through the clouds of dust are four orbs — two red and two blue. Bofus sees them immediately and panics. The professor and the queen calm him down as Darius's eyes, once again, begin to glow as he goes to the rear car, looking in the direction of the explosion. The two figures halt immediate-ly. Not a word is spoken, but it seems as if some mutual communication is taking place between the boy and these strange beings. They do not come any closer as the railcar powers up and speeds away in haste.

"That was close!" the queen exclaims.

"Not really," Jones-Bey replies.

"What do you mean?" Simeon interjects.

The professor thinks for a moment before giving his answer. "Those things seemed to recognize the prince in some way and even listened to his command. Nobody finds that odd? The eyes seem to signal some type of relationship. Could these be kin to your people?"

Irate, the queen responds, "Those creatures are of no relation to my son or our people! How could you think that? They are abominations of nature! I would think someone of your academic standing would recog-nize that."

The professor quickly tries to diffuse her anger. "I meant no offense, but the report from Babylon mentioned that men were mutated giving credence to a commonality in all of our genetic origins. That first thing was found to be in the employ of the very being we were sent to find to corroborate Babylon's tale. Add that to the fact that my very own research gives evidence that the Kison Tantu, Limbia Johari, and the very people that oppress them are high matches in basic genetic code. The glowing eyes are a trait I have seen in only two beings before ... now three. Would it be too much of a stretch to draw a link in their ancestry and yours or rather...ours?"

Some of the ire leaves her eyes, but she still isn't able to believe they have anything in common with the beings that seem to be following them in the caverns. One looks like an animal vaguely from the description Simeon gave her, and the other is humanoid, but most of its body has been obscured by its garb, as well as the odd way it moves. Whatever they are, they are enemies, and the queen is not confident in the mysterious control

Darius exhibited earlier, as it did not stop the creature from pursuing them. Just as the car reached maximum speed, Bofus comes rushing into the main car. "That thang spoke to me without speaking! Did any of you hear it?"

Perturbed, the professor grabs him. "What in the world are you going on about? Would you have us believe that you experienced some telepathic communication with one of those beings back there? Preposterous!"

Bofus is nonplussed by the professor's doubt. "Man, call it what you want; the thing's name is Tyfoo or something, and he was coming to get the other one!"

Simeon thinks the whole situation over. It was true they were fighting each other, but that wasn't proof of anything. For all he knew, the victor would be after them next. In his mind, it didn't matter who they were or where they came from. The king needed to know about them and something would have to be done to keep the queen and the prince from danger.

Chapter Sixteen

ALL IS SILENT IN THE collapsed cavern. The dust has finally settled. Typhoon is the first to recover, opening his glowing azure eyes, giving some light in the dim, hazy, rubble-filled cave. Still disorientated, the mutated gorilla scans the wreckage for his quarry. Not far off, it recognizes part of a black cloak sticking out from beneath a huge slab of rock. With senses he never knew existed, he can feel that Malice, though temporarily incapacitated is very much alive. Clearing the pile of debris atop Malice with herculean strength and mercurial speed to avoid Malice awakening, Typhoon quickly binds the being.

Slowly, Typhoon begins to drag Malice through the rough dirt corridors of the deep underground labyrinth. After a while, Malice awakens due to the unkind handling. "Are you sure the master sent you? You still have to rely on brute strength? Mutated or not, you will always lack elegance. Once freed, I will enjoy killing you," he rasps.

Without a word, Typhoon stops and walks a few paces from where Malice lay strewn on the clay-like ground. Malice's body begins to levitate six feet above the ground. Just as suddenly as he rose, his body is instantly slammed to the floor, air rushing from his lungs to a resounding thud.

There seems to be a smirk on the silverback's face as he gets on all fours to put his dark, leathery visage inches from where Malice's face seems to recess into his cowl, his red eyes blazing even more brightly than they had previously. Typhoon's eyes begin to match his counterpart's in intensity as he speaks. "You seem surprised, disappointed even. Yes, the gifts of telekinesis and telepathy were given to me, just as they were to you. I believe the powers are wasted on menial tasks, such as carrying trash, and truth be told, I would rather drag you back to the master. Maybe the arrogance will rub off by the time we get to him. It shall be a rather long trip. Save your threats for someone who cares. If not for the pain I would endure, I would rip you to mangled shreds of meat and leave it for the scavengers."

Malice watches as the silverback walks over to his feet to grasp him by his bound ankles and resumes dragging him before replying. "He has given you powers and the mind of men, yet at the core, you are nothing more than a glorified beast. The only reason you exist as you do is because the master thought me missing or worse. You will endure pain, and if I have any say about it, it will be by my hands and these blades."

The gorilla chuckles as he continues to drag his prisoner into boulder after boulder. Casting a glance over his shoulder, he thinks, You don't look much like a man either from what I see, even if you used to be. The master knew you were not missing. He thinks you went rogue. Disobedience is not something he values. I learned that early in my new existence. What's your excuse?

* * *

Sitting on the bridge of the *Ex-Wife*, General Krulak reads the report detailing the attack at Saturn, along with the reports from the counter attack at Jupiter. This new ordinance the enemy had was not a good sign. The GMC needed an equalizer, and if that could not be accomplished, then, at least, there could be something that would discourage the use of this weapon, which had devastated a large portion of their facility on Saturn. It is going to take a lot of precious resources to build things back up there. Those are resources that may be better served as material for new weapons of their own.

First the inexplicably quick development of military-grade space craft, and now this so-called dark matter technology. A substance so unstable, that his own scientists are baffled and cannot work out how the rockheads were able to weaponize it. The counter attack is meant to send a message, and the commandant is not sure they got the right one across. Their research and development team needs to have a massive breakthrough as fast as possible. Things cannot continue in the direction they currently are. Krulak refused to lose to these people.

The hatch slid open and in strides Lt. Commander Jameson with a bundle of papers in hand. He stops before the command chair and salutes smartly. Looking up from his report, the general returns the salute. "As you were, Lt. Commander. What's the deal with our pilots going wacky during combat?" he asks.

"Well, sir, there was nothing found in the blood streams of any of the men in question. They did seem to be on something though. All were coherent but emotionally unstable at times," Lt. Commander Jameson replies.

The general gets up to pace back and forth a few times before turning back to the other officer. "Unstable, as in going between laughing to crying to paranoid?" Krulak inquires.

Surprised, Lt. Commander replies, "Yes, sir ... you know something about it? Very odd."

The general smirks. "I have an idea. There are these new nitroclubs that are really popular now. Supposed to be safer than the usual spirits and manufactured party fuel, if you know what I mean. They use some variation of laughing gas or nitrous oxide to give the user different euphoric states. We will have to start having more random health and comfort inspections. We'll have to keep an extra eye out for canisters that don't belong on ship. More importantly, I need your team to develop something that will take the teeth from the enemy, and I need that weapon yesterday!"

"Aye, aye, sir!" Jameson replies.

Shaken at the possibility that the order of things may be changing, the general dismisses Lt. Commander Jameson and goes back to reviewing his reports. This is an inopportune time to have intoxicated Marines during combat, but if they don't find an answer to this dark matter issue, the tables could turn very quickly. Then an idea hit the commandant. A temporary cease fire could buy them time to figure things out and design better fighter craft. After all, this is an unprecedented situation. General Krulak has always thought, if the GMC were to ever meet its match, it would come from outside their galaxy. Turns out the pressure of oppression may have made diamonds out of the rocks in their own backyard, and now those diamonds are spearheads pointed directly at them and their way of life. Time may be the only tool that will give them a chance to rebalance the world into its natural order.

* * *

A few days later, the news of a galaxy-wide cease of hostility is announced all over the sat-net. Many are surprised, and some are angry, but most don't believe it, not even for the briefest of moments. A large number of military personnel are given immediate leave or liberty. They are asked to go out and be seen in public having fun. A strange request to some, but others simply write it off as an attempt from the brass to raise morale after a few successive losses or, at least, what had been perceived as losses after basically dominating every engagement, previous revolt attempt, and skirmish up to this point in history.

Corporals Aragon, Simms, and Jordan are suspicious but glad to have some liberty after the recent events. They need some time to gather their thoughts and relax. A trip to a nitroclub sounds like fun, but they are also cognizant of the fact they are lucky not to be court-martialed after Petty Officer House's last little stunt. Luckily, "surprise" cannot be detected in the blood stream, and the effects wear off as they arrive at sickbay. The three of them blame the awkward behavior on nerves and stress before and during combat. Strange behavior is common when soldiers are in the midst of the "fog of war" as many clinicians have come to call it. Aragon simply gives no explanation for his peculiar abderian episode while he and others were under fire.

The whole base, or rather the entire GMC, is licking its collective wounds, trying to figure out the next move. The damage at the military installation at Saturn is considerable. It will take months to get things as close to normal as possible. The three Marines are sitting in Jordan's barracks room, contemplating how leave and liberty in the middle of a crisis do NOT make sense when the hatch burst open. In came Petty Officer House looking bedraggled, in blood soaked camouflage utilities.

"What the hell, House?" they all scream simultaneously.

"It's not like I knew we were going to get hit! I'm sorry," he quickly replies.

Aragon is the first to notice the blood on his cammies. Corporal Simms rushes up to snatch House up when Aragon steps in to intercept him.

"Wait! I want to talk to him before we pulverize him. Besides, he's right. He couldn't have known we were going to be attacked moments after he gave us the canister," Aragon stated calmly.

"Hey, look. I took a canister of the same stuff right before I gave you yours!" House pleads.

"True, but were you actually in the field when it kicked in?" Jordan asks.

"Unfortunately, yes. I had to go near ground zero after whatever the rockheads dropped on us went off, and it wasn't pretty. There were some weird injuries. Some were sad, but that didn't mean crying incessantly was appropriate, and laughing maniacally wasn't well-received either," House reports glumly.

Simms chimes in. "I bet they didn't think any of it was too funny with Marines bleeding out through wounds that acted as if parts of the body that were no longer there, never existed in the first place."

"Yes," agrees House, "which brings me to my next point, though you all may scoff at my suggestion."

Wary of what his suggestion might be, they cannot help but ask. "What is it now?"

Raising his hands, House says, "Look, they gave us libo for a reason, so we might as well take advantage of it. I mean, how long do you think this break in hostilities is gonna last? You know the commandant and the rest of the top brass are simply buying time before the next strike. Let's be honest."

They can't argue with anything House is saying, yet are still skeptical because his schemes seem to have a common thread...trouble. First, there was the flash training incident; then there was the surprise, and those are just the most recent ideas. There is a long list of small misfortunes, all stemming from something House has cooked up. The truth though is that he is right, and they have been robbed of their liberty before when Major Vashti interrupted them while they were enjoying the nitroclub back home. The only problem is that they are a ways away from Earth presently. Someone has thought of that predicament and has even invested in a solution that will furnish local entertainment to the military members deployed too far away from civilization. The cost is high, but the services would definitely be in great demand.

House had overheard an aide to some rear admiral talking about the existence of a facility built into one of Saturn's sixty-one moons. There is even supposed to be an actual live DJ playing music for the main club. The owner is rumored to have spared no expense.

The Marines are angry and are sure they will have to pay through the nose in order to get in, so if it is not worth it, House will have to foot the bill. They all have the money since saving up months of hazard pay with nowhere to spend it, but free entertainment is the best kind. House knows they will complain enough to guilt him into paying, but like them, money at the moment is not an issue for the corpsman.

* * *

The Sat-Net is abuzz with news of the cease fire. It is scheduled to be announced by the commandant of the GMC later in the week. Babylon, the king of the Kison Askari; Toshi, and the rest that accompanied them for the attack are not fooled. They know their enemies are simply making a tactical play, as well as a political one. If it looks to the public as if they are trying to be reasonable and put forth an effort to end a conflict that affects everyone, that could potentially ease the minds of those who disagree with the GMC's methods.

Omega respects the cunning move, yet knows that not all beings here are sheep that will simply take what is presented by the media. Some will see the truth of the situation. The questions are, will enough realize the truth to make a difference, or will they continue to fight a battle on two fronts, one from the people in power and the other with those who have continually been blind to what is going on before their very eyes? Complacency often leads to lack of action. There is a human in the company of his new son and wife. This man is reportedly one such person that the king hopes others will follow.

The king is not entirely convinced of his proposed theory of common genetic origins for all Earth's inhabitants, but if that theory can unite them against Pharaoh, then he will not deny it. The theory is actually corroborated by Babylon's tale. There is a report of his wife and son being pursued by unknown creatures through the interplanetary rail system. This does not sit well with the king, but the cease fire just may have given him an opportunity to reunite with his family. Transport may still be difficult with eyes on everything coming in and out of every system in the Milky Way, but it is known that Babylon has not shared all of the Atlanean secrets. There may be something the ancient sage can do to help preserve Omega's lineage.

The shipyard jumps to an undisclosed location along with some fighters in case the group runs into trouble. Whether or not there is an actual cease fire, the Kison Askari are sure the GMC is still smarting from being taken by surprise and kicked in the teeth, militarily speaking. Any opportunity to avenge the string of recent events beginning with the revolt will be taken advantage of. The main deterrent to an outright frontal assault is the new weapon that has just ravaged the military facility at Saturn. The Kison Askari are new players to the idea of an arms race, but they are fast learners, and they have good help. The source of that help brings about a curious question.

If the Atlaneans have always been here, and are privy to knowledge and technological advances that rival what man has developed, then why have they waited until now to intervene? The reasoning behind this question is the crux of all the mistrust some have for Babylon and his people, yet they need them. Maybe they have something more to do with what has happened to all the other oppressed people, and only now have the courage to come forward in an attempt to rectify things. Whatever the reason, Omega is glad Babylon has, in fact, come forward. Without that fateful gathering, they might still be slaving away in mines throughout the galaxy.

***

Sitting in a hidden wing of the medical facility on Saturn, Sgt. Garrison is having his legs recalibrated along with the neural systems that helped him control them. He has no idea what has gone wrong with some of his men during combat. It disturbs him to his core. This is not a game, and there is nothing funny about war. He has lost his legs and, to some extent, his humanity, fighting these beasts. Garrison will do anything to make as many of them pay for what has been done to him. There has been an announcement of a proposed cease fire, and he will have none of it. He will wage war by himself, if need be. The entire GMC can go on leave for all he cares, but he will continue to fight.

He has a cache of weapons in a crate, as well as codes for ammo storage facilities throughout the galaxy. Garrison knows there are some men still faithful to the fight that will go with him. He could put together a small force with a plan to take out the other side's leadership. Cut off the head and the body will follow. The rockheads believed they can win this war. That is not acceptable. He likes the idea of guerilla tactics being used. Swift, silent, and deadly — that will be their motto. Some modifications to the hardware on his legs will make him more deadly than before. Garrison has a hook up with a guy in R&D who is working on a prototype for the GMC's version of the plasma cannon.

He will have to get in touch with his contact before taking off. The SpaceHarrier assigned to Garrison is a custom job that no one else can fly anyway so he might as well take it. Getting it off the flight deck without authorization could get hairy. A troop transport would be handy as well but is even more difficult to get a hold of. Garrison is sure he can get his hands on a decommissioned transport and have it repurposed to fit his needs. It seems the sergeant has some logistical planning to do, as well as assemble his team. They will spend their leave doing something useful. The commandant can thank him later.

* * *

The railcar carrying Tunisia, Simeon, Bofus, Professor Jones-Bey, young Darius, and the rest of the refugees rescued from the prison camp arrives at an outlet leading to the surface. It is decided that they will take their chances with those who might be hostile to them up there, rather than deal with what is chasing them below ground. Once they reached the entrance, their personal comms are able to receive signals as well as gain access to news feeds. The professor is giddy with excitement. "Great news! There's great news!" he exclaims.

"What are you babbling about?" Simeon demands.

"There is a cease in hostility! They have seen reason! My evidence has won out!" Jones-Bey fervently exclaims.

Simeon takes a long hard look at the teacher as he thinks of him before replying. "I would think someone of your supposed intelligence would not be so naïve."

Bofus begins to laugh. "Yeah, man, don't be so nave ...what's nave?" he mumbles.

The queen listens to the conversation in silence while holding the sleeping Darius in her arms. "What Simeon means, Professor, is that this must be a ploy to make us let our guard down. They have no intension of relinquishing control so easily. Something must have happened that has not gone in their favor. Simeon, see if you can communicate with our people both on planet, and off world. I know Darius is still young, but we may be better served by being where our warriors can protect us. Running constantly is tiring, and eventually we will have to stand our ground. I am not sure we have the resources to keep this up, and fight when the time comes," she suggests.

"Yes, my Queen," Simeon answers and then sets off to do as she asked. The response is quick, as if someone is waiting at the comm stations everywhere. That is likely the case as the king is probably worried about his queen and his heir. A pickup is to be arranged with the help of the Limbia Johari, who have access to high profile transport, and the only reason they will likely not be questioned is because of who owns the transports that are to be used. It is kind of ironic, being as the politicians who are so quick to condemn them will now unwittingly play a hand in their escape.

Chapter Seventeen

Sitting on a shuttle headed to Titan, Corporals Simms, Aragon, and Jordan are headed to the newest club in the system. Petty Officer House is somewhere in the back among other service members looking to get some recreation after recent events. Not many of them wanted to pay for a hop back to Earth. As expensive as the amenities are supposed to be here, there is the added advantage of being close to their duty station. Cease fires do not always last long and the announcement does not say they are looking specifically for a peaceful resolution, so the fight could realistically reconvene at any time.

Aragon takes a moment to look at himself, as well as his companions. Jordan looks over and gives him a smart knock in his helmet.

"What gives?" he asks.

"Just thinking about how much things have changed. I didn't mind the juice when we got to Saturn. The atmospheric color took a little getting used to. Why purple? I know that the dust in our atmosphere makes a prism through which sunlight shines and blue shows up most, which is why we see the sky as blue, but purple? That's not even a primary color. Weird, I know, but the suit is starting to get to me. I feel claustrophobic."

Simms leans over to put a hand on his shoulder. "I know how you feel, but we can't breathe this crap, so it's better than the alternative. They'll have the climate and atmo controlled in the club, so we can, at least, take our buckets off."

Further back in the shuttle, Petty Officer House is getting a head start on his companions with a spare canister left over from before hooked up to his filtration system. He doesn't think anyone else wants to sample another dose of "surprise," so he just keeps it to himself. In other words, this particular concoction takes a special level of appreciation. It is like life all wrapped into one singular experience, and others have a hard time noticing that. House likes surprise because it supplies an instant emotional roller coaster, and you never know which part of the ride you are going to be on from one moment to the next.

The shuttle settles on the surface, and the service members file out in full vac suits with Petty Officer House bringing up the rear, staggering one moment, marching smartly the next. Dust settles after the shuttle takes off again, leaving the men to follow a lighted walkway into a cavern that leads to a lift that will take them below the surface to the main club. Simms, Aragon, and Jordan get out of line to wait for their navy compatriot, who notices them and burst into tears, embracing them harshly.

"I love you guys!" he exclaims.

"Yeah, yeah, must be the nitro talking," Simms responds.

The landscape looks drab and desolate but, at least, the skyline isn't deep purple.

* * *

Giza is a long ways away, and Typhoon keeps his promise by dragging Malice a vast majority of that journey. Malice has sworn vengeance so much that the threat now rings hollow. The fact that some part of Typhoon actually enjoys meting out pain bothers the Gorilla deeply, and he was confused as to why this is so. During moments of silent introspection, Malice would try and sew discontent in the beast's heart. In response Malice would be treated harsher, and dragged more abruptly, leaving Typhoon feeling guilty. This has been Malice's plan from the beginning. The Gorilla now wishes for his simpler past.

"You love the power, don't you? Inflicting pain is intoxicating, is it not?" Malice rasps.

"You know nothing about me. Don't try to make me out to be a monster, as you have become. I have base desires as most creatures do, but I do not delight in this. I do what I must to rid myself of this imposed servitude.

Your treatment is a result of your own thoughts toward me. I know what you would do if you had your way, and I also feel your jealousy. Mockery will get you nowhere," Typhoon replies.

Malice's body is racked with uncontrollable laughter as he contemplates the absurdity of the concept this beast is proposing. Leaving the service of Pharaoh is simply not possible. There is nowhere master cannot reach, and he is not likely to simply let any of his servants go. Finally able to control his laughter, Malice replies, "The cliché does not fit you. You ARE actually dumber than you look. As hard as that is to accomplish. No matter how hard you try to hide these whimsical thoughts, Pharaoh will know of them. Forgiveness is not exactly his strong suit."

Typhoon stares balefully at Malice before answering with a slight smile of his own. "Let's hope, for your sake, he has a change of heart. Obedience, after all, hasn't exactly been your strong suit, now has it?"

At this, Malice has no answer. They simply allow silence to prevail for the rest of the trip. Their master will have the final word, and both want to save their energy for what is to come. No matter who the conflict will be with, they will need to be up to the task. Relenting, Typhoon begins to levitate his captive, not out of mercy, but to speed their travels along.

* * *

Toshi heads back to Earth at the request of Hironike. The expansion of the Kison Askari's space fleet is well underway with the help of the Atlantean contingent, as well as instructions Toshi left them to lay the foundation for designs, weaponry, and other technical specifications. Babylon is still enforcing their advancement with restrictions, but that doesn't agree with Toshi's sensibilities. Dark Matter is far beyond anything the rest of the galaxy has seen with the exception of a few. The proverbial cat is out of the bag in his opinion. Once fire was discovered, it was not like man could just go back and un-discover it.

The one positive is that because of its destructive power, the GMC and whatever scientist they have working on it will have the near-impossible task of trying to reverse engineer it. Literally everything touched would be destroyed, including the vessels that carried the ordinance. If General Krulak wants this technology, he will have to steal the weapons before they are used. Based on the previous attempt on Omega's life, Toshi thinks the chances of success getting in and out undetected will be slim to none. Add to that, the task of actually obtaining and transporting a live dark matter shell back to be studied without killing themselves in the process, and that brings a whole different level of the complexity to the mission.

Yet the leadership on both sides know that's exactly what this ceasefire is about. The GMC is trying to buy time in an effort to either steal the tech that outgunned their own, or to develop something just as devastating. Simply put, these people will not take a hint. Just because open hostility has stopped does not mean the effort to topple leadership will halt. Senator Levine and the rest of her bigoted ilk still remain in power, and are in agreement with the GMC and their strong arm tactics. The media still paints the Stone People in a monstrous light, as if they and others should simply accept their oppression as the natural order of things.

In some ways, there is a natural order to things, but this situation has taken a very unnatural turn as the ancient people of light (one in particular) has purposely unbalanced things in favor of one group over the rest, and then further manipulated things so that they have to be continually tweaked in order to keep them interesting. That's if Babylon's tale was actually true. As farfetched as it seems, something in it resonates with Toshi. He believes the story, but that still doesn't relieve those in power perpetuating an unfair societal imbalance. Toshi believes right and wrong are universal no matter what side of the railcar you were born on.

A full-scale war might be avoided if the present government can be brought to their knees in addition to crippling the military so that peace can rule. The politicians the Jade Assassins took out were writing the laws and signing off on immoral military actions. Far from innocent, they were paid for their participation. As things have escalated and relations between various groups have become strained, the high-level bureaucrats have attended in scarcer numbers as of late. Hironike needs to come up with a plan to continue their work.

Toshi lands near Kyoto and takes a taxi to meet Hironike at his favorite spot. The flying theater was left in port for renovations since shows were few and far between, as war has forced business to slow down. Hironike is found meditating at the Yasaka Shrine in the Gion District. Toshi goes into the shrine and quietly sits beside his leader, mentor, and friend. Not wanting to disturb him, Toshi sits in silence until, without knowing it, he begins to chant in unison with Hironike. The head Jade Assassin finishes his meditation and opens his eyes before getting up to help Toshi to his feet.

"Watashi no tomodachi, o genki desu ka?" Hironike asks.

"I am well. It's good to be home for a change. How many targets have you taken since I left?" Toshi responds.

"Twenty, but not the most important targets. They have gone into hiding it seems."

Hironike looks at his friend before continuing. "We need to start going after them. Bringing the field to us was convenient, but we are skilled enough to go out and get our prey. Put together whatever gear you think will help us achieve this. The hunt is on. We should go straight to the top. Senator Levine's time has come. She has a security detail that we will have to observe and work around, but I am betting we are better than anyone she could have hired."

They would have to wait for Megumi and a few others from the team to come back from various reconnaissance missions.

A lot of the political figureheads have gone underground in light of recent events. Hironike had taken the initiative to keep tabs on their movements. They will take advantage of this lull in action. Assistance from the Limbia Johari would be crucial to operations as they have eyes and ears on most of the people on the Jade Assassins' list. Perhaps the Kison Askari could deal a blow powerful enough to make these people see reason and make the assassinations unnecessary, but until that actually takes place, it will be business as usual. Hironike and Toshi catch another taxi back to where the theater was docked.

Once there, Toshi heads straight to his lab to take inventory of what the best tools will be. Neurotoxins and other poisons would be useful as they can often be confused with natural causes, if mixed properly. This would be a method for some of their targets, but Toshi knows that will not be the case for Levine. The new laws she has recently passed, along with other heinous actions she has personally sanctioned behind closed doors, ensure that Hironike and others will want her to die in a suitably unpleasant fashion. Blades, most likely along with a slow acting and vicious poison, or perhaps fire will be what she gets in the end. Even though they will be operating outside of the theater, in his mind, there will still be an artistic element that needs to be executed.

* * *

While her demise is being plotted, Senator Levine somehow knows something is wrong. Her security detail has tripled in the recent months, especially after hearing about the deaths of Senator Beasely and Cyndi Nguyen, one of the head legislators. Levine wants desperately to stay off the growing list of casualties. A stream of rotating guards and constant surveillance does little to ease her mind. Business has slowed down for various headlining shows and more attacks are happening at seemingly random places. Before, there was a pattern developing, and that theory was being destroyed by reports of deaths occurring at restaurants, during morning walks, and other scheduled outings that were supposed to be known only to the dignitaries and their highest staff members.

The senator can't hunker down in her estate and not come out, so something has to be done. Perhaps decoys and traps will have to be set in order to catch these assassins. It's obvious that's what's at work here. These are no random acts of violence by common street thugs, but this has to be the work of trained killers, plying their trade, at times, in broad daylight in full view of the public, yet witnesses have very little to contribute to the investigations. This is a very disturbing development, to say the least. The CSO will be tasked with putting together a team to combat this new threat that seems to be bent on toppling the government, one member at a time. It is only a matter of time before Levine's name comes up on the hit list, and given the fact that she's been thrust into the role of being the face of this administration, that time may come sooner rather than later.

* * *

Takimura and Megumi of the Jade Assassins, along with Angelo of the Limbia Johari, have been tasked with resuming the search for the elusive Pharaoh. Since they had first encountered a possible henchmen or associate of his at the Valley of Kings and Pyramid in Egypt, it made sense to comb other similar structures on Earth to see if they could pick up another trail to the original malefactor. The brute strength and fighting prowess of the Kison Askari would be missed. Their members that contributed to the original group assigned to go with them were currently off-world fighting, so they would have to make do without them. Their absence did, however, make disguising the group easier. Hiding strange features under cloaks or baggy clothing works well, but massive statures are not easily hidden, and people can guess who you are. Kamal and Nefer will always be recognized as Stone People, no matter how well shrouded they are.

They begin their renewed search at the White Pyramid, located near Qian Xian, a small Chinese village. Megumi figures it would be best to start at lesser known pyramids. Pharaoh has to be aware that he is being sought after, and may stay away from more famous structures similar to those found in Egypt, Mayan lands, and other places around the globe. It made sense that, if he created Egyptian society and the pyramids found there, then there had to be a connection to pyramids found in other places around the world. Perhaps these structures were built to help harness his remaining power while exiled to Earth.

Taki has tried to contact the professor that guided them last time but has gotten no response. There are reports that he had been arrested and sent to a detention center. The two assistants closest to him had died in Egypt at the hands of the thing they found waiting for them in the bowels of the pyramid. Essentially the two are on their own, blindly looking for clues, and the pyramids seem as good a place to start as any. It turns out that Megumi's guess was a very good one.

Each structure they visited is a chore. Finding the secret entrance that will lead to the labyrinthine paths deep inside the Ob-pyramidal section below ground proves difficult. The more famous and oft visited locations in Egypt have been painstakingly gone over for centuries by people trying to find the treasures or valuable secrets the ancient buildings are rumored to have. Sadly after a lot of studying, nothing of lasting consequence has come of these repeated studies that has not already been discovered long ago. To Angelo, the similarities in the decoded messages in cuneiform and hieroglyphics denote a relationship shared by all of the pyramids.

That relationship is a good one, but time is of the essence and they have no idea in which of these structures Pharaoh could be found, and may not be able to wait too long at one while he languishes at another location. Besides, things are about to get ugly, and this ancient being could be the key needed to stop the recent hostilities. It is likely that even, if found and brought to light, the GMC and the rest of the government will claim it is all a fabrication to justify the violence committed against them despite that violence being a result of unjust oppression. In the end, it will not matter as all avenues to peace are to be explored, and Omega has ordered this search continued, so they will do their best to bring this being out of hiding.

* * *

Sitting before a console jacked into the records system, Sgt. Garrison is going through a list of Marines who were traumatically injured during the initial conflict on Earth. The start of the most recent rebellion has created a lot of people similar to him — Marines who have been augmented due to severe injuries suffered at the hands of these beasts. He starts to mentally and electronically put together a list. If the commandant is going soft, he will be prepared to wage war with his own band of brothers, men who hate these monsters as much as he does, and who will ride proudly at his side. This is the way it should be.

There are a few names that came up on various operation casualties lists. A Private Cooper was hit in the chest and lost his upper extremities. The chest wound was properly attended to, but the young Marine would either be up for prosthesis or discharged. Lance Corporals Jennings and McNamara both suffered head trauma and would likely each lose an eye. Rounding out the group of potential recruits is a Private First Class Long, who is little more than a torso with a faint heart beat at this point. That poor young man will need more than everybody put together. Sgt. Garrison knows he has to come up with a plan, and the first thing will be to approach Lt. Commander Jameson.

The medical officer is the only one he knows that has enough pull to have this done, but there would be rules to follow this time, at least from an integrity standpoint. These men, if possible, will be fully informed of what is about to be done to them before the procedures begin. Garrison wants to make sure they aren't blindsided as he was; they will be given a choice. He knows the pain of what has been done to them will make that decision an easy one, but they have to be given the option of saying no. Injuries like what they have suffered will either knock the fight out of a man, or it will stoke the fires of vengeance in their souls, and they can be given special tools to exact that vengeance.

Chapter Eighteen

UPON ENTERING HIS OFFICE, LT. Commander Jameson notices deep scratches on the marble floors in his foyer. From touring this military installation, the officer is familiar with these tracks, which announces that Sgt. Garrison has either paid him a visit or is waiting for him in the conference room. Opening his door, he finds the latter to be the case. The cybernetically enhanced Marine sort of sits before the lieutenant commander's desk. Garrison is not in a chair, but his mechanical legs are bent as if there is an invisible seat holding him. Jameson understands what he is seeing but the sight is still slightly unsettling.

There is a series of buzzes and whirs as Sgt. Garrison quickly stands upright, smartly saluting the lieutenant commander.

"Good afternoon, sir!" he promptly bellows.

"At ease, Sergeant. Good afternoon," Jameson replies, while returning the salute. "To what do I owe the pleasure of this visit, Sergeant?" the officer asks.

Sgt. Garrison hands him a folder. "I want you to help me assemble a small unit of Marines like myself. I am guessing I was a trial run. With a few more, we could be the scalpel needed to take out the leadership of the enemy. Here is a list of good candidates, sir."

Lt. Commander Jameson looks over the list and then hands it back to Sgt. Garrison. "These men are all unfit for duty," he opines.

"Yes, sir, as was I before your intervention. The only option they have is to be shown the door, discharged, and given some sort of disability pay. If given a choice, I think they would choose to get back into the fight. Prosthesis similar to what I have been given is the only way they can do that, sir," Garrison replies.

The lieutenant commander seems to think it over before responding. "Where would we get funding for this, Sergeant.?" he asks.

Angrily, Sgt. Garrison answers, "With all due respect, sir, where did the funding for my legs come from? I looked into my medical records, and there is no mention of the procedure, only the injuries I suffered, so either there is a private investor, or some back channel funding. I suggest we go to that source to get these men back on their feet and in the game. The only thing I ask is that they are made fully aware of what will be done before they go under the knife! It's only right."

Mulling it over some more in his head, Lt. Commander Jameson turns to Sgt. Garrison and says, "I'll see what I can do. You go to these men and brief them. I want thorough psyche evaluations on them, and everyone will not know of this, but some of the brass will have to be informed as they were in your case. Come back when you have confirmation of who is on board, and we'll go from there. Dismissed!"

Saluting in response, Sgt. Garrison rises before about facing and leaving Lt. Commander Jameson's office, scraping the floor as he did so. Cringing at the sound of alloy on marble the officer shakes his head but refrains from berating the NCO about it. The prospect of experimenting further intrigues him more than his annoyance for now.

* * *

After finding a hidden entrance to the pyramid using scanning equipment that sees various spectrums, Megumi, Takimura, and Angelo enter, hoping to meet their elusive quarry. The stone work below ground has somehow become heated, as if it could siphon heat and energy through the portion of the structure that was above ground. This was a phenomenon they have not noticed at the Egyptian locations. The equipment picks up signs that these corridors have been used recently, but not as recently as the party would like. This trail is not really a cold one, but it wasn't hot either. They are still in a global game of cat and mouse. Guessing would waste time if they keep guessing wrong. There has to a way of tracking

Pharaoh. Perhaps Babylon would know of a way. Of course, if this is the case, questions will be raised as to why that information hasn't been passed earlier, just like the ones out there now about the people of Atlantis and their technological advancements that have not been shared until recently.

Megumi decides the topic has to be discussed either way. The reasoning can be discovered after their mission is complete. Gathering all the useful information from the lesser known pyramid in a small Chinese province, the group packs up and prepares to check a Mayan location before heading back to arrange a meeting with Babylon. While they are out, it is possible to catch a break, and she will take the chance on one more stop before seeking help. A contract is out on another prominent senator, and the team works best if they are all together. Hironike is capable on his own or with what is left behind of the Jade Assassins, but this time, they will be operating outside of their theater.

An uncontrolled environment with a moving target can easily complicate things and add any number of other variables that have to be taken into account. Everyone's expertise and opinions will be needed to ensure a clean kill. The importance of leaving no witnesses or clues behind is paramount. Loose ends are the bane of many assassinations, and the patrons who ask for them. Since the Loyalist Act will eventually target Megumi and her people after all, they are not a part of the "normal" population. Given the fact that it is only a matter of time before the government will see their differences as a threat despite their value as entertainers, the politicians will have to be taught a lesson that force them to accept everyone, or their bigoted leadership will be systematically eliminated.

* * *

Athena sits in one of her many offices, looking over conversation manuscripts and intercepting travel plans for government officials and other various dignitaries. Senator Levine must know she is on a very bad list and has taken steps to be discrete with her whereabouts. The problem with that strategy is that, very often, with the right person, searching omissions can sometimes tell a far more accurate story. Security details will be given an itinerary to make sure each destination is checked out before the official arrives. Usually it is easy to target them while on their way to or from an event, but as a result of people dropping like flies, the government is trying to keep their collective heads down.

They won't be able to bring the targets to them, but Hironike assures her that they can just as effectively eliminate them with the help of their travel plans. Angelo has sent Athena a message detailing the progress of the team. He is a part of continuing the search for Pharaoh. Discouragingly, they are not having the success initially enjoyed when they encountered the strange being that was likely in the employ of their quarry. Angelo reports they will be searching another pyramid before coming back to regroup to see if any further information can be gathered. The so-called cease fire has given all a lull in the action, but it is a ruse used by the government to recover from being blindsided by the entry of new and vastly more dangerous technology than they are accustomed to seeing.

The Jade Assassins would be fully intact with Takimura and Megumi at Hironike's disposal, which raises the chances of successful missions out in the field. Athena has some doubts, but they have previously proven that they can handle business outside of their theater in the past. Legislator Nguyen and a few others were proof of that. Local law enforcement is still baffled as to how she was beheaded in broad daylight in a restaurant full of customers. It is inexplicable how the wait staff, hostess, and patrons knew nothing was awry until the ghastly head softly thudded on the floor. What weapon was sharp enough to cut through muscle tissue, bone, and sinew quickly and silently? Athena is curious but also knows she should never ask Hironike what was used. There is a light tinkling sound as she gathers her hair thinking of their odd friendship.

Hironike often needs the information only Athena and her people have access to in order to carry out his missions. She knows what handing over that information will most likely mean to the target, and never wants to know the intimate details of their eventual demise. The targets are always beings who have shown that they cannot be reasoned with, and are usually doing things severely detrimental to others who are not in a position to defend themselves against tyranny. The Jade Assassins have become an anonymous swift justice system, but that comes with a colossal moral obligation to be right about the target.

What if one day the reports of an official's involvement in oppression are inaccurate? That is a doubly troubling question. If that were the case, it would mean her information was bad, and should, therefore, not be given to Hironike unjustly sentencing someone to death. If it still somehow gets into Hironike's hands, she would have to withhold information on the politician's whereabouts, limiting his ability to tail and eliminate a target. She is sure she would have the strength to do so, but would the Jade Assassin's leader understand her stance and why she is blocking him? Athena hopes she doesn't't have to find out.

* * *

Typhoon has gone back to dragging Malice, and they are cresting a dune from which they can clearly see the pyramid at Giza. Bending down to untether Malice's feet, the gorilla roughly tugs his fellow minion to his feet.

"You can, at least, walk in with some dignity, and we are close enough where I am sure Master can feel us. Even if you could outpace me, I am sure you could not escape him," the simian intones triumphantly.

Glowing red eyes lock with Typhoon's glowing blue eyes. It nods beneath the hood of its black cloak but gives no verbal response. Seemingly resigned to its fate, Malice trudges behind the ape, formulating a feasible story that master will accept, and not having much success.

Malice is determined not to let this be the end of the legend it has become. Defeat at the hands of an ape? No, it cannot end like this. If death is to come it would have to be from a being far nobler than that. Attacking Pharaoh is the only acceptable alternative. Malice has always wondered how such a battle would go. The answer seems obvious, but at least, now there would be no question. The minion will, of course, report all that happened including the nearly successful attempt at fulfilling the duty given, if not for this meddling muscle-bound oaf leading them into the stronghold.

"Ape...Master will hear of your interference," Malice rasps.

The growl of the gorilla turns into a soft chuckle before responding. "Your failure, I assume, is what brought about my ... transformation. If not for your ineffectiveness, we would likely never have crossed paths."

To that, Malice has no reply for the beast is correct in that assessment. Malice will still present his case. All is not lost. Master cannot hope to replace Malice with this abomination, and if he wishes to eliminate Malice for failing, that is easily accomplished, or at least, one would assume given the disparity in power. Something else must be in play. Soon they both will find out. Approaching the entrance, sand flies aside revealing an entrance few know about. Typhoon lumbers inside followed by a seemingly cowed Malice.

* * *

Sgt. Garrison and Lt. Commander Jameson wait in a chamber deep in the hidden part of the medical bay at the military facility on Saturn. Luckily this portion of the base is untouched by the dark matter ordinance dropped a few weeks ago. The GMC is still scurrying to repair the damage which was proving to be a daunting task to say the least. As they wait, four hover-gurneys floated in. On the first is Lance Corporal Jennings who'd lost his left eye during the initial skirmish near the copper mine in Zambia. There is also some burned skin tissue on his chest and facial area that has to be scraped away, leaving nerves open to the air. Jennings is in constant pain.

Next floats Lance Corporal McNamara, who had a strangely similar experience in South Africa, near an old diamond mine, but he has lost his right eye, in contrast to Jennings. The first wave of the revolt had been armed with some crazy looking hammers and stolen military rail guns, in addition to the sonic weaponry favored by the overseers at mining facilities on Earth, but the second wave of attackers came equipped with some makeshift weapons using some of the very mining tools the government had given to these animals. They had also fashioned a shoulder fired plasma cannon fitted to their bodies. The new weapons made a mess of things.

Private Cooper floats by third. Most of his red hair had been burned off, including his eyebrows. His legs are fully intact, and Sgt. Garrison is envious of that fact; however, his arms are completely gone. The powerfully built chest and legs suggest he is one of the many trained right here on Saturn, but the injuries did not seems as if they have occurred in the most recent attack. He will be questioned later as Garrison doesn't recall the specifics in his file. The name and listed injuries are all he remembers.

Bringing up the rear is the worse of them all, Private First Class Long, who is nothing more than a head and torso floating on the gurney. Pain and rage seem to erupt from his brown eyes, and he cannot vocalize it. All that comes out is a sort of raspy growl. Long had the bad fortune to be flying one of the Space Harriers during a training exercise when they were surprised by the arrival of enemy ships wielding live weapons. He flew virtually toothless with nothing more than training rounds to return fire with. The results were less than favorable, but he at least, escaped alive, just not in one piece so to speak.

When all four gurneys are in place before them, Sgt. Garrison stands to address these men. The floor screeches as he stands to his full height, making the Lt. Commander cringe. "Believe it or not, I laid in similar conditions as you, Marines, months ago after being sent to deal with the initial revolt in Africa. This was before the other skirmishes at other planets broke out, so I know, at least, some of what you're going through. As it stands, you are not fit for duty and will, in all honesty, be medically discharged, given military service connected disability stipends and sent home to lament what could have been." Garrison pauses to lock eyes with each of the tortured souls before him.

After a lingering moment staring into the depths of Private First Class Long's pain-stricken and fierce gaze, Garrison knows he has them, has their allegiance, and they are one in their hatred for those who put them in this condition. They have what it takes and are willing to get back in the game no matter the cost. He continues, "Some civilians will honor, even dote on you at times, while others will spit in your face and call you names. Some will forget that the freedom they enjoy comes at the price of our sacrifice, but it doesn't have to end this way. This is Lt. Commander Jameson. He gave me legs after the rockheads took mine. He can fix you up and we can get back in the fight, but I need you to know what lies ahead, and you must accept it before any procedures begin."

The lieutenant commander rises with a clipboard in hand and approaches the first gurney tailed by Sgt. Garrison. "What say you, Lcpl Jennings? You want to get back in the fight?" the officer asks.

With arms clenching the sides of his gurney, Jennings replies, "Yes, sir!"

They step aside to stand before Lcpl McNamara, and with tears in his eyes, he replies in kind, "Yes, sir!"

As they move down to Private Cooper, he bellows "I'll fight, sir!" before they stop, so they continue at last to stand before Private First Class Long. Studying him for a moment, the lieutenant commander speaks, "I know you cannot speak, but we can fix that as well, blink once for yes and twice for no."

Long turns his gaze back to Sgt. Garrison before giving him one long, hard blink. Pleased Garrison says, "Very well, men! Go back to your med quarters, and we will begin the paperwork for your procedures and get orders drawn up. We will be the tip of the spear, gentlemen, aimed directly at the heart of the enemy. Dismissed!"

The hover-gurneys swing round and file out of the room. The sergeant turns to Lt. Commander Jameson and says, "Sir, we are going to need some heavy fire power for our kits. We need to be able to take out the head, so the body can die. Reinforcements may not be available in time for the missions I have in mind. I am hoping you can make this happen, sir."

Staring curiously at the sergeant, Lt. Commander Jameson assesses the NCO before saying "I'll see what I can do, Sergeant. They'll be in much better shape than they are now with the prosthetics, and I'll need you to help train them and walk them through the process of getting used to the neuro-processors. It could shave some time off their readiness for battle. I admire your code of honor, but the formality of asking was an unnecessary step in my opinion. They would have been on board, just as you are now."

Garrison returns the scrutiny with a steely gaze of his own before replying, "A formality we all deserve...sir."

Sgt. Garrison slowly turns on his metal heals, scraping the floor as he does so and loudly storms off. Once the noise has receded, Lt. Commander Jameson goes to his office to draw up schematics for prosthetics that will make up for the injuries and even enhance their capabilities. There also needs to be fail-safes in place to ensure their compliance with his orders. There is already a group of unruly beings of higher capability running amuck. The officer does not want to be blamed for another in the midst of all the turmoil the top brass is in after the Stone People decided not to be free labor.

The first step will be to get funding, which might prove difficult, but given the relative success of his experiment with Sgt. Garrison, Lt. Commander is fairly confident the commandant will see this as a good risk, especially since they are currently looking for anything to even the odds, and that includes upgrading the quality of the Marine they are putting on the battlefield. The orders are drawn up, and *the Mechanics* are born. Now it is time to bring them to General Krulak and convince him to sign off on them.

Chapter Nineteen

BACK ON TITAN, THE SERVICE members board a lift that takes them below the surface of the moon. The underground facility makes it easier to insulate the club, and atmosphere control here allows them to take off their vac suits. Corporals Aragon, Simms, and Jordan place their suits in lockers while Petty Officer House chooses to stow his gear separately. Upon removing their helmets, they can hear a rhythmic pounding. They walk a long corridor toward the main club entrance, and the closer they get, the more they begin to feel the music pounding as well as hear it.

They file in as the corridor narrows and widens at a pair of double doors where a massive android awaits with a small retinal scanner in hand. As service members come up, he scans their eyes for identification purposes, as well as payment. Retinal scanning through the years has become the most reliable method of identification, and people's credit is also linked to their retinas. After all, you could lose your license or identification card, but you should be able to keep your eyes, at least, in most cases. When House gets to the front of the line, he has the bouncer scan his eyes four times, paying for himself, as well as Corporals Aragon, Simms, and Jordan.

Once inside the double doors, a cavern opens up, revealing a string of stalagmites too evenly placed to be natural. They have lights posted atop each formation. There is a dais at the end of the cavern, opposite the entrance through which they came. Standing in front of a table on the dais is a small but highly animated man wearing illuminated glasses and a cap. Oversized headphones worn half off are over his cap and a ridiculously large chain hangs nearly to his waist. As he jumps and sways to the music playing on the digital turntables, the medallion bounces, jiggles and cavorts reflecting light from various laser or light displays throughout the club.

There are private cabins cut out and sealed with thick glass enclosures and familiar openings where canisters can be affixed just outside the hatches. Seeing the canister placements, Petty Officer House perks up and speaks, "Nitro anyone?"

Glancing over at his navy compatriot, Aragon replies "Later, House. Let's check this place out first."

The others agree as they watch their fellow service members dancing and jumping to the sporadic and thunderous music. That's when Jordan notices the lack of cameras at the entrance while there were plenty throughout the cavern.

He points this out to his friends.

"No ethnicity scanning?" Simms asks.

House sees where his friends are looking and pointing and guesses what the discussion is about. Screaming to be heard over the music, House explains, "This club is using an old technique for music provision...an actual DJ! With virtual DJs and ethnic musical profiling, I thought they were all gone but apparently not."

Aragon squints and veils his eyes in an effort to make out the lettering on the DJ's medallion to see three gleaming letters, H M N. The crowd is working itself into a frenzy, so they decide a private chamber might be best. They could enjoy some nitro and watch the party from a safe distance, as well as have some privacy.

Once in their private chamber, Jordan orders four various nitro canisters from the androgynous android servers standing outside of the entrance. The hatch seals, and for a second, there is no sound until Aragon finds a control panel embedded into the table in the middle of the small chamber. From this console, they can control the sound, as well as make the sliding doors opaque or translucent. They leave them translucent to view the craziness happening on the other side. There is an option to use ethnicity scanners, but they chose to listen to what the DJ was playing.

"Anyone know what HMN stands for?" Aragon asks.

When no response is forthcoming, a sultry female voice emits from the speaker system in the chamber. "Those are the initials for the last known DJ. DJ Hot Monkey Nuts."

All four men stop glancing around and look at each other before bursting out in uncontrollable laughter as a soundbite comes through in rhythm with the music "S-S-S-Straight out the jungle. Make it funky!" The nitro canisters have not even kicked in.

"You have got to be kidding me!" Simms exclaims.

* * *

Senator Levine feels like a dear in the wilderness. Constantly skittish and frightened, a comic once remarked that "it is a miracle they are ever able to take a drink of water." The worst part of this is that she is largely to blame for the target on her back. She has, after all, signed off on a corrupt bill, along with a large contingent of the government. Of course, at the time, she thought it was the right thing to do. That was what she is constantly telling herself as the fear for her life builds up, threatening to throw her into a panic attack. CSO Thomas has noticed the gradual change in her charge. She is worried that if an assassination doesn't kill the senator, depression or anxiety will.

The itinerary has not been made official, and therefore cannot be leaked. Transportation solicited is not the usual government vehicle. The senator is on her way to visit a museum exhibit that usually calms her nerves. The new Smithsonian has a collection of stardust combined with some exotic lichen which glows. The rooms are kept completely void of outside light sources, giving the rooms an otherworldly feel to them. She is taking this trip against the advice of her security team, but Senator Levine needs a temporary escape, and Thomas has agreed only because this is a battle the senator is not backing down from.

The plan is a good one overall with the exception of blocking off the exhibit from the public. Some of the parts are rare and really interesting to look at, as well as there is always the question of whether these have naturally occurred or if someone has taken it upon themselves to combine these elements. The exhibit has become rather popular as a result of this enigma, and therefore the curator and museum staff leave the questions vaguely answered. It is a common subject of debate, and so closing, even for a small measure of time, raised curiosity and suspicion.

Athena has people keeping watch over the senator and her movements, as well as her official itinerary. It was a relatively easy thing for them to notice the discrepancy in the lack of official movement on her part and increased vehicle traffic to and from her home or office. It is a well-known fact that she often visits the stardust exhibits and has not done so in some time. This information leaves a virtual bread crumb trail for the Limbia Johari to follow, who promptly pass the trail off to the Jade Assassins. This visit won't be as therapeutic as Senator Levine hopes it will be.

With Takimura and Megumi gone, Toshi has been thrust into a relatively unfamiliar role in the field. He is to maintain surveillance and monitor all communications coming in and out of the museum's network. It is from a safe distance yet closer than the technician is used to. Toshi has taken a liking to the growing technical side of the Jade Assassins' operations but is also skilled when it comes to the kinetic execution of their plans. Hironike knows how to best use the talents around him. This job should be rather cut and dry, even with the missing members.

This situation provides an opportunity they cannot pass up. With the travel route scouted out that the senator will likely take and the timetable they have to work with, Hironike has devised a plan to take her out during her visit under the cover of virtual darkness. The senator likes her privacy when visiting, and that will get him time alone with her, even though she has the security team nearby. By the time they know something is wrong it will be too late.

Inside the exhibit, the head Jade Assassin waits on the other side of a hidden service entrance. He is dressed as a custodian wearing full body makeup to hide his emerald skin and a wig over his customarily shaven pate.

Putting on what looks like ordinary spectacles, but are actually night vision glasses that give off no external light. He waits silently and patiently. On the other side, inside the exhibit, the security team comes through and sweeps the area to make sure it is clear before allowing the senator to enter. She comes in and finds her favorite spot in the middle section of seats, three or four rows back from the front, takes a seat and closed her eyes. As the music cues, her ears pop inexplicably. This inner portion of the exhibit is hermetically sealed when on display, so she looks toward the entrance but sees no one coming in. High above there was the stardust and an ethereal light coming off the lichen seems to react to the musical notes intermittently going off and on creating a light show within the darkness.

Hironike creeps up silently, pulls a small vile from his pocket and flicks a drop of liquid onto the Senator's forehead which quickly evaporates before she has the chance to wipe the dampness away. Senator Levinc feels the drop and then sees the shadow leaning over her. She tries to speak or cry out, but finds that her lungs cannot draw in air. From the seat behind her, Hironike leans in close to whisper in her ear, "Don't waste your breath. Quicksilver is a fast acting neurotoxin, as you can guess from the name. We didn't get a chance to put together any theatrics, but you only have an audience of one. Your lungs are failing, and you will soon asphyxiate. You deserve far worse, however, given the amounts of violence and oppression you have signed off on through the years."

The look of surprise, anger, and resignation goes over her face in a flash as she strains to look at her tormentor. By the looks on her face, Hironike guesses there is some kind of recognition of who he was or of her complicit guilt in the wrong doings of the government. He likes to think it is the latter. He continues, "You knew, didn't you? Of course, you likely lied to yourself over the years that the oppression was a necessary evil and you were simply doing your civic duty. In the end, only when it's too late, do you admit, at least, to yourself, because only you can hear your thoughts, how wrong you and the others were to simply go along with it all. Enjoy the show, or, at least, what you will be alive to see of it."

With that Hironike makes his way back to the service entrance and makes his escape out of the museum. By the time the security team finds the senator's body, he and Toshi are long gone. One short message is burst transmitted to Athena simply stating, "It is done."

Upon receiving that message, Athena makes her people aware of the possible backlash that is sure to come. Omega will be notified as well. Despite being off world, he would definitely get the lions' share of blame until those responsible can be found, which is not likely to happen. Hironike is not in the habit of leaving clues, but there is always a first time for everything.

* * *

Striding angrily away from the commandant's office, Lt. Commander Jameson is about to make his way back to his office. General Krulak had just denied him funding. The general feels it was a waste of funds that could be better used elsewhere. Just as he reached the end of the corridor the commandant burst out of his office nearly running to catch the lieutenant commander.

"Jameson!" the general blurts out.

Still fuming the lieutenant commander stops and turns. "Yes, sir?" he replies.

Gathering himself, the general straightens out his uniform. "There's been some news which changes things. You want to implement this crazy plan of yours. You have the funding, but if they fail or make an unsightly mess, we will deny any knowledge of their actions. Understood?"

"Yes, sir. What changed your mind?" Jameson asks.

Gritting his teeth, the commandant answes, "There's been another assassination. A senator was killed at a museum. No witnesses and no evidence found yet, but we know it was them. They are operating under the radar to try and blunt our effectiveness by eliminating our leadership. A tactic we have employed in the past. It would seem they are learning rather quickly. Put your tin men together and deploy." Turning on his heels, the lieutenant commander spun and took off at a semi-run toward his office.

Once in his office, he looks up the schematic plans for the prosthesis to be implanted, the necessary materials, neural processing units as well as the budget for all of it, and sent it to requisitions in S4. They might balk at the numbers, but that would be quickly silenced once they knew the commandant has signed off. Lt. Commander Jameson's work on Sgt. Garrison was done under the table, but with help from friends to get the needed material. This project, at least initially, will have official funding and support. The doctor will have the ability to truly create here.

* * *

A week later, all four of his patients are in their beds, but one is strapped in and awaiting the procedure. Lt. Commander Jameson decides to start with the most difficult case first. Private First Class Long is basically a torso sitting in constant pain. An exo-suit is built that will give him arms and legs, along with a retractable faceplate and helmet combination. He will virtually be a walking tank, able to dish out more punishment than he ever will have to take, for the most part. If the rockheads have found a way to fit their warriors with personalized versions of dark matter weaponry, it won't matter what the lieutenant commander creates.

Long has nubs or stumps with just barely enough muscle and bone tissue, but to ensure he will be secure in the suit, some of the alloy and circuitry has to be inserted into that tissue. This is going to be a major source of pain, even long after he has healed. Measures are taken to counteract that pain, but the trick will be to numb the pain without negating what little sensitivity and control he has remaining. There is a chest plate that helps enclose the torso into the suit and also holds the face plate which would automatically deploy when Long's eyes see projectiles or other hazards flying toward him.

Nearly two days later, Lt. Commander Jameson stands back to look at his handy work. All of his aides have long since gone to other duties in the hospital wing. Many are frightened of this ... thing laying on the oversized gurney. The doctor is not, however. In fact, he is proud. What lay before him reminds him of knights from olden stories long since gone or forgotten. This knight, in contrast, will carry heavy weapons, weapons that will otherwise have to be mounted on an armored vehicle. Long's eyes flicker open, and all at once, his world is on fire.

Lt. Commander Jameson looks over at the monitors as Long's heart rate spikes to a dangerous level. A piteous squeal escapes Long's lips and turns into a crazy howl of rage and anguish. Sgt. Garrison, who has been waiting outside the room, bursts in to see what is wrong. The screaming was all the more strange as it was being aided by a digital vocalizer, which is also part of the suit which has been installed because his vocal chords have also been severely damaged. Jameson scrambles to sedate Long. Eventually his heart rate slows, but he is still quietly whining. Sgt. Garrison pulls up a chair and places a hand on the Marine's chest, looks into his eyes and says, "Use it. Keep it and don't let go. Don't let it control you, but save it for the enemy. When the time comes, we will need you to unleash it on the bastards that did this to you!"

The whining stops, and in Long's eyes, there is understanding and determination, but the pain also remains. Sgt. Garrison leaves his side when he has finally fallen asleep. Upon his exit, Lt. Commander Jameson is waiting for him.

"Sergeant, a word?" he asks.

Sgt. Garrison turns and begins walking with the officer. Curiously, there is no dragging of his legs to scrape and screech on the deck. Lt. Commander takes a mental note of that as he says, "You know, if he can't control himself or get a hold of that pain without help, he may go insane."

Garrison stops walking before turning to look the officer in the eyes. "Sir, we are all insane to some degree in my opinion. That Marine was blown to pieces, literally, and we just asked him to go back into the line of fire. He's not going to go insane, sir; he's already there. That's the kind of man I need, and I intend to ride that kind of crazy into the belly of the beast," he replies.

Taken aback by the sergeant's response, the lieutenant commander looks at this man with a new respect. "Very well, Sergeant. On to the next patient. You won't have long to train them. Any ideas on a code name for this one?"

Garrison thinks for a second before responding "Won't need time to train them in combat, sir. It will take them time to get used to the prosthetics though ...Berserker. That should be Long's codename, sir."

Pleased with that answer, the lieutenant commander goes to his office to write up the new file in the unofficial official records for the *Mechanics*.

Sgt. Garrison goes to the field house to get in some extra PT. He has a lot on his mind and a lot of plans to make. Once the rest of his crew is fitted and assembled, he will have to have the boys in R&D come up with weapons specially made for them. Regular issue will not do and likely won't be practical, given the modifications they are undergoing. Beserker is a nice start. Garrison is cautiously optimistic on how the rest will shape up.

* * *

Lance Corporals Jennings and McNamara have heard the screaming down the hall that has lasted for what seems like days. Both are nervous and are having second thoughts. They are both also strapped into their beds and heavily sedated. Neither can speak if they wanted to as they are wheeled simultaneously in the operating room where Lt. Commander Jameson waits fully scrubbed and ready to operate. Even though they are sedated, the officer can see the anxiety in their eyes. "Don't worry, gentlemen. Your transition will not be as...severe. Although I would be remiss if I told you there would be no discomfort. There will be pain, just not as much as your brother is going through. Be at ease. You are, after all, Marines ...suck it up."

Chapter Twenty

WITH TEARS STREAMING DOWN HER face, CSO Thomas is in the senator's office pouring over every security data feed that she can find in and around the museum. Ordinarily, she would have been at the exhibit with Senator Levine, but this time, her lover and charge had insisted that she go in alone. She said something about wanting to clear her head and to keep up appearances. The whispers were growing, and they did not need any bad press as things with the war were escalating. Well, none of that mattered now. All Thomas cares about is finding whomever did this and making them pay.

The video feed from inside the exhibit is of little use as the cameras in there have night vision, as well as thermographic sensors. Thomas can tell there was another person who had entered from a service entrance, but all of the custodial staff had been accounted for during the senator's visit and had had strict orders not to disturb her. From the feed, it looks as if the suspect had walked in, approached the senator, pointed to her briefly, and stood over her for a short time and left. Hard to tell from the footage, but there looks to be no reaction from the senator, and there's no sound, so Thomas cannot tell if there is a verbal exchange during the short encounter or not.

Through digital enhancement, they can tell it was a male who looks to be wearing glasses and a custodial uniform. Night vision is monochromatic and mostly bright green in color, so they cannot discern the complexion of the suspect, but, at least, the texture did not look similar to that of a Stone Person. If they didn't do this, you can bet they were responsible, and now it seems as if they have some inside help. It's a disturbing thought, but it's not surprising given the attacks lately on high-profile targets. Thomas doubts the Stone People would be able to pull an operation like this off. The question is, who is in their corner? She will have to find out.

There was a moment when Thomas thinks she will get a glimpse of the attacker when he exits the building when all of a sudden the external cam is flashed and the feed goes white. When the feed comes back up the assailant is gone, but it appears that he has dumped something in the trash receptacle outside of the door before the interference. CSO Thomas jumps up to call waste management, as well as the custodial crew. There might yet be a clue, and Thomas knows now she is dealing with a team, a well-informed team with access to a high level of technology, and they did their homework. She will not rest until she catches those that took her beloved.

* * *

Trudging along into a hidden entrance into the pyramid at Giza, Malice can feel his master's presence. Apprehension begins to settle in, but the minion refuses to give in to that or fear. In an almost hypnotized fashion Typhoon reaches over to take the manacles off Malice, and they both make their way through various corridors into a vast throne room, where Pharaoh awaits them. They both kneel in unison. Typhoon raises his eyes and makes as if to say something, but Pharaoh silences him with a raised hand. The brightly glowing golden orbs that are his eyes turn to bore into his other minion, Malice. "I would hear from this one first," he orders.

Grimly smiling and sneering at Typhoon, Malice keeps its head lowered to hide the delight beneath the hooded cowl before responding. "I nearly had my quarry, Master, but this beast you sent interfered, forcing me to deal with him, and they got away."

Pharaoh simply stared at his minions for a while, watching them stew. "Oh, I see. Was this before or after your failure at the detention camp? 'Cause I vaguely remember that happening prior to me having the need for another of your ... usefulness. Am I wrong ... Malice?"

Through gritted teeth Malice has to admit that is the case. "No, Master, you are correct."

"Good. Settle it then," Pharaoh slyly says.

Typhoon looks to his master inquisitively, but Malice instantly knows what's being ordered and launches itself at the other minion. They clash, and despite the surprise, the gorilla recovers quickly using the momentum of the attack to roll, throwing Malice off with his feet, tossing the crimson eyed wraith into a column. There is a sickening crack as Malice's body hits the column before hitting the ground. A howl of pure rage erupts from the fallen minion as it rises immediately, reaching out with a gnarled hand.

Tendrils of light flow outward from the fingertips toward Typhoon, who instinctively raises his hand and tendrils of light come forth in answer to the new attack. Malice screams in rage and delight, but that joy is cut short as they both inexplicably collapse. Pharaoh doesn't arise from the throne so much as he floats to stand between them. The light being gestures toward the minions, and their slack bodies rise off the ground to hover before him. "Neither of you knew you had that capability, I see, and that is perhaps a good thing as it drained you. The power struggle of a seeming rivalry between you two is negligible at best and ends now. The only power you need to be concerned with is mine and how I see fit to use it! Is that understood?" Their bodies collide heavily with the ground as he releases them.

Both minions struggle to one knee before simultaneously replying, "Yes, Master."

Balefully staring down the two before him, Pharaoh continues, "Good. We have too much work to do. I don't need to worry about where your heads are at. We all need to be on one accord now. I need to know what took place, Malice. A fabrication won't do." Placing two fingers at Malice's temple, both he and Malice freeze at the contact, seemingly sharing pain among other things. Typhoon sits there watching the strange exchange, contemplating whether or not to attack but thinks it better to wait instead.

Pharaoh stumbles after a brief flash as they break contact. "Ah, I knew there had to be something strange going on when I felt immense fear from you. Not the usual emotion that emanates from you. This ... child is strangely familiar, yet I can't figure out why. Looks like one of the newly anointed Kison Askari, but something is not quite right with him. I can now see through your eyes as if they were my own, Malice. Do not stray again, or I shall be forced to put you down. I still want the meddling professor taken out of his misery, but we must keep an eye on this young prince as well. His own seem to feel uneasy about him, as well, from the looks of those around him. That can be useful. Typhoon, you did well. Don't think I cannot feel the machinations moving in that brain of yours. Malice, you call him beast, but what of you? Are you not a twisted version of your former self? After all this time, he is likely closer to human than you. Leave me."

Pharaoh returns to his throne, sitting cross-legged and gazes upward. His glance is met with a blinding cascade of light. Shielding their eyes, the two minions do as they are bid and leave the chamber. Malice heads to one upper level room where he stores his prized blades, while Typhoon goes to explore and to be alone and contemplate the recent events. The gorilla knows he will need to be more careful now that some or most of his thoughts might not be private. If he chooses to rise against his new master, chances are Pharaoh will know about it.

* * *

Simeon leads Tunisia, Professor Jones-Bey, Bofus, and the rest of their group out of the hidden caverns. They have made their way through the intra-planetary rail system that is supposedly long since forgotten. The queen is holding a tightly wrapped Darius, who is sleeping soundly. They come out at the edge of a tropical peninsula. Simeon orders everyone to wait under cover of the jungle, like flora, while he signals the transport. Moments later, a long, dark, sleek, armored transport approaches and landed on the nearby beachhead.

Simeon goes ahead to the transport and, after a moment, waves them forward. The pilot tells Simeon, the queen, and a select group of the others in their retinue to board now, while those who are left will board another transport which was currently on its way. The queen does not like it, but her safety as well as that of Darius, is of the utmost importance to Omega, and she understands that. With Toshi's help, they have created a suit that will help Darius grow normally and not be adversely affected by the heavier gravitational pulls on the other planets.

Everything is in an unstable flux, and war is the main contributor to that instability. Omega yearns to be united with his wife and son. They initially planned to raise him solely on Earth, to avoid stunting his growth as has happened with other Kison Askari born and raised on off world mining colonies. Stopping ten meters from the transport, a look of dread comes over the queen's face.

"What's wrong, my queen?" Simeon asks.

Anger flashes in her dark brown eyes as she looks at the stout general before replying, "This is a government transport! How can you expect to get off planet in this? Are we not at war?"

"Yes, ma'am, we are. There is, however, a ceasefire at the moment, and it may be easier to travel as an envoy proposing terms of negotiation in a government transport than it would be with a commandeered military vehicle blasting our way through a blockade," Simeon answers. Begrudgingly she has to concede his point, so the queen hustled aboard with Darius, Professor Jones-Bey, Bofus, and a select few in tow. As they settle into their seats, the queen straps a still slumbering Darius in before heading up front to the pilot's cabin, and her heart nearly stops.

Manning the controls are two GMC pilots. Is this an elaborate trap? Have some of the military defected in light of all the injustice? All sorts of conflicting thoughts and questions are racing through Tunisia's mind. She begins to feel lightheaded when a steadying hand touches her shoulder.

"It's not as it seems, Your Majesty," Simeon reassures her. Then, he nods to the female pilot. The pilot stands to remove her cover, letting jet black hair that has been tucked into it flow down her back. Then, she takes two fingers and rubs her porcelain pale skin on the opposite hand until it reveals a deep emerald hue.

A confused look replaces the fearful one previously on Tunisia's face. "My apologies, Your Majesty. I am Megumi of the Jade Assassins, and I thought you knew of our involvement in your escape off planet. We may be questioned, and Omega and Hironike agreed it would be simpler to disguise Takimura and myself than Simeon or any of your Askari."

Any patrols around Earth's orbit would, in fact, request to communicate with vessels coming or leaving and, of course, they would see the pilots while doing so. Again, this makes sense, but there is too much that could go wrong for the queen to feel comfortable. She goes back to sit beside Darius as the transport lifts off.

*　*　*

Lance Corporals McNamara and Jennings wake up minutes apart in the back of the medical wing. Each, who is used to having the use of only one eye, is surprised when their monocular vision suddenly reverts to almost normal after a few blinks. Normal, as in, they now seems to have two eyes. Abnormal, in that, there is a steady flow of readings and analysis flashing before their eyes which disappears as soon as the brain recognizes and catalogues the data. Lcpl McNamara closes his eyes and tries to open the left eye independently since that is his real eye and the info stream goes away. He slowly opens his mechanical eye and hears a metallic shutter opening as the data stream resumes.

Across the room, Jennings is having a similar experience with the opposite eye getting accustomed to the prosthetics. Jennings holds his hand before the new eye and is amazed as its composition is analyzed in excruciating detail. Bone density, number of blood vessels, platelet count and various other minutia are taken in at an instant. He slowly swings his legs over the side of the hospital bed and prepares to stand, but there is a shooting pain up and down his spinal column that forces him to bite down to keep from crying out. He tastes coppery blood in his mouth as he looks up to see a similar pain-filled expression on McNamara's face, who is attempting to stand at the same time.

Both Marines, when finally able to stand, stop and slowly walk forward to examine each other, and it is strangely like looking into a mirror when face to face since they have lost the opposite eye, have shaved heads, and have also been similarly dosed with the special supplements common for those who trained on Saturn. McNamara is the first to speak. "This is amazing. Turn around, Jennings. Let me see what you're working with."

Shaking his head, Jennings complies. The Marine had an athletic build before but is now even more heavily muscled, but that isn't the most surprising change.

Starting at the small of his back, going all the way up to the base of his neck is a string of hexagonal plates. The plates are a mixture of plastic and metal somehow fused into one substance giving them strength and semi-flexibility at the same time. There are some kind of small computer chips imbedded under the skin close to the spine with silicone-coated circuitry laced in between their musculature, leading into the back, into the unit that must serve as an interface, controlling the prosthetic eye, helping it to function in concert with their natural eye.

All of the circuitry is internal, and the only external evidence is the back plating and the kind of reverse visor that wreathes the back of Jennings's head. Fighting the pain, McNamara reaches up to find the same apparatus on the back of his head. "Ok, your turn, Mac. I wanna see," Jennings says, but when their eyes meet before McNamara can turn around, the readings and schematics he just viewed are instantly transmitted to Jennings. "How'd you do that?!" Jennings exclaims.

"I didn't do anything. It just happened!" came McNamara's incredulous reply.

They both turned to see a Marine lying on a third bed in the room. Private Cooper lay still, knocked out from sedation, but where stumps had been slightly below his shoulders are two massive metallic arms. Through study with their cybernetic eyes, they can tell he had similar back plating and internal circuitry that connected his new arms to the spinal column and a small computer at the base of his brain stem. Jennings looks from Cooper to his new twin and asks, "Is it me, or does he remind you of a character from an old videogame?"

McNamara slowly nods his head before answering, "Dude, we all look like we could have our own videogame. Welcome to the freak show. I think I'll like it more if it stops hurting at some point."

As Cooper begins to stir, the hatch opens and Lt. Commander Jameson strides in, followed by the metallic thumps of Sgt. Garrison, and then there are much heavier metallic thuds as PFC Long makes his way laboriously into the room, having to enter sideways. The room seems to shake as he moves to adjust himself in order to face everyone. When he stops moving, a sheepish look comes over his face. "Sorry, sir, still getting used to ... this."

The lieutenant commander looks over at him and waves a hand. "No worries, Private. You will get used to it. As will you all. As soon as Cooper has recovered, you are to start training as a team. Sgt. Garrison is now your squad leader, and it looks like you won't have much time, which is why your supplement cocktails were given in the doses I prescribed. There's been another assassination and the government cannot sit idly by as they are picked off one by one. We need to answer, and you boys will be the instruments that communicate our discontent. Carry on." With that, the officer nodded to Garrison and left the room.

Sgt. Garrison looks over his squad and is proud of what he sees here — a combination of man and metal. These men will be the embodiment of the toughness the rest of the military and government should exhibit. "Tomorrow we will go get kitted with our new tools as soon as Cooper is good to go. We will get a crash course, which should be sufficient since the cybernetics should help with our proficiency. Any questions?"

McNamara raises his hand, looks over at PFC Long. "Sergeant, I think we'll need a bigger room."

Not even responding Sgt, Garrison stomps off angrily.

Jennings and Long look over at McNamara with smirks on their faces but do not dare to laugh out loud in case the sergeant is just out of earshot. McNamara holds up his hands innocently. "I was serious. Long barely fit in the doorway, and I hate to break it to ya, but there're only three beds in here."

Long shifts forward slightly to get further away from the bulkhead. "It's all good, Mac, I don't need a bed. This thing allows me to sleep standing up."

"Welp! Glad that's settled. Would hate to have wrestle for it. Plus I think you'd break a bed if you had one," Jennings quips before he and McNamara lay back down.

Tomorrow will be an early day.

***

Sgt. Garrison has, in fact, remained within ear shot. He knows he cannot be buddy-buddy with them, but it is good for them to bond with each other. Camaraderie is good for morale, and they will need to be a cohesive unit. Very soon, they will have to go into the lion's den. He will need to be respected and seen as hard-nosed which is easy enough since he is and his reputation seems to have preceded him. Sgt. Garrison will bond with them when they see his leadership. Tomorrow, the Mechanics will get their "tools."

Chapter Twenty-One

THE LONG, SLEEK BLACK TRANSPORT rises higher to escape the Earth's atmosphere as Tunisia sits in the back with Darius sleeping in her arms. Professor Jones-Bey reads quietly to himself, trying to ignore Bofus and his incessant questioning.

"Hey, man, where we going? The pilot looks like GMC. I don't trust her, man. You listening to me?"

The professor shakes his head and replies, "I am doing my best not to."

Before Bofus can respond, the hatch to the cockpit opens up, and Takimura strides into the passenger cabin, carrying a small package and presents it to Tunisia. The queen looks up at him quizzically.

She gently rubs Darius's cheek as he sleeps before turning to the contents in the package. She opens it; there is a small suit inside. Takimura explains, "Toshi came up with it at Omega's request. We understand there was some concern about Darius's growth possibly being stunted if he grew up on worlds with heavier gravitational pulls than Earth's. This suit can grow with him but will dampen the pull on his body, so he will grow normally yet still have the flexibility of movement." The suit was a bit heavy to Tunisia's mind for a child to wear, but if it would help her son grow normally, it might also prove to be a literal translation to what his small shoulders would bear in reality as he grew up.

The cockpit hatch slides open once more and Megumi sticks her head out to call to her fellow Jade Assassin, "Taki, up front we have a couple sentry ships hailing us. Show time! There's a small blockade to get through."

Takimura nods to her and places a hand on the queen's and squeezes it to reassure her before heading back up to the cockpit. Tunisia, Professor

Jones-Bey, Bofus, Simeon, and the other passengers all sit in their seats and strap in. This can get exciting. They all hope it won't get too exciting.

* * *

Aragon steps out of the private chamber to mingle with some of the other service members partying and having a good time. There is a thick fog floating through the huge cavern coming out of a machine at the base before the dais on which the DJ plays the music. The various lights play through the fog and shadows created by the dancing crowd. He stops at a small table a few feet from a wet bar. A dark-haired service member, wearing a suspiciously pristine vac suit and hood pulls up to the same table, looking oddly familiar to Aragon.

"Semper Fi," Aragon says, greeting the stranger.

"Semper Fi, brother," the man replies in a think Hindi accent.

Aragon's eyebrows rise as he tries to peer beneath the hood. "Major Vashti?" he asks.

Major Vashti pulls his hood a little tighter and admonishes Aragon, "Yes, keep it down and call me Vash while we're here." The major then reaches into a pocket and produces a coin, promptly slamming it on the table. He removes his hand, and Aragon sees the newly minted GMCAS Saturn coin, featuring an eagle with missiles and rockets clutched in its talons. He slowly eyes Aragon and nods for him to reciprocate. Aragon reaches into a cargo pocket and produces the coin minted for the new Recon Unit stationed on Saturn. It features an eagle, globe, and anchor like the traditional Marine Corp emblem, but it is varied in that the globe on this coin is Saturn surrounded by its ring, and the anchor is coming out of the planet rather than behind it. The insignia is encircled by nine shining stars.

"Well, since we both have our coins who buys the first round, sir?" Aragon asks.

Major Vashti shakes his head and says, "Don't call me, sir, and I'll get the first round if you promise not to blow my cover. I like hanging out with the enlisted. They know how to relax. The commissioned officers that can relax tend to take things too far. Plus, you know I have the money." They both chuckle briefly before Major Vashti waves an android over and orders two nectars. They're brought to the table, and both men clink heavily reinforced glasses before downing them.

There's a deep burn in Aragon's chest, but seeing the drink seems to have no effect on the major, he refuses to let his discomfort show. Aragon quickly stands, remarking to the major, "Thank you, sir, I mean, Vash. Nitro seems to be more my style. We have a chamber in the back if you'd like to join us so long as you're not here to revoke our libo this time."

Aragon is glad to see the major wince slightly before he replied "No, thank you, devil. I don't trust those canisters. Besides I heard you had a recent episode during that sneak attack. Sgt. Garrison was none too happy about it from what I heard. Long term effects?"

With that, Aragon doesn't respond to the last remark. He moves through the crowd observing the camaraderie and craziness happening all throughout the facility before making his way back to the chamber. When he steps inside, House, Jordan, and Simms are in the throes of uncontrollable laughter. House looks up with tears in his eyes. "New friend out there, Aragon?"

Through a slight giggle, Aragon shakes his head. "An old one, I think!"

They all pause briefly before bursting out in guffaws. It will be a long, joyful night. One they will need to savor as dark times are soon to come and without rest or respite.

* * *

Sgt. Garrison leads his new squad deep below Saturn's surface to a freshly excavated, powered, and finished underground training facility. They will be the first to use it since most of the unit commanders are suspicious of training directly beneath where the dark matter ordinance had hit. The engineers have assured them that it is deep enough for there to be no danger of a similar bombardment reaching them, but seeing as no one can be sure of the depth and power capabilities of the new ordinance, many are still skeptical.

The facility is a huge hollowed-out cavern large enough to house gun ranges for various weapons. Many of them look too large for normal men to carry and wield, as well as sprawling obstacle courses. The latter were built to help Marines get used to their new bodies with enhanced speed and prosthetics. The facility can vary the conditions to simulate different gravitational pulls, weather conditions, and other variables that they can anticipate including antigrav situations. The GMC has to step its game up if they are to regain the advantage. War is not only about technology but about creating a playing field that can be taken advantage of.

Space battles are new, so the SOP manuals are being written on the fly, and new strategies are being researched. How well can a behemoth of a stone warrior fight in an environment he cannot consistently gain leverage in because he's fighting in a vacuum? They don't know, but here, they hope to find out and have an answer before that question is answered in reality. The R&D department is rumored to already be working on mech suits with powerful propulsion systems that will give the Marines an advantage in antigrav environments. They are basically smaller versions of what is fitted to PFC Long's torso, but they will be wearing them and not grafted or fully joined to them.

Sgt. Garrison leads them to a large grassy field that looks like something a sporting event would be played on back home. Lance Corporals Jennings and McNamara simultaneously bend down to feel the grass, and both come up looking perplexed. PFC Long and Private Cooper look at them expectantly, silently asking what is wrong.

"It feels real, but it's actually synthetic," Jennings states.

"If you all are quite done taking in the sights, maybe we can get some training done today. Here we can get the look and feel of almost any environment without having to waste water or other materials to maintain the flora. Don't ask me how. That information is above my pay grade, and quite honestly, I don't care. I have had some various obstacle or confidence courses constructed for us to train on. You will learn to maneuver with speed and precision. Some of you will need to learn how to gauge your strength when moving to cover. We are not all armored, but I sense that is coming, and therefore are still vulnerable, at least, where there's flesh and blood exposed. You will be timed. Stand by!" Sgt. Garrison barks.

They all turn to look up-field as there is a deep rumble. Some of the grounds begin to shift as various walls emerge from underground at different heights and entire spaces flip to reveal hidden but already configured obstacle courses built more sturdily than the readily available courses throughout the facility. Lcpl McNamara looks over the changed scene and remarks, "Well, it seems we have our own little jungle gym, made especially for the cyborg kiddies."

Sgt. Garrison proceeds to run, jumping the first wall in a single bound, heading straight through some very high hurdles before leaping up to traverse a pit using bars overhead. At the last one, he slightly struggles with having to hold the heavy weight of his legs, which prove more difficult even with enhanced arms. The feat is still impressive as he jumps, climbs over, and crawls through the various portions of the obstacle course in record speed. Standing at the far end of the course, he turns back to the squad and yells, "Double Kill, you're up next, followed by Herc, and finally Berserker. Let's go, ladies!"

Lcpls Jennings and McNamara briefly look at each other before hitting the course slowly at first and then gaining speed as they get used to using their enhanced muscles and ocular guidance systems, which gives them the best routes to take at lightning speed. It is noted that they are fast, but slower than Sgt. Garrison. Private Cooper takes off as soon as they are done at about the same clip until he gets to the overhead bar swing section where he was able to use his cybernetic arms. He finishes slower than Sgt. Garrison but faster than Double Kill. Herc smirks at them as he lands on the far platform. They all turn expectantly to see what Berserker will do. He does not disappoint.

Clenching his titanium fists and flexing his pectoral muscles inside the mechanical casing that serves as the rest of his body, PFC Long presses buttons inside the chest plate stopping the flow of pain meds and releases a primal scream of rage before the face shield comes up and the helmet encases his head. He, then, runs through the first wall that the rest of them clamored over. There is a faint whine as the hydraulic systems store energy as he squats before entirely leaping the hurdles to snare the first rung of overhead bars. He bends it as he swings. Berserker is true to his new code name as he crawls, runs, and smashes through the rest of the course, meeting the rest of his squad mates on the other side, all standing with their mouths agape.

As he bends over to catch his breath, PFC Long flexes his pectorals again, once more pressing the internal chest plate buttons and returning the flow of pain medication into his system all the while laughing maniacally, saying "I beat you ... I beat you all!"

Jennings is the first to recover from the initial shock. "Um ...you sure did, but what the hell was that?"

Sgt. Garrison steps in to place a hand on Long's shoulder. "You steady now, son?" He asks.

PFC Longs nods his head affirmatively. He is now able to stand with his helmet and face plate fully retracted. "Yes, sergeant. I have to temporarily stop the pain cocktail, so it can fuel me. Feels like hell, but it's ... a kind of freedom I've never felt before," he states, looking at Jennings and the rest.

"All right, gentlemen. Let's run through this a few more times, and we'll call it a day. Double kill and Herc will have more PT. We need to ensure the flesh and blood can work in unison with all the mechanical prosthesis we have. We also need to work on being silent when we need to be. You seem to have the swift and deadly parts down. After we learn to maneuver as a cohesive unit, we will learn to add the fire into this equation. If you think Berserker is badass now, wait till you see him fire the M-1500

Dragonslayer the boys at R&D cooked up for him. We all have some nice new toys, but that one has a special place in my heart. All right ... again!" Sgt. Garrison barks, and they make their way back to the beginning to run through the course several more times.

*　*　*

Upon reaching the blockade, Takimura and Megumi answers the hail from a patrolling Space Harrier. A Lieutenant Markham is asking them to identify themselves and explain their business for leaving the planet. Megumi identifies herself as Captain Obu and says that she is headed out to deliver terms of negotiation to the Stone People for the senatorial committee. Markham tells them to hold on as he checks out the registration of the vehicle, and it does indeed belong to a senator, has no weapons that he can see or identify through his scanners, so he let them pass. He does, however, make note of it in his logs to be passed up the chain. There has been no announcement of a delegation, but there is the announcement about the cease fire that came from the commandant himself.

Nervously Tunisia, Simeon, Professor Jones-Bey, Bofus, Darius, and the rest of their group wait as Megumi pushes the throttle forward to speed away from the planet. She is picking up speed but holds back so as not to look as if they are trying to run. They have no idea if the fighter pilot has messaged back to the main force belonging to the blockade that might soon give chase. The GMC will realize too late that something is amiss. Finally, far enough out of the gravity well, Megumi inputs commands into the nav computer to initiate a hyperspace jump.

Aboard *The Ex-Wife*, the Centurion class warship orbiting the Earth, Vice Admiral Featherson is sitting in the officers' quarters going through the mundane task of perusing various log entries. Other lower ranking officers have already gone through these entries and highlighted what could be discrepancies or anomalies, but the admiral is one to stay on top of details personally. The good thing is having the potential problems already noted for him to look at, yet the bad thing is that this report has literally thousands of entries. No enemy vessels are reported or even glimpsed. In fact, pretty much no traffic at all is mentioned with the exception of one.

Vice Admiral Featherson runs his fingers over his salt and pepper, closely-cropped hair and narrows his coal black eyes as he goes directly to that log entry. It is entered by a Lieutenant Markham toward the end of his shift hours ago. It mentions a senatorial vessel en route to deliver a message pertaining to negotiations during the cease fire. That, in itself, is not alarming. What is alarming is who the vessel is registered to. There's no way Senator Levine is aboard that ship; she's deceased, which means someone else is headed out to either deliver that message or for some other purposes. This does not look good. The heavy brass will have to be notified but Featherson will have to do some homework first. Featherson presses a button on the console, opening a line to the duty deck far below, and a female voice answers, "Good evening, sir or ma'am. Be advised. This is an unsecured line. This is Lance Corporal Williams. How may I help you?"

"Is this the deck near the birthing area for junior officers?" Featherson asks.

"Yes, sir," the young Marine replies.

"Good. Have Lieutenant Markham report to the bridge."

Sounding befuddled, the lance corporal sputters, "Sir, Lieutenant Markham just got into the rack and left orders not to be disturbed..."

There is a long pause, and Lance Corporal Williams is sure she can hear the veins about to pop out of the neck of the officer on the other end of this communication console.

There's an audible inhale right before Vice Admiral Featherson explodes, "This is Vice Admiral Featherson! I don't give a damn about his beauty sleep! You tell him to get his ass to the bridge, or so help me I will invent space barnacles and write up orders for you to be on a cleaning detail searching for these mythological creatures on the outer hull! Is that understood?"

Nearly tearful, Lance Corporal Williams says, "Yes, sir! Right away, sir!"

"Good. Featherson out!" the admiral exclaims and shuts down the console.

Williams, still shaken, gets up and marches straight to the birthing area where the junior officers are quartered aboard the ship. Walking through various narrow corridors until she stops at a top rack in the rear of one of the birthing area wings where the metal name tape is partially covered. Lieutenant Markham is deep in the coma of good sleep as she nervously shakes the officer with little response. After getting lackluster results, she closes her brown eyes and resigns to accept whatever the response will be to what she is about to do. Grabbing a handful of the olive green blanket the officer is wrapped in, she proceeds to yank down hard. Startled by the unexpected shift, the lieutenant attempts to sit up a little too quickly. There is a loud clang as his head collides with the overhead in the birthing area. "Ow! What the hell, Marine?" he screams.

Helping him down and trying to assuage his pain, she blurts out, "I am so sorry, sir! Vice Admiral Featherson ordered me to get you up. He wants you on the bridge!"

Mention of the order and who gave it quickly quells his anger, but snickers from other officers sleeping or those pretending to be sleep does not help. A feeling of dread comes over the young officer when thinking of reasons why a Vice Admiral would want to speak to him. The only thing that comes to mind is the government vessel he stopped earlier that night. Everything checked out as normal, despite no previous notification of the diplomatic mission, which is not an unusual thing for government officials to move about, letting as little people know as possible. Hopefully, it will be something else, something meaningless or administrative. That hope will not come to fruition.

Chapter Twenty-Two

SITTING IN TWO SEPARATE CHAMBERS, Malice, and Typhoon hear Pharaoh mentally call for them. Each breaks from their private meditations to go meet their master in the uppermost chamber in the enigmatic pyramid. These are a mystery to most of the inhabitants of this planet but not to the one who created them. The floor is of marble and gold. Some of the structures inside are made of granite and other substances unfamiliar to most men. There, in the center, is a set of golden sculptures that look like ancient idols sitting upon a dais. Just in front of the dais is a throne-like chair, smaller than the one Pharaoh usually sits upon in the lower chamber.

The two minions file in, still wary of each other. The tension between them is palpable, yet they know acting on their feelings, after being instructed not to, could prove fatal. Pharaoh does not mind the rivalry as long as it keeps them focused on carrying out his instructions, and avoiding failure. Malice has lost face, and now that there is another to consider, the hierarchy isn't as secure, except, of course, Pharaoh's supremacy. That will never be in question. A disturbing development has come to the ancient's attention. Through various mental probing, Pharaoh has received a more detailed glimpse of the being that, for lack of a better description, frightened Malice into obedience. This is a surprising anomaly, especially since the being is a stone being who can be no more than a toddler.

Something is not right, and this child needs to be found and dealt with. Pharaoh will not brook any usurpers to his power or authority. The list of targets is growing, and Pharaoh needs to get a firm hand on the conflict so that he can guide the action. Peace will result if these beings ever realize their common origins, but this new being could possibly pose a bigger threat than the professor. There is something oddly familiar when staring into the child's eyes through Malice's mind. The contemplation is interrupted when the two minions kneel before Pharaoh.

"Malice, Typhoon, now that we are all on one accord, I have an errand for you both. I can see that you fear this child, and that irks me. Find and kill the good professor as previously instructed and bring the child to me. You will work together. Do not fail me," Pharaoh threatens.

"Yes, Master," they chorus and rise to leave the chamber as quickly as possible.

When they are gone, Pharaoh sits back down in the seat before the dais as the door slides shut behind them. The two minions have felt the hum of energy in the chamber but have no clue as to its significance. All living things are masses of matter and energy, and this chamber serves as a conduit through which surrounding energy flows into those who know how to focus it. Every living being on the planet has the ability to do this but has either forgotten or never learned to do so. This is one of the many disappointments Pharaoh has in man. A few might believe if retaught their full potential but a vast majority of the masses will ignore this knowledge. This is proof, in his eyes, that they do not deserve it.

* * *

Back at the barracks, after their jaunt at the new e-club, Corporals Aragon, Jordan, and Simms get ready for another PT run. Jordan sits down, confusedly browsing at a data chit.

"What you got there, J?" Simms asks.

Jordan looks up at the rest of them and says, "According to this missive, we can choose whether to PT and serve with this unit or with the fighter jocks in the air wing."

"That's odd," Aragon replies.

Simms thinks about it for a second before pointing out, "No, no, that makes sense. We have basically been given a de facto promotion since we are technically pilots, which under normal circumstances would be commissioned officers."

Jordan looks up at Simms in amazement. "You know what? He's right. The question is, what's it going to be, boys?"

They both turn to Aragon, who catches their eyes and states, "Kill that noise. I am recon all the way. When ordered to do so or in times of need, I will gladly deliver death from above, beyond, or whatever space warfare classifies as, but until then, I would rather have my feet firmly on the ground with a rifle in hand."

Simms grabs the helmet to his vac suit and proclaims, "And here I thought I was going to get to lounge in a flight suit this morning. I guess it's PT with the recon roughnecks and ground pounders."

Aragon touches him on the shoulder and says, "That's a choice you still have."

Jordan stands with his gear, shaking his head. "Negative, Aragon. Where you go we go. We started together after losing our original units, and I, for one, am not starting over with a new group of jarheads, unless I have to."

They fall into formation and begin stretching in unison with the other Marines gathered. Everyone is called to attention and roll call begins. With that formality out of the way, a short, stocky, dark-skinned man steps out to the front of the formation, placing his helmet on the deck to his right. Looking over the group, he bellows, "Good morning, Marines! I am Staff Sergeant Armstead! Until further notice, I will be your new platoon sergeant! Sergeant Garrison has been reassigned. We will now begin our daily seven! The first exercise will be Marine Corp pushups! Marine Corp pushups are a four-count exercise! I will count the cadence. You will count the repetitions. We will do thirty of them! Pushup positions!"

As one the one hundred twenty service member formation falls to the ground in position and begins exercising as he called out the cadence, and they responded in kind. Many are curious as to what happened to Sergeant Garrison and where he went. None more so than Corporal Aragon who still feels deeply connected to the man since they made it out of the jungle during one of the initial attacks in the most recent revolt. He feels uneasy since they did not part under the best of circumstances.

***

The streaks of light that are stars recess back into singular points of light as the government transport with the queen, young Darius, and the others travels with them and drops out of hyperspace. They stop just short of the gravity well of Jupiter. A fleet could be hiding on the night side of this galaxy's largest planet or spread out among the many moons and other sizable satellites. Megumi pulls back on the throttle, leaving them at a slow floating pattern in orbit while Takimura sent out a quick burst signal, and waits as Simeon is instructed. The passengers notice that they have stopped moving more or less, and all wait in dreadful silence for what seems like an eternity. But it lasted mere moments. Later a chirp of burst communication is returned to the government vessel. Takimura deciphers the communique which is quite brief but a very welcome message that simply says "stand by for escort...familia." Shortly after that a WarDragon jumps in system, followed by a flight of Shibokaze fighters. Darius is now wide awake and peering outside the portside portholes in awe of the huge metallic monstrosity that seems to appear out of thin air a few hundred yards from them.

"Wow! What is that, Momma?" the boy asks.

"I don't know, dear prince. I only know it is one of ours for it has not attacked and has a different look to it. Not like the craft I would often see of GMC vessels. It looks almost...alive," Tunisia responds.

Professor Jones-Bey, Bofus, Simeon and a few others press their way to the porthole to see what they are discussing. There is a swift intake of breath as the professor sees the large ship.

"Ah, I see it was made into the likeness of a mythical creature popular in many historical tales and fantasies. Quite beautiful in a horrific way, if that makes any sense." Bofus just looks the professor upside his head with a quizzical look on his face, listening to him.

Takimura walks in from the pilots' cabin. "It's a WarDragon, the Interceptor class fighter for the Kison Akari fleet. Fast, agile with an assortment of weapons meant to combat multiple targets in a dogfight. The smaller fighters are Shibokaze, I believe," he explains.

They get into a diamond formation with the government transport in the center and make a few jumps together to be sure that they aren't being tailed before rendezvousing with part of the main fleet at Mars. Once there, they are met with a sight that, while less organic looking, is possibly the most awesome thing anyone there has ever witnessed.

Floating over the small formation come the colossal Dreadnaught. This capital ship is the Kison Askari answer for the Centurion. It is a large ship shaped like an elongated pill with the back end chopped flat, where the main rear thrusters are placed. The ship bristles with weaponry and communication arrays. Among some of the pulse cannon placements are reflective and refracting shield placements, but the technology isn't completely worked out, but their scientists, in cooperation with some of the Atlantean developers, are working on them.

As the smaller vessels approach, it is akin to a human swimming up to the largest blue whale in an ocean on Earth. With faces pressed to the portholes, nobody on the government vessel says a word but simply stare in awe. Massive panels toward the rear of the ship slide open beneath shield emplacement with articulated arms attached to them. These shields can move to block or deflect fire coming in at ships coming out of or going into the docking bays. It amazes the professor that they seem to have thought of many possible scenarios that might come up during a space battle. The lack of experience has not hindered their ingenuity.

The four vessels surrounding the government ship with the WarDragon in the lead all sweep into one of the hangar bays and land with soft thuds as magnetic clamps come up to secure each craft to the deck. Inside the hangar, there is a bustle of noise and movement as technicians carry parts for various ships and work on others. There is a mix of Kison Askari,

Altlanteans, and, strangely enough, Ongakujin represented throughout the hangar. The professor has never witnessed such a large mix all at once. It seems that all groups have joined the fight for equality.

Standing tall before the main entrance to the ships berthing areas is Jared Omega. His slate gray features are absolutely still as he watches people file out of the ships that have just landed. Last to come off the government vessel is Tunisia and trailing her is young Darius. The boy is looking around at everything with the delight and curiosity you would expect from a child, and his eyes light up at all the new things in this strange environment. Then his gaze comes to rest on the tall being at the entryway. Taking in the great stature, thick build, long flowing cloak and ash gray skin. This being would hold the attention of many if he walked anywhere. His dark eyes, not so unlike Darius's own, are what catch the boy purely off guard, and he knows instantly who this man is.

For some reason, everyone in the bay seems to take notice despite the whole long distance exchange being silent. Neither has called out to the other as Darius slowly lets go of his mother's hand. She releases him and feels tears well up in her eyes as this is the first time they have been in each other's presence. The new suit makes Darius's steps awkward, but they slowly gain speed and momentum as he begins to run toward the elder Omega. The king moves the cloak back further, so he can kneel down and spread his arms wide as Darius runs headlong into his father's grasp in a huge bear hug to pick him up and spin around. Darius squeals in delight.

Tunisia walks up to the king and their son hugs them both, and says "Glad to be back with you, my love."

"Good to have you home, my dear queen," Omega replies.

Darius raises his head from the boulder like shoulder of his father and asks, "Home?"

The King chuckles deeply and says, "Yes, my son, you are home now. Home is where you make it and with your family. Your days of running through the underground tunnel systems of Earth are at an end. How do you like your special suit?"

Darius looks at them both and gives a small shrug before saying, "It's heavy."

Jared Omega laughs again and thinks, This is good. The boy will grow up carrying many burdens and not many of them will be light. Better to start him off early in as gently a way as possible.

Simeon salutes the king as the rest of the people file in to find berthing accommodations aboard this huge ship. There are places for non-military personnel, and that's where most are going. There are others who have been on the run since the revolt and are looking to enlist and join the fight directly. Among the non-combatants are Professor Jones-Bey and Bofus, who both come up to greet the King. The professor bows graciously while all Bofus can manage is, "Damn! You big!"

Jones-Bey tugs down hard on Bofus's arm, forcing him to bow slightly, and they make their way into the ship being directed as the people before them had.

Tunisia, Simeon, and Darius stay behind with the king as he watches three of his best pilot and crew deplane from the WarDragon that has escorted them in. Nefer, Kamal, and Muturi walk down the ramp after it is lowered and extended from the rear of the WarDragon. Simeon greets Muturi vigorously, and they all shared pleasantries, but Omega just holds tightly to his son. Tunisia looks at them and then around at the hangar before remarking. "This is a humongous vessel. It must take an awful lot to build and maintain something like this."

Omega takes her hand as he states, "Yes, there are four more currently in production along with other vessels. The engines are fueled by reactors, so they will never run out, and the materials to build are helped by us controlling a majority of this galaxy's mining operations, as well as taking a page out of the GMC's operational manual. There are materials to be gathered from the ring around Uranus that have been very useful in shipbuilding. There were a few more pickups from Earth in addition to your group. Not all of them made it, but the ones that did brought soil samples, plant life seeds, and other organic materials that we will need in order to sustain ourselves out here if it comes to that. We were pretty self-sufficient anyway being the only ones, for the most part, able to brave this last frontier and survive."

* * *

After going through the obstacle courses multiple times, Lance Corporals Jennings, McNamara, PFC Long, and Private Cooper are exhausted. The only parts of them that are not fatigued are the mechanical prosthesis. Sergeant Garrison seems utterly unaffected despite going through the same courses and, for the most part, posting the faster times. It is starting to annoy Cooper, who feels that, although his augmented body is stronger now, believes he is carrying the heaviest weight among them technically. Sergeant Garrison's legs are just as heavy, if not more, but they are doing the lifting, running and jumping. PFC Long's suit serves as a vehicle for what is left of his body. For Long, these exercises are more about control and gauging what he can do.

The only respite Cooper gets is when portions of the courses permit him to use the new arms they have given him. Those portions are difficult for Sergeant Garrison as his arms must bear the formidable weight of his robotic legs, but that is beside the point for Cooper. No one should look that smug after a grind like that. Sgt. Garrison seems to know his thoughts and smirks as he moves to stand before them. "Alright, ladies, we will do this pretty much daily until it's time for us to ship out once we get our first target which I will assume should be the head rock. In order to complete our missions, we need the proper tools. In other words, you don't come to the party without party favors. Check it out!"

A large rectangle of field behind him recedes below ground to be replaced with a platform with stacks of crates. On the far end of the platform, there sits an enormous cannon of some kind that looks like an oversized rifle that could have been easily mounted on an armored vehicle or ship emplacement. There are other weapons that look like hybrids of rifles and rocket launchers with seemingly complicated guidance systems. There is an assortment of attachments displayed next to them. In between some of the crates, there is another strange looking heavily chromed assault rifle of size. Not as big as the cannon at the end but big enough to question if normal people could shoulder it.

Lance Corporal McNamara looks at the biggest weapon he has ever seen sitting at the end, then glances sideways at PFC Long and says, "I'm going to hazard a guess and say that one is yours, Berserker."

Sergeant Garrison walks toward it, and they follow. He looks over his shoulder and begins to tell them what he knows about some of the weapons. "That would be correct, Mac. This here is the M-something or other. I don't care what the pencil necks that designed it call it. We are going to designate it the dragonslayer. Berserker is the only one that has the ability to carry this monster but does not have to as it is fitted with a propulsion system that allows it to be moved from place to place, but when firing it, it's best to do so while stationary. This behemoth was designed with you in mind, and for all intents and purposes, you as well as that mechanical wonder of a suit you are in will become the tripod. Coop, the long rifle in between the crates is yours. It's not as powerful as the dragonslayer nor as big, but don't be jealous because his is bigger than yours. Just know these are all designed to do the same thing more or less, and that's to put large holes where they don't belong in angry beings who happen to be a threat to most of mankind, as well as any vehicles these malicious individuals have built and are likely designing right now. Berserker, I am not sure if that beast can bring down the crazy looking ships we saw during the attack, but if given the chance, we will find out. Lance Corporals Jennings and Mac, the two crazy looking long-range weapons with the erector set of wild attachments are yours. I am told, once you scan them with those special eyes of yours, you will immediately understand how they work. There are lots of other goodies here for all of us to get familiar with. A lot is custom to us, and some things we can all use. I am going to find what works best for me and become proficient, as we all must, at using this new kit. When not at PT, you can come down here and get range time in whenever you feel the itch to shoot. Look them over, gentlemen. Tomorrow we will come back."

As he walks away, Jennings shouts, "Hey, Sergeant! What are the names of the other weapons?"

Sgt. Garrison stops, turns around, and says, "Make 'em up. Just don't come up with anything stupid." He continues on back to his quarters, leaving the squad to dig in and familiarize themselves with their new toys.

Chapter Twenty-Three

THE GMC AND GOVERNMENT AT large are not happy with the way things are developing. Some want to press the attack now and seek out where the main force of the Kison Askari are gathering their strength to ensure they do not advance too quickly. It is shocking to most that they have developed any tech at all in such a short time. For the most part, their people are happy with the natural state of things and have not previously sought out technological toys and such. So it is doubly dismaying to see these people amass armaments and a space navy equipped with weapons that rival some of the GMC's most recent developments.

The most bothersome thing is that nobody knows who is helping these barbarians. Dark matter and the example that they have somehow managed to weaponize it is the crux of the winning argument for the cooler heads among the government. This is what makes the GMC hesitate to go in, guns blazing. For the first time in history, it seems someone else has the better guns, and this has to change before they can go in. So for now, they will wait and let the government dignitaries come up with a plan for peace while they try to come up with a counter measure to this new threat. Taking out their leadership could buy some time for either or both plans. Only General Krulak, Lt. Commander Jameson and a few other members of the top brass know of the mechanics.

Images of a huge ship orbiting Uranus have been spotted by satellite feeds relayed back to the comm stations at Saturn and Earth. Orders have been given to keep an eye on this ship from a distance. The speed and depth of the development of this space navy is horrific to say the least. This new arms race has gone to a whole different level. It has turned into a chess match where each side is creating one piece to counter what the other player has placed on the board. Lt. Commander Jameson is in a bit of a strange situation. The commandant could demand details on the new covert unit at any time, but is less likely to do so seeing as they want to deny any intimate knowledge if things go badly. The public eye can be a strange jury at times; history has proven that. Most people want freedom and other things in life, but they will also naively deny the nasty necessities in order to make that life possible.

Sergeant Garrison isn't a believer in the sheep dog mentality, at least not for himself. He is not here to protect the herd. He knows there are members of the military that think of themselves in that light, and act accordingly. He thinks of himself as more of a wolf. Now the group he has formed is his wolf pack, and they are going to bite the heads off of a stone-headed dragon. These are the thoughts running through Sgt. Garrison's mind as he watches PFC Long bore holes into huge alloy target sheets. It is quite a sight. Everyone in the facility stops training or whatever they are doing when Berserker begins firing his dragonslayer.

The noise that is created when the energy pulses through the enormous cannon cannot be ignored which is what catches everyone's attention, and when they turn in the direction of the sound, it takes them a second to realize that this isn't simply an animated tripod. The metal legs dig into the ground and become more entrenched with each shot. The two metallic arms are pulling the dual triggers. Inevitably each onlooker will visually follow the arms back to the body where you could clearly see a human head with tear-filled eyes wide and his mouth agape in what looks like frenzied screaming through each trigger pull.

For most, it is really weird, but Sgt. Garrison thinks of it as a kind of therapy. Lance Corporals Jennings and McNamara simply look at each other and shake their heads as they watch Long during target practice.

"Sometimes that guy kind of scares me, and I am man enough to admit it," McNamara says. Private Cooper comes walking up to them holding the newly dubbed "big bad wolf" and replies, "It looks like that guy scares himself. Glad he's on our side."

* * *

Forensic evidence is minimal at best as CSO Thomas continues to investigate the murder of her former employer and lover. There, however, is residue found at the trash receptacle. There are no prints to speak of, and the local law enforcement has all but given up. Luckily for her, she has friends that will take an under the table job to do some further digging. What is found is puzzling. The residue is of a resin, specifically found in certain makeups. There is only one known use for this resin. Often theater players or motion picture make-up artists will use it to make masks to change features on an actor or actress. Skin tone can be changed, blended in, and it can often even fool people during an up close inspection.

Since there are no shows nearby or any scheduled filming going on by the museum to explain it randomly showing up in the trash in the back alley exit, narrows down who would have use for this stuff. Ongakujin had a show a few months prior and another senator met his end there. This group is the chief buyer for this stuff, and Thomas doesn't think that is a coincidence, given the recent deaths, including Senator Levine's. There is a definite connection. Now all she has to do is trace them all. The Stone People have to be involved as they stand to gain the most by toppling the government or, at least, weakening those who believe in the current structure of power and influence. Business has to be slowing during the current conflict. Could they be taking out contracts to make up the loss in revenue? Thomas will find out.

She will need to get outfitted for this next phase. Under previous employment, she had use of non-lethal weapons, and other preventative measures. Whoever is at the end of this trail is out for blood and shows no concern for positions or titles. She will have to be ready to deal in the same currency as her foes. She has an old shady contact who will be able to get her what she needs. It isn't a relationship she wants to rehash, but times are desperate, and Levine is no longer here to be jealous.

Some of her other inquiries also turn up some other interesting finds, and Thomas passes along the information to her friends in local law enforcement. It seems that personal information is being passed along to people or groups that are looking to take out high-profile government targets. That means the Limbia Johari have to be involved somehow, and Thomas knows the blame has to lie with Athena. She is, after all, their financial leader and does most of the procurement of special servants that cater to the wealthy households.

They will all have to pay. The Loyalist Act is needed more now than ever, and there will be more people added to the list. Some of the upper crust might not like their servants and entertainment being rounded up, but it is for the safety of all. Athena will be brought in, and questions need to be answered. This will be no easy feat, but she is used to having some influence and also has access to resources that will give her decent security as well as some extensive tech. Whoever went to apprehend her will be seen coming which could lead to complications. Either way, it has to be done.

* * *

Sitting in his quarters aboard *The Ex-Wife*, General Krulak is going over the recent reports and wondering if they will ever get a firm grip of control on this situation. Someone has escaped off planet, and nobody can nail down whom exactly as they have used a deceased politician's transport on some phony diplomatic mission. Admiral Halsey has heard it directly from the pilot that let them through. There are reports of the Stone People continuing to build and gather arms, but they are being smart about it. The fact is that they are not as far ahead in this game as is usually the case. Space travel is old news, but space warfare is still relatively new, and until now there has only been one side to speak of.

Krulak simply stares at the monitor, hoping some semblance of a plan will magically come to him. There is a strange rippling effect in the air behind his desk, as a doorway forms. Out steps an older, blue-skinned humanoid with long white locks. Startled, the general reaches for his sidearm, which is absent from his holster as he stands up. The mystical doorway closes behind Babylon as he turns to General Krulak. "Don't worry. Not here to harm you. I undastand why you would be troubled by me sudden appearance. Don't call. I can be gon for anyone come runnin'," the Atlantean stated.

He doesn't believe this ...whatever it is before him but has no choice right now but to play along. "If you're not here to fight or kill, then what business do you have here?" General Krulak asks.

Babylon walks a few feet away from the desk and proceeds to sit on some invisible chair, which disconcerts the general but does not distract him from the potential danger he could be in.

"I am here to try and talk some sense to you, but I know you won't listen. I know the cease fire was only announced, so you could buy some time, but peace is a real option if you would honestly seek it, ya know?" Babylon rasps.

General Krulak shakes his head. He cannot believe what he is hearing. These savages have broken the peace that previously existed. "Are you serious? These same people who started an uprising and slew hundreds of mine overseers? We are supposed to extend the olive branch of peace to them?" The general asks incredulously.

"Funny thing about oppressors. They always think life is good when they are on the right side of the advantages. Call the overseers what they really were ... masters ... they are in every era in history that there are slaves. And there is always a rebellion against it sooner or later. The oppressed will either be freed or die fighting for their freedom. I may not always agree with their methods but cannot blame dem. Peace is your best option, and these people will not bend the knee any longer. De winds of change are comin'. Don't be sitting in the wrong direction when dey blow."

With that, another doorway opened up, and the stranger stepped through leaving General Krulak fuming.

* * *

An elite law enforcement task force has secretly gathered outside of Athena's estate. After finalizing their breach tactics, the men are stationed near all access points to the property, in case she does not come willingly. The queen and leader of the Limbia Johari has to have known it would come down to this someday. Why else choose such an obscure location, so far from most of civilization? Opulence is sure to be prominently displayed inside, but the fact that you had to wade through Siberian tundra to get there is a statement in itself.

Captain Federov is a local policeman who is not happy with being assigned to this detail. He is familiar with the lay of the land, leading up to and around the compound Athena has built here. This placed from the outside looks ostensibly like an old abandoned fortress holding very little of value inside, except shelter from the frigid temperature outside. Inside, however, it is a hub of technology and surveillance with what looks like one way in or out. The compound is built at the back of what looks like a big manmade ravine with steep icy walls leading to the front entrance. Federov has told them as much when both his commander and a group of government security officers first approached him days before.

He had said, "It's impossible to go in unseen. They will see you and know you are coming. I don't know what or who is inside, but whoever it is, they have the resources to keep things quiet and keep to themselves. There is very little traffic, so for the most part, we keep away." Federov saw no reason that he needed to go with them, but his commander had insisted. They supposedly only want information, but people who only want to talk do not go in heavily armed and do not ask if they can covertly enter.

Federov is not familiar with the senate but knows that even their security does not move, dress, talk, and act like these men. Even the personal security of senators and ambassadors are not like these men and it makes him suspicious. These men look like they are going to war and a former military man, such as himself, easily picks up on that. This is an overt show of power with the intention to intimidate whoever is in that compound. If this is a response to whoever in particular owns that place, does it mean that they are dangerous or have people in their employ that are dangerous?

Captain Federov looks over the men tightening up their gear, ammo, and weapons then looks down at his prosthetic hand. The hand reminds him of why he exited the military after his fair share of war, mining revolts, race riots, and other conflicts between supposedly rational beings over the years. He is dressed in white and gray urban camouflage, common to the area. The men with him, aside from another of his police unit, wear dark flacks and utilities over some new body armor. Protective, no doubt, but they stick out like sore thumbs. Overconfidence is another bad sign. Federov looks over at his young Corporal Yevgeny. He is dressed in the same manner as his captain. His green eyes with bright red eyebrows are knitted together in worry. Apparently he has the same bad feeling.

* * *

There is incredible unrest on Earth as people of the mutated races are indiscriminately taken into custody by security forces. There is no grand announcement of why this is being done, and the people are furious the world over. This is going to be a problem as most of the military has been deployed to deal with the revolting Stone People, and now there are uprisings of the other mutant races, as well as some of the privileged, who are now opening their eyes to the events taking place and seeing injustice.

This war could potentially have many fronts now, and General Krulak is infuriated. Up to this point, there was one fire to put out, and they were having a hard enough time dealing with that. Now that Senator Levine has been killed, it is a scramble to see who will fill that void in their leadership to help reign in this mess before it is too late. All execution of apprehensions in the name of the Loyalist Act should have been on hold during the cease fire, but someone had obviously ignored that fact and taken things to another level.

If the situation with the Stone People is currently under control, there should be no trouble in dispatching units accordingly to deal with this situation, but the GMC doesn't have the time nor the resources right now with the threat of armed and powerful beings out of control at the moment and the ever-present threat of weaponized dark matter hanging over their heads. The general has made some calls and figures the assassination of Senator Levine is likely the catalyst for this knee-jerk reaction. Threats from some white-haired, blue-skinned freak, and now this on top of all that is going on is threatening to topple all they have worked to build. Lt Commander Jameson might have to put his boys in play quicker than expected. This is a risk, but it is a necessary risk at the moment.

*　*　*

There is one more group of beings that Babylon can appeal to in an effort to stop this madness before it goes too far. The ancient beings of sentient light who have come so long ago to this small galaxy, in all likelihood, know very well what is going on and, for whatever reason, see no need to intervene. He will try nonetheless. It is only right to, at least, make an effort when he has not so many times before. He and his people have sat back in seclusion, watching the drama unfold, just as Pharaoh has. The difference in Babylon's mind is that they are not orchestrating it as Pharaoh is, and so are somehow less guilty.

It is often the case that simply witnessing wrongdoing without doing anything about it bestows just as much guilt upon the witness as the perpetuator of ill occurrences. This effort to enlist the help of others may help but will certainly not wash away that assumed guilt. Standing aboard his Manta-shaped personal ship, Babylon keys in the commands on a console at the back of the bridge. Void walking is both a technological advance and an arcane art which seems to be at odds as an explanation and not many humanoids have the stomach to deal with travelling this way. In some ways, the mind is an essential part of the process, and disbelief, when using it, can be fatal, at best.

It is, also, the means by which Babylon and his people were able to stay hidden but within reach of the world, for so long. Many olden tales of extraterrestrial visits were bungled uses of this means of travel witnessed by bewildered people who were laughed off or ridiculed after telling what they had seen. Babylon straps on an EV suit with a helmet specially fitted so that his long white dreadlocks fit without hindering his vision or breathability. There is a slight crackle in the air, and an opening appears in the transporter room. A dark rip in reality coalesces into a makeshift doorway. Babylon straightens out his brown robe over his suit, closes his eyes, and steps through the doorway.

His first footstep touches down in the city of light, on the home world of the ancient light beings. He leans heavily on his trident scepter for balance and to shake off the slight nausea that has come over him. It passes quickly as he is used to it, and his body has learned to recover in a decent amount of time. There have been instances where others have been sick or incapacitated for days after stepping out of the void. Blinking his eyes, Babylon changes the setting on his helmet, so it is slightly opaque, shielding his eyes, at least, partially so as not to be blinded by the inhabitants and their architecture.

The ground is solid and made of some kind of rock similar to Earth's surface, but the buildings are clear or prismatic refracting the light of the beings inside each dwelling. A globe of light floats up to Babylon and speaks directly into his mind, and he has to gather himself as it sounds as if they are mentally screaming at him. *What is your business here?!* Babylon starts to shout an answer back, but the helmet only makes things worse. Now he is screaming at himself. When he realizes the problem, he simply thinks his reply. *I need to see the council.*

The being flickers, which Babylon guesses is the equivalent of a nod and floats away. Shading his eyes, Babylon follows the being to a large crystalline temple. Once inside, the halls and walls are opaque and the only light source is a gathering of beings that approach Babylon, stopping ten meters or so before him. Babylon uses the trident scepter to help him kneel before the council and thinks at them. *Greetings, blessed ones. You may or may not know who I am. I be Babylon of the former colony of Atlantis. The Earth is in trouble, and I believe it is because of one of your own left there long ago. Your guidance is needed.*

Chapter Twenty-Four

SITTING ON ONE OF THE lower chambers, Pharaoh waits as two thin pillars rise from the floor before him. Light from each pillar spills out toward the other, coalescing into a makeshift screen. On the newly made screen, footage from the event months earlier plays out as he watches the new craft created by the Stone People dropping ordinance on the military installation on Saturn. Malice glides into the chamber, followed by Typhoon, who lumbers in his wake to wait slightly behind their master who has telepathically called them to see this.

They all watch as the Morningstar bomber, accompanied by a few other attack vessels, jump in just outside of Saturn's gravity well. The GMC is caught off guard and scramble to head them off. There are a few brief skirmishes, the bomber swoops in, drops ordinance, and then the attackers quickly jump back out before the GMC knows what hit them. The devastation is immediate and a bit strange to most who view this footage. There is no bright explosion, though there is a rather large dust cloud. Once the dust settles and clears away, it looks as if some giant artist simply took a pencil and erased part of the planet's surface, along with some of the facility built there.

Pharaoh leans in and points to the damage, waving his minions forward. "That is dark matter being put to a very dangerous use, and it's absolutely thrilling! These beings are obviously getting help, and I think I may know from whom. I did not teach many about this matter because I knew most beings here would not know how to control it and would likely destroy everything the way they almost did multiple times with nuclear power. These imbeciles can destroy themselves if they wish, but I would prefer to have vacated this galaxy before they do!" he explains.

"Master, what can we do?" Malice asks.

Pharaoh turns to both of them. "First you carry out my initial task of eliminating that meddling professor, the Stone People's king, and then come back for further instructions. My former disciple may prove too difficult a target to just go after without a strategy. Do not fail me," Pharaoh says.

In unison, both Malice and Typhoon reply, "Yes, Master," and turn to leave.

Malice is intrigued as to who this former disciple could be, and is ready for the challenge. Typhoon feels trapped and simply wants this ordeal of servitude to be over with. Life was so simple before. Knowing what he does now, he would rather be content in ignorance of all these conflicts than enlightened yet unwillingly involved.

* * *

Vagrant Kison Tontu, Limbia Johari, and any groups of mutated beings are being randomly picked up and detained at various facilities on Earth. There might be a cease fire with the Kison Askari and their mining contingent turned militant, but back on Earth, the government is taking the opportunity to clean house and squash any hopes of remnants revolting locally. Despite the media's attempt to paint things in a more positive light, for the most part, the public at large sees the injustice for what it is. In some cases, they aren't just detained; there is often brutality of unarmed beings and even deaths.

Things are spiraling out of control, and riots are breaking out across the world. It is growing so large that General Krulak fears that, if the war starts back up, it will basically become multiple fronts to handle. Local law enforcement is ill equipped to handle the amount of activity all over, which could be a factor as to why the harshness on their part has escalated to this boiling point. There is a mission currently running to get a hold of the Limbia Johari's leadership, to see if they can be linked to the recent high-profile deaths that have plagued the government in the wake of the announcement of the Loyalist Act.

Senator Levine, who spearheaded the passing of the act, was the most recent victim. Something has to be done, and the general is beginning to worry since no news has come back since a task force, in conjunction with local law enforcement, was sent to apprehend and question Athena, who is holed up in Siberia. The breach has just started and is not going so well. General Krulak will not like the report he is to receive in a few hours.

* * *

Captain Federov has advised the government task force to attempt to find a way up the steep ravine walls at the sides. They will possibly find a less direct route into the compound and avoid the bottleneck a frontal attack would march them straight into. A broad-shouldered man with dark hair and shiny emblems on his lapels says he will take his advice under consideration but later is told the sensors in their helmets don't detect any spaces over top that they could get to without being vulnerable for too long before being in a position to take advantage of higher ground, so the frontal assault is still in play.

He looks over at Corporal Yevgeny, whose green eyes are still full of worry, yet straightens his gear and nods to his captain, signaling his readiness. Federov clasps the young man by his shoulder, looking over the task force once again, shaking his head. These men rely too much on their equipment to the point that a lack of common sense literally negates all of their advantages. He sorely hopes that will not be the case this time. Corporal Yevgeny will be with the vanguard because he has some knowledge in this area, while Captain Federov will have to hang back and help oversee the mission unfold and advise if necessary.

They have marched toward the entrance of the ravine, electing not to use vehicles, unless needed in support and when it is time for evac hopefully with their target in tow. The huge steel double-sided doors to the compound stand closed in silent defiance of the approaching men. Corporal Yevgeny is sweating beneath his armor. It is soaking his body glove and uniform. He does have admiration for how silent these men move for how heavily equipped they are.

On the approach, everyone notices an immediate problem if things go south on this mission. There is absolutely no cover to speak of, heading toward the entrance. Federov has told them all of this, of course, before but now sees that the reality is finally sinking in when he catches the eye of the officer he spoke to earlier, looking back over his shoulder. Federov picks up his pace to catch up with the man. The officer slowly nods, saying, "Go ahead, Captain. I hear I told you so coming."

Federov simply shrugs and is about to reply when a small opening appears in the left door and out floats a hover cam.

The officer raises his hand, and the men all froze in place with the front row taking a knee to shoulder their weapons. The hover cam pans left and right before a metallic voice blares out of it, saying, "State your business here!"

The GSO looks toward the hover cam and yells, "We're here to speak with Athena, and to take her in for questioning. There's evidence that suggests she may have had something to do with the passing of sensitive information leading to the deaths of government officials."

There is an awkward silence as the hover cam pans back and forth over the gathering of men. The front row has now deployed large personnel shields, and has formed a phalanx at the head of the formation with rail gun muzzles protruding from between the shields.

Athena's sultry voice echoes out of the hover cams speakers. "You boys don't look as if you came to talk, and I'll not be joining you. If the government is finally reaping what they have so foolishly sewn, then so be it. Kindly leave please. This is your only warning."

The GSO looks at Captain Federov, who shrugs slightly, and the officer nods to a group of men at the rear of the formation. Eight men come up as the formation opens up, carrying a large cylindrical machine with four handles on each side. They set the machine down a meter from the door, and legs extended at its side, so it stands up in front of the entrance.

Federov gives the officer a questioning look. "That door looks to be a bit more formidable than what that ram can knock down easily," he states blandly.

The officer waves him off, saying, "That, my doubtful friend, is a quaker. Once it gets up to full capacity, it can pack a punch almost capable of shifting tectonic plates."

There is a thunderous boom as the ram draws back and drives the head into center mass between the two vast doors. The men are rocked back on their heels from the sound alone yet when they regain their equilibrium the doors seem unaffected.

One of the men presses a series of buttons on the ram, and there is a whirring sound as it begins gathering energy for the next strike, a more powerful strike, Federov is hoping. Inside Athena, Angelo, and other close members of her household watch on monitors as things are unfolding without. The crystalline tresses hanging from her head shimmer in the light and make tinkling noises as Athena shakes her head in disdain. She turns to Angelo. "Let's see how they react to us disabling their toys," she says coolly.

Angelo smiles, revealing pearl-like teeth inside of his faceted head and begins inputting commands on a console on an ornate desk. As weatherworn as the exterior of this compound looks, the inside is the exact opposite — lavish furniture and a computer system that can outdo some command centers are in evidence.

After finishing the commands, both Angelo and Athena sit down on an elongated lounge chair with various interfaces built into the arms to watch what is happening. Outside, some of the men point upward as slats at points high up on the doors open up. There are heavy floodlights that light up the entrance area. These are shut off immediately, and there is sudden darkness, and the men can still hear the whirring of the ram, but there is relative silence aside from that. The helmets that the task force wears have HUD displays and night vision, which automatically compensates when light is scarce. The officer heading the task force begins to laugh. "Let's get this over with!" he orders.

The men go back to work, and the whirring comes to a high-pitched whine and will strike any second. Before it does, several objects fall from the slats in the doors and hit the ground with small metallic thuds before exploding. Multiple flash bangs go off and all hell breaks loose. Corporal Yevgeny and Captain Federov are disoriented more from the noise than anything, but all the men wearing the high-tech helmets are screaming in agony as the night vision amplifies the light, effectively blinding them. Federov can see everyone is in total disarray and also notices another object as it is dropped to the ground nearly next to the ram and the eight-man team writhing next to it. There is a large electronic pulse, and the ram goes dead just as the arm begins to drive forward, stopping it inches before making contact a second time.

As the men are starting to recover, the massive doors swing open, and fifty Limbia Johari walk out headed by Athena. All of them are wearing light armor and harnesses with anti-personnel canons mounted on the shoulder pads of the armor. They are similar to the plasma cannon harnesses created for the Kison Askari troops but smaller and they have various settings they can choose from. Athena looks over her men and women gathered behind her and orders "Stun setting only," and saunters off. Her people follow and fight off task force members as they leave a mass of groaning stunned men in their wake. The doors slam shut, and a booming voice announces something in Russian that they cannot understand. One of the task force members crawls to where Corporal Yevgeny lay recovering from the stun bolt that hit him squarely in the chest.

"What is that thing going on about?" he asks.

Yevgeny looks at the man and says, "That went well, yes? It says security protocol has been initiated. Not sure what that means, but I do know we don't want to stay to find out."

They begin to pick themselves up and leave to lick their wounds, which luckily are not fatal. The government has no idea how serious a threat these people could be seeing as they had no idea they had the resources to produce such weaponry. Captain Federov is frustrated at his prosthetic hand. The electromagnetic blast shorted out the internal circuitry, and now he cannot manipulate it. It is stuck grasping the trigger housing on his rifle. It is going to cost him heavily to have it repaired. He knew this was a bad idea.

* * *

It doesn't take long for the news to get back to General Krulak and the rest of the government on what happened in Siberia. Athena is now at large and likely going to attempt to flee the planet. There is another recent incident where someone has gotten off world, and the troubling thing is they have yet to identify who exactly it was in a senatorial transport supposedly carrying terms for peace negotiations to the Stone People. The young officer that let the vessel pass has been severely reprimanded but cannot be held totally responsible as there is no protocol to stop diplomats during these trying times. This is a no-win situation. Had he erred on the side of caution and detained a dignitary unlawfully, it would likely not have bode well for his career. Admiral Halsey and General Krulak understand that, even if they found it hard to agree with.

Sitting, once again, at his desk in his quarters aboard the *Ex-Wife*, the general is staring blankly at holographic images of high-ranking government officials all wanting to know how this latest fiasco has been handled. These people disgust him. Pontificating from their positions of safety and security, and they only come out of the woodwork when they feel that status is in jeopardy.

General Krulak pretends to listen; he nods at all the appropriate moments and assures them that everything will be handled. Most don't look or sound convinced, but the general doesn't care; he simply wants them out of his virtual presence. At this juncture, he has nothing to lose. Lt.

Commander Jameson's crew will get their chance and soon. Training will have to be cut short. They are Marines, after all, that have been previously trained to fight. Now they simply have new kits to get used to. On the job training was sometimes the best training. After the rant session is over General Krulak types up the orders and then deletes the file. This is going to remain off the books as discussed.

* * *

The benefit of being able to base on a planet that most beings could not endure the conditions on is that anyone here will be able to train in peace. The Kison Askari take that advantage one step further. They delved deep below the surface of the planet and built their training facilities far underground where they are relatively safe from planetary bombardment which would come into play very soon. The GMC is still nervous over the dark matter technology that has eluded them yet found its way into the arsenal of the Stone People in a controllable form.

The volatility of the substance is what gave them pause to use it in retaliation. Omega knows they are simply buying time to either develop their use of it or find an equalizer. Both sides are now using the reprieve time to make more in-depth preparations. His people have fought out of anger and frustration but now need to add skill to that mix if they are to survive as free beings. Their warriors are now organized with military structure complete with ranking, chain of command, and much needed weapons training.

Few of these men had fought recently, aside from the latest revolt as they always had their hands tied, resulting from the electromagnetic systems throughout most mining colonies in the galaxy. Now their hands are free, and for the most part, their families have gone to ground if they cannot get off planet, so the chance of them being hostages to force compliance is minimal. Countermeasures are being developed to overcome this new freedom they have discovered, so now that their hands are free they have to be taught to use them along with the very new technology.

It is a popular belief in society that the Kison Tantu are slow-witted people. That is not the case. It is simply a matter of those in control limiting the education they have access to. The wages paid to "miners" are laughable at best and basically a system of glorified slavery. Education depends highly on where you live, and if you can't afford to live where the highest levels of education are being provided, you get a less than average skill set. People only see the immediately obvious. They are tough, big, and strong people who seem suited for labor or fighting.

Not long ago, there were fighting arenas where they could gain a little more of a living from if they survived, but it was mostly fighting themselves, and eventually as their expertise in martial arts became more evident, these games were eventually stopped altogether. As entertaining as they were, the powers that be did not want these games developing a growing field of potential warriors who at some point would realize they should not be tamed. In a sense, Omega was going to bring these games back, but for the purposes of helping his people get stronger.

They would train in hand-to-hand combat, weaponry, and study tactics. Babylon has reluctantly given him much knowledge on tactics after they came back after the strike at Saturn. There is also old knowledge that has been passed down through certain families through the years, who have not abandoned their history, despite being displaced and oppressed. In celebration of some of that lost history, the Cgyab games were born anew as a sort of right of passage for the warriors, where the best at hand-to-hand would fight in a tournament to see who the overall best was. The winner was instantly promoted, so lower ranking warriors would see this as an opportunity to rise before their time. They would fight for glory, for honor, and most importantly, they would fight for family.

That is the crux of this whole war. The imbalance in this galaxy, and the society that inhabits it have caused war all throughout history. The choice to live life as you see fit, and for that same choice to be available to your loved ones is all any being wants. The constant denial or degradation of that choice is the consummate enemy of peace.

Chapter Twenty-Five

A BABY ARMORED SNAKE, THAT'S what Sgt. Garrison wanted to call the ship they had been given. That is a stupid name, and he knows it, but it is the concept that he likes. It was heavily armored, built with the remnants left over from the manufacturing of the GMC's other military vessels. It is small and will not outrun anything but will be able to take a pounding. Roughly diamond- shaped like the head of a poisonous snake, yet nobody would call it sleek with five laser canon emplacements, one at each point, and one that comes out of the belly.

The Adder was the name they tentatively agreed on because snakelet or neonate weren't menacing enough. PFC Long is cleaning his dragon-slayer heavy canon in their squad bay when he glances over and sees Sgt. Garrison getting his kit together. They will be leaving soon. According to Lt. Commander Jameson, the timeline is to be sped up as a result of current events. "Sergeant, why were you so hellbent on the baby snake thing?" Long asks.

Looking up from his gear Sgt. Garrison replies, "A baby snake doesn't know how to control its use of venom when it has prey. Adult snakes know and have figured out just the right amount to take down their quarry. We are small, and when we get to our prey, we will let them have it with everything we have. I thought it fit but the options sounded too pansy ass."

Lance Corporals Jennings and McNamara file into the Adder to stow away more of their gear. Hidden compartments open up from a myriad of different locations in the flooring and overhead areas. Watching his brothers in arms, Private Cooper folds his huge alloy arms and comments, "Hey! If we don't make it big with intergalactic wet work, perhaps we can make some money smuggling."

Sgt Garrison looks over at Cooper and asks "What, pray tell, would you have us smuggle, Coop? Arms? There are currently only two sides to sell to in this galactic conflict, and we can only get weapons from one of them, and there's only one group of people looking to sneak in or out but mainly out from Earth. Those people being our enemy ... doesn't sound too lucrative an idea."

The rest of the group simply bows their heads and keeps stowing their gear, but no one can argue with Sgt. Garrison's point. Tribalism still exists, yet there are fewer groups than ever before. Previously there were a lot more fringe groups that arms dealers could sell to for a big profit. For Sgt. Garrison and his "mechanics," there is only one viable source of arms, and they are highly dependent on that source through unofficial channels. Even off the books, operations would raise eyebrows if too many resources were funneled their way.

It is almost time to ship out on their first mission which will basically be a warm-up/training exercise. This is actually a misnomer since it will be against real enemy forces. There are some surveillance shots of perceived troop movements in a few locations in the galaxy off planet they can initially target before going after their leadership, which would be more heavily guarded. Drones with artificial intelligence are nice to practice on, but nothing beats real life experience. The newly assembled unit with new equipment will likely get to start off facing opposition that is training, as well, to get their feet wet. At least, that is the strategy they are hoping to implement. Time will tell very soon.

* * *

Athena does not try to make it off world as many have thought she should. She, instead, goes to take refuge in the huge subterranean network in which Tunisia has taken refuge in to have her son. Plus, her people are in the most danger here on Earth, where the authorities have begun to try and further subjugate all mutated races. She will not abandon them when she is needed the most. Angelo watches her closely throughout this strange journey. They are not used to being on the run or without access to the best available technology.

The queen of the Limbia Johari is thinking of ways to remedy, at least, one of these problems. "Angelo, I need you to find a way to send an encrypted message out. See if you can get a hold of Toshi," she requested.

Angelo goes to do as he is bid but first turns back to ask, "What should it say?"

Athena thinks for a second before responding "First ensure that the line of communication can be consistently secure. We need to find a way to marry the rustic look of this underground network with viable tech and yet leave it looking old and unused. Toshi should be able to figure out a way to do that for us."

Looking around at the dusty caverns and worn, rusty-looking rail system they had been travelling, Angelo agrees something has to be done. Modernizing this network while making it look decrepit will help them speed up travel and strengthen communications while leaving a less visible trail for those hunting them, and more mutants may have to make use of this new underground railroad. With his orders clarified, Angelo goes to work with a small satellite link that will send a burst signal that few will pick up on. Hopefully Toshi is monitoring somewhere.

They have weapons to protect themselves, some supplies, and the run of a network few surface dwelling non-mutants will hazard, but given the way events are going that advantage might not hold up for long. Pockets of resistance will get smaller as more mutants are rounded up and the authorities have to have an approximate census and when they figure out they aren't fleeing off world, there is only one other direction to start looking.

* * *

Darius loves running through the cream-colored corridors of the Dreadnaught capital ship they had boarded weeks prior. This has, in fact, become his home. A flying city capable of housing thousands with docking bays for a large assortment of other vessels. The young prince is determined to learn every nook and cranny of the giant ship, which has gone from the Mars system to drop troops off at Uranus. Another training facility is to be built there to diversify their forces and not give the GMC one target to take out. There is talk of a suspected attack coming soon, despite what is being publicly announced. Omega is going to make sure his forces are prepared for any forthcoming possibilities.

Tunisia is trying to keep a close eye on Darius, who has grown very quickly, and there are plenty of suspicions and theories as to why he has grown the way he has. One theory is that, since he was born on Earth under a lesser gravitational pull, it put less stress on his skeletal structure, and another is that the suit has helped do the same, even when he is on worlds with heavier gravity. Less gravitational stress on the body would let it grow to abnormal proportions. Given the size of his father, no one would be surprised if Darius ended up a huge man, but nobody expects a boy of three or four to look like a child twice his age.

The other children are curious but wary of him because of the whispers going around. It is said the boy is either possessed or has powers, so most are on the fence in regard to their young prince. Darius runs through the lower decks, which he is forbidden by both his mother and father to go to. As with most children given direct instructions, he has simply became too curious to abide by them. There are many different rooms on the lower decks built for all manner of combat training, as well as agricultural classes, and the housing of the reactors are in the lower decks, as well deep inside the ship to protect them from attack.

Darius hears strange noises coming from one of the large enclosed areas, so he goes to see what is happening. Although he is big for his age, he can't quite see into the room as the porthole looking into it is just high enough that he can only see the overhead in the chamber. There are flashes, but he isn't sure what they are coming from, and there are grunting noises with accompanying cracking sounds. Darius isn't sure of who or what is being hit, but he loves the sounds. Finally unable to contain himself, he looks around for something to stand on, so he can get a better view.

Finding a small pale in a maintenance closet nearby, he turns it upside down and stands on to look down through the porthole. The deck is a lot lower than he expected, by around ten meters or so. There he sees Simeon wearing a strange respirator mask, wielding both his hammer and a long staff with veins of electricity pulsating at each end of it. There are about fifteen or so Kison Askari surrounding him armed with similar staffs and shoulder-mounted canons. Simeon smiles menacingly twirling his staff in one hand. Darius notices his mounted canon is lowered on his harness while the others have theirs up and are actively targeting Simeon but have not fired.

"What are you waiting for?" Simeon bellows.

The shout seems to stir them into action as one of the canons targeting Simeon fires. Two of the warriors rush in to attack. Simeon easily deflects the charged projectile, and it ricochets into the overhead, as the smaller statured Kison Askari jabs into the first oncomer's stomach while simultaneously spinning and deflecting a blow from the other attacker, sending him flying with a swift swing of the hammer in his other hand. The others gather to strike when there is a shrill whistle, and they unexpectedly start to float, stealing any momentum they had gained.

As their momentum carries them forward toward the center of the chamber, Simeon leaps upward gracefully floating toward the ceiling and pirouettes while twisting to have his feet hit first. The previously dormant canon on his shoulder comes to life and begins targeting all the warriors on the deck, stunning each, one by one, until there are two left. There is another shrill whistle, and before the tone ends, Simeon throws first his hammer and then his staff at each. There is a mean thud as the hammer connects with the still disorientated warrior and sizzling noise as the staff reaches the last man who has not yet fallen. Both collapse as the gravity returns to the chamber, and Simeon lands, catlike, on his feet.

Darius's mouth is agape, staring as the men all around squirm and struggle back to their feet as Simeon calmly strolls to pick up his staff and hammer before helping some of them stand up. "That, men, is why you should always be prepared. There is a reason why we have chambers like this one. With new wars come new problems. What if we fight while being boarded? It could happen during a hull breach or through an open air lock. You will be thrust into a vacuum, and the loss of gravity will nullify your strength and size advantage in some cases. Trust me when I tell you, the GMC will have tactics with just this kind of scenario in mind. Be ready for it!" he commands them.

The warriors all stand to attention and answer "Yes, Sir!" before exiting through a hatch on the opposite side.

Simeon sees the small head in the porthole and waves to Darius who sheepishly thinks of ducking before returning the wave. Suddenly the deck in the chamber begins to rise, bringing it to the level of the hatch Darius is watching from. There is a hiss as atmosphere is brought into the chamber, and Simeon takes off his mask before opening the hatch and stares directly at Darius's small chest. Seeing the quizzical look on Simeon's face, Darius remembers he is standing on the pale and quickly steps down bringing him to stand a head shorter than the general. Simeon lets out a deep heartfelt laugh, saying, "I knew I was short, but if you had caught and surpassed me this quickly, I would know something was definitely wrong!"

He hugs the boy before admonishing him. "You know you're not supposed to be down here."

The boy stares at the ground and says, "I know, sir, but that was amazing!" He beams. Darius continues, "I want to train and learn to fight as you do! I think I can be good at it. Don't you?" he asks expectantly.

Simeon pats him gently on the head before answering with sadness in his voice, "Of course, you will be a great warrior and king one day, but while you still can concentrate on being a boy, go play, have fun, run amok, and cause trouble. You will have plenty of time to train and fight. Did the men you saw today look like they were having fun?"

Darius takes a while to answer, thinking it over. Recognition comes into his eyes as he looks and replies, "No, not really, but that was because you beat them all. They weren't very good now that I think about it."

Simeon laughs again before explaining, "They are fierce and very good, but I put them in a situation they were not prepared for which gave me the advantage."

Confusion comes over Darius's small face as he asks, "Isn't that cheating?"

Simeon smiled at that. "Yes, in a manner of speaking, but better to be unprepared against someone who is teaching them a lesson than against people that are trying to kill them. This is not a game, young one, and even if it was, you are not yet ready to play. So run along and play as you should for now. When you are ready to train, I will be here to teach you!"

With that, Simeon turns in the direction of the lifts and smacks him briskly on his back. Squealing Darius jumps and runs toward the lifts, laughing all the way down the corridor, making up his own battle sounds and fighting along the way. Simeon is happy to see the boy joyful, yet sad because he knows the imaginary enemies will likely become real, and he has a feeling that day will come too soon. Hopefully, he is wrong.

* * *

Babylon leaves the home of the ancients furious! They did not listen to reason, and worse it seemed as if they knew what was transpiring all along and saw no reason to intervene on behalf of the beings in that galaxy being manipulated for trivial pursuits of entertainment for lack of a better description. He is not sure, but he could have sworn one of them had mentally whispered that there was another already there to remedy the situation, but that was during a moment that had seemingly erupted into a telekinetic argument.

It is a small relief that, at least, some of the ancients believed something should be done, but the reigning council had all decided against direct intervention. This is a strange stance to take in Babylon's opinion since obviously the inhabitants of Earth and the Milky Way have already been interfered with. What is the problem with trying to correct a past wrong? The GMC and the ruling government are hellbent on returning the Stone People and all other mutants to a subjugated existence. The mutated races are fed up and want equality, and the ancients seem content to sit idly by, as if this were all some sort of grand scale drama unfolding. Which he guesses it is, but real lives are hanging in the balance.

* * *

The former CSO Thomas has gone back to her old street identity and called in some favors built up over the years. No matter how much the world has advanced, there will always be seedy places where illegal weapons and substances can be had if you know where to look and who to ask. She knows where to look and who to ask. Extensive research has found a few possible sightings of where the Ryoko-gekijo might be docking these days now that war has taken over, assassinations have been running rampant, and show times just aren't a priority anymore. It isn't as if she has to dig too deep. A floating theater isn't hard to spot. Word is it is keeping close to the islands of Japan as of late.

CSO Thomas, or Sparks as she was known now, is going to meet with some of her old contacts to get some weapons and other needed gear before paying the Ongakujin a visit. She wants answers, and they will either have them or know who does. The trail to Senator Levine's murder points in their direction, but she has to be prepared. There has to be more than meets the eye with these theater players and musicians. It isn't until recently that Sparks has unearthed an alarming amount of deaths that just "happened" to occur at or suspiciously close to one of their shows.

There was speculation about this years earlier by media outlets because most of the targets were high profile persons who were known to frequent the highly sought after events they performed at. The theory was that someone was already targeting these people and the concerts or plays made it easier for a hired gun to get at their marks, knowing in advance where they would be. What didn't make sense was the strange ways in which these people were killed, and not all targets were high profile, but they were all people of influence. The common denominator in Sparks's mind is the Ongakujin themselves.

They stay in the spotlight, giving them even more fame while somehow avoiding blame for these outrageous fatalities. For some of their more morbid fans, it was a running joke for a while, which led to a gambling site called Blood Money. A list of ticket purchasers was made available on this site, and you could literally bet on who would die at their shows. The site was banned a few years back, but there were rumors that it was up again and somehow encrypted so that law enforcement couldn't get in and you had to have an invitation. Maybe one of her old friends would be able to find out. It could be another lead to follow. If nothing else, it proved how sadistic and cruel some had become.

Sparks had enough money saved to last a long while. During her tenure as a chief security officer on Senator Levine's staff, she was paid very well and rarely had to spend anything. This was an advantage of mixing business with pleasure, and now she is taking some of those savings with her to Max on the Southside of Chicago, who is sure to have a good selection of weapons in addition to gear that won't blow up on her in a fight. Plus some of this stuff has to be tailored to her. She doesn't want it to look obvious that she is wearing protection and packing.

Media types aren't known to pack heat, and they also wouldn't come in full body armor for a supposed interview which is the closest thing to a believable cover she could come up with on short notice. Sparks assumes, sooner or later, Hironike will see through the ruse, but hopefully, by then, she will have some answers. If it turns out he is the one responsible for Levine's death, she wantes to be prepared to take him out.

Chapter Twenty-Six

CORPORALS ARAGON, SIMMS, AND JORDAN sit in the mess hall eating whatever slop passes for food on Saturn. Looking up from his bowl, Aragon says, "You know, I get it. We are vastly more efficient than ever before, and there is supposed to be an optimal amount of nutrients in this stuff, but shouldn't we enjoy eating sometimes?"

Sourly glancing into Aragon's bowl as if he suspects the contents are different than what's in his, Simms replies, "No, sir. We are clothed, armed, and ready to fight. Enjoyment will be issued when they deem it necessary, Marine."

Jordan chuckles but stops when a familiar screeching invades accompanied by more ungodly noises. All the servicemen and women turn in the direction of the ruckus as Sgt. Garrison marches in slightly dragging his feet just enough to scrape the deck as he walks, followed by what appears to be a mech suit, transporting a head and torso, and finally a guy with cammie pants, a utility vest, and huge metal arms. Corporal Jordan swallows before saying "They've multiplied? Hey, Aragon, maybe if you'd got hit back when this started that could be your unit."

Shaking his head at the thought, Aragon has no reply.

A steely glare from Sgt. Garrison makes most avert their eyes, at least, temporarily. There have been rumors about these men, but nothing was confirmed which was strange given that the men and women here are attached to recon units which fell under the umbrella of black ops on occasion, and yet they seemed to be more secretive than usual with what these guys were doing. Marines and other service members couldn't help but notice them training, which often was distracting given the noise of their equipment, and you couldn't help but watch them traverse the incredulously difficult obstacle courses designed specifically to help them get used to the new prosthetics.

Staff Sergeant Armstead had taken over temporarily as platoon sergeant because Sgt. Garrison was reassigned. It looks to everyone as if they are getting cranked up for something, but nobody knows what. That also raises alarms with most people since they are technically at a cease fire. Corporal Jordan nudges Aragon and Simms. "Hey. I'm going to go ahead and say it, but why is the guy in the full suit always crying when at the range? I mean, I know he has this crazy war cry thing going while he shoots, but if you look, those are real tears ... it's kind of weird."

Just then, two more men from their group walked in. The new arrivals are not quite as augmented as the others. Aragon notices they have been normally supplemented by their builds, but there is a hexagonal plating going up their spines similar to what he assumes is some sort of neural interface that Sgt. Garrison and the rest of his new squad have, and they are each missing one natural eye, which has been replaced by a mechanical upgrade. Corporal Aragon and Sgt. Garrison have not had the chance to fix the rift that came between them after the surprise nitro incident that unfortunately happened during a combat situation.

Sgt. Garrison nods at Corporal Aragon and takes his tray, moving to a nearby table to sit and eat with his new band of brothers, none of which seem inclined to socialize with the other recon Marines. There are plenty of people curious about them, but not enough to actually approach them. Aside from their brief long distance acknowledgement, there are no further interactions between Sgt. Garrison and Corporal Aragon, so the hatchet is assumed to be buried. Corporal Simms nudges Aragon and says, "Hey. At least, he's not trying to rip your head off anymore. With his new buddies, I don't think everyone in the chow hall together could stop them."

* * *

Typhoon follows Malice into a small chamber near the top of the pyramid. Malice turns to his reluctant simian partner and rasps, "I know you are used to lumbering along through the jungle, so this mode of travel may seem unsettling at first."

Looking around the chamber and seeing no vehicle in sight, Typhoon is confused. "Does this chamber turn into a ship?" the gorilla asks.

Malice chuckles, oddly melodiously. "No, my sublunary counterpart, there will be no rudimentary modes of travel used from now on. We don't have time to chase these beings from planet to planet. There is a faster way, but we must take a few test walks to get your mind and body more used to it before we go to take our prey."

Typhoon looks even more bewildered as he asks, "How is walking faster than a ship?"

There is a needle sharp glisten beneath the glowing orbs within Malice's hood as he menacingly says, "We will not walk on land; we will be walking voids."

Seeing further confusion on the large gorilla's face as well as a hint of fear brought a sense of sadistic joy to Malice, and they would speak no more until it was time to leave. Strange looking runes on what appear to be a stone desk in the chamber begin to glow as Malice places claw-like hands over them, inputting commands into an ancient computer that looks arcane but is obviously far more advanced than anything being used today.

Moments later, a dark silhouette of a portal formed with strange lighting around the edges. Malice simply looks to Typhoon and then back at the portal. Not to be intimidated by this enigma, Typhoon walks toward it but a surprisingly slender yet strong vice grip of Malice's hand stopped him. "Steele your mind and envision the uppermost chamber at Giza. Only after you hold that vision firmly in your mind should you step through that door," he states and lets Typhoon go.

Closing his eyes, Typhoon tries to recall what the uppermost chamber at Giza looks like, and when he is sure he has it, he steps forward and walks through the portal.

Everything seems to be going fine, and then all of a sudden, Typhoon's body is assaulted with what could be only described as extreme discomfort but not quite pain. Squeezing his eyes shut again, he tries to reclaim the vision of the chamber, and the feeling abates some, only to be replaced with the worst case of nausea the gorilla has ever known. His body seems to be rejecting something, and Typhoon feels as if he is about to vomit, just as he heard the grating voice of Malice in his head. *"I wouldn't do that if I were you. Hold on until you reach your destination. You may unwittingly let go of more than undigested food here."*

With a new resolve born of fear of not wanting to find out exactly what that means, Typhoon clamps down on that feeling until suddenly he is on all fours within the chamber at Giza. Unable to hold it any longer he begins heaving. A few moments later, Malice appears behind him, cackling maniacally. Gathering himself, Typhoon wipes his mouth and stands, not wanting to give his fellow minion more satisfaction, but his innards are still warring with the trauma of this new method of travel.

Angry, blue, glowing eyes lock with baleful red eyes as Malice announces, "We must do this until you can get to and from our destinations without becoming a sickly mess or destroying yourself during the journey. Do you need time to rest?"

The sarcasm angers Typhoon further, and he takes this as another challenge. Nodding at Malice, he states "Let's go again." If he had eyebrows that could be seen, they would be raised.

Malice simply replies, "Very well." And opens another portal.

* * *

Sparks was unsure but needed the armaments. All her reservations resurface about this meeting with Max. On the ride to meet him, she calms down and sets aside any uneasiness. She only thinks of the end goal. Finding the senator's murderer is all that mattered. She quickly traverses the seedy streets of the Southside of Chicago, making her way to an old club, which from the outside looks shut down. There are three huge letters in lights outside. BIZ doesn't look like too fancy a name for a club, but she is sure there were once other letters at the end of the sign which have somehow fallen off or been taken down.

Once she reaches a thick rusted metal door, she taps five times quickly on it. There is a pause and a peephole opens up as a hovercam floated from some unknown place to scan her.

"What do you want?" came briskly from the peephole.

Swallowing, Sparks looks into the hole and says, "It's Sparks, here to see Max."

Another pause, but this one is longer, and she begins to wonder if she is lost or perhaps at the wrong spot. It has been a very long time since she has came down this way and with good reason.

There is a horrible grating and grinding sound as the door methodically slides open, allowing about three feet of room to slip in sideways. Inside, there is a behemoth of a man in a respirator mask and helmet who dumbly stands there. Sparks can't tell which thing is more off putting — his size or his silence. A much shorter man with dark hair wearing an old Kevlar vest over a heavily muscled frame walks in with an awkward gate as it is obvious that one leg is cybernetically enhanced. Max has fallen on hard times but is somehow able to recover as he always does.

"Sparks ... now that's a pretty face I haven't seen in a long time. Told you you'd be back," Max states smugly.

Biting down on her anger, Sparks smiles and replies, "Yes, you did, but it's not because I had to. I have something I need to do, and I may need your help to do it."

Max seems to think this over and gestures for her to follow him to the back, when the giant man stirs giving her reason to hesitate. Max gestures to the man with one hand palm held flat toward him. "It's all right, Argos. She's with me."

The giant man kind of grunts and then goes back to stand by the door. Sparks follows Max back through a maze of weapons and various prosthetic parts.

Finally coming to an office area, Max sits down behind a large glass-topped desk and offers her a seat in front of it. They sit down and look at each other for a moment, each assessing the other and having similar thoughts. She thinks that his place of business has become a shambles and must not be doing too well, and he thinks she must be in quite a pickle to be sitting before him now after leaving the way she had. She is the first to break the silence. "So I take it business took a hit once more folks united against mutants, instead of fighting with each other, huh?"

Max just shakes his head. "Not at all. In the aftermath of the devastating wars before the unification, we built a new business, selling after-market prosthetics. Not much of a market for weapons, but it looks like that may change now that we are clearly starting to purge mutant races or, at least, the ones that stayed planet side."

A fire lit in Sparks's eyes as she asked through gritted teeth, "Which side are you selling to?"

Max chuckles. "Come on now, darlin'. You know me better than that. I am selling to whoever is paying. Don't get all emotional about it. I know you are here for some payback of some sort, and I can give you what you need, but don't think I take sides in any of this. I am merely a man of opportunity. We have been riding on the backs of these peoples for a long time. Everyone ignores that fact until they start kicking up dust as if it's for no reason."

Not wanting the anger to distract her from her purpose, she quickly changes the subject. "You sell prosthetics, but wouldn't pony up and get two legs?"

Max softly chuckles again before answering. "No, I just don't believe in the equilibrium theory. Besides, having one leg gives me character. I wanted to stay as human as possible. Some of the vets end up more machine than men."

Sparks understands that. She decides to get down to business. "You were right. I need to settle a score, but first I have to narrow down who to take out."

With a slight smile, Max asks, "Any good leads?"

She is not sure how much information she can share and trust Max with since he may be available to the highest bidder, and if the people she were up against can take out members of the government in high positions, it may be likely they have some pretty deep pockets. On the other hand, she doesn't have much choice. Max will have to know who she was feeling out in order to properly outfit her. "Ever hear of Hironike?" she hesitantly asks.

With an incredulous look in his eyes, Max just stares at her before replying. "The crazy flying theater guy? You can't be serious." Max knows there is obviously more to it than that. Even he couldn't ignore the body count surrounding the infamous theater, but he always figured the Ongakujin either knew of the hits or simply sold the information to those targeting the victims. Never once did he think the owner and manager of Ryoko-Gekijo was a major player in these deaths.

"So you think they have a side business dealing in wet work?" Max asks. Sparks seemed to take a moment to compose her thoughts before answering. "I have evidence that points to them either doing some of it themselves, or if they're not directly involved, they must be funneling info to whoever is pulling the hits off. Either way, I need to find out and question him, and, if they are as dangerous as I believe, then I need to go in with some fire power. I need to look as innocent as possible though ...that's where you come in."

Max thinks for a second before laughing hysterically. When he sees that she is not as amused, he puts on a hurt look before saying, "Oh, come on! You don't see the humor in that? You want to go into what you think is potentially an organization of assassins armed to the teeth without looking like you're armed to the teeth! If you are right, this is a group of beings that go around performing concerts and laser-lighted ballet shows all the while disguising what must be some pretty good weaponry to take out some very high-profile targets with big time security...If that's not irony, I don't know what is."

On many levels, he is right, but she doesn't care. Evidence doesn't lie, and all things point to the Ongakujin being involved somehow at the very least, and she will have her answers. Seeing that she is not going to budge on this, Max takes a deep breath and asks "Ok, so what's the play? You have a cover in mind?"

With a confidence she didn't feel, she said, "Reporter looking for an exclusive interview is the best I could come up with."

Max just shook his head. "Sparks, you're killing me."

A few hours later, Sparks is dressed in what looks like a smart tailor-made black business suit, and Max is obviously happy with his handy work. Catching him looking at her rear, she turns on him and says, "A little snug don't you think? Damned uncomfortable as well. What's the ribbing in the undergarment?"

Max grins with pride as he explains, "That is a plexi-alloy of my own invention, so it shouldn't raise any eyes at the metal detectors or cam scans. Not tough enough to stop a rail gun but should hold up to most other high speed projectile weapons and large blades they may have, and you still look like...a lady. We can have Argos heat it up for a bit, and you'll have to wear it to let it conform to your body better."

Max is enjoying this, and she is letting him, for now. If this stuff will protect her in a scrap, then she will tolerate his nonsense. She was just about to ask about weapons when two hovercams floated in. "Um...I have some of those already," she states flatly.

"True, but they, I am assuming, won't have any anti-personnel capabilities undetectable by most scanners. Now bear with me as these will have to be nonlethal countermeasures while you're in the lion's den. Once outside, you can pack more punch."

Sparks lets out a deep breath. "That's not good enough, Max! These people are serious. I'm not going in there to play footsie!"

Exasperated, Max responds, "I know that, but they are likely to have some good equipment to check you out. One cam will spray a liquid coolant, and the other will discharge a large burst of energy to incapacitate anyone in the room with you. This should give you time to get out of there and get to your vehicle where you will have heavier weapons I can supply you with and even outfit so you can fire on the go. That's going to cost you extra by the way. The suit has boots and thin gloves to go along with everything else. They are super insulated and will be able to protect you from the charge, yet are thin enough to look pretty much like normal accessories for a fashionable badass anchor."

Sparks stands there with her arms folded, thinking it is likely the best she could find on short notice and under the circumstances, but that doesn't mean she has to like it. Max seems perturbed at the lack of gratitude he is seeing. "Hey! I was even able to build you a solid cover complete with ID, credentials that should hold up under light scrutiny and my team was able to release some fake documentaries and exposé pieces in your name, so you'll have some buzz when they look you up, and they will. So let's try and be more grateful here."

Sparks walks over to try on the boots and gloves that Argos has just walked in to set down on the table at the other end of the office. As she slips one foot into a boot which is surprisingly comfortable, Sparks looks up and asks "Team, huh? All I see are you and Big Foot here. What's the skinny on my cover?"

Max walks over and hands her the freshly minted media creds for her examination, explaining, "You will be Amelia Jorgensen, GMC Vet turned war correspondent. Being a former chief security officer, you should be able to put up the stuffy bearing you law enforcement and military types have and stay on topic for as long as you can with him."

The name Jorgensen sounds familiar but she can't quite place it. "Why does that name sound so familiar, and what topic?" she asks. A screen lights up behind Max's desk and the face of a young blonde woman appears, but they can't hear her because the volume is turned down.

Looking at the woman, Sparks notices for the first time that they kind of favored each other.

Max points at the running video and explains, "That is Karen Jorgensen, a pretty, well-known live news anchor that you kind of look like you could be related to. So...you're her older sister who chose to enlist."

She doesn't like it, but it just might work, so she has to accept it. There are other options, but Sparks knows Max did good work and will be there when she needs him to be. She is paying after all. "Max, if this doesn't work, I'm going to kill you..."

Max simply smiles and says, "I love you, too, and ... that'll cost you extra."

Chapter Twenty-Seven

BACK ON SATURN, PETTY OFFICER House gets up early in the morning to squeeze into the body glove that he wears under his vac suit in order to go for a run. During his run, he notices they are trying to rebuild parts of the facility that were hit months ago; in addition to that, there seems to be a plethora of strangely large construction projects going in multiple locations around the existing facilities. He wonders what the GMC is up to, or has some corporate giant decided to wade in and try and take advantage of all the military members here with a nearly untapped source of disposable income? The inner hustler in House says the second option is more likely.

The run seems even more taxing this morning, and he wonders if he has skipped a dose of the special supplement members of the military have to take while on this planet to sustain their augmentation and ability to function here. Things are heating up back home, and the action could start back up in full swing any moment. In space, it will be a battle of machinery and experience, but if they are to go toe to toe again back on Earth, the GMC is hoping this augmentation will put them on more even footing, at least, physically with the Stone People.

It turns out that the GMC sees things exactly as Petty Officer House does. The construction is for additional barracks and training facilities to accommodate more of the current active-duty military members that are to come there for supplementation in an effort to even the odds further. The strategy, from General Krulak's perspective, is that, since the Stone People are catching up and even in some ways surpassing them in the technological sense, they will have to try and do so physically. When

House gets back from his run, he does some digging and finds that there is a new initiative that will be coming down the pipe soon from headquarters called the Ascension Protocol. This could turn out to be really good or really bad. Time will tell.

* * *

Deep below the surface of Jupiter, Simeon is watching a fierce competition of warriors in the latest cygab games. Jared Omega has given him permission to start the arena-based competitions up again with added events that will focus on tactical prowess, as well as individual performances in hand to hand combat, in addition to marksmanship. From these competitions, they will assemble their elite warriors. This will also help keep them sharp during this cease fire. Although it is for a relatively short period of time, being on the run with the queen and young Darius has taken a toll on Simeon.

Seeing these warriors totally in their element, fighting for recognition and in the spirit of competition, is good for his soul. No lives will be lost today, and for that, he is thankful. The king has taken a small group to see if any of the outpost and mine on Pluto can be salvaged. Most have opined the king should go with more than his personal guard, but he refuses, saying it is unlikely there will be any trouble. Pluto is viewed as a wasteland now, a mass unmarked grave and a reminder of the lengths the GMC would go to in order to bring the Kison Askari back under their collective heels.

Tunisia asks why Omega has to go himself in the first place. Why not send someone else to look, assess the area, and then report back? The king explains that those who were lost were his people. He needs to personally pay his respects to those that suffered. Simeon understands even if no one else did. It may have been a formality and somewhat ritualistic, but it is also the reason these people will continue to fight for their king. It is why this proving ground will succeed in finding the very best warriors, allowing them to fight the injustice that has been heaped upon them for so very long.

One day they all hope there will be no need for war and fighting, but until then they will do what is necessary. Noticing a very tall warrior being absolutely dismantled by a shorter but more robust Askari brings Simeon out of his introspective thoughts. The taller, dark gray Askari is powerful, but his opponent is just as strong yet faster. There is a fluidity and beauty to the way he fights with absolutely no wasted motion. Simeon goes to where some of the judges are watching and instructs them, "When the preliminary competitions are finished, send him to see me."

"Yes, General!" they reply in unison.

* * *

After a few months of running through the Earth's underground, grabbing as many of the muntant races as she can, Athena is tired of running. Toshi has returned her message and walks some of her technicians through upgrading lines of communication and surveillance throughout the network while simultaneously linking some of their equipment to satellite and camera systems used on the surface without visually changing anything. A local security forces or GMC detail patrolling the entrances or even upon entering the underground rail systems would notice nothing different.

As for the people themselves, the mutants have become incredibly good at hiding their tracks. Some patrols have resorted to destroying these entrances, but it is soon deemed a waste of ordinance. There are also too many for them to viably blow every entrance. Excavating tunnels for a mine or underground rail system is child's play for the Stone People compared to that same process on some of the other planets in the galaxy, so even if they could all be destroyed, they will just as soon be rebuilt or replaced. With the horrific treatment her people and other mutated races have endured recently, Athena wants to go on the offensive.

This is the ideal time for that with the military spread so thin, but lack of weapons for a large scale battle ensures that any attacks on Earth's soil will be more of a nuisance or distraction. She has concentrated on keeping as many mutants free as possible, and rescuing as many captives as she could. Being able to monitor the communications lines enabled them to intercept prisoner transports, but the more they did so, the tighter security around them became. At least it was a start. Omega and the bulk of his revolutionaries will have to do something soon, and she is curious when the government would turn their attention to Hironike and his crew.

Many believe them to be un-mutated humans with a constant coat of green makeup on. Admittedly, Athena isn't sure herself if that is not the case, but the fact remains that he and his people have always sided with the Kison Tontu, Limbia Johari, and other people the general population frowned upon when it became convenient or necessary during certain circumstances. Athena trusts him implicitly, even if they do not always agree on his methods.

* * *

After about the tenth experience with void walking, Typhoon is a lot more stable upon his arrival in the next destination. Stepping through the void behind him comes Malice. "Good timing. You have taken this surprisingly well. This Omega, along with the young one, seems to be on a path toward Pluto, or what's left of it. Take a moment to rest. When you have fully recovered, we shall go do our master's bidding," he hisses.

Nodding, Typhoon lumbers off to find a place to rest. They have void walked to various locations on Earth, but this time will be a far greater distance, which is sure to make it a more intense journey.

Malice knows the repeated walks have to be taking a toll on the gorilla yet it has made them in spite of the difficulty. A begrudging respect is growing between them. Hopefully that will translate into a successful mission. Once securely back in favor with master, Malice will revisit the slight of the existence of this perceived replacement. For now, they must concentrate on eliminating Omega, the young one, and the meddling professor. When all that is done, things should go back to normal, and master will be content watching his manipulations unfold on this planet.

Pharaoh observes them as they prepare to go out and knows the alliance between his two minions is tenuous at best, but that does not matter. Getting things back to the way they were is the most important thing. He does not want this professor helping the Stone People unite all inhabitants of this insignificant galaxy. These beings are best as a form of entertainment, and they threaten to take that singular form of pleasure away. This new being could prove to be a problem, as well, but Pharaoh cannot quite specify why. Looking into his young yet somehow old eyes through Malice foretold this being could be his undoing. That is enough to know he needs to be eliminated as well.

* * *

While sitting in the waiting area, Sparks is nervous. Max has somehow gotten her the interview she needs to feel out and confront Hironike about the assassinations and murder of Senator Levine in particular. The security detail at the entrance to the theater has scanned her and the equipment she brought along and let her through easily enough. For some reason, it doesn't feel right. Either security is lax because these people are no more than what they seemed, in which case she is looking in the wrong place, or they knew what she has and let her through anyway, meaning they could be more dangerous than she thinks.

In her head, she is rehearsing her introduction which has slipped out verbally a couple times as she waited. "Hello, I'm Amelia Jorgensen. It's nice to finally meet you!"

Nervously, she glances around to see if anyone has caught the strange greeting to no one, since she is the only one in the room. Sparks looks around to see if she can spot any hidden cams. Her nervousness can be easily explained as anxiety over meeting such a famous persona. Hopefully they will buy it long enough for her to get the information she needs.

The door slides open, and a tall emerald-skinned woman seems to glide in. She bows respectfully as she places a tray with tea and refreshments on the table before bowing again, then leaving. It has not been long, but

Sparks wonders how long she will have to wait. The anxiety is building, and what is only a few brief moments seems like forever by the time Hironike confidently strolls into the room and sits down on a couch in front of the table where the tea is. Sparks awkwardly walks over, extending her hand. "Hello, I'm Amelia Jorgensen. It's nice to finally meet you."

Hironike stands in his finely tailored suit and takes her offered hand while bowing slightly. "Nice to meet you as well. Although I must admit I am more familiar with your sister. I had no idea any members of the media were that interested in my troupe with everything else currently going on."

With a nervous giggle, Sparks nods toward the hovercams and asks, "May I?"

Looking over the hovercams before turning back to her, Hironike says, "Of course, this is an interview after all, right?"

Sitting at a local bar in Kyoto, Max listens in on the exchanges between Hironike and Sparks. Argos sits on a stool next to him. The stool is straining under his weight and is threatening to crumble, which would leave the huge man sprawled on the floor. Max would be glad for the entertainment as he is nervous about both situations. Funny as that might be he doesn't want to pay for the stool, and Sparks sounds nervous enough to start snorting in the midst of laughter which could blow her cover.

Back in the small conference room aboard Ryoko-Gekijo, Sparks anxiously activates her two hovercams, makes a show of straightening up her hair as they float into place, so she can begin interviewing Hironike. She looks straight into the first hovercam and begins her opening for the fake show. "Good evening. I am Amelia Jorgensen, and tonight we are live at the infamous Ryoko-Gekijo, the floating theater that brings phenomenal beauty, and entertainment to various locations around the globe. Hironike, the owner and manager, was gracious enough to grant me an interview. Thank you so much for sharing a little of your time with me!"

Hironike smiles and pauses to stare at the hovercams curiously before speaking. "Not a problem Amelia. It's good to get some kind of coverage with all that's going on today. We here are hoping a civil resolution can be found soon. War is, after all, bad for business."

Each time he stares at the hovercams, there's an obvious uncomfortable reaction by Sparks, who lacks the composure of a seasoned media personality, but she keeps up the charade anyway. Max's fears seem to be coming true as Hironike looks to be calling her out without actually saying anything.

To her credit, Sparks keeps the interview going. "Bad for business is an understatement, I am sure. How is the theater coping with the loss of revenue resulting from less shows, and even when you have shows, attendance is declining?"

Hironike noticeably turns in his seat before answering. "There, of course, has been a dip in business, but fortunately there are some patrons that remain very loyal to us and our brand of entertainment. We still receive enough in donations from loyal fans to keep this theater alive and well."

This time, it's Sparks who turns to stare directly into the hovercams for effect. "Alive and well is an interesting theme as there have been times when some of the most notable fans have not left your shows in those conditions. Any thoughts on why that is?"

Back at the bar Max nearly chokes on the shot he has just taken. Argos stood immediately, but Max waves him off. "Get the transport ready and prep the weapons systems, she may either get the information she seeks, or we may have a fight on our hands to get her out of there!" Max commands.

The big man barely grunts in acknowledgement and goes to do as he was bid. Max just shakes his head in amazement. He thought she would play nice a little longer before going into the meat of what she wanted to know. It is obviously a touchy subject as others in the media have asked things along those same lines but are consistently stone walled. The difference here is that she is asking them in person in contrast to a general question asked for the public to ask online. The only thing on their side is that hopefully Hironike believes they were being recorded and broadcast. That should limit how he can react or retaliate.

They are in truth being recorded but not broadcast to any major media outlet. If the hovercams are shut off, he may not play so nice, especially if Sparks is right about whom they really are. Her ending up missing would be easy enough to cover up since, at this point, no one would be looking for a fictitious media personality. Her closest ties are to the senator she had shacked up with who is already dead. Max doesn't want to have to go on a vendetta without knowing everything, but the fact that he thinks about doing just that if things go wrong tells him he has a soft spot in his heart. After all these years, he thought that spot had been burned out.

* * *

Malice steps into the chamber where Typhoon is resting. "It is time to catch our prey. Prepare your mind for the journey, beast," he hisses.

Just when Typhoon thinks he feels a minute amount of respect from Malice, it's immediately dispelled. The gorilla merely grunts in acknowledgement, partly to play up his role and also to show a little sarcasm which Malice does not appreciate. The crimson-eyed minion continues, "I have located the leader of the Stone People and his ... son heading toward the dwarf planet with a smaller group than what the little one was travelling with when you thwarted my efforts to kill that meddling professor."

Typhoon pounds the ground with a great fist and is about to respond as the dust settles in the chamber when Malice raises a gnarled, thin hand to forestall him "I know master ordered you to come for me, but it doesn't change the end result. I don't blame you. He can be...persuasive."

This somewhat calmed the gorilla, but Typhoon still has a bitter feeling when it comes to his new partner. "How do we attack once we find them?" Typhoon asked. "You will run in first when we find a good spot to ambush them, but not to attack directly. Not yet anyway. With their attention focused on you, I should be able to get in and hit their so-called king. If we are fortunate, the professor will be there as well," Malice explains.

The gorilla's bright azure eyes seems to burn as he asks, "Why is it that I have to be the distraction? I understand I am a beast to you, but let's be honest. You're not exactly...human." Malice laughs gratingly before answering. "My origins are of no concern, and also not the reason for why you will be a decoy initially. We have other ... skills that you have no knowledge of yet. Had you been trained, we could have attacked as one, but you have just barely mastered void walking, have physical prowess, but there is more to me than this physical shell, and that is where you fall short. There will come a time when we will share equally in the responsibilities of carrying out the master's wishes, but for now duties will be split according to our ...talents."

Cryptic as that is Typhoon has no choice but to accept the word of his fellow minion. Void walking is a new thing to him, so it is very possible and even likely there are other things to learn and gain command of before he can truly challenge Malice in any meaningful way. Typhoon will play along and bide his time. Right now, he has no choice in the matter.

The gorilla sits and meditates, waiting for the time to depart as Malice gathered weapons for the task. Typhoon is curious that Malice seems to favor blades of various kinds. He wants to ask but changes his mind. Since his fellow minion seems opposed to the use of ballistic projectile or energy weapons that are stored here, that's what Typhoon chose to arm himself with. Some are archaic and some seem more advanced than what the humans have been using recently. Another curious observation, but perhaps once this is all over he will be able to arm others of his kind against poachers who still threaten to make some animal species extinct.

Chapter Twenty-Eight

DARIUS LOVES THE TIME SPENT with his father. They have been travelling in a new prototype Toshi is working on before having to go back at the request of Hironike. They are aboard a Tiger Shark, a medium-sized destroyer class warship. Only about half of the elite guard has come along for this journey to Pluto. Omega wants to take the time to pay special homage to those that lost their lives there while there was still a lull in the action. Tunisia had advised against this trip, along with Simeon and some of his other generals, but the king would not heed their advice. It is important to him, and Darius is just as adamant about going along.

Once they jump into the system, the dwarf planet looks desolate even from a distance. The surface has lost its glowing blue hue it usually displays when the sun hits it. It seems that the planet itself remembers the tragic event from the start of their galactic conflict and mourns the loss of life that occurred there. Stroking his son's head, Jared Omega watches him curiously as his eyes begin to grow sad and glow slightly.

"What is it Darius?" the king asks.

Shaking tears out of his eyes, the boy replies, "I feel pain and suffering from this small world. Why?"

In amazement, the king just stares at his son before answering, "That's impossible. The event that happened here took place before you were born, but a lot of our people, good people, died needlessly here, son."

The boy simply nodded and leaned in to hug his father. Embracing the huge man made him feel safe and gave him some comfort despite the aura he felt from the planet. Kamal walks onto the bridge where Omega and Darius are observing from to notify them. "The habitats built here are likely ruined, sire. It's recommended we wear full evac suits or, at least, sealed helms."

Omega nods at him and gives the order for everyone to suit up.

* * *

Sgt. Garrison walks into his squads' sleeping quarters and bellows, "Skids up in one hour, ladies! A small group of ships was just spotted heading to Pluto. It may be some of their own going to pay their last respects, but just in case it's someone important, we will be there to properly send them off, getting our feet wet in the process. Let's get ready to rock!"

There is a hiss as PFC Long's suit comes up to fully encase his torso. He flexes and stretches his robotic body as he and the rest of the squad chorus, "Yes, sergeant!"

Sgt. Garrison nods to them and then proceeds to scrape his way back to the Adder to power up its systems and to perform the pre-flight check. Yawning, Private Cooper looks around before saying, "Anyone else notice the fact that he didn't scrape the floors on his way in here?"

Lcpls McNamara and Jennings look at each other briefly before Long responds, "He does it more for effect, but it's not as necessary with us. Besides, we're all use to it now."

They all nod and go about collecting their things before boarding the Adder. It will be a long trip, so PFC Long is tasked with getting provisions from the chow hall.

The rest of the squad goes ahead to the ship to make sure all their gear is secured properly inside the ship. Jennings and McNamara use their cybernetic eyes to check the outer hull. There are some plates that have been welded on to shield them from detection scanners, as well as sheets of a material previously used in experimental wraith suits. According to rumor, the first field test hadn't been too successful. Depending on who they were going to be confronting, they may need all the help they can get. Perhaps the bugs have been worked out or, at least, they could hope.

Long returns with hermetically sealed crates with fresh provisions which he mag locks next to the crate of MREs. It is then he notices five eerily coffin-like containers sitting at the back of the ship next to the bay door. The engines roars to life and Cooper slides into a seat to strap himself in as Jennings and McNamara do the same. Seeing as there is no seat large enough to accommodate him, PFC Long simply picks an open space on the deck in the rear compartment where they were and mag locks his legs to the deck.

They are all still getting used to being able to interface with computers, ships, and electronic devices in general. Finally Lcpl McNamara asks what has to be on all of their minds. "Who is to be flying this stealthy space bucket? We were all in various states of disrepair when the new pilot initiative kicked in."

Before anyone can answer the rear hatch opens and in stalks Sgt. Garrison. As he steps around the coffin-like containers, he answered them, "I will be our pilot. Lt. Commander Jameson and I had discussed bringing a pilot on board, but since I was not in a state of disrepair as you so eloquently put it. You could in fact say I was the first of us knuckle-draggers to go through the flash training program. Besides we are all capable of remotely controlling this thing whereas a regular pilot cannot. All boots can be on the ground and still have air support as well as evac solutions at our virtual fingertips. Don't worry, boys. I'll be gentle."

With that, Sgt. Garrison marches through the rear compartment up to the pilot's cabin, straps in, and they soon feel a slight weightlessness as the Adder lifts off. They are pushed back in their seats as the ship begins picking up speed to push through and escape Saturn's atmosphere. Long isn't sure, but mixed in with the roaring of the engines, and the noise of the various layers of atmosphere trying to burn them, he thinks he heard the sergeant laughing maniacally. Almost as one, the rest of the squad and look to the rear of the bay. Nobody asks what the strange containers are for.

* * *

Max doesn't know how much time he has to get Sparks out of there, but it seems to him that the interview is going to take a turn for the worst sooner rather than later. He hopes he is wrong, but she rushed into a more direct line of questioning quicker than she should have. Perhaps Hironike will be as cool as his demeanor sounds, but if not she is definitely in trouble. It is only a hunch, but Max hasn't survived the rise and fall of many criminal organizations, corrupt law enforcement groups, and some crazy para-military groups he has been a part of by not following his gut.

They dropped her off in what looked like a luxury transport as befitting a budding media starlet or, more realistically, the big sister of one at least. As they sped toward a place closer to the theater, Max put his earpiece back in to listen back in on the interview as Argos drove.

Luckily, Hironike still sounds calm. "You seem to be fishing for something Amelia, and I am not quite sure what that is, but we have had nothing to do with the coincidental deaths at some of our events. Powerful people often make enemies that either already are powerful or become powerful. It's a scary universe out there sometimes, which is why we enjoy bringing some beauty and joy to it."

Sparks nods her head calmly before responding, which is a miracle considering how angered she is right now. How pompous and arrogant this green-skinned fool is! She thinks to herself. She continues her line of questioning, "You mentioned having nothing to do with deaths at some of your events, but there have also been some questionable deaths, at least, near your events. Prominent political figures, litigators, military leaders, and you would have us believe you have no knowledge of how any of this came to be? It has to be hurting your bottom line and I find it hard to believe someone as smart as you wouldn't be concerned, unless, of course you were involved in some way..."

Hironike takes his time straightening up his suit this time and does not rush to answer. Sparks takes that as a sign of guilt. He makes as if to reach for something but stops short. Sparks's hair stands up on the back of her neck as she almost instinctively arms the hovercams, but she waits. She wants to hear what he will say.

"We provide art. That is what we do. We all in one way or another reap what we sow. Many of the people you mentioned have a lot to atone for. Perhaps karma has seen fit to pay them a visit, and in some cases, they were lucky enough to enjoy something like one of our shows before death took them. I have had no personal vendetta against any of them, so why do you insist we must be involved?"

Sparks smiles evilly as she says, "You still haven't said yes or no, Hironike. What was Senator Levine's crime? What was she atoning for when she was poisoned?"

Again, there is a pause, and Sparks can swear his eyes were dilating. She has him! Hironike returns her feral grin as he says, "From what I hear, she died of a heart attack or respiratory issue. I suppose someone disliked her politics or her bigotry or maybe she just was uncaring to the wrong people. Who knows? It's of no concern to me. Art is our lives. We are done here, Miss Jorgensen or whoever you really are. I expect I won't be seeing you here again. This can be a dangerous place, after all, according to your research."

Hironike stands, goes to the office door, holds it open for her. Sparks decides to take the cautious route in this situation. As much as she hates to admit it, there isn't a mountain of evidence for her to go on, but his responses do merit further investigation. Before she exits the office, she turned to Hironike and says, "I know you had something to do with her death, and I will find out how."

He merely chuckles and says, "In some cultures, death can be an art form, also; we must be careful of which art forms we embrace. I hope you find what you are looking for."

Before she can respond to the veiled threat, a large Ongakujin appears out of nowhere in a suit, shades, and wearing a strange earpiece. He points down the hall and instructs, "Down this way, your transport is waiting outside the west terrace, Miss Jorgensen."

She has no choice but to follow his directions since Hironike has disappeared as quickly as this guy has popped up. The armored limousine they have acquired from one of Senator Levine's homes pulls up to the terrace and the door slides back. The hovercams float over and rests in the trunk which has opened as they approach. The side door opens up, and Sparks nervously steps inside.

Once it slides shut, and the vehicle floats off, Max yells, "What the hell was that?!"

Gathering her thoughts, Sparks replies, "I was close to getting him to admit it! I think he did, through some vague comment about art, but in so many words, he was letting me know they are a part of all this."

Shaking his head, Max is amazed at her audacity or stupidity, depending on how you look at it. As they head away, Max orders Argos to take some scans in different spectrums of the theater. "I am glad we didn't have to blast in and rescue you," he stats blandly.

"But what if I'm right?" Sparks shoots back.

"Especially if you're right! Didn't we already go over the absurdity of you waltzing in there to see if they were some group of master assassins? If you're wrong, you come off as slightly crazy, but if you are right, then you may be a bit worse off than that. Suicidal would be more accurate. Some of what he said in response did seem a bit odd, so I will help look into this a little further, but only if that means you'll take it easy and not put yourself at risk like this."

Leaning back into her seat, she looks at Argos piloting the transport and then at Max before pouting, "Aw, Max, I didn't know you cared."

* * *

Malice steps into the chamber where Typhoon has been meditating, waiting for them to depart. The crimson-eyed wraith is carrying an oversized helmet which he hands to the gorilla. At the inquisitive look from the beast, Malice explains, "It's hard to know what conditions we will be stepping into, and I doubt you would function well in an atmosphere comprised mainly of methane."

Nodding, Typhoon tries on the helmet. It's a snug fit, but it's not too uncomfortable. He does notice that it does not completely seal around his neck as there is indeed a lot of space for air to get in.

Before he can ask, Malice answers the next question. "There's a suit with it, of course. I wanted to see if this was a good fit first."

This makes sense, but then the gorilla looks around before asking, "Where is your helmet and suit?"

Malice chuckles and it sounds like two pieces of sandpaper lightly rubbing together. "I have no need. There will come a time when you don't as well ... if you last." With that, Malice goes to retrieve the suit, and Typhoon shrugs his big body into it.

It looks like leather but is not. The suit is dark and has an almost organic quality to it, as if he has just put on a symbiotic being, instead of an inanimate object. The feeling makes him uncomfortable, in addition to the amusing glances his partner is giving him. He cannot actually see Malice's face, only those two burning orbs within the hood, yet somehow he knows there is an expression of smugness he would love to slap away, if he could see it. Malice stepped around to place the helmet over Typhoon's head and seal the clasps.

"The suit is made from the skin of a beast long extinct that could live in vacuum, and its skin had transformative properties which could filter out certain substances and change them into what the animal needed. Hard to explain, but that's the closest I can give you. It will, in essence, take what you cannot breathe and make it breathable. You should feel it slowly conforming to your body. It is durable, and should allow you to move unencumbered."

Typhoon stretches out his arms and legs, feeling the suit writhe as it adjusts to his muscles, fur, and contours of his body. The gorilla swears he is hearing something but can't quite make it out as speech, but feels it is communication of some kind. He looks at Malice and says, "Are you sure this is a dead animal? It feels alive, and it's a bit ... unsettling."

Malice runs a slender clawed hand over the material before responding. "Many that put these on have said they felt what you are feeling. I did not. My only theory is that the suit can form another pathway through which you can communicate with your own body that's different from the neural pathways you're used to. Just a theory, but yes I am sure it's dead."

Malice turns to leave again but instructs, "When the suit is done conforming, we will step back into the void and follow our prey. The suit may help insulate you from the effects this new mode of travel will have on you. There may be fighting, so I cannot have you incapacitated when we step out, but you also needed to feel void walking in its purest form first. Gather what you need and be ready." With that, Malice left to gather the last of his tools for affliction.

* * *

Nervously waiting in their old quarters on Jupiter, Tunisia lay in the bed, trying not to worry about her son and husband. She did not think it necessary for them to go to Pluto and see firsthand the decimation left behind. The findings there were not worth the risk of being there, and her people were always the ones risking their lives for the gain of others. This was a sentimental trip, and she understood that, yet also saw that Omega would be a target.

Refusing to take more than his elite guard and a handful of ships was a dangerous risk and one that could create an opportunity the GMC could not pass up if they found out he was, indeed, travelling so lightly. Whatever weapon they had used the first time would surely be enough to wipe him out and anyone foolish enough to go along. That was, also, another reason for great anxiety. Darius was there with him! She had not been away from her son until this point, and it was hard to deny him time with his father having spent so much of the beginning of his life away from him.

Tunisia has a bad feeling about all of this but has to remain strong, at least, outwardly. They should be back in a few days, and the king will chastise her on why she shouldn't have worried in the first place. Trying to get some sleep, she fights to force her mind to hold on to that thought, hoping it will come to fruition. Nefer, when she isn't training, often comes talk to the queen in an effort to console her. During the downtime, they have become fast friends as she is one of the few pilots who have seen real action against the GMC, even if it was short lived in the Mars skirmish. She is often called in to consult with the generals on the formations she saw or perceived tactics.

Both sides still have very little to go on, and the GMC has a slight advantage as warfare is what those employed there have studied for a long time. The problem is their old data is of very little use now. Previously, wars had been fought between countries on Earth, whereas now the world is, for the most part, united ... unless you were one of the mutated. Then you are considered to be so different that you are to be used. Equality is not to be spread among everyone. Tunisia has often wondered how it is that they have come so far technologically, yet remain so in the dark morally, spiritually, and mentally. It is like handing immature beings weapons of mass destruction, and today, they just might be aimed at her husband and son.

Nefer is on standby with her WarDragon. It was a crazy idea, but if something goes wrong, they have devised a plan to go get them. Kamal, who was ordinarily her gunner/navigator while she pilots, and Muturi, who manned the rear gun of the craft, have gone off with Omega. Nefer won't admit it, but feelings had developed between the two which explained why she so eagerly agrees with the queen when the plan is brought up in jest.

One thing Tunisia knows for sure. If anything does happen to them during this supposed cease fire, there will be no quarter given, no mercy, and she will try to burn everything in her wake across the galaxy. This is her family and her people who have spent too long being the downtrodden, offered backs on which others stepped on to lift themselves up to higher standards of living while constantly looking down upon the people that were essential in getting them there.

Chapter Twenty Nine

MOST OF THE GMC's HYPERSPACE technology have been set up to make jumps in unison with other ships as units that have been moved to various parts of the galaxy. In emergency cases, they can jump alone. The Adder, used by the Mechanics, is an exception to that rule. Sgt Garrison and his crew can jump where they want, when they want without being linked to any other fleet of ships. As they make their way to Pluto, it is the first flight for this highly experimental ship not currently on any unit inventory, and for the most part, the small unit itself is a ghost or rumor. After all, aside from the commandant and Lt. Commander Jameson, who assembled and modified each member, nobody knows what is to become of them.

Most of the Recon Marines who had seen them train thought it was the beginning of an MRP unit or that they would be given a new B billet somewhere. They have been given some new tech, but that could all be for show or a new propaganda campaign meant to distract the public from what was really going on. Stranger things have happened before.

Sgt. Garrison stops just outside of Pluto's gravity well and waits among some debris. With the engines off, he orders LCPL McNamara to initiate stealth protocols which shut everything off but essential systems and activate the plates on the Adder's hull, which will reflect or refract light around the ship, making it virtually invisible. Hopefully the ships heat signature will be similar enough to the debris it sat among to fool any scanners.

Huddled in the center of what would be considered passenger cab/ bay, Sgt. Garrison addresses his men. "Well, boys, now we wait. There's a small group of ships that jumped here, and a few of them made planet fall not too long ago. We are waiting because we don't know if more are coming, and I sure as hell don't want to run headlong into a hornet's nest. We know their so-called king is here, and he is target number one. Once we know there's no cavalry, we are going to use the drop capsules to make a less noticeable planet fall near wherever the king goes, take him out, and then remotely call the Adder down for our extraction. Some satellite feeds are still active in this area, so we can access them to get a picture of what's approaching as well as what's going on planetside. Any questions?"

There were none.

There is a brief debate on whether or not one of them should remain with the ship in case things go so wrong that they need extraction sooner, but the fact that all of them can remotely interface with the ship makes it unnecessary. One of them should be coherent enough during this operation to make the call, and if they were all down simultaneously, then obviously the mission is a failure and extraction would be a moot point. Private Cooper walks over to the drop capsules and runs a metallic hand over one of them. "So these, I assume, can withstand breaching the atmosphere and get us safely on the ground?" he asks no one in particular.

LCPL Jennings comes up to Cooper and clasps him on the shoulder and responds, "Safely? Not sure if you noticed, but the Marines are not too big on safety. Effectiveness, yes, but safety, no. I, my friend, am confident it can withstand breaching the atmosphere and all the loud heat exchange we will endure on the way. It's the welcoming grasp of gravity pulling us ever so closely to the surface and landing in one piece that's kind of got me a little apprehensive, but we did sign up for this. I'll take this chance over sitting on a gurney any day."

The talk doesn't exactly instill confidence, but they all agree with the last sentiment.

* * *

On Pluto's surface, Jared Omega and his son walk hand in hand, looking over the devastation visited upon this small planet. They have to keep their helmets and suits on as the enclosed habitats are still structurally erect but have been thoroughly cleansed of any life as the thrusters from the ordinance dropped ignited the atmosphere, creating a planet-wide inferno, immolating anyone on or near this surface. Once the portholes and hatches had been breached, the flames rushed in, along with the methane, and the habitat had been built to keep out.

Strangely enough, Omega looks at young Darius and sees complete understanding of the situation. He can't explain how, but the loss and the gravity of its meaning are etched on the boy's face as he looks over the destruction. Omega tugs him into a hug, and through the helmet, he can see a quizzical look in his eyes, which the King is grateful to see. There are moments he has been seen at play, but for the most part, it seems that Darius has skipped childhood. He has been thrust into a life of conflict seeing and understanding way too much for a child his age.

Within the helmet, the boy's eyes begin to glow as he casts his glance skyward. Omega follows his gaze but can see nothing out of the ordinary.

"What do you see, son?" he asks concernedly.

The glow subsides as Darius turns to his father and answers, "They come for us."

The boy points in a different direction than he was previously looking at what appears to be a dark shooting star. Omega chuckles and puts a hand on his son's shoulder. "I don't know who they are, but that is a shooting star, and I don't know what else you think you saw over that way, but there's nothing out there. Nobody's coming for us, and if they are, we'll be ready!"

As they walk through the desolate facility, a small portal opens a few clicks away on the surface. Through this portal steps Malice and Typhoon. Malice watches with unbridled yet silent joy as Typhoon clamps down on nausea from this void walking trip. They begin to slowly make their way toward Omega and his son. Darius, once again, feels the rift in ethereal matter as the two minions step through the void and turn in their general direction. Again, Omega turns to see what the boy is looking for and sees nothing as he doesn't have the senses his son does.

Mentally, he dismisses it as childhood paranoia. After all, the boy has seen a lot in his brief time, and not all of it has been imagined according to accounts given by the queen, her retinue, Simeon, Professor Jones-Bey, and all who accompanied them through the underground rail system that has long since been abandoned. Had this been the account of one imaginative child, that would be one thing, but a lot of people, some of which are close told similar stories. There had to be some truth to it. Whether or not those accounts had anything to do with what was haunting the boy now, Omega didn't know.

The boy moves around, placing his hands over various surfaces like walls, melted consoles, or chairs. Omega feels for him and hopes he isn't disturbed in some way, but he doesn't seem so. There are also rumors going around about his son being vastly different from other children. From Omega's perspective, this is expected. He is a prince after all! He could never be considered ordinary. It seems as if his wish for his son to enjoy his childhood will be cut short. The boy stops and begins to tear up, prompting the king to rush to his side.

"What's wrong, son?" Omega asks. With shaking hands, Darius's frightened reply is "I can feel them and the echoes of their pain!"

Omega grabs Darius in an embrace, just as the boy reaches back out to touch the chair again. Before the King can ask what he is talking about, they are suddenly transported into a dream-like environment.

Smoke filled the air as the temperature continued to rise. Alarms were blaring and there was screaming, so much screaming. Nothing but pain and confusion permeated everything. Then there was just silence. An absolute void of nothingness, and that transference of something to nothing in an instant was worse than the pain.

Darius releases the chair, and Omega finds he has not been transported at all, but is standing exactly where he last remembered. Looking around, he recognizes that what he has just seen and felt have actually happened in reality not long ago. Briefly they had just witnessed the atrocity visited upon his people here by the GMC.

* * *

Still orbiting with the debris, Sgt. Garrison monitors the scanners and a strange anomaly briefly pops up on his screen. He is just about to order his men into the drop capsules when the images pop up. Sgt. Garrison yells back to the rear cabin, "Lcpl Jennings, get up here!"

Jennings yells back up front, "Aye, aye, Sergeant!" and runs up to see what the commotion is.

Once he gets there, Sgt. Garrison turns the monitor toward him and says, "Tell me what you see."

There seems to be a bluish-purple streak that enters the system and then turns toward the surface, but there is no ensuing breach of the atmosphere, so it's obviously not a vessel which is what they were on watch for before heading down to the surface. "Unless they have a new stealth ship of some kind, I don't think it was a ship at all. Plus, there's no visual evidence of anything entering the atmosphere, Sergeant."

Garrison agrees that he sees the same thing, but there is definitely something. "Rewind it. Change speeds, and do whatever you have to do to figure this out. Either way, we are still on mission, but if I can avoid surprises, that would be nice," he orders.

Instinctively Lance Corporal Jennings runs the footage back, and this time slows it down while letting his cybernetic eye break down what he is looking at. "Huh..." he says.

Sgt. Garrison comes up beside him and asks "What do we have?"

As Jennings once again replays the footage Private Cooper and PFC Long squeeze into the pilot/scanner cabin, making things a bit tight, but they say nothing as he describes what is playing. Pointing to the screen, Jennings says "Look at this streak entering the system. At first, I thought it was a shooting star, an ion trail of some sort, or a combustion trail from some sort of stealth vessel the rockheads may have come up with. Once we look at it slower, you can see there are several breakages as if whatever is moving is constantly stopping and going, but in real time, it looks like one smooth flight path. The trail disappears once it heads into the atmosphere."

Lance Corporal McNamara overhears and sees everyone has piled into the front, so he comes to join them and looks at the footage as well. Perplexed, he points out, "Whatever it is, it's making holes in space if that makes any sense at all, and then keeps moving forward repeating the process. So....what the hell is it?"

Sgt. Garrison shakes his head and says, "I don't know, but it's not a ship, and we may have a short window of opportunity here, so everyone gear up and head to the drop capsules. Mac, calibrate them, so we land nearest to where the last known surface activity took place." Nearly falling over, everyone struggles to do as ordered.

* * *

The gusts of wind and temperature are making the short trek to their quarry difficult for Typhoon. The suit does nothing to stop the unforgiving bite of freezing cold that permeates this landscape. Frustrated, Malice stops and turns to his unwilling partner and travel companion. Angrily, he instructs the gorilla, "By now you should realize you are much more than you seem as a result of the master's manipulation of your molecular structure. Use it to control what's within you, and do not become a victim of these elements! Prove you are more than a simple beast worthy of what was bestowed upon you!"

They are close to their prey and cannot afford to have a weak link going into this confrontation. The Stone People are formidable, and the child is another unknown entity they would have to contend with. Typhoon closes his eyes and looks inward, ignoring all the external elements hindering his movement and concentration on the task at hand. Surprisingly, he finds that Malice is correct. The winds are far stronger here than on Earth, yet when he thinks of himself as a more dense being, it is so. Next he mentally commands some of the molecules within his body to move at a faster rate than usual, creating more energy that translates into heat.

Now that he does not feel frozen to the bone and is not buffeted about by the winds, Typhoon opens his bright azure eyes and locks gazes with the cold, glowing crimson stare of Malice and asks, "Why did you not tell me of this before?"

Dismissively, Malice turns away and begins anew their journey while replying, "I did not know you needed to be told what you should have felt was possible within you. I was given no such guidance. Notice the beings that are here rely on manufactured habitats in order to dwell here. They are unaware, as you were, of their full potential and capabilities. This is why we will defeat them."

The two minions trudge on toward the facility where Omega, his son Darius, and a small contingent of his elite guards are sifting through the rubble that was left of the main facility there. A few of the modified mining devices float around the entrances, monitoring for any unexpected traffic. Following Malice's lead, the duo easily avoids the scanners and makes their way inside but are met with resistance from guards posted further inside.

When Malice runs into the Stone People in the caverns on Earth, most of them are fleeing refugees with no arms to speak of, aside from a small group of soldiers travelling along as escort. This is a totally different situation. They are all armed with no worries about collateral damage. Aside from the job of protecting the king and prince, they can eliminate anyone else in the vicinity with extreme prejudice. Once they realize they are not alone, the air comes to life as energy and projectile weapons fire simultaneously.

The energy projectiles mix with the exposed atmosphere that has leaked into the facility creating long streaks of fire from their shoulder-mounted cannons that trail behind the rounds as they fly toward their intended targets. Typhoon struggles mightily as he scrambles to find cover before returning fire with the ballistic projectile weapons he has decided to carry with him. That decision proves to be a valuable one as his weapons create less of a spark and therefore do not ignite as much of the ever-present methane in the air. They will still have a good indicator of where he is firing from.

This may be the distraction Malice needs to get closer to their prey, which moved deeper inside the facility as the battle begins. Perhaps, if most of the guards concentrated on eliminating the newest minion, Malice may be able to sneak around and take out the king and his bothersome child. They have no knowledge of the professor being here, but they will catch him soon as well. Noise does not travel well overall in the environment where the fighting is, with the exception of the com units within the helmets which were situated right next to the shoulder-mounted canons.

Simeon feels as if fireworks are exploding right next to his ears and all the Askari planet-side are experiencing the same horrible surprise when the fighting started. The short general runs full speed to see if the king and prince are unharmed. Omega and Darius look at him confusedly when he rushes through the open hatch, skidding to a halt. "Sire, are you and the prince all right?" he asks desperately.

Still holding Darius, who was staring in the direction of the fighting, somehow Omega replies, "We are fine. What is happening?"

There is a deep thud that comes through their in-helmet comm systems and they all rock slightly as if hit.

"Attackers suddenly appeared through the north entrance. The guards there began to fire upon them, but that has slowed as we don't know how it affects the atmosphere. We don't want to create another deadly explosion here! There are only a few we think, and we should have them soon, but I think it best if you and the Prince get back to the ship now," Simeon suggested.

It is hard for the communications officer aboard the Dreadnaught in orbit to hear what the pinned down guards are trying to say over the fighting. Not all of them have heard the order that Simeon has given to cease or, at least, slow down their fire, so as not to bring about another tragedy. The message does not need to be clear for them to know that the king might be in danger, so a transport and more guards are already en route to pick them up. Hopefully, they will make it in time.

* * *

Sgt. Garrison, along with Private Cooper, Lance Corporals Jennings and McNamara are strapped into their drop capsules and are awaiting verification that PFC Long is secure in his pod so that they can initiate the drop to target.

"What are you waiting for, Long? An invitation?" the sergeant bellows.

There was one drop capsule bigger than the rest, but it lacks the seating rig and straps the others have. After hearing the reprimand of his squad leader, Long turns around to back into the capsule. When the hatch shuts, his mech suit moves of its own accord. The face plate, which is normally retracted into his chest armor that encases him, comes up over his mouth and nose while a rear skull casing rises over the top of his head, meeting the plate for a fully enclosed helm.

Parts of his new arms and legs extend to brace against the walls and door of the capsule effectively holding him in place. The pod may be buffeted or banged about, but inside he will not move. They are all securely strapped inside, but that doesn't mean too much of an impact will not come with a nice concussion, but that is a danger they have signed up to risk. Once the ship's system verifies they are all secure, the drop will commence. The rear bay hatch opens as the Adder adjusts its attitude, pointing the nose away from the planet, and the mag locks holding the capsules in place are disengaged, allowing them to gently tumble out into the vacuum.

There are a few gentle bumps as the pods exit the Adder. Lcpl Mc-Namara comments, "This isn't so bad." The attitude and main thrusters on the pods are located on top, above where their heads were situated. The smaller attitude thrusters kick on, effectively pointing their feet toward the planet. Then with a roar, the main thrusters kick on. Momentum picks up as they speed toward Pluto's surface. The rest of the Mechanics are thinking, Mac is right; this wasn't so bad. Sgt. Garrison knows better than to expect a smooth ride the whole time. He is just glad they aren't going in head first.

The cybernetic interface they all have allows them to open their comm frequency through neural command. Sgt. Garrison orders comm silence until they hit the dirt and have one last parting message before then, "We are not flying the friendly skies, boys! Here comes the fun part! I'll meet you on the deck. If not, I'll see you in hell!"

They wonder what he means as he laughs hysterically. Understanding comes when the pods are greeted by the thunderous noise of travelling from vacuum into planetary atmosphere.

Chapter Thirty

INSIDE THE DROP CAPSULES, THE Mechanics pierce their way through Pluto's troposphere with the outer hull of each pod seeming to scream in protest. Most have their eyes clamped shut inside their helmets. PFC Long still feels relatively protected as he is the most armored of the group, technically speaking, but is still having his share of reservations about his decision to get back in the fight. Then he remembers what took him out of it in the first place, and his anxiety turns to rage. Inside his mech suit, he presses the button to stop the pain meds flowing into his body. Embracing the pain, his scream joins that of the pods hurtling at breakneck speeds toward the surface.

The comms should have gone silent at this point, but Sgt. Garrison thinks he can hear Berserker screaming in his pod and joins his screams with periodic hysterical laughter. Lance Corporals Jennings and McNamara are simply holding on for dear life during the plummet. Strangely enough, Private Cooper is the only one holding on to his sanity, at least, for the moment. His eyes are wide open but staring stoically at the display in front of him as it counts down the distance to the surface. He has decided he can freak out after they reach the surface. If they reach the surface in one piece, there will be nothing to freak over, and if they don't ... well if they don't, they can all argue in the afterlife, if such a thing exists.

There's almost a hush as they reach the stratosphere. There is a slight jolt as the thrusters above them shut down and the attitude thrusters below them ignite in an effort to slow their descent. Watching the indicators on the display, Cooper begins to feel a little better as there was obviously more planning involved than he at first thought upon entering into this "flying coffin" as some of his squad mates have dubbed them. An aperture opens up at the center of the bottom of their pods, and ejects massive globs of some gelatinous substance.

When the hell ride has calmed down some, Lcpl Jennings opens his eyes and begins watching the displays as the rest of the squad has. Everything that happens outside of each pod is being recorded and displayed in real time as it happens, so that they can monitor their progress and prepare for ground-fall when the time comes.

"Um ... what the hell was that stuff?" Jennings asks no one in particular since comms are in fact silent. The globs descend ahead of the pods as their thrusters continue to slow their fall, but they are still travelling at great speeds.

The globular projectiles expand and blanket a wide swath of land that the pods are speeding toward. A couple of the capsules are off-course, but the attitude thrusters make minor adjustments in time to get them back on the right path. The countdown is getting smaller and smaller. Cooper finally closes his eyes as the inevitable collision is almost upon them. They hit the blobs, and there's a brief sensation as if they have landed in water. The craters that the blobs create upon their impact create a large pool of sorts which briefly solidify around the capsules, slowing their momentum. Once they are still, the pools shatter. In warmer temperatures, the substance would have liquefied. On Pluto, it makes a strange gelatinous ice or snowy substance.

The Mechanics are able to climb out and pull their gear from the pods, but it is difficult. At least, they are alive. Groggily, Sgt. Garrison is the first to emerge from the frosty rubble. He checks himself over and adjusts his helmet, then turns to watch the others climb out from short distances away. PFC Long is the last to come out. It takes him longer as he is more cumbersome and his weapon is stowed in a back compartment on his capsule along with the hover sled that will carry it for most of the mission until the fighting begins. Huddling at a nearby ravine, Sgt. Garrison says over the comm, "Sit rep! Everyone fully functional, men?"

After physically and visually checking each other over, they are confident they are able to continue to the target. Remembering the Stone People might have a way of listening to their comms, Sgt. Garrison goes silent again and begins using hand signals, ordering them to rely on the HUD inside their helmets to get their bearings. They are less than a click away from the facility. Lance Corporals Jennings and McNamara survey the quickest route and give thumbs up to the rest of the squad. The march doesn't take them long, but once there, it is obvious that the party has started without them.

There is some smoke coming from the facility, and given the composition of the atmosphere, that isn't a good sign. Sgt. Garrison signals for them to be cautious with their rate of fire when they go in. Jennings and McNamara will set up outside the facility with two tripod weapons systems in case the target tries to flee which was likely given that there is some kind of battle in progress as the Mechanics arrive. Private Cooper and PFC Long will go in with Sgt. Garrison to take the top rockhead out, and anyone that stands in their way.

The hatches have been blown off their hinges from the explosion set off by the attitude thrusters of the ordinance dropped off here by the GMC, after the initial revolt began. Most of the methane must have somehow burned off or, at least, lost some of its potency somehow. At least, that's what Sgt. Garrison and the rest of his mechanics are hoping. If not, it is a miracle that they reached the surface at all without simply becoming part of the conflagration as did the mjollnir bombs. It's likely they exploded without ever touching the ground.

This line of thinking also brings up a curious thought. How are the Stone People and whoever they are currently fighting able to reach the surface without worry about igniting the heavy methane content? It could cause a problem when it is time to be extracted. He put the thought out of his mind as they enter through what used to be the main entrance. Walls are charred, and it has to be an illusion because everything is being filtered, and they are breathing air supplied by their suits, but he can almost smell burning flesh.

There are plenty of bodies evident, but most of them are unrecognizable. Some look like silhouetted stains on the floor or draped over consoles in that facility. The sounds of fighting draw closer as they move deeper into the facility, but have become somewhat muted and less frequent. The combatants have to be aware of the potential dangers here as well. Another factor to consider is the gravity difference here. Beings from Earth weigh one-fifteenth of what they do on Earth, making them lighter and faster. Private Cooper crawls up the corridor leading into the chamber where the fighting seems to be happening as Sgt. Garrison, and PFC Long change the rounds in their weapons to ballistic rounds, instead of any energy projectiles they were carrying.

From behind a frozen lump of melted slag, Cooper peaks into the chamber and has to blink to believe what he is seeing. A group of rockheads with shoulder-mounted canons are fighting with what looks to be a gorilla in a spacesuit. For the most part, they are swinging at the beast with long gilded hammers, and it is retaliating in kind with swings of his own assortment of rifles and some weapons that Cooper couldn't put a name to. Every so often, a shot goes off from either party, and they all cringe and duck as sparks ignite.

Cooper sees it is at a stalemate, and perhaps one that is being manipulated to remain that way. There is another player who seems satisfied to sit back and watch the whole thing unfold from a dark corner. Private Cooper doesn't have any enhanced eyes to see everything, but there is something alive in the shadows. That is for sure. Just when he is starting to doubt himself, part of the shadow shifts, and there are bright red glowing orbs boring holes into him. Cooper, at that moment, turns and crawls back as fast as he can to report to Sgt. Garrison.

PFC Long and Sgt. Garrison look on as Cooper tries to signal what he saw. So far, all they can get is that there are five or six combatants and possibly a seventh, but it is hard to decipher what he is trying to say. Finally Sgt. Garrison grows frustrated and breaks comm silence. Chances are nobody is listening. Even with the verbal explanation, "red eyed ghost-like being" doesn't quite ring a bell. Perhaps it is another mutant type they had yet to see before. In any case, it doesn't change the fact that the king is holed up in the back and will need to get by the fight in order to exit.

Perhaps they can sneak by and get to him while the battle is taking place. The downside to that plan is that someone else had thought of exactly that. Sticking to the shadows as Typhoon and the elite guard try to find openings for either physical blows or clear shots, Malice finds himself near the other entryway and slips inside. Simeon, who is waiting just inside the chamber, nearly takes his head off with a swift hammer blow, but the minion ducks with minimal clearance while unsheathing gleaming blades to parry the follow up swing.

Stepping in front of his son, Jared Omega undoes the clasps holding the ceremonial cape to his shoulders and lets it fall to the ground. He brandishes a large staff with metallic balls attached to the ends. Darius has never seen this weapon before and wonders where his father got it from. The wraith that has just come in to attack them is familiar to the boy. He recognizes him from their encounter on Earth. Darius's eyes begin to glow slightly but stop when his father places a hand on his chest, commanding him, "Stay put, son. No matter what happens, I will need you to find a way to get to the transports."

Tearfully Darius nods as he watches his father jump into the fray. There is a canon mounted on Omega's shoulder as well, but he has been warned of the dangers of using it here, so he goes in with a quick thrust of his staff into what should have been the midsection of the strange red eyed being but feels no indication that he hit his mark. Perhaps the dark robes hide the being's true form, but it looks humanoid in shape as much as he can tell. Darius watches as the three battle and can tell that, although Simeon and his father are fast and powerful and also helped by the conditions, this other being is, in fact, faster.

They are vigorously fighting with a being that seems to be dancing through the fight, striking, parrying, and reposting. Simeon's energy is dropping, and it is only a matter of time before the glancing blows become more serious. That's when Darius notices there has to be something different about the blades being used. There are noticeable cuts and scrapes on both the king and Simeon, and that should not be the case. These are no ordinary weapons. They are laced with something.

Back in the previous chamber, Typhoon is frustrated at having to be the decoy and begins opening fire with his entire arsenal and throwing caution to the wind. Sgt. Garrison decides they can wait no longer and do the same. He has no idea how they will get off planet either way. The chamber nearly erupts as everyone follows suit. Shoulder canons come to life, spitting hot plasma at Typhoon, forcing him to duck for cover while firing at the party crashers. The air is alive with energy, but no huge eruption of flames so far, so they continue to fire and return fire.

Using a different tactic, Sgt. Garrison goes back to ballistic projectile rounds and aims for the tubes leading to air supplies on the Stone People suits. Once the threat of asphyxiation comes into play, the battle calms some, and he is able to sneak past them as Typhoon continues the firefight with the remaining guards and Cooper. PFC Long follows the sergeant, charging through the fight, oblivious to rounds flying past and around him.

As they crash into the rear chamber, the king is just beginning to slump down to one knee with the ghost-like being Cooper has described raising a strange looking sword for the killing blow. At the last moment, the king slams a staff to the ground, and there is a blinding flash, and everyone is thrown wide, as if there has been an explosion, but there was no evidence of such an occurrence. Darius who has been hiding behind a control panel is the first to awaken. He runs to his father's side. Simeon, who is a few feet away, struggles to his feet.

There were two men in what look like mechanical suits. They are laid out in the entrance to the chamber. Simeon quickly gathers Omega's cloak and wraps the still unconscious king in it. He is alive but seems to be fading. They make their way to the outer chamber where the firefight is taking place, and the small blast seems to have reached them as well, but there has been no smoke or burning. Darius is carrying his father's staff. There is another man, prone, near the corridor to the main entrance with metal arms, similarly suited to the others.

A couple of the guards have died, so they gather the remaining ones and go to the transports, which are luckily already on their way. No one notices the unconscious gorilla, strangely enough, on their way out of the facility. Waiting a few hundred yards away from the facility in opposing directions are Lance Corporals Jennings and McNamara, who have, moments ago, experienced a very unpleasant high pitched squeal in their helmets and then nothing. They can see with their normal eye that the rockheads are leaving the building. They have had no communications with the others of their squad inside, but they were not in pursuit of the target, and to make things worse the interface controlling the mounted tripod weapons systems they have set up for just such a scenario is not responding.

Malice wakes up to find that his prey has, in fact, left, but he holds on to the fact that the king will not live long after his dark blades takes effect. Making his way back the way he came, he sees his fellow minion and begrudgingly picks the beast up who has served his purpose after all and steps into the void, leaving this forsaken place.

Cooper who is just coming to catches the very end of that scene and doesn't know what to make of it. His arms, which had inexplicably gone limp before he passed out, are just now coming back online.

Sgt. Garrison, in the rear chamber, stands over PFC Long. The entire suit has shut down in the process of whatever the hell just happened a few moments ago. As he comes back online, a primal scream erupts from him, causing the quad to cringe as the comms are now back online as well. Sgt. Garrison calls for a sit rep and all report they are fully functional, but have no explanation for what happened. Jennings reports, "A few of them left, Sergeant, moments after all our equipment went haywire. Since their transports were safe to come down, ours should be."

Sgt. Garrison shakes his head and, after some hesitation, asks, "Did you see a being in dark garb with a gorilla leave with the target?"

Stifling a laugh, both Jennings and McNamara respond, "No, Sergeant!"

McNamara adds, "There was one being carried in a shroud of some kind. He looked unresponsive, but can't confirm who it was."

That may be the best thing about this mission. Plenty had gone wrong, but they may have had some help completing this assignment. It doesn't matter to Sgt. Garrison how the job got done, so long as it got done.

"Roger that. Sit tight for a bit. Then let's blow this joint. Monitor all satellite surveillance available to track the possible trajectories of their ships. The unresponsive one, I believe, was our target. Someone else dealt the killing blow, if it is though. We may need to follow up, just in case. Garrison out."

Everyone double clicks their mics in silent response, to acknowledge their understanding of the orders. True to the theories, the Adder is able to enter the atmosphere and pick the squad up. They retrace their steps and pick up the drop capsules to leave as little evidence of their having been there as possible. Once they are out of Pluto's gravity well, they watch footage of the battle from the ship's vantage point and analysis of the data reveals that there was a big electromagnetic pulse at the end of it which caused all the system failures.

Their weapons systems, suits, and cybernetics would need to be insulated further to protect against future uses of that kind of technology. At first, Sgt. Garrison thought Cooper was being funny or speaking figuratively when he described the other two attackers present when they went into the facility. That is a mystery for another time. More than likely, the rockheads were headed toward Mars, according the satellite footage they looked at so that was the next destination. The only problem is that means they could be running into a much larger force. There might not be another chance to catch the king. At the very least, Omega was likely mortally wounded and that meant he would be more heavily guarded. Sneaking in would not be easy. It is rumored that they have attempted and failed to use wraith suits to get to him before. That, coupled with their use of EMP tech, didn't leave a lot of good options available. They could always hope that he is, in fact, terminated and go report that to Lt. Commander Jameson, but that could bite them in the ass if Omega resurfaces. The only viable option is to take the Mechanics in to finish the job or verify that it was, in fact, done. Either way, they would get credit for it, even if only the top brass knew about the op.

* * *

Running alongside the gurney, carrying his father to the medical bay aboard the Dreadnaught, Darius is tearful and angry. He remembers the two beings fighting his father and Simeon from before, and he vows that, if his father dies, he will eradicate them personally. The king is rushed into a special chamber to analyze what is being done to his body, which cannot be explained right away. The cuts look as if there should be minimal damage, but he is having different reactions throughout his body, as if allergic to something.

His skin is softening where the blades touched him. Simeon is suffering similarly but is recovering and has not been affected to the same degree. It is obvious to Darius that this is on purpose. The king is the target and not Simeon; therefore, the reaction is not as severe in Simeon's case. The Dreadnaught is to rendezvous with the main force at Mars where they will get together with their other leadership and decide what to do next. If Omega passes on, the queen would be regent until Darius is fit to rule their people. Until recently, the ruling house of Omega has hidden in plain sight as a beacon of hope to the Kison Tantu.

They have risen up out of bondage and to continue their race toward freedom and equality in this galaxy. Their house cannot fall at such a pivotal time. Too much is at stake. Darius will not let that happen. Somehow, despite his age, he knows the importance of all that is going on and knows what must be done. He can feel the evil beings going back to Earth, as well, as the lost one gathers there unaware that this is all a game in which one being is responsible. He doesn't know why, but he knows he must speak to Babylon. Perhaps the old Atlantean could clear up a few things for them.

Darius can feel someone else. His mother Tunisia, along with all of her rage, is on her way, hurtling through space to see her son and injured husband. The rage he feels from her might need to be controlled, as well, but he isn't sure that he wants to. Maybe it is someone else's turn to burn as his people on Pluto have been made to burn.

Epilogue

THE MILKY WAY IS IN a state of disarray and turmoil. The Mechanics' suspicions are confirmed as they surveil the Mars system and verify from a vast distance that the king of the Stone People has, in fact, fallen. They are able to patch into satellite feeds still active and monitor images as well as some message traffic. However, they cannot go in to verify things firsthand. The forces gathered on Mars are too much to handle with such a small force. The Kison Askari are licking their wounds, but it will not take them long to mobilize and retaliate in kind, likely with a determination and ferocity not seen before.

This is why, after a small contingent from the highest levels of HQ GMC received the report, General Krulak decides this is the best time to break the cease fire, to go crush this latest revolt, and end the war once and for all, while the Stone People have a void in their leadership. There were some who think they should wait to see if they sue for peace first, but the commandant will not hear of it. The Mechanics are having their systems upgraded with some added protection and insulation. They will likely be needed again soon.

There is another reason the GMC is determined to end the conflict with the Stone People. Their fears have come true and open revolution by the other mutant races has begun on Earth in earnest, creating multiple fronts to worry about. That will have to be quelled, as well. What is left of the upper echelon of government seems safe for now, but with all that has transpired, it is only a matter of time before the remaining leaders are to be targeted again. They are all spinning into chaos.

* * *

Sparks, along with Max and Argos, come up with a plan to dig up more connections between the Ongakujin and the recent rash of deaths in government officials. They pour over video footage, literature, and any media they can get their hands on to find any corroborating evidence that will support her theory. Max promises, if they find tangible evidence, that he will help her exact justice, but he in turn, makes her promise to give it up if what they found turns out to be a pipe dream fueled by anger over a lost love.

Meanwhile, back on Mars, there is a huge funeral procession marching through the underground facility built there. Most of the Kison Askari not employed as sentries on Mars or Jupiter, where the other portion of their main force is, are there for the death of their king. At the head of the procession are young Darius and his mother, the queen, dressed in royal purple and old gold. Tears are streaming down their faces. Songs are sung but not too many words are said. There are none needed.

Everyone here on Mars and those on duty know what happened. They also know the GMC will soon be coming for them. They are all willing to fight and die to the last man. Those who have chosen to strike down their beloved leader will pay dearly for it. Despite what they thought they are not truly leaderless. For these people have been blessed with a new one. The Kison Askari just hadn't discovered him yet.

Upon the dais, where Jared Omega's casket sat, stands young Darius who has gotten up without knowing why he did so. His tears are soon burned away as his eyes begin to glow so brightly. He stares out at the vast crowd before him. Because his eyes are so bright, some of them have to look away. From the middle of the crowd, an old miner among them, who has hopped a transport from one of the smaller facilities on one of Jupiter's moons to be there, points at the boy and yells, "Kuongoza Mwanga!"

Soon others pick up what he said and chant the words over and over. A large group of Atlanteans enter the large hall they are in and the crowd parts to let them through, approaching the dais. Leading them is a tearful

Bablyon. Long white locks sway back and forth in front of his wizened blue face as he walks up to the young prince. He briefly hugs Tunisia, who crumples into his embrace before recomposing herself.

"I'm so sorry for your loss, Tunisia," he tells the queen.

Then he turns back to look at Darius, who says, "I know you. You're Babylon."

The sorrow in his eyes is met with equal sorrow in Babylon's amber gaze. He kneels down to pat the boy on his head and asks, "You hear that?"

Darius peers around Babylon at the still chanting crowd of mourners. Sheepishly he looks back at Babylon and says, "How can I not? What does it mean?"

Chuckling lightly, Babylon replies, "True, true. They believe you ... are their leading light."

Glossary of Terms

Ancients — Sentient beings of pure light with the ability to change form and manipulate things on a molecular level.

Atlanteans- Blue-skinned people from the lost city of Atlantis. Thought to be gone but still exist, often hiding in plain sight in disguise.

GMC — Galactic Marine Corp, united military force in the Milky Way galaxy.

Kison Askari — Stone warriors, mutated race of beings who throw off the mantle of being oppressed to fight for freedom.

Kison Tantu — Stone People

Limbia Johari — Walking jewels or common servants in the homes and businesses of the upper echelon of main stream society.

Minion — Maliciously mutated beings used by the original Pharaoh, an Ancient exiled to Earth.

Ongakujin — A group of musicians and playwrights that operate from a flying theater.

Rockheads — Derogatory name for Stone People.

Ryoko-Gekijo — The flying theater.

CPSIA information can be obtained
at www.ICGtesting.com
Printed in the USA
BVHW071146220522
637685BV00005B/16